THE MURALIST'S GHOST

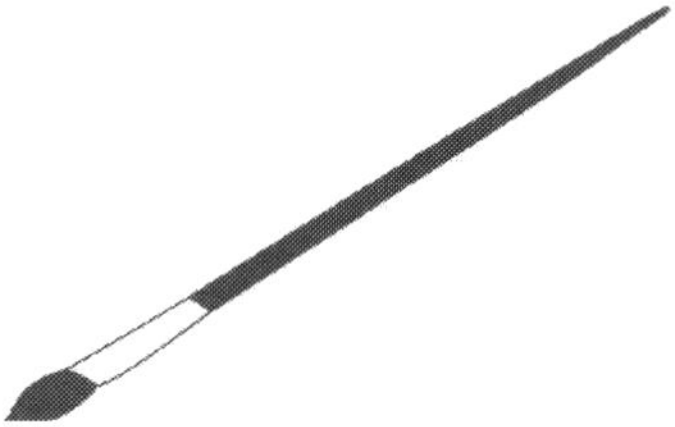

Karen Mocker Dabson

Covered Bridge Publishing
Columbia, Missouri

Covered Bridge Publishing
1001 W. Covered Bridge Road
Columbia, MO 65203

The Muralist's Ghost
Karen Mocker Dabson

© 2014 by Karen Mocker Dabson
All Rights Reserved

Editor: Nicholas S. Hrenda

Cover Design: T.A. Potts
Cover: "Self Portrait" by Maximilijan Vanka by permission of the Croatian Academy of Sciences and Arts.

All rights reserved. This book is published courtesy of Covered Bridge Publishing. No part of this book may be reproduced in any form by any means without the author's express written consent. The author may be contacted at www.mockerdabson.com/contact.

This is a work of fiction. Names, characters, places, and incidents either are the product of the author's imagination or are used fictitiously, and any resemblance to actual persons, living or dead, businesses, events, or locales is entirely coincidental.

Published in the United States by Covered Bridge Publishing.
ISBN-13: 978-1503144569
ISBN-10: 1503144569

For Brian

and

For Mitzi

AUTHOR'S NOTE

MAXO VANKA LIVED from 1889 to 1963 and as an artist, found fame in both Europe and the United States. Perhaps best known for the murals that he painted in St. Nicholas Croatian Catholic Church in Millvale, Pennsylvania, a few miles from Pittsburgh, this story features Mr. Vanka as its main character. Some of his life experiences have inspired the writer, but that is where the resemblance ends. *The Muralist's Ghost* is entirely a work of fiction garnished with conversations and circumstances of the author's own making. As is the fiction writer's tendency, time, dates, personalities, and situations have been bent or invented to suit the story line.

ACKNOWLEDGMENTS

NO BOOK IS EVER CREATED by only one person, and mine is no exception. The making of *The Muralist's Ghost* relied on the help and support of so many. To my extraordinary editor, Nick Hrenda, thank you for sticking with me during all the years of revisions and changes and for your good humor throughout. For all the people – family, friends, and supporters of Maxo Vanka – who gave generously of their time as I researched the artist and his life, I offer simple and heartfelt gratitude to Marya Halderman and Elena Rozbicka, Mary Petrich whose tireless assistance, advice, and encouragement went way beyond the call; Louis Petrich, Josephine Nagel, Nena Komarica, and Walt Supina; and Alice Snyder and William Lafe; to everyone who welcomed us to Croatia, especially Stanka Kraljevic, retired Director of Tourism on Korcula, who opened so many doors for us, including the Vanka home and gallery; Rafaela Petric of the Korcula Cultural Center; and to Nikolaj and Stanka Adlesic for a great taste of Slovenian hospitality in the countryside similar to Maxo's early days.

Many, many thanks to early readers Janet Brown, Shirley Campbell, Elizabeth Slosar, Pam Harvey, Brian Dabson, Mary Petrich, and Louis and Marlene Petrich for their wise observations, prevention of awkward mistakes, and strong support; to Gayle Dixon for her marketing ideas and help; and to Tracey Potts and the Croatian Academy of Sciences and Arts for the beautiful book cover. Also, I am so grateful to local friends Rexanna Ipock-Brown, Frances Reynolds, Sandy Ward, and Amy Lake for their ever-present enthusiasm.

Finally, dearest Brian, I cannot say thank you enough. This book truly would not have been possible without your love, patience, and understanding; your partnership in research, adventuring, editing, and marketing; and your unfailing willingness to provide me the freedom and flexibility to create this novel. You make my heart and mind sing.

TO LEARN MORE about the writing of *The Muralist's Ghost* and the life and times of Maxo Vanka, please link to www.mockerdabson.com/category/backstory. To view the Millvale Murals, go to www.stnicholascroatian.com or check out http://www.vankamurals.org. Special thanks for background provided by docent emerita Mary Petrich of St. Nicholas Croatian Catholic Church, and the James A. Michener Art Museum.

CHAPTER ONE

SHE HUNG IN CHAINS. The dull metal links snaked across her body like a boa constrictor. They coiled around her knees and twisted her wrists behind her back. The white of her gown rippled under the tight bonds, and the blue sash of motherhood cinched her waist just below the breasts. More painful yet, she was suspended by her elbows. Someone had forced them backwards, up and over the arms of a crude wooden cross. That caused the woman's face to fall forward, disguising her age. The fiends had not killed her, but she was completely helpless.

The choir director gasped and slewed her eyes to the floor. With an about turn, she steered her young charges to the rear of the church where they sat, a cluster of small, frightened faces floating above the pews. Two nuns tidying the apse for evening prayer froze in place. Their hands flew to their mouths, but nothing could block the horror that hissed through their fingers.

A dusky gloom had gathered in the church, and the choir shrunk deeper into the wooden bench as a metallic screech assaulted their ears. The sisters in the nave grabbed each other's arms. The scraping intensified, and now they could tell that it came from the rear hall. The choir director's jaw dropped as a thick, plank door opened to reveal a black void.

Dry rot and shellac invaded the air. The odor of urine joined the mixture as Billy Jones' bladder let loose.

"Not now, Billy, please," Miss Janko whispered, mainly to herself. She tried to gather the eight choristers in her arms and move them in silence toward the front door of the church, but before they could exit the pew, a footfall sounded on the threshold of the cellar door. A man stepped into the hall.

"Dear God!" Miss Janko leapt upright. "Father Žagar – you scared the dickens out of us!" A tumult of voices crashed in a wave around him. "Father, did you see…?" "It's horrible, terrifying." "What can we do?" "What could he be thinking?"

Patting the air in front of him, Father said, "And good afternoon to all of you, too. Ooh, Miss Janko, what's that smell?" She cocked a head toward Billy, and with a wave, he indicated that the situation required immediate attention.

"Now, then, one at a time. What seems to be the problem?"

The elder of the two nuns pointed to the southwestern corner of the nave and shook her wimple at him. It clicked with starch and accented the stern lines on her face.

"Father, by all that's holy, do you really think - " she said, but he laid a restraining hand on her arm before she could finish.

"Hold on a second, Sister Mary Martha, and let me see what is what here." He moved into the corner that she had indicated and stood with his arms crossed for some time.

Father peered upward at the form of the woman, and his face crimped in concern. In the deepening shadows of the afternoon, he could feel the censure of the old nun, her eyes boring into the back of his neck. "Father," she said in a terse undertone. "This is the worst yet – abhorrent. Such irreverence surely cannot be tolerated."

He glanced to the ceiling and sighed. Dozens of angels gleamed faintly from the transepts, their stares pouring down from every corner of the darkening church. Like an admonishment, they seemed to defy him to take in the woman's pain and find the courage to set things straight.

Father Žagar mashed his lips like he always did when a difficult problem presented itself. Hot air rushed out of his nose as he thought that this time, things may have gone too far. But just as surely as he planned to express this point of view, he felt certain that Maxo Vanka would have a compelling argument that would override his objections, making them seem pathetic and groundless compared to the ardor of his own beliefs.

Father released the clamp of his lips and puffed a hasty farewell to the nuns. With determined steps, he marched out the door of the church and across the lot to the rectory. He found the artist in a casual slouch against the kitchen sink, taking tiny, quick sips from a cup of steaming hot water.

"Ah, good afternoon, Father, were you looking for me?" The priest grunted, and Maxo said, "And those thunderclouds trailing over your head, are they meant for me, too?" He gave a small grin that somehow combined friendliness with concern. Maxo felt comfortable in making this small jest, as the two men had been close ever since the last time the artist had painted for the parish.

"Well, Maxo, my friend, you may well have sunk me this time." The priest's lips twisted. "And yes, the clouds are for you."

Maxo reached for the kettle, and placing a tea egg in a second cup, poured boiling water over it. He invited the priest to sit at his own table and handed him the teacup. "There, there, tell me, what is all this about?"

The cleric cleared his throat. "Maxo, it's this. Several people, including some of the school children, were frightened by the life-size sketch that you left in the church this afternoon."

"Oh, that." Maxo nodded with some vigor. "I can explain." Words spilled from his mouth. "And I am so, so very sorry to have startled anyone. I carried that pastel sketch into the church this morning, you know, to see how it would go on the wall, to get a perspective. As usual, no one was around, so I left it for some refreshment," here he lofted his teacup, "never thinking it would a problem. I am so…"

"Bomé! Maxo, listen!" Father interjected his words hastily. "What you are asking for is really too much. You know, we are a very open community here, but this new mural could be seen as an affront. You have to admit, it's drastically different from anything else you've put on the walls so far." Father wiped his brow. "And you know we believe in you. Everyone is so committed to this second round of murals, and some good money's been put behind it."

"And for that, my heart is deeply, deeply grateful," Maxo said. "To be given the opportunity to create such messages … such a dialogue in paint and imagery so that all can grasp its meaning … it is a gift, I tell you, a gift. I swear."

The priest did not doubt that Maxo's words and intent were absolutely sincere. His own words could gain no ground except to stir the artist into further discourse, defending what Father could now see was an *idée fixe* in his mind.

"Father Žagar." Maxo ran a hand across his mouth, and then whipped open his palm in the priest's direction. "Please, please. It is completely important to include the Mati Croatia figure on the walls of the church. Nothing will more readily show the people the plight of our dear Mother Croatia. Here it is – 1941 – and a people who have withstood the onslaught of so many others, who came through the Great War, who fought for their rights and their lands with the Serbs and the Bosnians, who put up with a traitorous king – and now, now they are being rolled over, Father. Literally! Flattened by the horror of the Nazi machines and their soulless soldiers. Imagine if you will, Father," Maxo panted. "Imagine if you can … whole towns vanished from the face of the earth – every stick, every morsel, every human, every child, and, and," here he gestured wildly, "Mati Croatia sold out in a despicable deal negotiated by her so-called leaders and the evil Germans."

It was Father who took his turn to entreat his friend to sit and draw breath, but Maxo stamped past the chair and continued.

"For these so, so pressing reasons, I am creating this

portrait – a true representation of our poor motherland – bound and hopeless, trapped and helpless unless others – other nations – come to her aid."

"Father Žagar, my good friend," he had smiled. "Think of how wonderful, how very wonderful it is all going to be." Maxo had never quite shed his Croatian accent, and it added to his charm. "You have come so far, brat moj. It would be a shame not to complete this work. We must…I say must…represent the evil side of things as well as the good if we are to wake people up to the work…yes, the good work that is still left to be done … by all of us."

Father dipped his head in rapid pecks. Once more, Maxo's passion had converted his thinking. The intense portrayals that Maxo had created for the walls a few years ago already beamed an eternal reminder that man can never rest until justice is served. This new mural would add a critical message to the church's walls. Unconsciously, his lips tightened again, for now it would be Father's duty to convince his parish council, the parishioners, and possibly the bishop that the Mati Croatia mural was a good idea. Father's eyebrows peaked. *No doubt easier than shifting Maxo*, he thought. He rose to his feet. "All right, Maxo," he said, "Okay." He patted his shoulder. "No promises, but I'll see what I can do."

The parish had invited Maksimilijan Vanka to return four years after his engagement with them in 1937. That year, he had created murals of extraordinary meaning and luminescence that people adored and children feared. They had also brought him a small measure of fame. Landscapes and portraits of Croatian peasants shone upon the anterior walls of the tiny, cruciform church. The largest mural wrapped the altar. From left to right with some parts hidden on the curved wall behind the altar, an observer could follow the plight of the Croatian immigrants as they sacrificed the pastoral beauty of the Old World to endure the long sea voyage to the New World with all of its opportunities. When they arrived, it was only to learn that they had exchanged the lush fields of the countryside for the grimy and often dangerous steelworks and industries in and around Pittsburgh. They had traded the hard but beneficial farm life for the grind of the factories where many were worked near to death. Woven in and beside the colorful murals and their social commentary were figures and emblems related to Christian subject matter. Only the dullest person would not recognize the contrast that the artist drew between the spiritual mores of Christianity and the people's suffering.

Father Žagar remembered the usually peaceable, but sometimes contentious dialogues with Maxo Vanka as they had looked over the artist's sketches for the 1937 murals. The man was inspired, there was no denying that. But Maxo, in making his points, often pushed concepts that strained the good Father's convictions.

This latest set of mural sketches raised the pitch of the discussion to a new level, however. Vanka's main plan involved painting a visual diatribe against the atrocities of war. The woman in chains, called Mati – for mother, Mother Croatia – would stand as a bleak reminder that Croatia was now embroiled, harnessed, bound – whichever word one chose – in a world war not of her making, but from which she was helpless to escape.

Some of the drawings ran dark with the blood of Croatian sons that women had lost to war. One sketch caused Father Žagar to grind his hands one against the other as he watched the Virgin Mary seize the barrel of a rifle, mightily angry and frightening in her resolve. Yet another picture did little to disguise the artist's views on the division between rich and poor.

Was the public to draw the conclusion that rich men carry out wars on the back of the poor? Father wondered as he walked back to the church in time for evening prayer. It was just one of many questions that churned through his brain as the last of the sunset leaked around the vestry door.

Maxo Vanka grunted as he adjusted his back against the boards of the scaffold later that evening. For a moment, he almost wished that Father Žagar had not been so persuasive in gaining the church leadership's approval for this second series of murals. But the best way to paint a mural on a ceiling was lying down, and he felt that this precise spot was where the wrathful Mary would have the most effect. Every time the parishioners exited down the center aisle of the nave, they would be confronted anew with her message and their duty.

And wouldn't you know it? The priest had successfully negotiated a contract for the entire body of work. But – and there always was one – like the last time, the parish needed the work done in a matter of weeks instead of the months he had been hoping for. Soon they would hold a grand celebration on the Feast Day of St. Nikola Tavelić, and the church leaders insisted that the walls be completed for the important event.

Once more, Maxo found himself locked in the church, alone, and working fifteen to twenty hours every day in order to fulfill their wishes. *Well, I did it in 1937, and I can do this again,* he thought. Four more years had gone by though, and at age fifty-two, his bones protested against the hard bed of the wood, and at times, his right shoulder flamed from the effort to hold his brush aloft for so many hours. The parish council had allotted an increased number of weeks over the last time he had completed a job for them, which would give him some reprieve. But painting eleven larger-than-life murals in eighteen weeks was asking a good deal.

No matter. All in all, Maxo contentedly pursued his work at St. Nicholas Croatian Catholic Church in Millvale. The earlier murals had made more than a small splash in Pittsburgh and the arts community, and several other commissions had arisen on that account. But more importantly, Maxo felt that his work at the church was unfinished, and he liked the direction he had created for the new set of murals. It was essential that their message be shared and broadcast.

He also welcomed the opportunity to renew his friendship with the Millvale priest. Father Žagar he found to be an intelligent spirit, and he valued his conviviality and trustworthiness. Besides, the priest was open and willing to engage in long discussions that ranged over matters both familiar and foreign.

Maxo looked forward to reviving their nightly talks. After he would quit work – no matter if it was the middle of the night – Father would be waiting in the parish house with cakes and fruit and coffee to wind down Maxo's work day. Though he could not imbibe at that hour himself, the priest remained awake with Maxo, chatting quietly while the artist chewed.

And Maxo could not disagree that the money was good. As in 1937, the parish had raised a handsome sum that told Maxo how much they valued his artistic ability. His wife, Margaret, had agreed wholeheartedly that he should take the job, and they both had concurred over dinner one night that it would be best to leave the family installed at their Bucks County home for the weeks that the work would take.

"My darling, it's not as though you're going away forever – or even that far. And neither we nor White Bridge Farm are going anywhere," his wife had said. The small town of Rushland where they lived sat in the county next to Philadelphia. "Peggy and I will be fine, and if not, why then you are only a train ride away."

"Well, my sweetest – you know that it will be hard to leave my pretty Peggies, and the gardens, *and* my studio for so long a spell, but," he had paused to take a mouthful of food, "I feel this opportunity pulling me in. It is like the church itself wants me to be there. It needs me to fill the remaining blank walls and finish the work that I started so long ago."

Margaret nodded and smiled a little crookedly. She was accustomed to the unusual way Maxo expressed things. "Truly, Maxo, I wouldn't want you to go for any other reason. I mean, it's not as though we need the money."

His cheek had ticked just slightly when she added that phrase. It was unintentional on her part, but he had never harbored plans to live off of the wealth of his father-in-law, and he was not going to start now. Especially when he was completely capable of selling his art and making good money doing so.

"Right. So I will retire to my study to write Father Žagar and let him know I will be coming, yes?" His knees pushed back on his chair as he stood, and Maxo placed a kiss on her head as he made for the door. In her turn, she slid a hand along his thin arm and gave his fingers a small squeeze.

"Yes, of course, my dear."

Like motes of dust, Maxo batted these memories away from his face as he studied the ceiling. Here he was now, and in fact, the commission with the church had satisfied him in every way but one. However, there was little anyone could do about that particular. Maxo blew a sigh through his lips. *Ah well, when was a job ever perfect?*

He resolutely composed himself and resumed his work on the first half of the ceiling beneath the choir. With a wide brush, he slashed at the ceiling, and soldiers' bodies began to emerge. With bold strokes of shadow amid the somber colors, they seemed to come alive, writhing in terror at the scene before them. Maxo could feel his chest rise. *The air inside my chest is smiling,* he thought. *This … this is what I want to achieve. The viewer should understand that the soldiers believe themselves to be in mortal peril, as indeed they are. Deserving of death when they have treated the gift of life with such cruelty and disregarded any moral teachings that their churchly upbringing may have endowed at some earlier time.* His dark eyes shone with satisfaction as he sculpted the soldiers' faces in the sickly greens he remembered from his experiences in the Great War. Next, he widened their eyes with white horror and dark frantic lines. The soldiers trembled in their place on the ceiling and looked as though they would bolt at any moment – far, far away from the angry Mother Mary.

Perched on one elbow, Maxo squeezed more umber onto his palette and selected a pointed sable brush in order to add detail. He scooted his shoulders across the scaffold to get closer to the first soldier. The work absorbed him now, pulling him along like a strong magnet, up and into the mural.

Somewhere a clock tower chimed three. Maxo woke with a start. He had drifted to sleep on the platform. It was the third night in a row that he had painted so late. Earlier, Father Žagar had said not to expect him as he rushed away to the bedside of an ill parishioner. Without his faithful friend to remind him that it was time to descend from the scaffolding to eat and rest, Maxo had painted on well past the midnight hour.

"Ai, ai" Maxo whispered to the ceiling as he creaked to a half-sitting position, propped on his elbows. He extended his limbs in a long stretch and groaned. His pectoral muscles and his neck shivered from the chill of waking up, but something else lurked behind the cool as though all the joy had been wrung from him while he slept. The aroma of cold stone wisped past his nose.

No, no! No, no, no! Maxo prayed silently to the image before him. *Please, please, not again.* An unpleasant tang coated the back of his throat, and he swallowed to push the acid back into his stomach.

The cold grew deeper, and a sly breeze stole across the nave, quivering his paint rags and ruffling his hair. The lamp altered from a bright beacon to a dull yellow glow. Previously sharp details morphed into the blurred outlines he usually associated with dusk.

More than any time before, Maxo felt stiff and helpless as waves of dread washed over him. Ideas raced pell-mell through his head, keeping pace with his batting heart. *It has come for me. I know it. Oh my God, now what? I simply cannot lie here all night*, he tried to reason. Maxo rolled over and pushed himself onto his knees. All the while, his eyes swept the vast dimness of the nave, but he could see nothing. He reached out for the pole of the work lamp and swiveled the beam. Like a shaking, halting searchlight, the dim lamp sought for intruders in the gloom of the church.

Maxo's eyes ached from the effort to see what could not be seen. He was near to giving up, but every time he thought of descending the ladder without knowing what might lurk below, his heart faltered.

The lamp's light bounced past the first pew. *Wait, what was that?* He twisted the pole counterclockwise so that it pointed just below the giant Mother Mary that floated above the altar. His tongue became thick, and the burn of bile was back in his throat. Situated in the front pew sat the tall, hooded figure. As if it were possible, it looked darker than it ever had before. Its regard aimed for the altar and the forward murals, but as a muffled gasp escaped the artist, it rotated to glare at the choir just above Maxo's head.

Maxo's heart beat wildly as the specter's stare froze his blood. Disturbed, the creature rose slowly, so slowly, an agony of slowness. At its full height, it floated down the aisle – down the aisle toward him.

Maxo clasped a hand over his mouth before another sound could burst out, but it made no difference. The dark apparition dissolved into the night shadows as silently and swiftly as it had come. Maxo fell back onto the boards as the work lamp flared brightly, and the warmth returned to his muscles.

"Dear God," Maxo muttered, "if it is the last thing I do while I am here, I will figure out who or what this spirit is, and why it is visiting me, and me alone." The vow hovered between him and the figures that peopled the walls of the church.

He had hoped against hope, but this was the very particular that no contract with the church council could circumscribe – this specter, this horrid, vaporous apparition that had first appeared in 1937 as he worked on the mural at the front of the church. It had persisted in visiting him during the wee hours of the morning, seeming to know when he was completely alone and most vulnerable. Back then, he had enlisted Father Žagar's opinion, but the priest had told him that no one else had ever witnessed the ghost's appearance. In fact, the priest had tried speaking to the blank air of the church one night in order to quiet the chimera, but that had worked for only a short period.

Yes, this time, no one could help him, especially as he would tell no one – not even Father Žagar – that the ghost had returned. Its past appearances had been so long ago that it seemed as though he must have imagined them. But no, unfortunately for Maxo, he remembered each terrible experience with all the vivid recall of an artist's mind.

In the drafty church, it was sometimes difficult to

distinguish between a light wind that trickled through the masonry cracks and the beginnings of a ghostly visit. At first, he would rub the back of his neck as a chill whiffle reached him upon the scaffold. It always began like that – the faintest stirring of air, so faint he could not be sure he had actually felt anything. He would carry on, but eventually the chill would wrap him, and the hint of a breeze might pass over his cheek or his forehead like someone deliberately blowing iced air his way. At the same time, an involuntary terror would wrap his chest. His muscles would ache and contract until he found it almost impossible to breathe. His lamp would dim, and without realizing it, Maxo would sink into a pool of panic that he could not control.

As he gathered his materials from the scaffolding, Maxo recalled the first time the ghost had appeared to him. He was completing the mural at the front of the church – the one that depicted Croatian villagers in the home fields of the motherland. Their white costumes were bright and cheerful with the reds, blues, and greens of traditional Slavic textiles. The women wore babushkas on their heads, and the men stood in stout boots. The lands were green and gold with the lushness of summer, and he could almost smell the fresh air.

Maxo stood near the top of a stepladder adding some fine detail when the tips of his ears tingled as though a sudden frost had descended. The smell of chilled granite invaded his nostrils, and his skin prickled. For a moment, he thought he glimpsed something moving out of the corner of his eye, but when he glanced down at the chancel, nothing stirred. As he shrugged, the light in the church flickered, and he remembered glancing toward the lamp he had rigged on a stand, worrying that the bulb was about to blow.

His heart jolted at the sight beyond the lamp. A dark figure, cloaked in black, its mantle much like that of a monk's robe, stood just beyond the circle of light. Maxo's chest seized around his heart as a cold horror set in. He grabbed a rung of the ladder to steady himself. He had heard no one enter the church. No aching sound from the front door hinges or the cellar door had caught his ear. No footstep had struck the stone floor. He had been the sole occupant of the nave up to that instant.

Despite himself, Maxo shouted, "Hallo! Hallo there! Who are you?"

No answer.

"Who are you? What business have you here?"

Silence.

"Father Žagar will return any moment now. If it is him you wish to see - "

Before Maxo could finish his sentence, the figure had turned and drifted into the front pew. It did not genuflect as it entered, but simply took up a post toward the center aisle. Frozen on the ladder, Maxo stared at where a person's face should be, but no light reflected from a glassy eye or heated cheek, nor did any breath move the cowl's folds about its head. Maxo tried to swallow, but his tongue and the roof of his mouth were as dry as desert sand.

"What do you want?" he croaked.

No answer.

Maxo could not beat back his dread long enough to move up or down the ladder. Finally, he swung around to the platform where his palette and brushes awaited his next move. Inhaling to the very bottom of his lungs, he grabbed his things and plunged down the ladder. As soon as he hit the floor, he whirled around, planning to make his escape through the vestry door, but there was no need. The figure had vanished, a shadow's shadow blending into the night.

Maxo shook off the old memory and straightened his shoulders. As an afterthought, he brought a brush back up to the ceiling and added some strokes. With a few extra weeks, he had the chance to outline his paintings – at least the main figures – before completing the murals. Laying back down and raising his knees to reduce the pressure on his back, Maxo continued to sketch lightly with the tip of a sable brush. While he worked, his mouth twitched side-to-side, his beard a pendulum pushing away things he would rather not consider at the moment. At least painting from this position, with only the ceiling, crossbeams, and corbels illuminated by his work lamp, he had no ability to see what might be going on below him. And the wooden planking of the scaffolding was pleasantly warm.

Though he sensed that not revealing the night's adventure to Father Žagar, or anyone else, might lead to unintended consequences, Maxo could not bring himself to tell the good priest when he returned home the next morning.

The priest clucked his tongue and asked, "Maxo, my friend, what have you been doing to yourself in my absence? If you could look thinner, I believe you do." He grabbed the artist by the right shoulder and stared into his face. "Tell me you are not ill."

Maxo shook his head. "Ne, ne, I … I am fine … a bit over-fatigued. Too many hours without my brother's keeper to tell me when to stop." A thin smile pushed up one cheek.

Father's eyes crinkled, and the air rushed from his nose. "It is as I feared. We are asking much too much of you. Perhaps," he hesitated for a fraction of a second, "perhaps we should reduce the number of murals from your contract."

Father Žagar lurched back as Maxo threw out both of his hands. "No! No! Impossible! That is not a solution. Father, you know, I have already made many plans, *many* plans for the walls. The paintings work together, they must all work together if we are to achieve unity, and … and … and our message." Maxo sank into a chair, out of breath. He rubbed his eyes. "Please, Father, I beg you, do not make such a decision."

"But, but, Maxo, dear friend, you simply cannot go on like this." The priest rested a hand on the artist's shoulder.

Maxo laid his hand upon the priest's in return. His eyes fastened for a moment on his teacup as though he were divining an answer there. Then, in one swift movement, he grasped Father Žagar's wrist and stood tall. A shot of energy rang in his voice.

"Please, Father, it is not for you to worry about me. You have far too many others who rely on your help, and I do not need to be taking, but giving to you." Without hesitation, he added, "The murals will be done for the fete, and they will be done by me, as we have planned all along."

He doffed his felt hat at the priest as he placed it on his head. "Adio, my friend," and he stepped briskly out the door.

The priest ran after Maxo and pressed a banana into his hand. "For quick energy. And no matter what, I'm pulling you off the scaffolds at eight o'clock this evening. Count on it!" He pivoted on his heel and darted into the rectory before Maxo could object.

Maxo gnawed on his lower lip as he entered the vestry door. Part of him would put the specter behind him, carry on with the work, and do it well. Another part wanted to go home – run in his fields, paint in his bright studio, eat strukli and pacenka and kamenice, hold Peggica on his knee and tell her a story, sink into his big, comfortable bed wrapped in the arms of his beloved Margaret – bathe himself in the smells and touches and sights of all that was familiar to him. His heart felt lighter at the thought of it. *After all, only fourteen weeks and a little more to go. I can do this.*

The last part of him wanted to put the apparition to rest permanently. In the morning light, Maxo promised the sun that he would keep a sliver of its brightness tucked inside his chest to ward off the chill of the dark, lonely nights in the church. In the light of day, he resolved to take his task seriously, and for this, he made a plan. It would involve searching back through time and space. He would make this part of his daily métier. The ghost clearly connected to his past, to some part of his life, else why would it appear to him and him alone?

More than most people, Maxo understood that logic and structure had its limitations, especially when it came to things metaphysical. Regardless, he was conscious of his shoulders relaxing, his lungs expanding, and his limbs hanging more freely. He had a plan. He had a plan.

CHAPTER TWO

HIGH ABOVE THE CHURCH FLOOR, Maxo lay on the scaffolding. The fingers of his right hand pushed into his chest, sculpting circles across the lean sinew. His muscles were tight, so very tight, and every time he thought of home, they contracted another degree. Maxo angled his shoulders to a different position across the rough boards. Only twelve more weeks until the murals would be revealed. He had to press on despite his worry.

Last night, in their usual way, he and Father Žagar had shared a simple supper of fruit and bread. Father's face had puckered when Maxo spoke of his pain. "Father, I know it is nothing a doctor can cure, but there is something in my heart – an ache most profound – worse than when you lose your first love."

The priest nodded intelligently, and reaching out a hand, pressed it against the painter's right shoulder. Then, silently he turned both palms toward the ceiling – a gesture to God, a supplication to the ages, or simply acknowledging questions for which there are no answers.

For a moment, Maxo's hurt lay between them like a dead rat on the kitchen table. The priest's heart panged with sympathy for he knew the cause of such angst. At first he could put no words to it, but finally, when he cleared his throat to speak, he was interrupted by the rage that spewed from Maxo's throat, sore and hot.

"Those bastards," he said, smacking the tabletop. "Have you heard the latest news? Oh my God, Father. Our homeland, our beloved Croatia has fallen, by acts so foul, they do not bear thought. It is horrible, horrible!" The artist pulled at his hair. Before his friend could breathe a word, he continued. "The Nazi scourge has crossed from Slovenia to Croatia. They are using this … this technique they call depopulation." Maxo sniffed. "Such a dry, sterile word for what they have done. The land. They have laid it bare, destroyed and uprooted as though some crazed machine has passed through, leveling hamlets, fields, and people before it."

Maxo paused to pass a handkerchief over his face. "Father, my good friend, Louis – you know, the journalist you met the last time I did the paintings – Louis tells me thousands, no, hundreds of thousands of villagers have been exterminated over the last three months."

"Dear God," the priest muttered into his own handkerchief. His head jerked up as Maxo continued.

"And do you know what is worse, Father. Worse than anything?"

The priest shook his head.

"The Nazi pigs in their evil cleverness have turned Serb against Croat, Croat against Serb so that their own killing can be magnified. And the Slovenes to the north? Poor souls - left to the Italian fascisti to suffer a different brand of cruelty."

He realized now that he had probably frightened his friend with his intensity. Maxo closed his eyes and pressed his lips together. His paintbrush rested by his side. The air flowed through the open vestry window. He half raised his eyes and watched as his cotton painting rags flapped over the bars of the scaffolding. A tear slid down his cheek as his thoughts beheld the shirts on Mati Dora's clothesline waving against the windswept hills of Kuplenovo. The Zagorje region of Croatia had proven more difficult to penetrate for the bestial Germans, but the news that they had received in the United States was not good. *Farms ransacked for livestock and foodstuffs. Houses razed, blown up, or torched. Males over the age of fifteen rounded up and slaughtered. Women, well, God only knew.*

Like the worst kind of indigestion, a sour lump caught beneath his breastbone. Maxo swallowed then belched without relief. A man of conviction but lacking the balm of religion, he never prayed. Yet now he did pray, and hard. He prayed that his sisters, Doritska and Maritska, had hidden in some nearby cave. He prayed that they had not been transported to the Russian front like so many before them. He prayed that someday he could rescue them.

Heat suddenly flamed through Maxo's body, polishing his thin cheeks a dusky red. In a flash, he seized his painting instruments and charged the entryway ceiling with a barrage of strokes. Bold lines and striking figures emerged. Beneath his brush, the Virgin Mary took shape and power – breaking guns and challenging soldiers. With frightening fury, she would vanquish anyone that dared to harm her sons and her daughters. This, then, would be the message that Maxo Vanka would send to the world. The wrath of the Virgin mother awaited anyone who waged war, and particularly those who fought in the name of Christianity.

A week later, Maxo breathed in the fresh air of the July morning. With any luck, he would finish the righteous Virgin Mary today. The job's completion would bring some joy as then he could begin his *Croatian Family.* That mural had the double benefit of painting a somewhat lighter topic while standing on his own two feet. His back had seen enough of scaffolding for the time being.

As he crossed from the rectory to the church, cotton ball clouds scudded across the azure plain of the sky. Maxo stood for a moment admiring their procession. They caused the sun to flicker, like the light between the blades of a revolving fan – one moment all brilliance, and the next, soft shadow.

Today's challenge for painting, the artist thought as he entered the church. Inside, however, the large windows welcomed the sunlight, and his workstation was well lit. Maxo climbed the scaffold and situated himself beneath the upper half of the woman's figure. Today, he would detail her face and hands and put the finishing touches on the soldiers' expressions. He would contrast her strength with their fear and bewilderment.

The open door to the churchyard magnified sounds from the outside. The birds were happy this morning, chirruping a greeting to the arriving school children. Maxo smiled. Nothing pleased him more than birdsong on a summer's morn.

A loud cry jangled the morning peace. "Mummy! Mummy!" Maxo craned his neck to see what had happened. He could just make out a small boy on the ground hugging one knee. His wailing climbed an octave as his mother approached.

"There, there, little Petar." Cooing, she gathered him into her arms. The boy snuffled into her chest, and Maxo's thoughts swirled away to his beloved Mati Dora, the woman who had raised him. He had come to her with no parents and no name, but no matter. She had christened Maxo as Mikula, and so he was to her.

"Mati! Mati Dora!" Little Mikula had dashed through the cottage door, tears flying off his face. "Mati, where are you?" His voice quavered as he called for her.

Dora Jugova emerged from the kitchen wiping her big hands on her flour-specked apron. She collected the five year-old in her arms, and he nestled into the soft place between her two large breasts. "Whatever is it, my little prince?" she asked. She rubbed a circle between the tiny wings of his shoulder blades, willing away his sobs.

"I saw it again, Mati. In the woods. Just beyond the ivy wall." Mikula stifled a rising sob. "And, oh, Mati, it was looking right at me." Fresh tears bathed his brown eyes and made the long lashes clump together in wet tufts.

She pushed aside the dark hair and kissed his forehead, checking for fever. However, even as she caressed him, Dora knew what he was talking about. She had felt the presence, too. Sometimes, on a sunny day, an icy breeze would lift the hair on her arms for no good reason. She had never seen the tall dark phantom the boy described, but still, she believed him.

It was hard to understand, and yet not hard, because she believed Mikula to be a special boy. Not because his parents had come from noble bloodlines, not because he was so very handsome for one so young, nor even that he could already do his letters and some simple sums. Dora had often struggled to come up with the right word. Mikula was special because he was sensitive. Even now she thought the word, sensitive. He amazed her on a daily basis with how well he fit into the natural world, never harming a fly and embracing all that was around him.

One day as she carried the washing to the clothesline, Dora had stopped, fascinated by the sight before her. Little Mikula stood by the garden wall at some distance, holding out his hand. A small brown bird – a sparrow, she thought – gently fluttered from the wall right onto the boy's palm. After resting there a moment, it had tip-toed up to his left shoulder where she was astonished to see it join two other birds that already sat on either side of the boy's head.

He was so at one with nature that Dora found it difficult to think why any spirit, bad or good, might want to bother him. Upon reflection, though, it could be that his sensitivity was the very thing that attracted their attention.

Dora's Baka – her grandmother, a wise woman of the village – had firmly believed in spirits and ghosts. The life force of friends would visit her right before their deaths. "On their way to Heaven," Baka would explain. She would tell young Dora of faces floating in the dark, an unseen hand that placed its cold fingers on her arm, or an unexplained weight in the bed next to her. Always, the room in which these visitations took place would grow cool, cooler, cold when the spirits came. Baka had never been afraid. She would talk to the souls and bid them farewell, helping them along their heavenly journey.

Dora supposed she had inherited a fraction of her grandmother's talent, and though he was not her blood son, she felt that Mikula had somehow become a spiritual guide, too, for people and animals. She had witnessed how he would lock eyes with old Brutus, the sheep-herd, who would then eat from his hand. Though the priest said animals had no souls, the boy somehow connected with that old fleabag in a way she never could.

Dora sat Mikula on her knee and clucked quietly. He ran his small fingers over her hands, outlining the knobby knuckles and curling his own little hand around first one reddened finger, then the next, as he listened to the soothing sounds she made. Dora breathed a thankful prayer to the good God for sending her this dear child, this special boy. He had made life bearable again after the loss of her only true son three years ago. Clutching him closely, she carried Mikula to the kitchen where the bread oven had grown piping hot.

"Soon there will be fresh crni kruh, Mikulek, brown bread, your favorite. Won't that be good?" She gave him a squeeze and set him on a stool by the stove. "But while we wait, shall I tell you a story?"

The boy nodded.

"This is the tale of how a poor peasant woman came to find the littlest angel, the best blessing of her life," she said.

"Do you mean me?" The boy's face shone and a shy smile glanced across his face.

"Listen, and you will hear …"

Down through the years, the low tones of Dora's voice reached Maxo's ears as he painted from the scaffold. As a child, the chronicle had become the salve that soothed stormy nights, scraped knees, and suffering at the hands of his siblings. He remembered how Mati Dora would always start the story.

"Many years ago," Dora would begin.

> Many years ago, there was a countrywoman who had a stepson and two lively twin daughters, but no blood son that she could call her own. Her own baby son had perished in the cold winter, and she had only laid him to rest a short while before the miracle came into her life. Funny enough, the woman had the same name as me – Dora Jugova.

On the day in question, this Dora Jugova rubbed the tip of her nose with her woolly shawl in an attempt to warm it. She stood at the snowy garden gate watching for the visitors. She thought it would not be right to make people of their class come through and knock on her door. She should be waiting for them.

With this plan in mind, Dora Jugova had risen early to mix the bread dough, milk the cow, gather the eggs, and brew her morning tea before swathing herself for the trek into the cold. She had pulled a boiled wool vest over her homespun dress. Part of her marriage trousseau, the vest was strewn with embroidered flowers sewn lovingly by her mother, the good God rest her soul. Over this, she donned her husband's sturdy brown cardigan – the one she had knit for his thirty-sixth birthday – and buttoned it up to her neck. A green and blue babushka covered her soft brown hair. Finally, the shaggy gray shawl topped this outfit, covering her shoulders and head. As a last thought, she had thrown a small cream-colored blanket of lamb's wool over her left arm.

Though her ears strained for any sound of the approaching sleigh, Dora heard only the wind making the last of the dead leaves chatter on their branches. A fresh snowfall the night before deadened all other sound. The visitors were late, but Dora enjoyed this chance for a pause in the middle of her busy morning. The air smelled crisp, and she inhaled its freshness, relishing the tiny icicles that formed on her nose hairs.

Dora surveyed the grounds beyond her garden fence. The familiar became unfamiliar under the mantle of snow, and it was like seeing their land for the first time. The lane formed a subtle crease as it wound out to the main road, and the log pile had changed into a mass of snow-crusted bumps. Dora turned to look at the copse of maples beside the cottage. Snow lay thick upon the tree branches, painted there by Grandfather Winter with a generous brush. She loved the way it outlined the dark bark and beamed against the blue sky peeking from behind the clouds.

A burst of wind whipped through the nearby pines and created a small snowstorm in the road before her. Dora daubed her eyes and wiped her nose, then clapped her reddened hands together until they grew warm. She peered across the wide, white valley and thought she could glean movement out beyond the Praljaks' farm, her neighbors to the north.

Funny how this morning's meeting – for it was more of a meeting than a visit, she thought – had come about. A week ago, she had opened the door to a stranger just as evening was sliding into night. Baldo would not have liked that, but what else could she do? Alone, with her light on, whoever it was knew she was home.

She had asked him in. He was an officer of some rank in the cavalry. She could see that by his smart red uniform and shining black boots. Captain … Captain Čović, that was it. The captain had been formal but polite and inquired after Baldo. Learning that he was in the mountains herding some stray sheep to lower pastures, Captain Čović asked if this was also the home of Dora Jugova.

"I am Dora Jugova," the woman said and extended her hand.

Captain Čović explained why Dora was wanted and gave her a paper outlining a very favorable payment plan in return. Dora did not read the paper – her reading skill amounted to very few words – but she trusted the handsome young captain and pledged to do all in her power to fulfill the commission. Far be it from her to refuse the request, seeing that it had come from such high quarters. In truth, she was happy to take on the task for reasons of her own.

That was surely the jingle of a sleigh bell. Dora roused herself from the memory of the captain's first visit. Time to be ready and present.

A half-hour later, Dora Jugova unwrapped the swaddling cloth of the small bundle. Captain Čović and the nobleman's sleigh had departed within ten minutes of its arrival after his one admonition.

"Are you clear on what is expected of you, Dora Jugova?" the captain had asked, his stern tone contradicted by the kind light in his eyes.

"Yes, Captain," Dora Jugova responded with a firm edge to her words. "I will feed and care for this child as though he were my own. A messenger will bring money and goods to help with his care. I will see that he receives them. I will keep him free from harm and mistreatment, but teach him responsibility. I will not speak of his origins, but from time to time, he may receive a visitor. I will give him or her every consideration when this is the case."

The captain passed a gloved hand over his chin and nodded once. "Thank you, Dora Jugova." He leaned down from the sleigh to shake her hand. As he did so, he held it for one second longer and looked into her eyes. "I can see that you have a true heart, and I am glad."

Without another word, the captain jolted backward as the sleigh's runners found traction in the deep snow. Dora Jugova stared after him, but only for a fleeting moment as the sky darkened and let loose a hundred thousand snowflakes.

The warmth of the kitchen was where she wanted to be, and she was anxious to regard her new charge before the other children returned from the village school. He had arrived in layers of down and silk and lace. She placed him in a wooden box on top of the stove and looked upon him for the first time.

"Why, you are as tiny and thin as a waif," she said, marveling at the baby. "Perhaps only a few days old." As she spoke, the infant opened his eyes. Dark brown, almost black, they studied her; and in some way, she felt like they looked straight through her, seeing her every thought and feeling. When he reached a tiny fist toward her and mewed like a newborn kitten, Dora Jugova fell in love.

"There, there, my little prince, there, there," and she lifted him out of the bed clothing, opened her blouse, and pressed him against the large gourd of her breast. After fumbling to position the nipple in his mouth, she felt the tug that told her the baby was taking milk. She smiled. Was there any better feeling?

"Praise the good God for sending you to me, dear tiny boy. Soon my milk will make you big and strong, but for now I will call you Mikula – small one."

Maxo remembered jumping down from the stool in the kitchen after Mati Dora had finished the story and wrapping his arms as far as they could reach around the big lady's legs. Almost fifty years later, his heart surged when he recalled the simple comfort her touch and her mother-love could bring.

The woman outside the church door had dried her boy's tears and walked him over to the classroom. The atmosphere in the church had lightened now that the sun shone steadily. It reflected onto the ceiling where Maxo worked, and all at once, he realized that he had completed the mural.

He scrambled down the ladder and canted his head up and sideways as he studied the completed picture. The scene was dark and forceful, the Virgin Mary the dominating figure, a mother fully furious with the war-mongers, slicing through them with her arms, frightening in her vigor, her determination, and her strength.

Maxo saluted the Virgin Mother. "This is the ultimate

battlefield, the one on which your deserving rage wins out. That is what I will call you," he said to the painting. "*Battlefield*."

As Maxo cleared his materials out from under the *Battlefield* mural, he continued to think about the power of mothers. It was not surprising, really, that his thoughts had drifted onto that old story of Dora's. Though it had been triggered by the little schoolboy's injury, he realized now that his thoughts unintentionally had begun exploring his own tiny beginnings and whether the church's specter stemmed from those days.

Well he remembered that dark shadow in the woods outside the cottage. A tall, faceless figure, it would slip from tree to tree so quickly that he could not be sure if he had actually seen it. As a boy, he would strain his sight peering into the leafy undergrowth where the green was darkest, hoping not to see the specter and yet somehow drawn to its presence. The sightings guaranteed that he never ventured further than the cottage wall, at least not on that side of the house.

But as the ghost had never revealed itself to him, what possible meaning could it hold in present day? Maxo waved a hand before his face as though swiping at a pesky fly.

More likely, the Millvale specter, if it was from his early days, represented something else. He ruled Mati Dora out as a possibility. She had been all things good and kind to him. He considered her his true mother, and he had to admit she had treated him better than her own children.

That had led to jealousy. Juro, the classic nasty stepbrother, discovered new ways to torture the pipsqueak orphan once he realized where Mati Dora's affections lay. As a tough twelve-year-old twice Mikula's size, he took every opportunity to blacken his little brother's eyes and box his ears. Maxo still bore a scar on his right leg from the time Juro knocked him into the haystack and started lancing it with a pitchfork. The outside tine of the fork had caught in his pants and ripped a wound from knee to calf. Mikula had screamed in earnest then, and Juro had run into the fields before Dora could catch him.

Perhaps Juro felt he had an old score to settle with Maxo. After all, Maxo had gone on to a life of success and relative ease, while Juro had inherited Baldo's land – a mean two acres with a half-dried-up creek where every day was a challenge. *Actually*, Maxo stopped in mid-thought, *I do not even know if he is dead.* He knew Juro had signed on with the military in the Great War, but his sisters had never written of him again. That might explain the ghost. If Juro were dead, his spirit could have tracked Maxo and now come for retaliation.

Maxo rubbed the beard on his chin. His stepfather, Baldo, had been mean enough to haunt people as well. From the day he had arrived in the household, Maxo could sense the brooding hulk's resentment and hatred of him. Mati Dora had said that as a babe, he would cry every time Baldo came into the room.

He certainly remembered the brute screaming at all of them and the beatings he had doled out. Sadly, Mati Dora was usually the first in line. Maxo distinctly recalled consoling her as he had wiped the blood from her lip the time Baldo broke her jaw. The fiend had little tolerance for the affection that could grow between a woman and a child, and even less for a scrawny fachook – a child he considered a weakling bastard.

Though he had forced Dora into wet-nursing for the money it could bring, it had been strictly a business proposition from his point of view. If the payment for Maxo's keep was one day late, Baldo went on a tirade, insisting that they leave the boy on some country road. Then Dora Jugova would be reduced to pleading on her knees as Baldo slapped her cheeks. "Please, oh please, Husband, please do not take my boy away. Have you forgotten –" the crack of flesh hitting flesh. Dora crying. "Have you forgotten the cow and the extra food that Mikula's benefactors have allotted? Ooph!" Such pleas often seemed to whet Baldo's temper, and his violence only increased as they went on.

The muscles on the back of Maxo's neck tensed in remembrance. If only he had not been so helpless in those days. That bad memory led to another.

In a fury one afternoon – Maxo could not remember what had provoked it – Baldo had seized the young Mikula out of Dora's arms and knocked her to the ground. Before she could claw her way up from the floor, he had bashed through the kitchen door and out into the fields. Clutching the five-year-old Mikula like an armload of kindling under his right elbow, he stormed past two neighboring farms and onto the steep bluffs of the Zagorje. There he stripped off the child's shirt and pants, and placed Mikula on a rocky shelf high above the ground.

Maxo recalled never uttering a word during the entire episode, but he had stared after Baldo as the man deserted him and stomped down the hill. When, after twenty paces or so, Baldo turned, he could see the boy's dark eyes, round and unafraid. Pointing a finger at his abuser, Mikula drew the sign of the cross backwards. Baldo stooped and picked up a rock, hefting it in his hand. It was slightly smaller than the boy's head.

He cocked his arm and shot the rock toward Mikula, but did not see it land. The force of the throw cost Baldo his footing on the loose gravel of the trail. The big man's feet flipped out, and he skidded down the stony incline on his back, cursing the rocks and sticks that poked into him. The switchback of the path arrested his descent, and his bottom crashed with a rough thud. A cloud of limestone dust closed around him. The pounding stunned him for a second, and Baldo shook his head.

The dust and his choler blinded him, but once he could see, Baldo pushed himself to his knees and slowly drew himself upright. His eyes roved the cliff face for the stone shelf, and he was about to bolt up the path and finish the child properly when he saw it. A small, limp arm hung from the lip of the rocky protrusion. Baldo shook a fist at the rock face, and then smacked his hands together with an air of consummation.

"Hah!" he shouted. "That is that, and a good beating will show Dora who is boss, God damn it. Not this, this," he waggled his hand at the overhang, "this strange, snotty rich fachook – little bastard – always looking at me funny." Baldo spat in the dust. He raised his fist to the ledge once more. "Guess you find out you cannot hex me, hey? Bah!"

Maxo's face grew hot as he recalled the appalling incident. Baldo had been a menace every day of his life. He had not been sorry when the big man fell, but when he had seen him get up again, the child, Mikula, had decided to play dead on the rocky shelf. The ruse worked. An hour later, he clambered down from the ledge, half skittering on the dusty, loose stones, but landing safely on the path. Though he was tiny, Mikula was wiry and smart. Instead of yelping as Baldo carried him away, he had been watching, noting this tree or that stream or the fence by the neighbor's barley field, composing a map in his mind that would lead him home again.

The strange thing was – Maxo snorted with an unhappy chuckle – little Mikula had managed to reach home, the Jugova hovel, before Baldo. In fact, they did not see his ugly face for another two days.

Dora Jugova had cried out when she spotted the wee boy strolling in the lane as naked as the day God breathed life into him. "Mikula! Oh, Mikula!"

She had pulled up her skirts and run to him then. Mikula leapt into her arms, and she wrapped him in her big white apron. Hurrying at once to the cottage, she barked orders at the girls. "Boil some water. Make some broth. Fetch me that stool there!" With loving care, she had bathed his little body and ransacked the ragbag until she discovered an old shirt of Juro's. It fit Mikula like a dress.

"No matter, my little prince. A tuck here and a tuck there, and you shall have a fine new shirt."

Dora instructed Maritska to pour a few cups of the hot water into a small basin while she stirred in some salts. Slowly, she eased Mikula's feet into the solution for a good, long soak. Gravel and nettles had bitten into them, and he winced as the welts and sores absorbed the saline mix.

As they sat together, Mikula told Dora the whole story. She gasped, and pink spots of heat rose on her cheekbones.

"Oh, Mikulek, poor, poor boy. To think that you walked all that way. Why it must be more than three kilometers to the far border of Bobrić's farm, if it is the spot I think you mean." She tutted over the cuts on his feet. "Small wonder your feet have suffered so, but this will help."

She stroked the little boy's cheek. "I will have to make you some new pants tomorrow, my little prince," she told Mikula. "I know not what good grace of God guided you back to me, but my heart is very, very full of thanksgiving at this miracle. We will go to the church on Sunday and spend a kovenica – a coin or two – on a candle to celebrate your return and to give great thanks."

Maxo laughed now to think of Baldo's face that Sunday evening when he finally drifted home. Crossing the threshold with his usual bluster, he had gulped air and staggered back a pace or two when he spotted young Mikula on his stool by the stove. Baldo's mouth gaped, a black hole with no teeth and breath as sour as a cesspool. He ran his hands down his dusty jacket, and his eyes swam with dark horror and disbelief. The big man crossed his burly chest and sank to his knees. All the while, his eyes never left Mikula's face, clearly afraid to look, but equally afraid to look away.

Dora entered from the sleeping area and crossed her arms as she spied Baldo. "Yes, you! You evil wretch!" she shouted in tones that rang with new confidence. "You … you … you stay on your knees, and beg the good God's forgiveness for your wicked ways." She stepped toward Baldo, and he shrank under the threshold. "And you beseech forgiveness from Mikula and from me!" Dora stamped her foot on that last word.

Baldo backed out of the cottage. "Go! Go! That is good. And do not come back until you are clean and sober … and, and penitent!" She slammed the stout oak door in his face.

Maxo grinned again. From then on, Dora Jugova's will ruled the family. Baldo had been beaten and broken by something he would never understand, but both Dora and Mikula took full advantage of his ignorance. If he chose to believe that the boy's ghost had come to roost in his home, for good or for ill, then so much the better for them. To Maxo's knowledge, Baldo never touched his mother again.

Maxo laughed quietly when he remembered seeing Baldo stuff extra tails of cats into the wattle of the hut – a belated gesture to keep the demons from his door - or the way Baldo's eyes rolled back in his head so that the veiny whites alone showed if young Mikula passed him by. Maxo passed a finger across his moustache as he wondered. *What if the frustration of Baldo's earthly existence had somehow transmuted into an evil spirit that wanted its revenge on the boy who had stolen his household authority?*

It was not a bad guess on Maxo's part, but he could not see the reasoning behind it. Why would Baldo have waited all this time to strike? How would his spirit have learned the truth behind Mikula's reappearance? Would Baldo have ever made the connection between Mikula Jugova and Maksimilijan Vanka? The artist thought not.

CHAPTER THREE

FOLLOWING A WEEK ON THE SCAFFOLDING, Maxo happily reassembled his materials next to the wall that would carry his portrait of a Croatian family. The flat plane stood perpendicular to the half completed *Battlefield* mural near the eastern entrance at the back of the church. *Beautiful*, Maxo thought as he stretched until his spine erupted with a series of cracks. He admired the vertical surface. It would be a perfect contrast to the work he had completed so far. The mural would express hope and normalcy even during a time of such ravaging changes.

From the front of the church, a tuneless whistling reached the artist's ears. Father Žagar, stopping by to see how the work was progressing, Maxo assumed, but also checking to see how he was doing. Not so very long ago, Father had caught him at a very bad moment. He had never had a minute to explain to the priest what had possessed him that afternoon. Father Žagar's actions had shoved all of his own concerns to one side. He remembered that he had been crying, again.

That day, tears had leaked from Maxo's eyes like a defective faucet dripping water. He could not turn them off though they bleared the wall painting before him. Drops slid down his cheeks, penetrated his beard and soaked into his collar. Paint smudged his eyes where Maxo mopped them with a shirt cuff that had recently made contact with his palette. A sobbing sigh hiccupped its way up his chest, and he blew his nose on a navy blue bandanna.

"Pull yourself together, Maxo," he spoke into the silent cavern of the church apse. "This will do no one any good. They are beyond your help." The thought caused a fresh outpouring as Father Žagar rounded the corner from the church office into the nave.

The priest heard the artist's snuffling and looking up, saw him cross-legged on the scaffolding, the heels of his hands scrubbing at his eyes. With his torso hunched over his knees, Maxo portrayed a sadder picture than any to be found on the church walls.

Father laid a hand on his heart as it pitched out of its usual rhythms. "Maxo, whatever is it?" he called to the weeping man.

Without waiting for an answer, Father seized the long ladder propped against the scaffolding and began to climb. It curved and swayed on its way to the scaffold's edge. Father Žagar closed his eyes, momentarily thinking how much higher this was than the stepstool in the parsonage kitchen. When he opened them, the church apse slewed and slid below him, a writhing whirlpool of pews and altar and aisles. Father nearly hesitated, but the crumpled figure of the artist compelled him onward.

Black thoughts rushed through his mind as he climbed. *Perhaps Maxo had just learned that he was seriously ill. No, Maxo would not weep for himself. His wife, Margaret, then. Injured in some freak accident, or worse, his daughter, succumbing to some dread disease. Or, bad news from the home front. That was surely it. Maxo spent much time thinking about Mati Croatia these days.*

Father sped his steps up, up, and up. Twenty feet above the hard tile floor, the ladder joined the scaffold and continued upward for a few more feet. Shaking, he grasped the nearest upright of the structure and swung a leg around the ladder to place one foot on the level boards of the platform, then the other. His right hand scrabbled to clutch another post so he was able to place his feet astride the scaffolding. Clinging with both hands, Father Žagar addressed the artist.

"Maxo. Maxo. It's me. It's Father. Please, please, won't you tell me what's wrong?" Moisture slickened the palms of his hands, and as Father Žagar's eyes flickered over the deep space immediately to his left, he froze.

The artist's swollen face lifted slowly toward him. A profound grief raged there, transforming his eyes and his cheeks, yes, even his jowls into something unrecognizable. A chill rippled across the priest's back, and Father thought he might be sick.

What had happened to his gentle, kind friend? What had disfigured that peaceful visage, those clear eyes, that smiling mouth? It was a force beyond understanding, beyond imagining. With an awful dread, the priest realized that he could not lift a finger to assuage Maxo's pain.

At the same time, comprehension nudged at the edge of Maxo's consciousness. He rose like someone burdened with a yoke of lead. The boards creaked beneath his feet as he walked stiffly to stand beside Father Žagar.

"God in heaven, Father, what can you be thinking to climb all the way up here? This," he gestured to the dusky cavity of the church's upper story, "this is not at all a safe place for you to be. I fear very much for you. Did you not consider that one of your dizzy spells might topple you over before you could help yourself? Please, Father, permit me to guide you once more to the solid earth below."

The priest straightened his knees and stood firm, his grip clad like iron manacles on the posts. "I'm not going anywhere until you tell me why you are so impossibly sad."

But Maxo shook his head. "You and me, Father, we are too old for such games. I am more sorry than I can tell you that I have caused you such deep concern, but it is of no matter at this moment. Of the first importance is –" and his eyes drilled into Father's, allowing no doubt, "we must return you to the ground."

Father Žagar tucked his chin back toward his neck in mute resistance, but just then his left hand slipped down the pole.

He flinched and with a curt nod, agreed with the artist.

Maxo checked his tears and reached for a long rope that coiled snake-like in a dusty corner. This he tied fast to the nearest upright with a knot worthy of Gordias. He tested its strength with his own weight and satisfied, encircled the priest with the rope's other end, fastening it securely.

Maxo smiled faintly at his friend. "A precaution only."

The artist stepped onto the first rung of the ladder beneath the scaffold. "Now, Father, you trust me, yes? As much as you have ever trusted, please give me your right hand."

The priest's body stretched out at right angles to the scaffold's edge with his back to Maxo. He would need to reach slightly behind his position to extend his hand. A hard lump formed in Father's throat. He closed his eyes and tried to swallow.

"I am right here, Father, right behind you. I would never let you fall. You know this."

A pause. Neither man moved. The tower clock chimed the quarter hour.

"Please, Father. Please, it will be all right."

Maxo reached up to Father Žagar's right wrist. "You are going to give me your hand, and I am going to move it, oh, about fifteen inches so you will be able to grasp the ladder. Okay? This is okay, yes? Okay. Here we go. One, two, three…"

The priest uncurled his fingers one at a time. A bead of sweat dropped from his forehead, making him blink.

"That's it. That's good, Father."

Maxo guided the hand from upright to ladder. "Good. Now we move the left hand, but you must also shuffle your feet to the right so they are ready to climb down."

Again, the pause. Father labored to breathe, his chest nearly paralyzed with tension. He did not look down. Instead, he stared straight ahead, blindly at first. Colors swam in a mixed fog before him, but as they cleared, he realized that he was facing the mural above the altar. Mary, Mother of God, composed and calm, gazed at him as she floated there. *You can do this*, he thought.

"You can do this," Maxo said, and the priest transferred his hand to the ladder, and then his feet to the first rung.

"Now, Father, just one more thing."

"Oh, God, what? What now?" The priest licked his lips and leaned into the ladder.

"The ladder cannot support both of us at the same point at the same time. So. So, we must space ten rungs, only ten feet between us at all times. I will go down ten steps and call for you, all right?" And before the priest could argue, Maxo started downwards. The ladder flexed and shook with the artist's weight. Father Žagar flattened his body against the ladder, pressing hard into the wood.

"Okay," he heard from down below. "Come. Come now."

Father glanced at the great head of Mother Mary. "Lord, give me courage; Mother, guide my steps," he whispered and dangled his right foot toward the rung below.

The descent began in earnest, Maxo moving down a rung for every step that Father took. The priest's feet touched the cool tiles of the church floor far more quickly than he had expected, and a wave of relief surged through him. He knelt at once, and with a flushed face, thanked God and Mary and all of the angels who had watched over him. Maxo thanked the priest for keeping his head.

"It is the Lord's will that I live to continue His work," the priest said to his artist friend. "Now, let us remove ourselves to the rectory for a warming cup of tea." The ghost of a twinkle lit Father's eye. "And perhaps a dollop of whiskey. I want to hear all about what is troubling you so."

As Father undid the rope from around his waist and dusted his cassock, Maxo noted the tremor in his voice, and a twitch seemed to have invaded his hands. Then, with a shake of his shoulders, the priest walked away, his right hand anchoring him to the prayer rail in front of the first pew. At the door, he turned and coughed. "Coming?" he said to Maxo.

Now Father's whistling drifted into silence as he stepped toward the back of the church. As happened most days, the enormous battle scene on the ceiling arrested his gaze. He stood straight and held his hands behind his back in a relaxed pose. *Maxo had been one hundred percent right,* he thought. *This half of the Battlefield mural works well here. Very well.* With intelligent eyes, he noted the final touches that had brought the portrayal to life.

Clapping his hands, Father approached the table where Maxo had arranged his paints at the rear of the church. "Magnificent work, my friend, breath-taking. There is no one who will not be moved when they see this painting."

The artist smiled into his palette as he mixed gentian violet with blue and ebon, and began outlining a seated child in the lower corner of the new mural. "It makes my heart glad to hear your words. Now, we will make some delicious colors, more uplifting perhaps, for this household scene. Do you not think it will make a marked contrast with the seething ceiling above? The observer's mind will have to hop, hop to make the leap, but it will be good, no?" He scratched a small stool beneath the child's bottom. "And while I have to bend to this part of the task, I will be able to stand straight and tall for most of this painting. Yes!"

He beamed at the priest, and Father Žagar could not help grinning back at him. "These are all good things, Maxo, all good." He pulled at his nose for a minute. "But don't be too late, all right? This is the night that our dear cook is making that special meal you requested. She told me to tell you that it shouldn't be more than an hour now."

To underscore the message, the delicious smells of roasted chicken and warm bread filtered from the rectory through the back door of the church. Father trailed back to the house. The clanging of pots and pans told Maxo that dinner preparations were indeed underway. Though he could not say that eating ranked high in importance for him, Maxo liked the cacophony of sounds and smells that preceded a meal. It brought familiar and well-loved scenes into his mind – picking strawberries with Peggica, watching lamb turn on a spit, or lunching with his friends in the early spring sunshine of Zagreb.

In his memory, clinking plates and the ting of silverware had chorused behind the conversational buzz of the café. The sidewalk tables had bulged with students taking a mid-morning break from the nearby School of Arts and Crafts. Despite the unseasonable coolness of the spring day, they huddled in groups of four or five or six, debating drawing techniques, arguing politics, or simply making plans for the evening.

Cheeks ablaze, Darko stole a chair from a neighboring table and pulled in next to Maxo. Instantly, a waiter appeared at his side, well attuned to the comings and goings of this crowd.

"Coffee, lots of hot coffee, and hot milk," Darko ordered. "Oh, and some of that poppy seed rugulach would be perfect," he called after the disappearing back. "Hvala! Thank you!"

Sun streamed thinly over the bowed head of his friend, Maxo. With a charcoal pencil, he sketched on the pad in his lap. His café au lait waited patiently at his elbow.

"What's this, my friend? Still working? Never a moment's rest, eh?" Darko peered over the edge of the table. A neat representation of the next table but one with its three female occupants emblazoned the center of the page. "By Jove, Vanka, you've captured their very essence! But won't you drink your coffee before it grows cold and sour?"

Maxo raised his head and smiled. It was as though the sun had come out in full spate. "You lead with your stomach, *tu sais*, Darko?" He chuckled softly. "But in this rare moment, I cannot pass up the chance to – well, you see how the light hits her shoulder, the one in green, I mean? And how it slides into darkness beneath her breast?"

Darko gave an approving look at the young lady in question and smirked at Maxo.

"This little sketch. It will remind me of that, that essence, as you call it when I get back to my paint box." Maxo's eyes gave a twinkle, and his long straight nose raised a smidgen along with his lips. He stroked his beard. "But I can see that you did not plop down at this table to discuss the question of chiaroscuro with me."

The big bear on the other side of Maxo grunted and spoke for the first time. A rich baritone outlined his voice. "How likely do you suppose that would ever be with our Darko Mislav, eh, Inri?" Like many, Grgur used the holy nickname for Maxo – a reflection of his abstemious practices as well as his gaunt, bearded, and somewhat hallowed appearance. Grgur puffed out a cloud of cigarette smoke and fiddled with a piece of tobacco stuck to his tongue. He slammed a hand on the table good-naturedly. "I can see you are bursting to tell us something, Monsieur Mislav. Fire away."

"Well, I do have some rather splendid news. It's this," Darko replied, glancing again at the table of pretty girls. "Aleksander Zadanska is throwing a huge dinner party at his parents' country estate this Friday coming." He gulped the steaming coffee that had arrived at the table. "They have a beautiful place near Ivanic-Grad – just thirty kilometers away, you know – and we're all invited. We can take the early evening train from Zagreb Glavni Kolodvor and be there in no time. There will doubtless be a grand smorgasbord and I am sure, excellent wine *and* dancing. We're each supposed to bring the prettiest girl we know."

At this, he prodded Maxo in the ribs and tilted his head toward the girl in green. The young artist received numerous jibes from his friends about his lack of interest in the opposite sex. It was not so much a lack of interest as a lack of time, the serious student had explained on more than one occasion.

"Hmmm," Grgur cleared his throat. "That does sound too good to miss. Will you tell him then from us that we'll be happy to attend?" He threw a playful arm around Maxo's shoulders. "And we'll be glad to help our friend here find a suitable young lady to escort."

Gently this time, Maxo smiled once more. "My friends, how can I ever thank you for this kindness? So good of you to look after me!" And with this, a hearty laugh erupted from his mouth.

Before he was done laughing, Darko had made his way to the nearby table of young women. He bowed to them and leaned in close between the lady in green and her friend.

"Darko," Maxo murmured. Grgur covered his mouth with a big burly hand. Maxo watched the green-gowned woman closely. She was smiling up at Darko, and the ring of deep brown curls that framed her face shimmered as she laughed at what Maxo could only imagine was Darko's version of a polite invitation to dine with a complete stranger. The curls graced a skin so pale, so pure, it could have been carved from alabaster, and only a hint of rouge rose on the cheek set beside the pert nose as she responded to Darko.

Without warning, she turned to gain a better view of Grgur and Maxo, but her intent was checked by the look in Maxo's eyes. He drank her in like a man with a terrible thirst and did not look away. The radiant smile was back on his face, and she became its captive. Maxo stood and bowed low with a slight flourish of his hand. She returned a gracious nod.

Darko rushed back to their table. "Isn't she a stunner?" he said. "And with a voice to match that dulcet face – sweet as a nightingale's."

All of the sudden, Maxo's tongue was a-rush with questions. "Did you get her name? Did she agree to attend the gathering? Does she dance? Would she really consider accompanying me?"

As his voice gathered speed, all three women turned to face the young men's table. They murmured to each other, and in their absorption, the green goddess' girlfriend dropped her handkerchief.

"Her name is Jelena, Jelena Petarsic," Darko shouted after him as Maxo sprang to retrieve the square of lace. "And she says yes …" but the rest of his commentary faded away as Maxo reached the ladies and their table.

With some fanfare, Maxo knelt and rescued the missing handkerchief. He restored it to its owner with a kiss of her hand. Then, he knelt on one knee before Jelena and adorned her hand in similar fashion. Their smiles burst forth, and the two instantly fell to chatting as though they were old friends. Maxo's smile surrounded the whole table, and soon all three young women were plying him with questions and offers of tea and invitations to bide awhile with them.

Darko shook his head. "How does he do it? One moment, he is the retiring ascetic; the next, the social center of the universe!"

"Well, what did you say to them?" Grgur asked.

"Little enough, really," Darko replied, "though they seemed terribly interested in the fact that Maxo had drawn a sketch of them. And naturally, I invited all three to Alek's dinner because they are all charming in their own way, don't you think?"

"Ah, little Darko, ever the romantic." Grgur patted his friend's hand. "Of course, of course, you have done well." In truth, Grgur had never dreamed of working up the courage to invite a young lady to dinner. He sat a little straighter, thumped Darko's back, and clearing his throat once more, said, "Yes, well done."

Friday night found the three comrades on the platform at Zagreb's main station. Grgur took quick puffs of his cigarette and stared at the tracks. Darko darted here and there, checking timetables, eying the clock, and scanning the crowded platform for their intended guests. Maxo leant against a pillar, reading a book, and occasionally following the pigeons that shifted back and forth on the station roof.

Darko, the stylish one among them, sported a purple velvet jacket with dark trousers and a crisp white shirt. A loosely tied scarf of mauve-and-black-patterned silk set off his ruddy complexion, and more than one woman graced him with a second look as he dashed up and down the trackside. In contrast, Grgur's city suit of chalk-striped brown muted his size and his personality, but a waistcoat of gold brocade that peeped from beneath his jacket offered a glimpse of something livelier. Meanwhile, Maxo's individuality in choice of dress allowed no mistaking the avant-garde artiste within. The soft felt hat, a silk shirt with flowing sleeves, and a pair of light-colored trousers favored his slender form. A matching jacket hung lightly around his shoulders, and a cravat of seaside colors fluttered from his neck to his waistline. By no means a man without resources, habiliment mattered little to him, and Maxo often selected his clothing from the gypsy bazaar where the colors and sounds and smells of the market place bore more import than any clothing he might find there.

Despite Darko's reconnaissance, Maxo spotted their companions first, around the same time that the train pulled in. Like fairies made of cake and icing, the three women floated toward them dressed in all the colors of the Spring – new grass green, daffodil yellow, tulip pink. Their big skirts ballooned in the breeze, and Maxo pictured the young women as enchanted sprites that had drifted their way on the wind.

After gazing at them for some little time, Maxo collected his friends, and they sallied forth to greet the young women. Maxo proffered an arm to Jelena, while Grgur escorted Valerija, the dark blonde beauty whose handkerchief was now safely secured in her evening bag. Darko brought up the rear with the petite Ana, a puff of rose tulle hooked onto his arm. He grinned happily.

After a brief search, the party found an empty compartment toward the middle of the train, and they were off. Sandwiched between the flowing chiffon of Valerija's dress and Ana's pink pouffe, Darko nestled and grinned even more broadly. Maxo smiled at his friend and then averted his eyes to the passing landscape. The afterglow of the setting sun tinted the hillocks and farmhouses in delicious hues of sepia and peach, like the colors at the beginning of a dream.

Jelena watched Maxo watching. His face reflected the quiet shades though his eyes shone light and white from the belated sunstreaks now curving over the horizon. Contentment colored his countenance, and she sensed that an interruption of his reverie might not be welcome. Instead, she turned to Grgur on her right and asked what the evening would bring.

Grgur immediately colored, and flustered, he said, "Er, well, you had better ask our Darko. He is the organizer of tonight's affairs."

Darko, quick to the rescue, said, "Aleksander Zadanska

you will find to be a most genial host. He is the son of well-to-do merchants that keep a summer place in Ivanic-Grad. Wait until you see the house. It is magnificent."

"Yes, but what can we expect?" Jelena really wanted to know more about her hosts. It would inform her behavior for the night. If they were wealthy, but uncultured, she would need to play down her own background. If they were well off and of high rank, she could draw on her own noble heritage to meet them on the same level and cultivate whatever opportunities might present themselves.

Of course, Darko did not interpret her question in this way. "There will be a grand entryway decorated with flowers and laurels, and we will no doubt be asked into the ballroom." At her quizzical look, he added, "That is, after dining. There is an immense dinner table that can seat forty, I believe, and Alek is sure to put on a banquet worthy of a prince."

Jelena's ears perked up. "Prince?"

"Well, you know what I mean," Darko said. "And the wine, oo-la-la, my dear, never less than the best."

Grgur smacked his lips in anticipation. Maxo's head cocked ever so slightly to his right as he followed the conversation. Then he glanced at Darko and said, "I do not believe Miss Jelena is asking about the refreshments. Are you, Mademoiselle?" He turned to face Jelena.

She had the courtesy to blush. "It's just that … it's … everything is so new to us. I mean, we have met all of you only for the first time the other day, and I want to know more. Umm, more about each of you." This last she added as she studied the lace trim of her gloves. She could feel Maxo's disbelief edging her hairline.

"Ah, well, if that is all, that is fair enough," Maxo rejoined. "Let me give you a brief histoire."

And by the time they had arrived at Ivanic-Grad station, the young women had learned that Darko, a city boy from Zagreb, studied art and art history with an eye to teaching some day. He did not actually need to worry about working as his parents were related to old Yugoslavian nobility, and he would inherit his wealth, just as they had. Grgur, on the other hand, grew up on the Dalmatian coast near Labin where he had learned to work stone at an early age beside his mason father. That had translated into a love of molding, touching, feeling, and shaping stone, and now the Arts and Crafts School considered him a first rate sculpture student.

Maxo, they already knew as a serious artist, but that did not stop him from waxing at some length about his interests. "It is essential that I, we, no, all artists experiment with many, many types of media," he explained to his companions. "At present, I have the great honor to study under the excellent Professor Csikos-Sessia. I wish to perfect my understanding of his classical approaches to peinture, and yes, some of the newer techniques as well. It seems that I have a penchant for the paint and the brush in particular."

"I'll say," Darko intervened. "Did you know that our Maxo has already won some recognition for his painting?"

Maxo ignored the remark and continued to discuss art for so long that the young women had no further chance for questions before they were climbing down the steps to the platform and the waiting hansom. Maxo smiled as he handed Jelena down from the train. He had never bothered to mention that his lineage likely extended to members of the Austro-Hungarian nobility.

As the carriage pulled up to the elegant three-storey façade of white stucco and red tiled roof, the house was ablaze with light. True to Darko's description, the entryway hung with a hundred lanterns that threw the surrounding greenery into relief. Skyrocketing arborvitae, pyramidal yews, and resplendent borders of King Alfred daffodils and lush early tulips laid a welcoming path for the visitors.

A solemn butler dressed all in black took the ladies' wraps, and they proceeded down the hall toward the music. On Maxo's arm, Jelena looked eager. "Oh, I love this waltz, don't you?" and she hummed along with the violin as it crooned out the bars of the Emperor Waltz.

Maxo's brows shot up. "Ah, you are a musician, then?"

She thought she detected a small note of approval. "Yes, well, that is, Mother made sure we all had musical training. I have been told I am rather good on the piano, but I yearn to master the pipe organ. There is nothing more magical than a large church organ in full thrust, its bass pipes trembling within your breast, its tenor the pure sound of reeds blowing in the wind. It enthralls me like nothing else." She paused, feeling she had said too much, but Maxo nodded, shaking his brown locks.

"Yes, yes, I understand you perfectly," he said. "As I was viewing the countryside tonight, the colors were so sweet, so mellow, such a perfect blend of light and dark. I – I was transported. Transported to another plane of existence. Music can do the same, I believe." He eyed his partner pensively.

"That's it exactly, Monsieur Vanka."

"Maxo, please, we are not so formal here."

"Maxo, then," she said. "But your point about being lifted up and carried away – that is what pipe organ, well-played pipe organ does for me. I often wish that everyone had this experience with something in their lives, something so uplifting." Her eyes gleamed in the candlelight. "But I'm not sure they do." She dropped her eyes, not wishing to avoid Maxo's gaze, but becoming rather sad at the thought.

"But isn't this what art does for everyone?" Maxo asked, as a firm hand clapped down on his shoulder.

"Asked like the true art student you are, my good friend." Aleksander Zadanska greeted him. "Only far too serious a question for tonight, or at least this early in the evening before we've had a bottle or two." His face smiled as he turned toward the attractive women filling the hall. "Now, please, do me the kindness of introducing your lovely acquaintances."

A few hours later, Darko and Maxo shared the remaining pour from the champagne bottle at their table. Both of their companions swept around the room, their skirts swaying gracefully from side to side as they danced the Viennese waltz. The dark-haired, dark-eyed Alek held the exquisite Jelena in his arms, while his younger cousin clasped little Ana. Maxo did not dance much as a rule, but he had been given little chance of a round with Jelena once the Lothario-like Alek had set his sights on her.

"Now we can see why Alek insisted on us bringing the prettiest girls we could find," he joked with Darko.

"Really, Maxo, it does not seem entirely fair, does it?"

"Do you know, my friend, I truly do not mind all that much. Beauty may be better observed from this distance, and in the end, I will have one less distraction from my work than I might have should things have grown serious between me and the lovely Jelena."

"You are the philosophe, my dear Maxo," Darko smiled softly. "I would that I could remain as calm about these things as you do. As it is, I think I have what you might call quite a little pash for dear Ana. Such a sweet little thing. Ah well, she has promised me the last dance."

"I have seen how she looks at you, Darko. I think you will have plenty of attention from Ana over time. She is probably wondering why you do not wrest her from this boy dancer right now," he said as the cousin trod on her slippered toe.

Darko tossed back his drink. "What a marvelous idea. Toute á l'heure, Maxo!" He marched onto the dance floor in pursuit of the whirling Ana.

Maxo stroked his nose and leaned forward. The exchange of pant leg and billowing skirt, the blur of faces and feathers and flying hair, the churn of dancers in and out of the lamplight, the scuff of soles in time to the gay music. All paraded before him. *As pretty a picture as Degas ever painted*, he thought and marveled once again at the artist's ability to capture the verve and motion and energy of the dance. In his head, he filed away the scene to be summoned again when he had need of interjecting its fluidity and its sanguinity into a future painting.

Returning to the present, Maxo rested his eyes on Jelena as she twirled below the arm of her partner. Here was a mystery, or at least, a mixture that stirred his imagination but gave few answers. Her beauty was beyond compare to any other woman's in the room that night, yet she had betrayed a surprising shallowness of character that had bothered him. Somehow, he had expected beauty of face to be accompanied by beauty of spirit. This had not been the case, or so he thought. Then in the entry hall, she had surprised him once again with her declared love of music – of organ music - which he thought to be sincere. Suddenly, she had looked into his artist's heart and spoken to it.

"Maxo!" Father called. "Maxo!"

The reverie burst – a thin bubble of time that brought pleasure and a little regret.

"Maxo, we're about to eat," the priest shouted. "Come on, man, it's an hour and a half since we spoke."

Maxo covered his palette, slipped his brushes into a jar of turpentine, and arranged his rags over the end pew after checking to make sure that no paint spatters touched the wood. "Coming, Father! Goodness, coming as fast as I can!" He plunged through the rectory, gave a quick wave into the kitchen, and said, "One more moment – I cannot present myself at such a grand meal without the proper attire."

The artist slid into the bathroom for a hasty wash. He was not long in his ablutions, but he took the time to laugh at himself. It had been forever since he had thought about that dance at the Zadanska residence, and even longer since he had contemplated the mysterious girl's beauty. *My mind, you take charge of my work for me, do you not?* He chuckled, realizing that now he had started the search for the ghost's origins in earnest, it appeared his brain was going to leave no corner of his memory unexposed.

"Yes, Father, I come!" He thrust the face towel onto the rack. "Coming, this instant!"

CHAPTER FOUR

"I THINK HE MISSES HIS FAMILY," Mrs. Dobrovic told her daughter as the lard in the pan sizzled behind her words. "It's the only possibility of why he don't eat more of the good food I make for him, eh?"

"Oh, Mamma," the girl sighed, but he did not catch the rest of the sentence. It was enough to hear the exasperation that coated her words.

Maxo chuckled. He had slipped into the house to use the facilities, and now as the water from the bathroom sink lapped his hands, he overheard their discussion. *Well, not much of a discussion*, he thought, *more like Mrs. Dobrovic thinking out loud like she does most days*. Once more, his cheeks fluttered with quiet laughter. *Young Cara does not often intervene in her train of thought, oh no. It is likely she has learned that her mama would pay her no heed in any event. Not an inconsiderate lady, so engaged in her own conversation, nothing else filters in.*

Maxo examined his moustache in the mirror for paint flecks and reflected on his own daughter, Peggy. *Cara is no match at all for ma petite sprite – not a bit. You do not catch my Peggica waiting to say something.* Though he considered that she must be four or five years younger than Cara, Peggy was as full of thoughts and excitement as one girl could be.

A brief smile flitted past Maxo's lips as he remembered the

day she had dashed up to the breakfast table, already out on some great exploration before the meal had been spread. Her mother had tugged one of her plaits playfully and reminded her to give him a good morning kiss before Peggy had burst out, "Oh, Papa, guess what I've discovered down by the barn?"

"Why, whatever could it be, my little petal? Is it a big, black bear?" he had asked.

"Papa! No, you *are* silly, not a bear!" She had shaken her head.

"What? Do you mean – do you mean it was the giraffe I saw down there just the other day?"

Peggy had shrieked with laughter. "No, Papa, you must come and see for yourself. It is something much sweeter than either of those." At that, she had grabbed his long slender fingers and pulled on them with both her small fists until he rose and escorted her to the barn. His wife, Margaret – or Peggy the Elder as he sometimes teased – had bestowed an indulgent smile on both of them.

"Peggy, don't keep Papa away too long lest the nutkins spirit away his toast and jam, and yours, too!"

Maxo recalled how the morning had greeted them as he opened the front door. The early sun warmed the grass, and scents of hay and loam rose like invisible smoke as they stepped outdoors. Peggy had frisked down the stone path ahead of him. Like a frolicsome colt, she skipped and spun her way to the barn, her braids flying in all directions, and he had fallen under her enchantment all over again. He remembered rubbing the hair on his chin and wondering. *Could such energy be captured in a painting? What colors and what brushstrokes could possibly do it justice?*

As they neared the silo end of the barn, Peggy pointed upwards. Maxo lifted her, and they moved in for a closer look. What looked like a thick daub of mud had been caulked into the joint between roof and siding. Sticks and strings gave the rounded mass a curious texture, like a basket embedded at the bottom of a streambed.

"Oh, well done, my dearest Peggica," Maxo had whispered

with a tone of reverence. "You have discovered the house-making of Mr. and Mrs. Swallow – Mr. and Mrs. Barn Swallow to be exact." He watched as one of the adult birds emerged from a hole in the nest and zoomed away. He breathed out. "Oh! Oh my!"

"Papa, did you ever see anything so beautiful in your life? Did you see the flash of purple in the blue as the father bird flew away?"

Maxo passed his hand down the back of his head as once more he met his own eyes in the bathroom mirror. Real happiness crowded his chest as he remembered Peggy's bright eyes and how clever she was, already seeing life from a deeper perspective than most people ever would. Perhaps she would befriend the swallows much as he had the small brown birds living in the rectory garden.

As pots and pans clanged in the kitchen, the happy feeling slid into an ache that stretched through him like a long, taut muscle. Mrs. Dobrovic had been right about one thing. He missed his girl fiercely. Fiercely.

His stomach panged with hunger as a raft of good smells shifted his thoughts back to the kitchen. The cook's recipes were good. On this he concurred with Father and anyone else who might join them for a meal. Thick-sliced brown bread generously spread with butter, peas in white sauce, roasted chicken, boiled new potatoes – all good, hearty food offered in plain but quite satisfactory style.

Maxo realized he would need to do something to avoid injuring Mrs. Dobrovic's feelings. He did not know how to make her understand that when the painting was going well, it consumed him and eclipsed any idea he might have of eating her good food.

The work truly did absorb him. He licked his lips and pressed them together. *Bože moj – to have an entire church for one's canvas. To lavish color and texture and light and shadow in bold, strong strokes.* He swallowed as he walked out of the bathroom. *To fashion a statement that was the soul and embodiment of what needed to get onto those walls. To snare the energy – no, better words, the force of the action – with figures, faces, and hands and feet that demanded the viewers' attention. Forcing them to look. Making them fear and yes, think. Think what was happening. And think what must be done to stop it. Mati Croatia was suffering, sinking, bound, and they must do all they could to rescue her.*

"Oh! Mr. Maxo, you scared me, hunkering there in the hall like that!" Mrs. Dobrovic said as she came through the kitchen door wiping her hands on her apron. "Was you wanting something?"

Maxo's fright had been equal to her own, so deep had he glided into his own thoughts. He shuddered but it was more an act of coming back to present time than shirking off fear.

"Oh, oh, oh, Mama Dobrovic, I am so dreadfully sorry if I startled you," he bowed slightly toward her stout figure. "Actually, I was washing my hands and coming to see you, with a little surprise, I hope."

"Ooh?" The cook rounded her lips and looked at the hem of her apron. "What sort of surprise would that be, Mr. Maxo?" Hesitation hovered at the back of her words.

"I am going to buy for you the most special thing," he said, waving a hand as if to shoo away her doubts, "and you, you with your great culinary expertise, will make it into a chef d'oeuvre!" To the puzzled look in her eyes, he explained, "What you call a masterpiece!"

"Oh, what would that be then? I know how to cook most things."

"Well, it is ultimately delectable. In Croatia by the sea, we call it škampi. But here, it is shrimp." Maxo extended the word into two syllables – sha-rimp – savoring the word with the same relish he reserved for the sweet meat of the shellfish. "A little beer, a little bay, a little butter, and voilà!" The artist kissed the tips of his fingers and offered them to the air.

"That is a new one on me, Mr. Maxo, but I'm game to try it," Mrs. Dobrovic said.

Later, she confided her unease to her daughter in another one-sided conversation. "He was so enthusiastic about it, I couldn't hardly tell him I'd never cooked any of his shrimps before. But there, you see, there's not much I wouldn't do for Mr. Maxo, he's so kind." She pooched her lips thoughtfully. "He's different, you know, Cara. I feel like he's the first person that I've cooked for who ever really listened to me. And that includes your father."

Cara nodded. If she had known how to express it, she would have told her mother that Maxo Vanka was equally kind to her and had taken an interest in her schoolwork and what her favorite books were. He made her feel like a real person instead of a shadow against the wall, which is how she thought most people saw her.

The next night, true to his word, Maxo delivered three dozen shrimp to Mrs. Dobrovic's kitchen. At first, she stood hands on hips, her nose crimping into wrinkles between her small eyes.

"Them's an awful lot of legs, Mr. M." She poked the tip of a knife in and out of the pile of shellfish. "And heavens, they do smell, and what are these stiff feathers at the ends? Do we eat those?" She wiped her brow when Maxo explained that they were the tails and could be cut off.

"Ah yes, but the legs. All the better for stripping the shells, my friend," Maxo had said to her earlier remark, and he plopped the meaty sea creatures into the boiling kettle she had prepared at his instruction.

For once, Maxo sat to eat with gusto, but not before he had made Mrs. Dobrovic and Cara understand that they would eat with him and Father Žagar. The unpeeled shrimp steamed on the platter before them, flanked by bowls of fresh green beans and yellow corn.

Everyone sat and stared at the mound. With a glint in his eyes, Maxo flashed a smile that lit the room like the sun coming out at night. He laughed. "Here, if you please, let me demonstrate." He selected a shrimp and grasped the back of the pinky-coral shell in one hand and the weedy looking legs in the other. A quick twist and a tug, and the curl of white flesh popped from its jacket. Maxo repeated the action several times, and then wiping his hands on a napkin, he asked for the sauce.

Melted butter flaked with parsley filled the gravy boat that came his way, and he dribbled the golden liquid over the shelled shrimp with a practiced hand. Immediately, he forked one into his mouth. He leant back and closed his eyes as he chewed the rubbery meat. His mouth popped and smacked as the succulent shrimp roused juices from his tongue and cheeks.

"My dear, dear Mama Dobrovic, you, you who are such a marvelous cook at all times, you have outdone yourself tonight. Superb, absolutely superb!" He looked at his friends. "Oh, but please, please help yourselves, do – plenty for all." He nudged the shrimp platter toward the cook.

Mrs. Dobrovic tucked her chin into her neck, and the dimpled folds of her cheeks wreathed a smile that was a cross between approval and satisfaction. She spooned some of the shrimp onto her dinner plate. Soon a general chorus of chewing and slurping sounded around the table as the diners devoured shrimp well doused in the liquefied butter.

"And how anything that smelled that bad could taste so good on the other end is beyond me," Mrs. Dobrovic commented to Maxo a little later. "Though if this funny kind of food can get you to eat, I'll be more than happy to make all you want and then some." The artist laughed as she concealed a burp behind her napkin.

He reflected upon the noisy and cheerful scene at the rectory dining table before him. Everyone seemed to have learned the knack of peeling the warm shrimp, and it became a race to see who could do so the most quickly. Father Žagar, it had to be said, showed real talent for this new skill and had come out ahead, judging from the stack of discarded shells in the bowl next to his plate. A close second was the cook who had surprised everyone by sucking on her empty shells to catch every drop of the delicious flavor.

All told, Maxo thought, *an unqualified success.* Mrs. Dobrovic now knew that he appreciated her cooking, no matter what she was making, and to a person, everyone enjoyed being introduced to the new food.

With some gallantry, Maxo stood and turned to the cook

with a slight bow. "Dear Mrs. D., I hope by now that you can understand that it is not your cooking that keeps me away from the table most nights, but simply my vast, vast hunger to create something special on the walls of the church. And the platters of fruit and cheese and bread you put together, even if I eat them so, so very late at night, are a cherished part of my day."

Taking her hand, he saluted it with a small kiss. Mrs. Dobrovic fanned herself with her apron and pushed him away. "Go on, now, back to your painting then. These dishes won't wash themselves, you know." With a meaningful look in Cara's direction, she retreated to the kitchen with a stack of soiled china. Cara clinked after her with handfuls of cutlery.

After the feast, as the good cook had suggested, Maxo returned to the church and resumed his work. He stood on a lower scaffold tonight as he studied the wall where a mural that he called *Greed* was beginning to take shape. He sniffed quietly at the contrast between it and the meal that they had just eaten. This mural depicted a rich man of uncertain age seated at a solitary board while a sad servant and a sadder mendicant looked on and hoped for some crumbs to fall from his table. Tomorrow, when it was not so late and he could climb higher, he would paint the devil's hand at work in the tableau.

As he sketched on the wall, Maxo's cheeks clucked with another chuckle. How Margaret would have loved the evening and the exchange. A fine lady in every respect, she was not above indulging in good fun when it came her way. Maxo's smile tucked toward his eyes and tinged them with something sad as he thought of his Peggy – Peggy-starija – Peggy the Elder. He shook his head. He missed her ready laugh and the way her head threw so far back, he could count the fillings in her teeth and practically see the mirth curling up from her belly. Low and forceful, it reminded him of a mezzo-soprano's aria forte – loud but musical.

They kept in touch by letter reasonably well, meaning she wrote long, detailed letters from home weekly, and he sent brief notes and cartoons for Peggica when the mood swept him. Maxo found it challenging to put to paper the discussions that he longed to hold with his wife about what he was trying to convey on the walls of this mighty little church.

They had mutually agreed that he must travel to Pittsburgh alone while she and Peggica stayed on the farm – after all, Peggy must attend school – but it was more for his benefit. *No*, Maxo thought, *not quite right. It benefited all of them. Well, honestly?* He tugged his right ear. *It is like what I just tried to explain to Mrs. D, how absolute my absorption can become once I begin the work – its conception, its drafting, its outlining, its painting, its completion. If I am truthful,* he grimaced at the thought, *precious little time remains for anything approximating family life after one of my days on the scaffolds.*

Margaret and he had covered this ground before. Both recognized the truth of the matter, and it was a testament to her good nature that she understood and fully supported what he needed – *good word, that, needed* – to complete his work within a confining deadline. Maxo sighed.

All logical, all sensible, all well thought out, and all of which meant utterly nothing when he felt his loins contract just at the thought of her. Or, he could be passing by a rose in the vicarage garden whose fragrance instantly transported him to the back of her neck where the sun caressed the bronze summer skin. There, his nose could nestle among the tiny hairs that played beneath her hairline. There, the sun's warmth gave rise to the rosewater scent of that morning's bathwater, lifting it from her skin and wafting it straight into his soul.

His blood pulsed in his belly. He imagined her curved into him, lying face away in their big bed and snoring lightly. And her taste – his tongue humped against the roof of his mouth. Maxo bit both lips together tightly and closed his eyes. *Neck of musk and mouth of sleep's salt and a hint of the preceding night's honey-drenched confection.*

A bittersweet aftertaste tipped his tongue and snapped Maxo back from his musings. He gulped heavily and straightened his shoulders. *Another reason for handling the work alone. I simply must not suffer these distractions if I ever plan to finish the murals.* Mentally, he set aside the beauty and the attractions of his other life and slipped back into the current familiar of ascetic artist.

Maxo stretched and then resumed his standing position on the scaffold, palette and brushes in hand. Tonight, triggered by thoughts during dinner, he had moved back to the *Greed* mural for some added detail. He would focus on the servant, paint him black as the night, paint him sad as the greatest sorrow, paint him supine and supplicant, paint him the way he saw Negroes in American society, still enslaved by public opinion though their emancipation was nearly eighty years old.

The slightest movement of air, cool as a winter's breath, whispered across the back of his neck. Maxo shivered despite the evening's warmth, then flapped the air before him, swatting dust motes and his own fear like pesky flies. He did not bother to turn around, knowing full well that no one would be there, and that this tiny church – well, rather its duplicitous drafts could fool the fearful into believing that they might have substance and form.

The chill reminded him that his quest for answers, for why the ghost had made its reappearance, had yet to be satisfied. This time, however, his mind did not wander too far from the present.

As Maxo combined sienna brown and ebon together on his palette, he examined the question with fresh eyes. What if the spirit was not from his distant past, or even his near past? *What if he or she*, he thought, *is a messenger sent to me regarding the subject matter that I portray on these very walls? But if that is the case, what is it trying to tell me?*

Maxo used the boar bristle brush and stroked in the skin of the black man on the wall. He would pick up a finer brush to supply the details, but for now, he worked on achieving the right colors. The skin should shine with distress and by contrast, the man's eyes must stand out – dull, but white and anguished.

If, stroke, stroke, *if it is about my paintings, then surely*, he cleaned a spot with his rag, *surely, it would be to support the lessons depicted.* Maxo could imagine no other possibility. *But why then*, here he struggled with an idea he loathed to consider, *why do I have such a feeling of froideur, of fear, of fate knocking on my door?*

As if in response, the faint tingle waffled his neck hairs once more. This time Maxo reeled around, but the perfidious atmosphere of the church displayed nothing. Only deep shadow crouched beyond the working lamps he had erected to shine on the mural of *Greed.*

CHAPTER FIVE

"OH, I'M NOT SO SURE about calling this mural *Greed*." Father passed the blackberry jam to Maxo. "The word doesn't feel," he mumbled while chewing his toast, "big enough."

"No? Well, Father, I must say, greed seems to me a global concept," Maxo said, "in two ways." He dipped a spoon into the jam jar. "One," he spread the confection on a corner of his bread, "there is no place on earth – no place, I tell you, in the whole wor-old" he endowed the word with two syllables, "where greed does not exist. And two," he laid down the spoon and shot Father a look from under his brows, "greed has led to the destruction of men and families. No truer examples can be found than the ones here in Pittsburgh, especially as we arrived in the new century."

Father raised a hand to protest. However, Maxo's hand flew up at the same time with his own exclamation.

"But, but we would be most foolish to think that despite the recent victories of the steel unions - " he munched on the bread, "that is, we would be deceived if we thought that greed did not yet promote the causes of the rich men, don't you see?" Maxo dabbed a few crumbs from his moustache as Father leaned back in his chair, wiping his buttery fingers on the linen square in his lap.

"What I started to mention before," Father Žagar smiled,

"is that I think you have captured something else, something more complex than the notion of greed in your painting. If you were to pull out your sketch, or if we took a stroll to the church and looked at what you have completed so far, we would see that you are expressing multiple themes." Father grabbed his coffee cup, but set it down again. "The painting has a bit of everything – the Negro's plight, poverty, the devil's hand at play, a certain lack of charity, the, the …"

"The forcing of people to become supplicant?" The artist cocked his brows.

"No, what I was about to say had more to do with what I see as the aloofness of the rich man – his obvious disregard," Father blew on his coffee and sipped cautiously, "maybe even his distaste for things that are beneath his notice." He rapped the table, and his spoon jangled to the floor. He grunted as he bent to pick it up, and his voice came muffled from the folds of the tablecloth. "Like people who are indigent, and especially the man of color. It's all right for them to wait on him, but he has no intention of interacting with their like."

Maxo's eyes glistened as he heard the priest's words. "Bože moj, how you make me see my own work from a new perspective. These ideas, these thoughts are well considered, Father, well considered and well put. So then," he leaned toward the plate and tore off another morsel of toast, "what do you suggest we call it?"

The cleric cracked a broad smile and laughed. "I was afraid this conversation might turn in that direction! And I confess, though I have given it some deliberation, I don't have an answer for you. At least, not yet."

The two friends chuckled and clinked their coffee cups against one another. "Here is to a search for the best, or at least a better title for the *Greed* mural," Maxo toasted as Mrs. Dobrovic entered to clear away the breakfast dishes.

How companionable it is to have such a friend, Maxo thought as he stood at the screen door and gazed at the sunny patch of lawn just outside. The move to America some years ago had separated him from his old Croatian colleagues – they had dubbed themselves the Group of Four – who had challenged his ideas and whetted his appetite for intellectual exchanges.

His old school days ambled back into his mind, and the shared laughter of chums younger than these rang in his memory. *Mikal Koltska had been such a card.* He remembered him as the comic of their small group. The clutch of boys had not welcomed him to begin with, but soon, the other three lads understood the value of the short, rangy boy who had arrived mysteriously one day at the boarding school.

Maxo's mind skipped to an image of his young self on the day of his ninth birthday. Mikula had stood in the kitchen and puzzled at the scene before him, seeking to take it in. Mati Dora had collapsed onto a corner stool, weeping and moaning. By the door, a fine man dressed in a spotless uniform ordered a young servant to pack Mikula's clothes. In less than five minutes, the lad handed the officer the small bundle. For a moment, Mikula's back stiffened as he took in the room. Then, he flew to Mati Dora's side and latched onto one of her stout legs. With an aching throat, he cried, "Ne, ne! My Mati, my Mati! Ne, I won't leave you!"

Mati rose then, scooping the child into her arms and holding him close to her chest. She raised her face to the officer as tears poured from her eyes onto the boy's head. Before she could speak, the man handed her a crisp, cream-colored card. An ornate crest of twining leaves and regal lions adorned the back flap of the envelope. The dark green seal reflected the emblem.

Dora sat down once more. With one arm around Mikula, she rubbed her thumb over the waxy sheen of the seal.

"Go on, it is for you. Open it," the officer said in a quiet voice.

Dora Jugova wiped the tears from her eyes and unfolded the paper. It was only a sentence or two, but the upward slant of the lines and the incisive curves of the letters told her as much as the words. Their meaning pulled at her heart. She knew she could not fight against such a formal missive.

Dora's bottom lip trembled, prelude to a new fall of tears.

In silence, silver pools lined her bottom eyelids, breached their rims, and flooded down her cheeks. She shook her head right and left. "Ne, ne, ne, not possible." With damp fingers, she clutched the letter, and tiny wrinkles rayed across the paper like a spider's web. She tilted her head toward her left shoulder, her face drooping.

"Sir. Umm, Captain," she hesitated.

"Colonel Salvić, Madam." The officer inclined his head.

"Yes, please sir, sir, Salv – Colonel Salvić." Dora held three fingers to her lips to stop their quivering. "You see, you understand, I am," she licked her top lip, "a simple woman. A simple woman with simple needs."

"Yes?"

"It is but this. I love this boy. This boy, he is mine, as much as he ever could be. I, I love all my children, but this boy, he is special." She caught a sob in her throat. "I had never thought the time would come so soon." She swallowed like it was a burden. "I never planned to give up my boy so soon." She dropped her eyes. "That is all." This last remark fell to her apron.

The young military man stroked his beard. To his credit, he did not remind Dora Jugova of her position. He did not reproach her with the terms of the arrangement agreed so many years ago. He did not mention that Mikula was not her boy. Instead, he regarded the youngster with interest. He stepped toward the mother and son and crouched on bent knee so that he could look into the boy's dark eyes.

For the first time, the lad heard his new name. The colonel uttered it softly, like the sliding notes of a tamburitzan. "Maksimilijan, Maksimilijan. Monsieur Maksimilijan Vanka," the young officer said. "For this is what you will be called from now on – Maksimilijan Vanka. Sir, has no one ever spoken to you of the true story behind your birth?"

With the backs of his delicate hands, the boy rubbed his eyes and then gazed upon the soldier. He liked the face he saw. The blue eyes were kind, and the long, straight nose led to a handsome, brushy moustache and a well-trimmed beard. They framed a gently smiling mouth with rows of even white teeth. Mikula shook his head.

"But I have told you some of this," Dora Jugova said, her voice notching up a degree. "Mikula, have I not? Have I not always called you my little prince? And explained where your cow came from? And, and …" She dissolved into tears as the colonel raised a hand for her to stop.

"Please, dear lady," he said, "do not distress yourself further. The boy is young. It is possible that he does not remember every detail. He – " The soldier stopped talking when the lad tugged at his tunic. He turned to him.

In a tiny voice, Mikula said, "But I do remember. Everything. Everything Mati Dora told me. It is only that, th-that I thought they were fairy tales. Mati Dora is the very best story teller ever, are you not, Mati?"

"Ah, I see," the bearded man said. "Well, you shall hear the entire story once again by the time we reach your school."

"School?" In that one syllable, Maxo mixed excitement, alarm, and interest.

"Yes, my young man, it is high time you were off to boarding school." The officer stood then and divided the morning. In its earlier hours, Maxo had been Mikula, young lad of Kuplenovo; now he became Maksimilijan Vanka, student, set to take on the next chapter of his life.

"Hello! Welcome back," Father Žagar grinned across the table at Maxo. "Where have you been? Some far flight to distant lands, eh?"

The faintest sniff issued from Maxo's nose. "I am sorry, Father. Not a very courteous manner in which to end a stimulating conversation, is it? Truthfully, I was contemplating the gift of friendship, and how blessed I am to have yours."

Father colored slightly, but before he could speak, Maxo added, "And then, well, then," he laughed, enjoying the joke that his mind had played on him, "then, I drifted away to other friends, other times, other places. And you are more correct than you know. I did travel back to the beautiful Zagorje, and the second beginning to my life."

"That sounds intriguing," the priest said.

"Dear me, let me be the last person to bore you with my daydreams," Maxo said. "And anyway, look at the time. The morning is ticking by, and I have yet to raise a paintbrush." He knotted a bandanna around his throat. "A dio, Padre. May your day be filled with sunshine and wonder." He swung through the screen door of the kitchen.

"And yours, my friend, and yours." Father tidied away the cups and saucers, filled a glass with water, and moved toward his study. Sunday's homily waited to be written, his second meeting with two young people eager to marry was at ten, and he had promised to look in on old Mrs. Barnes. "And so another day begins," he said to the house.

Maxo erected a tall ladder against the scaffold by the painting of *Justice. On such a day as this*, he thought, *a somewhat gentler subject is warranted.* Though the figure in the painting appeared serious, the message it issued was a good degree more positive than many of the other murals, and Maxo felt the need to escape the heavy subject of *Greed,* at least for the remainder of the day. He prepared his palette with a lighter array of the egg tempera hues – Chinese white and cadmium yellow, cerulean and viridian, a touch of bright red. He could bring all the freshness of summer to the painting with these selections.

Because of the fine weather, Maxo propped open the doors on opposite sides of the church. The wind burst past them in uneven gusts, and warm currents dashed into the church along with it. Sunshine splashed through the windows on the east side of the building. Maxo breathed deeply. *That's better.* The old stones needed a scrubbing from the wind, and the sun-warmed air introduced fresh flavors. New-mown grass and mint and heated plinth swept the must and the dust before it and out the church's eastern portals.

Maxo could hear a mother's pitched voice from the schoolyard. "Doreen! Maureen! C'mon, girls, let's go. Hurry! Say good-bye. Say good-bye to Father."

Without encouragement, that day in Kuplenovo rose in his

mind once more.

"Doritska! Maritska! Come, come now, there's my good girls. Our Mikula is going away, and we must bid him farewell."

Mikula's sisters had come at their mother's bidding, but Doritska, ever the shy one, stood behind her mother's skirts when she caught sight of the tall colonel. She pulled at Dora's sleeve. "But Mati, where is Mikula going? And why does he have to go? Why?"

"This man is taking him, can't you see?" Maritska said. A few hours older than her twin, she took the lead on all of their play and work and supplied the answers when a problem presented itself.

"But why, oh why?" Doritska's lips pushed out, and her brows drew together. She and her sister had loved playing with Mikula when he had first arrived, a real live baby instead of the cornhusk dolls that Grandfather had made for them. What a story they could tell their friends, though at five years of age, they were seldom allowed out of Mati Dora's sight. Growing older, their affection for Mikula had taken the form of merciless teasing, tickling and pinching, and the little boy had been happy to escape them whenever he could.

Regardless, there remained a strong bond between them, and Doritska, in particular, had adopted him as her pet. It was she who would sneak him a bit of bread or bring him a tiny toad that she found in the garden to make up for the times when they had teased him to tears. Plus, as he had grown older and stronger, and perhaps a bit wiser than them, too, Mikula had defended the two sisters against Juro and his nasty disposition.

Horrid Juro, they had called him. Horrid Juro, four years older than the girls, believed they had been sent by God to be his servants. If they did not do what he told them, retribution arrived within moments. Both girls bore the scars of his beatings, and frequently, he attacked them without provocation. He had knocked out two of Maritska's teeth and slapped Doritska so hard one time, her left cheekbone collapsed permanently. His favorite torture was to capture one of them between his knees and clap both sides of her head again and again until her ears rang with pain. As a result, both girls strained to hear at times.

Juro had a wildness in him that Dora could not control. Baldo merely laughed if she complained to him. "Hush, woman! What do think? He is learning to be a man. Juro will be a man, not some pussycat, not some weakling fachook. Leave him alone!" He would clump a big hand on the older boy's shoulder as if congratulating him on a job well done. Juro would cross his arms and stand tall and broad next to his father. His eyes defied any of the household to cross him.

Such cockiness on top of the brutality only made Mikula despise Juro more. He, too, had been the recipient of many blows from the brother who was nine years his senior, but it did not prevent Mikula from plotting to avenge his sisters. What the little brother lacked in brawn was easily compensated by his intellect. He could set traps for Juro, so clever in their device that the brute never knew it was Mikula. He had rigged the woodpile so that when Juro went to fetch the firewood one evening, the entire cord tumbled down upon him. He had positioned the rake on Juro's usual route to the garden shed in a way that it sprang up and smashed him in the face. With fine thread, he had sewn Juro's pant legs together when he sprawled on his pallet snoring in the night, so that he crashed to the ground as soon as he rose, cracking both kneecaps hard against the solid earthen floor.

Sometimes, however, there was no time for subtlety. One day, Mikula had come around the corner of the house to find that Juro had both sisters pinioned below his legs, and he was dealing blows to their stomachs. Both girls were gasping for air and croaking for help. In a flash, the blood rushed to Mikula's head. The next thing he knew, he had girdled Juro's neck with his legs and was squeezing them together as hard as he could. At the same time, he scratched Juro's face, his cheeks, his nose, his chin, anything he could think to do. Suddenly, it came to him. With his right hand, he jammed his handkerchief into Juro's mouth while his left pinched the big boy's nostrils.

Juro rose up, snorting like a bull and flailing his arms. Maritska latched onto one of his boots and bit into his calf. Juro swiped with his free foot, aiming for her head. She ducked, he missed, and the momentum of the kick took him over. Mikula jumped clear as Juro's head slammed into the hard earth. He did not get up.

Doritska rolled onto her side and curled into a tight ball, moaning and crying out for Mati. Mikula ran to her and cradled her head in his lap. He brushed the hair from her face and stroked her cheek.

"Maritska! Run! Quick as you can! Fetch Mati!"

He returned to his ministrations and crooned a lullaby to quiet the sobs of the broken girl.

"Good lord!" Maxo said. "Perhaps I should have been painting something else." He stepped away and regarded the work he had completed on the Justice figure. The brushstrokes were brilliant, long and thick, and bold – and a shade more vigorous than he had intended for this representative of righteousness and all things fair. "Perhaps I should have been thinking of something a bit more calming, even though my thoughts did relate to a certain type of justice." He shook his head. "Ah well, nothing a little paint will not fix."

Maxo dug in his paintbox and selected some clean brushes. He squirted some ochre onto the palette and then rested the palette, the brushes, and a rag on the nearest pew in readiness for the afternoon's work. He moved across the lawn now shaded by the church and entered the back door of the rectory. A quick wash, a brief lunch, a good stretch, and a cup of tea, and he felt eager to get back to his painting.

Maxo grabbed an apple on his way out the door. They were early apples – red Empires - the first of the summer, supplied from Mrs. Dobrovic's garden. The tart flesh tingled on his tongue, and Maxo found himself dabbing at his mouth to catch the juice.

Back inside the church, he suddenly recalled the enormous apple that Colonel Salvić had given him at the beginning of their journey together. To this day, he could remember the dappled glow of the apple's skin. It had been striped with reds and greens as though watercolors had drizzled over its head. Maxo remembered thinking about painting, then, possibly for the first time. He longed to capture the image of that apple so he could save it and savor it long after its disappearance.

"Is this for sharing?" the boy had asked the colonel. "I mean, please, would you like to share this?"

The colonel barked out a small, tight laugh. "Ha! No, no, my boy, that apple is for you, sent along by your benefactor. And see here," he pointed to a sack beneath the seat where Maksimilijan sat, "Here is a bagful for you to enjoy at school."

Maksimilijan could hardly believe his luck. Never in his entire life had he eaten an apple all by himself, and now here sat an entire bag of the fruit to call his own.

"That is too kind. Thank you so much, Colonel." The boy spoke with a simple grace that came as naturally to him as breathing.

"Now," Colonel Salvić said, "Do you find yourself well situated?"

Maksimilijan nodded. Perched high next to the wagon's driver with a cushion below his buttocks to ease the bumps and a backboard on which to lean, he could imagine no greater level of comfort. Cushions had never arrived in the Jugova household. He nodded again with some energy.

"Very good then," said the colonel. "Once we are underway, I will ride alongside and tell you the story I promised. How does that sound?"

"Oh, yes, please, colonel sir, I would like that very much," and for the first time, Maksimilijan smiled at his new friend.

And what a story he recounted for me, Maxo thought as he added shade and dimension to *Justice*'s flowing gown. Princes and palaces, mysterious disappearances at night, a baby with no name, a secret benefactor, the woman in the distance. The story so closely resembled a fairy tale, it had been hard for young Maksimilijan to believe that the words were actually about him.

Now as the western sun streaked evenly through the

church's windows, Maxo looked again through memory's eye at the woman in the distance. He remembered her, and he had seen her more than once. But the moment the thought crossed his mind, a thin finger of air prickled the hairs on the back of his neck. At the same time, a pungent scent stung the inside of his nose. It was like opening a dusty old box of clothes where the mold has gotten in. Without any forethought, Maxo associated the odor with burial cloths, or at least what he imagined their smell might be like.

A slight tremble rattled his spine from bottom to top, and he glanced around. Nothing – as usual. No one there. Only a missal, left open on a pew, evidenced the passing of the wind. It turned its own pages in concert with the breeze. Maxo had not seen the red book lying there before, and he walked over for a closer look. As he sat on the pew, frostiness rushed right through him as though he had stepped into an icehouse. The cold shrammed him in a glacial sweat, and the leaves of the book fluttered. Just as suddenly, the book's pages stopped turning. Maxo's gaze dropped to the passage on the page that remained open, and his eyes froze to the spot. He covered his heart. The missal lay open to the *Prayer for the Dead.*

Maxo hastened to the rectory for a glass of water. The churchyard, gilded by the setting sun, placed a reassuring distance between him and the little red book in the church. He sat on the stone wall that edged the church's garden and tilted his face to the warmth. *Never, never has the spirit visited me in the daylight.* Maxo pondered. *What has happened to change this*?

He had been daydreaming about the journey with Colonel Salvić. With the clarity of a child's recall, he remembered every detail, especially the story that the colonel had woven. "There really was not any mistaking what happened, actually. The moment I thought about the woman in the distance, the ghost had manifested," Maxo said very, very quietly to himself. "True, it was not the dark specter of earlier occasions, but the cold and the feelings of dread were the same, for sure."

The woman in the distance had been an object of mystery for most of Maxo's lifetime. With fresh eyes, he contemplated the few instances when she had appeared. The first time had occurred when he was still quite a small boy. He remembered the day particularly because Mati Dora had scrubbed his face and hands until they glowed pink. She had exchanged his every day shirt for a clean, white garment with flowing sleeves and colorful embroidery at the neckline. He loved those sleeves. He could zoom around the cottage, arms flung wide, and pretend that he was flying.

Mati had taken him into the garden and told him to stand by the garden gate. In harder words than he usually heard from her, she said, "Mikula, if I see one speck of dirt on this garment, it will be the worse for you. Now go stand and wait, and do not play among the garden rows!" This last admonishment came with a slight shove toward the gate. Mikula sensed that no other explanation would be forthcoming. Being a child who generally tried to please his mother, he walked to the gate and stood on its lower rung so he could see out to the road.

Maxo recalled that day well. It had been mid-morning in late summer. The view from the gate had always enticed him, and now he had an excuse to perch there and take in the sights without interruptions from teasing sisters, nasty brother or chore reminders from Mati. The dirt track stretched west toward the purplish blue horizon of mountains and clear sky. To his left, it followed the wheat fields around a curve that he knew led to the Praljaks' farm.

The grasses of the field opposite vibrated with activity. Grasshoppers, their wings finally dried from the dew, bounded under and between stalks. Brown-flecked sparrows darted, pecking for seed, while the glorious goldfinches balanced like circus performers on the waving heads of the coneflowers. Beetles' backs flashed rainbows as the sun stroked their wings, and ants trailed a long, orderly line back to their hill with bits of treasure clamped in their maws. The hum of bees making their rounds of the blooming clover permeated the scene.

Mikula's enchantment grew the more he looked. Stories whirred through his brain, and he stood on tiptoe to see more.

All of the sudden, a rabbit skipped from the brush and raced pell-mell down the track to the west. Little Mikula watched the white of the bushy cottontail bob and swerve in defense of suspected predators, though the boy could see none.

At a far fencepost, perhaps thirty meters down the road, the rabbit disappeared into a tangle of blackberry bushes. Mikula began to turn away, when a flicker up the track just beyond the fence caught his eye. He could feel his eyes grow wide for never had he seen such a sight in his life, let alone on a lonely country road. It was the last thing he had ever thought to see.

She looked like an angel with her gown of cream and peach layers trailing out behind her in the breeze. She stood straight and still as a statue. The boy realized she was more solid than a vision as she adjusted her parasol against the growing brightness of the day. Its silver tip glinted in the sun. The fact of her mortal existence did not reduce his awe at her appearance. She was the most beautiful woman he had ever seen. He had no words at that time to describe the ivory complexion, the faint blush of the cheek, the mound of soft, chestnut curls that peeked from her bonnet, the arch of fine brows, nor the dark, inviting eyes that stared intently his way.

They stood locked in position, the woman in the distance and little Mikula - two animals accidentally encountering each other, not daring to move a muscle nor lose eye contact. For the little boy, whose dark brown locks danced in the wind and matched her own so exactly, the moment was magical. He could neither go forward, nor leave his position at the gate to retreat into the cottage. His heart batted against his chest, a trapped butterfly of curiosity. Something else – longing, maybe, or a feeling of connection – hovered beneath his breastbone. For her part, the woman in the road seemed to be breathing him in, taking in as much as she could see of him above the garden gate, etching him upon her memory.

Then, as swiftly as she had appeared, the woman turned to walk toward the blue haze of the Zagorje. Though strictly prohibited to venture outside of the garden by himself, Mikula struggled to slide back the hasp on the gate. With every ounce of his being, he wanted to run to the woman and ask her a thousand questions, and perhaps, grasp her gloved hand or better, touch her soft skin.

"Mikula!"

He looked around as Mati Dora emerged from the cottage.

"Mikula! Stop! You must not!"

He looked again, but continued to battle the stubborn latch. Mati arrived at his side and said quietly, "You must not, my little prince. This is not for you to do. Not at this time."

"But, Mati …" The boy whipped around to point down the road, but she was gone. The woman in the distance had vanished into the mountain air.

Maxo's shoulders lifted in a deep sigh. He stood and rubbed his bottom where the hardness of the stone wall had pressed in. *So many years ago, so many memories*, Maxo thought, *but what did it all mean in the end?*

The grown artist admitted that he had substituted the word "connection" for what the boy Mikula had felt that long ago day. Maxo could remember that he had been filled with longing and curiosity. He also credited his sixth sense. Something had stretched between him and the stranger. He knew that he had sensed some attachment between himself and the woman in the distance. If he could have sketched it back then, it would have been a picture of two figures – a lady and a boy – with a pulley-like device strung between them. Any movement of the strings would affect both of them equally, but it would never bring them together.

And yet, here, inexplicably, thinking about her had triggered the connection in a strange and powerful way. It was especially odd when he considered that she had played only a minor part of the story that Colonel Salvić had told him. However, it had been enough to cause a new wrinkle in the behavior of the church's ephemeral visitor.

Maxo shook his head. He could not take it in, and he could not resolve it. Of one thing he felt certain, however. He could control it if he thought about something else.

Maxo threw back his shoulders and walked into the twilit church. He busied himself for a while rigging the portable lights so that his work could continue well after darkness fell. With some focus, he could finish a good portion of the *Justice* figure this evening. With similar intention, he returned to the conversation with Father Žagar this morning, the one that had led him into today's jumbled pathway of memories. He had been grateful for the priest's thoughtful remarks and for his friendship. That had guided him to thoughts of other friends, and now, with a degree of purpose, he revisited those early school days. He picked up his palette and dipped a rounded brush into the China white.

His memory arrived at Lepoglava Gymnasium for Boys, but not among friends. For some reason, it deposited him in the middle of a squabble with boys that loomed over his scrawny frame. He had met his tutors for the first time and performed reasonably well in his morning classes. While his teachers had been impressed, the gang of boys surrounding him clearly had not.

"So, Herr Maksimilijan, don't you have the grand name?" one of the boys taunted. "Do you think you're big enough to live up to it?" "And a show-off, to boot!" a boy named Branko shouted. "How many questions did you answer for old man Kravic?" He shoved Maksimilijan into one of the other boys. Karl chimed in, "Trying to make us look bad, that's what. Eh, boys?"

On and on, round and round, the comments went. No matter which way the new boy turned, he was greeted by a snide remark or an ugly sneer. The boys circled up and pushed Maksimilijan into the middle to face a bruiser named Brucic. Tall and square with a crooked nose, his mean little eyes squinted at the skinny boy before him. The circle started chanting, "Brucic, Brucic, beat him! Beat him! That's right, give him a real lesson!"

Brucic cuffed Maksimilijan on the shoulder and prepared to take a swipe at his head with a hand that seemed as big as a frying pan. As he swung through, Maksimilijan ducked and using his head, plunged into the big brute's stomach. The crowd heard the "oof" as air exploded out of Brucic's mouth. He bent over to catch his breath, and the smaller boy scuttled behind him. With a running leap, he planted both of his feet squarely on the back of Brucic's knees, and the giant slumped down in a heap.

A cheer of appreciation rose from the circle. Brucic spat dust from his mouth and pushed onto all fours, his face a glowering mask that appeared to bode the new pupil no good. However, before he could rise to his feet and give chase, five or six of the older boys encircled the victor and told Brucic it was over.

Maksimilijan's lips puffed out relief even though the big boy muttered something as he stalked away. A number of lads closed in, slapping the newcomer's back amid congratulatory noises. One boy, Mikal, who later became his closest friend, asked, "Where did you learn to do that?"

Everyone laughed when Maksimilijan explained how he had developed survival techniques while living with his older brother. "Just so," someone hollered. "I have two big brothers like that."

"Come along, Maksimilijan." Mikal pulled at his sleeve.

"Just Maxo," Maxo said.

"What?" Mikal scratched his head.

"I say, no need to call me anything but Maxo," Maxo said. "That is what everyone calls me." Or at least, it was what he planned to have everyone call him from then on.

"Very well – Maxo, it is!" Mikal gave him a friendly punch on the shoulder. "And Maxo it shall be from now on. Come on. Let's go get lunch. I'm starving."

A good laugh ripped its way through Maxo's chest. *What silly creatures boys are, and what fun times we had being silly together.* After that first day, life had become easy for the new boy. The other lads soon had learned that he was more than willing to help them with their studies; better yet, he could hold his own when they played cricket or football. For a small boy, Maxo had been wiry and quick and brought intelligence and strategy to the games he played. Other students competed to place Maxo on their teams. Mikal won out and also had the prescience to choose Brucic for their team, much to everyone's surprise. But as Brucic liked to win, having "the pipsqueak" on their team pretty much guaranteed that they would surpass all the other teams. The bully soon forgave Maxo for their initial encounter.

Maxo counted those days of his life as the last ones that were utterly carefree. His only responsibility had been to achieve well in his studies, and this he considered more entertainment than task. He sailed through his studies, his mind hungry for the new subjects presented to it. Latin, Greek, mathematics, literature, and geography – all opened new doors in his mind. He received individual tutoring in music and art. Soon, the young student fell in love with the notion of capturing what he saw and what he perceived on paper. One night in bed, he tried to explain it to Mikal in veiled whispers after the lights-out bell.

"Mikal, it is so amazing. I feel the greatest joy when I can sketch or paint a bird or a tree or the sky."

"Your work is good," Mikal yawned, "but it is hard to understand. For me, I mean. Of course, I never had much luck drawing things myself."

"Oh, bless me, Mikal," Maxo said. "Let me see if I can explain. It is like, like – well, you know when you are so, so hungry, and you are willing to shove anything or anybody that gets in your way when you are walking into lunch? Well, this is like that for me. Creating art is my food, Mikal. It is what feeds me. I feel like I must have it."

"Shhh," Mikal said. "All right, I get it. Though I have to tell you, I'd never trade food for paint." He laughed. "We better get to sleep now before the proctor comes around," he said in a final, tight whisper. "Good night, dear Maxo. And dream of your next great painting."

Maxo had whispered a breathy good night and rolled over. The clean, firm bed reminded him of yet another benefit of coming to this school. He could count on a bed all to himself, three changes of clothing, and food from the commissary that proved tasty and filling. *Every need attended*, Maxo thought. *What brilliant freedom, to learn and to create without limitations.*

Sometimes, though, Maxo yearned for the good soups that Mati Dora cooked every week. He smacked his lips as he thought of her potato and leek potage, his favorite. A good son, he wrote to his mother every week, telling of his adventures at school and sharing some of what he was learning. He wrote short notes in simple language that Dora and the girls could read. Maxo knew his family would never have the same opportunities as him, so often he spoke little of school, but wrote things that he thought would amuse them.

My sweet Maritska, Joze is a tall boy with silky dark hair. I am sure he would like you, if he could see your beauty. You would like him because he knows magic – he can pull a coin from behind your ear, and he also writes poems. I know you would inspire him! And dear Doritska, Mario would admire your blue eyes and blonde curls. I know, for I have seen him watch the girls in town, and the blondes are always his fancy! Dearest Mati, I miss you very much and your wonderful soup! Hope I can visit soon, Your Loving Son and Brother, Mikula

Good lord, that all seems like a million years ago, Maxo thought as he cleaned his brushes for the night. He fully expected Father Žagar to appear in the church door any second now. Besides, it was a good time to stop for the evening. The outline and some of the detail for *Justice* peered from the wall. Any onlooker would be able to tell that the mural was at least halfway complete. What the casual observer could not notice, though, was the resemblance between the angel's face and the countenance of the mysterious woman in the distance. Quite unconsciously, Maxo had portrayed *Justice* in her image.

Two days later, on a Wednesday evening, Father assembled the entire group of church school students – about seventy in all – and their parents. They arranged themselves in the pews of the tiny church and spoke in low tones, now telling a child to be quiet or to straighten his collar, now wondering about the frightening new paintings on the walls.

"Perhaps they're not done yet," one mother whispered to

her husband. He did not have a chance to reply as Father strode in from the rectory side of the church. He walked directly to the lectern. No greetings were issued, no hands shaken, no youngsters smiled upon. The nuns entered behind him and went to stand behind the rear pew, looking in turns, concerned and dejected. Only their head, Sister Mary Martha, stood tall with crossed arms and a stern line drawn across her mouth.

"I have asked you here tonight, parents, students, and teachers, to deal with a situation."

Almost at once, a cluck of alarm passed through the crowd.

"Please, your attention, please." Father Žagar rapped firmly on the lectern with his left hand. He nodded toward the front pew. "As you know, over the past couple of months, we have been privileged to have as our guest the renowned artist, Maksimilijan Vanka – or perhaps known better to many of you as Maxo Vanka." He motioned for Maxo to rise. The artist stood and made a stiff little bow before reclaiming his seat. Every eye revolved his way until Father pounded on the lectern once again for their attention.

"As I was saying, we have been privileged to have Mr. Vanka here as our artist in residence while he completes the final set of murals for our wonderful church. Mr. Vanka has been nothing if not steadfast in his work over the past several weeks. Often, he works a sixteen to twenty hour day, recognizing that the diocese has a rather tight turnaround time for the production of these paintings. And for that we are most grateful." Father bowed his head slightly in Maxo's direction.

"But it is with enormous regret that I have to tell you that someone has seen fit to tamper with – " Father hammered the lectern till it boomed through the church, "that is, to vandalize one of the paintings, and thus set our schedule back by possibly another week. In addition, Mr. Vanka's art materials were discovered in great disarray. Apparently, the same night the delinquents decided to ruin the mural, they meddled with the paints as well. This is disaster. Mr. Vanka's palette as well as one mural has been thoroughly destroyed."

A collective gasp rippled through the crowd. Father Žagar drew up to his full height and folded his arms across his chest. The toe of his right shoe tapped an angry tattoo on the tile floor.

The priest grabbed both sides of the lectern. "I have asked you here to get to the bottom of this. I am deeply sorry to have to say that someone in this room must be the culprit." His jawline pulsed as he clenched his teeth. "Mr. Vanka, on behalf of the parish, and in front of all these parishioners, I beg your forgiveness. It is my understanding that this has never occurred in your experience before. Am I right?"

Maxo nodded and looked into his lap.

Father looked down upon his audience. "The reason I am suggesting that someone in this room has information about this incident – no, let's call it what it is, this crime – is because no one else had access to the church. Ordinarily, the school children are not permitted in the church during the hours that Mr. Vanka is working, but that would not prevent one or more of you," and his eyes searched the face of each child, "from sneaking in here and hiding till Mr. Vanka took a break."

"Likewise, you parents are similarly responsible and would have a similar opportunity. And some of you have keys as aldermen of the church." A roll of grumbling rumbled like faint thunder across the room. "You are right to be angry," Father said, "as angry as me, or as disappointed as Mr. Vanka. And I realize that not all of you support the creation of these dramatic illustrations on our walls. But I do beseech you to come forward now or to help us identify the offenders. Please put forward your ideas at this time. The sooner we resolve this, the sooner we can move forward."

Like a flock of sheep, the parishioners stared toward the front of the church in mute dismay. None of them had ever seen Father Žagar in such a rage. His was a personality that did not allow for irrational behavior and black moods. In a way, it made his words worse – more frightening – since they had never heard such tones from his mouth before.

"Questions?" the priest demanded.

A gentleman in the back row stood, pinching the brim of the brown fedora he held in his hands.

"Yes, Mr. Bostay?"

Mr. Bostay was a church council member. "Yes, please, Father," he said in a quiet voice, "what night did the damage take place?"

"The crime happened sometime between the time Mr. Vanka left work this past Monday night, about midnight, until after matins on Tuesday, the next day," the priest said.

"Father, please forgive this naïve thought, but wouldn't it seem unlikely that any child would stay in this church in the blackness after midnight, especially with these scary pictures staring down at them? Why, my own Mary Louise says she can hardly stand to come in here during the day for choir practice, let alone at night."

A chorus of agreement rose to support this claim. Many of the parents admitted that they themselves would hesitate if they ever had to come into the church after nightfall when all the lights had been doused.

Father held up both hands. "Please, please. All right. All right. These are legitimate claims, and perhaps in my anger and disappointment, I have made the mistake of jumping to conclusions, but I need your help. We simply must identify who has done this. If not, how are we to prevent them from damaging Mr. Vanka's work again, perhaps destroying more this time? Also," and he swept his hand toward the artist, "it is essential that Mr. Vanka feels he has a safe and comfortable setting in which to work. Can you imagine how he feels?"

In his seat, Maxo bit his lower lip. He had reported the vandalism to Father Žagar on Tuesday morning following the morning prayers. Over a cup of coffee, he had explained why he might be slightly late in making a start that morning.

"The palette is a huge loss, I have to tell you," Maxo said as he stirred the teaspoon round and round in his coffee cup. "One mixes the colors just so. I had come up with a delicious range of grays to define the skirt of *Justice*, and now I must start from scratch. Creating color is an essential part of the painting process, but now I will have to start," he paused, "how do you say, start from square one."

When the priest had decided to confront the congregation and the children all at once, Maxo declined to comment. He feared it would only breed anger and more challenges, not answers. He had attended the assembly with his heart low.

Now, in addition to stirring up the parishioners, and possibly without foundation, the priest remained ignorant of the one thing that Maxo still could not bring himself to share – the reappearance of the specter. The whole incident began to loop in crazy eights, like rope tricks above his head. There was still a specter, he knew. However, he also knew that it had never harmed him or his work physically in all the time that he had worked in Millvale. If it was the ghost, then strange that it obliterated such a beautiful face. And why would it destroy the palette, unless it was to block any attempt to recreate what he had painted originally.

In and out, up and down, his thoughts coiled until they toppled into a huge tangled knot of jumbled ideas and theories. Maxo once more found himself longing for home, for comfort, and for understanding the environment around him. Tonight, the end of this job could not come soon enough.

Tomorrow morning, he would telephone the Peggies. That would give him strength and reassure his heart.

CHAPTER SIX

IF HE CLOSED HIS EYES, he could almost smell Korcula. There, the salt-bleached rocks emitted lime and granite and sun, and the skirts of seaweed dancing below the water spiced the surf with that faint odor of decay that he always associated with the sea. But it was not Korcula here on this pebbly beach alongside the Allegheny River, and Maxo missed the sharpness of the salt in the air and the way it filled his saliva glands. However, the aroma of the wet rocks soothed his senses.

Father Žagar had suggested that Maxo close up shop early that night as the weather forecaster had promised fair skies for the evening. "You look as though you could use some fresh air," the priest had said, "and a few hours on the riverside always buoys my own spirits, and anyway, don't you love to be by the water?" Maxo knew it was the closest Father could come to an ocean visit, and he noted the relief that exhaled from the priest's chest when he finally agreed to come.

Mrs. Dobrovic had fussed around the kitchen, clucking like an old hen as she converted that night's dinner into a picnic. She had bowed readily to the task when Father explained why it was needed. "We'll make it all as nice as nice can be for you," she had said to Father, including her daughter in the effort with a wave of her hand. Cara folded and handed her the napkins, and grabbed a large pie basket from the shelf above the kitchen cabinets.

Daughter and mother packed the pannier to the rim with slices of roast chicken, a mound of potato salad, two shining apples, a thermos of coffee and a Mason jar of water, two healthy slices of peach pie, and plates and cutlery. She wedged two drinking glasses into the corners of the basket where they would be safe from breakage. Finally, she layered a worn checkered cloth over all to shield the contents and buffer the basket's travel to the riverside.

Now, Father smacked his lips over his final morsel, and Maxo ran his fork around the plate once more to catch the last of the peach pie filling. Afterwards, he dribbled water over his fingers and dabbed them dry on one of the napkins. A burp rumbled its way from the bottom of his belly.

"Oh, I beg your pardon," Maxo laughed. "What a sumptuous repast. I think perhaps that is the most I have eaten in a week. Maybe a month!" This time, they laughed together. "Please do tell the good Mrs. Dobrovic how very, very delicious it all was, and how exceedingly grateful I am for her kind flexibility." He paused for half a second. "What am I saying? I will tell her this myself at breakfast tomorrow!" He flashed the priest one of those dazzling smiles of his. Father's lips rose in return, his heart warmed by Maxo's grin. It had put in far fewer appearances lately.

After this, they lapsed into a silence, the comfortable kind where friendship was enough on its own. The two men, the artist and the priest, rested their backs against the sturdy oak that towered above their picnic cloth. They closed their eyes and breathed in the gentle evening air. The scents of river and stone and woodland filtered past. The plash of the river's current as it drifted by the picnic spot stroked Maxo's ears.

Maxo stood in the water, the mild surf gurgling around his calves. A hand shaded his eyes as he looked up at the villa. Margaret was shouting something from the veranda, but he could not hear her above the commotion at his side. His daughter, little Peggy – his Peggica – squealed and dragged on his arm.

"Come, Papa! Come! You promise me. Swimming. Peggy swim. Now!" Peggica's words pierced the air, her toddler pitch one note below unbearable.

The sun poured warmth down his back while the waters cooled his legs. He looked down into the aqua pool and watched Peggy hang on his arm as her little legs kicked. *How she makes me smile. Not even three, but the determination of – God forbid – an adolescent! She will keep me young. And busy!*

"Maxo!" It was Margaret from the rail of the terrace. "I say, not too deep now, all right?"

He nodded in firm agreement and waved. Their only precious jewel, he would never put his little Peggica in harm's way. In fact, he felt driven to teach her to swim. Living on an island, water all around, anything could happen, and he wanted her to be prepared for it.

"Papa, swim!" the little girl cried and tugged on his arm once more. "Then, pirates, okay?" A gleam in her eye turned the princess into an imp in the space of a moment.

"Yes, yes, as you say, but even pirates need to learn to swim well."

The marble villa on Korcula had been a summer home to the Vankas for a few years before the advent of their parenthood. It served as an escape from the heat and bustle of Zagreb, and eventually, they began to spend more and more time there. The sea, the rocks, the rugged terrain, the olive groves inspired Maxo in his work.

He squinted at his home while he whished Peggica in the azure waves, hand-to-hand, round and round his legs. The house's white walls gleamed back at him in the afternoon sun. He could make out the tip of Margaret's sunhat as she sat on the broad veranda that opened out from the lounge and ran the entire length of the villa. The large terrace was like having an extra room, and the family spent many a pleasant hour dining there, reading, or simply enjoying the glimmer of the sunset that tipped the wavelets between their island and the Peljasic Peninsula.

The lounge itself spanned the length of the house and

offered a splendid area for receptions. Three French doors breathed in air and marvelous views of the sea, so it was not at all difficult to convince friends to visit. More often than not, the promise of fresh seafood and island wine had tantalized even the most entrenched city-dwellers, and the certainty of stimulating discussions had made the villa's lure irresistible.

"That's a big sigh," Father leaned over and grabbed a scrap of chicken he had left on his plate. His brows, like two question marks, stood poised to listen.

"Ah, Father, once more you have caught me. Yes, I am dreaming of Korcula again." The artist smiled gently. "How I wish I could take you there someday." He inhaled. "Yes, I know you have been to the Dalmatian coast, but this island – it is special, I tell you. Of surpassing beauty. And, and something magical. The old city, the sense of times long past, the knowledge that this same scent of heated stone – the scent I imagine as the fragrance of Korcula – belonged to some wayfarer from ancient Greece, and then later, some rich fellow from Venice, and let us not forget, Marco Polo himself!"

"Yes, my friend," Father said, "you paint pictures in the mind almost as well as the ones we can see on the walls. I feel as though I'm coming to know the place through you." He sipped from his glass and paused. "And these notions of times past and great explorations connected to Korcula," he shook his head. "Small wonder that you long for its shores."

"Dear me, Father," Maxo replied. "I would never for anything have wanted to miss this friendship with you, but let me share that one of my true regrets in life was leaving Korcula. I believe I might have stayed there forever if I had been given the chance."

The two friends fell silent once more. Father had stretched full length on the cloth and tucked his hands behind his head. Maxo ran an index finger down one side of his mustache and then the other. *If only they could have stayed.*

"And then there was such a clashing of swords as no one had ever seen before!" Maxo feinted and bobbed around the veranda, slicing through invisible foes. "The battle was so fierce, and the clashing went on for so long that the people in the town thought it was raining knives and forks."

The children giggled at the image.

Suddenly, Maxo plunged his arm into the bough of a pine tree that brushed the top of the stone wall. "There, you scoundrel, now we have you!" He clapped his hands loudly, and young Marko jumped.

"Papa, is this the yardarm part? Where they take the pirate?" his daughter said.

"Peggica, always you jump to the end of the story, but yes, this is the part." Maxo gestured to the old juniper that dominated the promontory. Its silvery outline gleamed in the late rays of sun that cut across the water. There it stood, tall in the evening sky, and a long, menacing arm stretched out from its trunk, pointing a gnarled finger toward the sea.

"Yes, mes enfants, may you well be afraid," here he performed an amazing impersonation of the tree, "of the evil that still lurks," a dramatic pause, "at Pirate's Point!" And here, Maxo let loose a loud and frightening cackle. Without taking his eyes from the tale-teller, young Marko inched his hand into little Peggy's.

"Maksimilijan, darling," Margaret's voice took on a chiding tone. "That's enough now." She turned to her friend and Marko's mother, Marija, and said in her ear, "He never fails to take the story a little too far."

He pulled at his lips with his teeth as he remembered the scene from what must have been eight or nine years ago. Maybe he had crossed the line once too often in spinning the scary yarn for the children. Could he have somehow insulted the spirits in an unwitting way? Though no ghostly visitor had chilled his neck or watched from below for more than a week now, he still puzzled about the origins of the phantom. Its genesis had become a sort of game for him. No, more than a game. More exactly, the spirit's visitations were a full-blown enigma, one that pulled and gnawed at him. The mystery had grown into an obsession he would sooner have dismissed given the amount of work he still needed to accomplish.

Maxo grimaced into the darkening waters of the river. "Don't be ridiculous, old man," he whispered to the evening. "How could Korcula have ever produced such terrors?"

His mind drifted away from the apparition as the remembrance of mild Adriatic breezes carried him to a gentler and calmer place. He stood once again on the veranda of their villa on Korcula, but this time, he was alone. Peggica was attending the good Sisters' school, and Margaret had tootled off to play bridge with some of the ladies from town.

The day was fair, and soft winds ruffled the sleeves of his peasant shirt as he worked the palette. To capture the feel and smell of that morning in this painting, now that would be something. Somewhere, the air carried a hint of sun-washed hay, and the sunlight glinting through the tree boughs bounced the light from corner to wall to floor to wall again. He licked his lips, and even the salt was light upon them.

Maxo wondered how he had ever lived away from his beloved Korcula. The years in Zagreb, to be sure, had been good ones, exciting ones, in many ways. He sometimes missed the buzz and hustle of trains, trams, and hundreds of feet tramping through the squares or the marketplace. And the conversations, the heated discussions, and the arguments he would hold at the cafes with his friends had invigorated his mind and his wit. The big city had teemed with light and color and sound, but it had never offered the balm of Korcula that was as natural as breathing itself.

Every day offered a new awakening. Birds flickering in and out of the wild oaks or the fronds of the palmettos he had planted along the walkway. Fresh fish and škampi and polpi from the fishmongers. A cooling swim in crystalline waters, clear and delicious, the small swells holding him up in their salty palms. The glorious stone buildings beaming with the morning light or glowing yellow and ochre in the sun's after-light as it sunk into the west. Always, the kiss of the wind as it surfaced from the sea or the hills. A new awakening for this island, too – every day for hundreds of decades, for thousands - new and yet, so old. His, and yet, no one's; or everyone's, depending on one's perspective.

The taste of sunshine and salt filtered down through the years and caressed his tongue. So much time had gone by and yet he so well remembered these details. The island's character had inspired some of his best work.

He recalled another occasion when he had invited a number of students to come to Korcula for a week of creation. Now that had been a perfect combination – students and Korcula and the time and leisure to create freely, far from care, and far from home and its inevitable tasks. The joy of the memory sat in his heart like a miniature sun. He remembered Georg – tan and full of the good Posip wine – letting loose on his canvas and producing work far superior to what he had yet painted. How they had laughed and lived that week – good-natured joking, long bouts of studied work, refreshing dips in the sea, late night dinners of seabream and tomato salads.

He believed Margaret had been happy on the island, too, and little Peggica. For Margaret, plenty of old families and an educated lot made for good soirees. Peggica ran around like the little vixen she was, prancing through the shallows, piling shells and pebbles into small cairns, balancing carefully on the stone walls, climbing trees to peek into sparrow nests, and drawing pictures in the sand with a piece of broken shell.

The will of the island infected all of them, and given the choice, they would have lulled away the hours there until they became months and years. However, events intervened most cruelly and jerked them onto another path.

Maxo's heart wrenched as he pictured that scene around the dining table, the Thursday evening they had finally acknowledged the danger knocking at their door. Louis had come to dinner. An unforgettable exigency had colored his friend's voice that night.

"Maxo, you know I would never ask it if things were not getting so bad." Louis puffed on his cigarette while Maxo's head shrunk further between his shoulders. His jawbone went rigid with the onset of stubborn resolve.

Maxo spoke to the floor. "Louis, Louis, Louis. This is our

life, our home, our haven. How are we to leave it, hey? Are we supposed to throw a few things in a bag and bid farewell to our beautiful Korcula?" He looked his friend in the eye. "Are we to desert Mother Croatia? And what about the rest of my family?"

A cloud of smoke blasted through Louis's lips, and a thread of hard fear thrummed behind his usual honeyed tone. "Maxo, we have had this discussion, remember? Many, many times before. Up to now, you have been able to get by. But now, tonight, the risk is too great. The danger is too close. It is only natural that the Germans will march to control the sea as their next move after Sarajevo, and then what? It is a stone's throw to Korcula or any of the islands after that."

Margaret listened carefully from her side of the table. Now she jumped into the conversation. "Tell us, Louis. What is it? What have you heard?" Her clear voice commanded attention.

"Oh, Margaret, dear," Louis turned to face her. "I would spare you the details, but layer upon layer of horrific stories are reaching us daily. It seems impossible to believe that things could be any worse than they were say, even six months ago, but they are."

"How worse?" Maxo's voice chimed in as Margaret shivered in her chair.

Louis reached for Margaret's hand. "They are conducting a crusade to eradicate every Jew in any present or former Yugoslavian territory. Göring himself vows that he will not rest until every person who is Jewish, every person who looks like a Jew, acts like a Jew, speaks like a Jew -" he bit his lip for a moment, "- smells like a Jew, thinks like a Jew, eats like a Jew, and prays like a Jew is exterminated. His very words, or so they tell me." Louis patted Margaret's hand and said quietly, "I am so sorry, my dear." Then he wiped his brow with his large, light blue handkerchief and leaned back in his chair.

The bronze of summer slipping from her face, Margaret froze in place, still and white as the villa's marble. Maxo raced around the table to clasp her shoulders. He pressed his lips to her forehead and knelt beside her. "My darling?" he said.

After a few seconds, Margaret sighed and looked at them

both. “I, I guess I knew it was happening. Simply hearing you put it into words,” her hands gestured helplessly, then found her chest, “feels like a mountain crashing down on me.” Her shallow, stilted breaths punctuated the silence that followed this remark.

Abruptly, she rose. The backs of her knees pushed the chair away from the table, and it screeched along the floor. “I – I can’t breathe. Must get out, must go.” She bumped past Maxo, shoving him away when he tried to help. “No, no, leave me alone,” she said and fled out the French windows. Through the twilight, they could see Margaret’s dim form leaning over the terrace wall.

Maxo stepped toward the open door, but Louis grabbed him by the elbow. “No, my friend. Bide here awhile. Give her some time.” He crushed the end of his cigarette into the tray. “But now, dear Maxo, do you comprehend why I have been pressing on you all these months?”

The artist slumped into Margaret’s chair. “I realize, dear Louis, that it sounds incredibly stupid, but somehow I thought that all this –” he waved his arm in a wide circle that took in the island and the sea, “ – I somehow thought that all of this would keep us safe. And, and it is all so beautiful, I have had a hard time imagining that anything bad could happen here. Why would the hateful Germans want to destroy a wonderful island like Korcula?”

Louis Adamic lowered his head, and then looked up into Maxo’s eyes. “I know, my friend, I know.” He paused to light another cigarette. He inhaled deeply and tapped the ash thoughtfully on the edge of the tray. “Why indeed? None of it makes any sense at all. The only logical thing to do now is to leave. You must make plans to come away – come away, almost at once. There is no certainty, no ability to predict when the Gestapo or their foot soldiers may be upon us. Come to Stella and me in New York. We will see you well situated once you are there.”

Louis tamped the smoldering cigarette stub into the tray and stood. “I will go and say good night to Margaret, and then retire. I do hope I haven't upset her too much."

Maxo clamped his friend's left bicep, gave it a little shake, and nodded. He had no words. He did not trust his voice after such news, but he was grateful for Louis's offer.

Once Louis departed, Maxo's immediate thoughts leapt to Peggica. After checking on Margaret, who shooed him away once more, he had run to his daughter's side. She slept on her small white cot, heedless of the moonbeam stroking her pillowcase. A light cotton sheet covered her legs, and her walnut curls lay tousled on the pillow, a dark halo that complemented the dark brows and eyelashes. *Peggica's Jewish blood was less than half of her make-up, but still – would they be willing to take her away based on looks alone? And what did a Jewish person look like – or smell like, for that matter?* Maxo asked himself. Such questions had answers that did not bear hearing, and Maxo did not intend to wait for them.

These many years later, Maxo's heart still sank when he thought of that difficult evening and the wonderful life that they had been forced to leave. The enemy soldiers swarming the hills near Sarajevo had all but eliminated any choice in the matter.

The clock tower gonged midnight. Maxo's head lay on his pillow as his slender fingers fretted with a feather that poked out at one end. In the narrow bed at the rectory, he listened to the hour slip by as so many had on other nights. Bidding the priest a fond thank you and good night, he had brushed his teeth and reached his bed by 10:30, but his eyelids had refused to close. Often the sixteen-hour stretches of mural painting that Maxo undertook became the thieves of sleep. Those hours bulged with activity and flew by at an intense pace that would flatten most people. Small wonder his mind struggled to settle after the long days of concentration.

No surprise then that sleep would not come, though Maxo knew the cleric had hoped the fresh air of the picnic would produce a full night's rest for the artist. A chuckle rattled in his throat. It had certainly worked for Father. Maxo could hear the good priest's snores sawing through the walls from two rooms away.

Maxo Vanka never permitted this wakefulness to disturb him, however. Far from it, some of his best ideas came at that moment, that nexus when waking folds into slumber. If anything, he tried to encourage those slivers of light – for that is how he saw them – to arrive.

He waited, therefore, with the natural ease that had been his since childhood. It allowed Maxo to drift in a dream-like state, his thoughts gliding around corners of his life or wafting through his day. They traveled far and near as thoughts often do when left to their own devices.

Back on the sunlit veranda of the Korcula villa, the students from the art school, had disappeared to select a site and paint *en plein air*, all save one. Georg remained on the terrace with Maxo, nibbling at some leftover fruit from the luncheon buffet table. Maxo had asked him to stay behind, and now they engaged in a vigorous discussion about the painting he had developed over the past few days.

"Vraiment, Georg," Maxo converted to the French language to aid his student from Provence. "This is your best yet. The colors, oo, la, la, I can almost taste them, and their freshness. You have truly translated Korcula onto the canvas – une petite miracle, my dear Georg! La plage, the sea, the sky – merveilleux! Wonderful!"

Georg smiled into his chest while he removed his eyeglasses and polished them for the second time in ten minutes. "Merci, Professor Vanka." He breathed in deeply. "What you told us earlier seems to have come true. I have fallen under an enchantment – the fairies of Korcula? In any event, I only know that I feel somehow freer, happier here. My arms and hands seem to have a life of their own, and I am happy to be their means of conveyance between canvas and palette."

Maxo placed a hand lightly on the student's shoulder for a moment. "Ah, and a poet, too."

Georg's chest received another smile, but his chin jerked up at the tiny, sharp intake of his teacher's breath. For a minute, his face wrinkled with a puzzled look as though he was not sure he had heard anything. The sound had been inconsequential, and the artist showed no sign of indisposition or concern. But he had repositioned himself in front of Georg's painting, his nose nearly pressing the canvas.

Maxo stroked his beard till it pointed to the ground. He seemed to be talking to himself.

"Professor," Georg finally managed, "are you…?"

"Un moment, s'il vous plait," and Maxo flung his left palm in front of the student's face. "It cannot – it is preposterous," he murmured to himself.

Georg followed the tip of the professor's nose. Like a classroom pointer, it rested near the portion of his painting that was predominantly sand and beach. In the distance, an attractive woman strolled along the strand. She had dark hair and a slim figure. Garbed in high style, her dress and hat hailed back to an earlier generation. Though distant, Maxo could discern her beauty despite the kiss of middle age. She was diminutive compared to the sweeping and vibrant seascape that had come alive under Georg's bold brush. None-the-less, he seemed unable to escape the feeling that the woman was watching whoever viewed the painting. Now she studied Maxo and Georg.

A hollow feeling scoured a patch in Maxo's chest. "Dear God," he said under his breath.

"Excuse me, sir," said Georg. "Did you ask me something?"

Maxo wiped his brow, unaware he had spoken aloud. He gave a little cough and cleared his throat. "Pardonnez-moi, cher Georg. Tell me, dear fellow, where were you the day that you painted this, this …?" His index finger circled the air in front of the woman on the beach.

Georg blushed, mystified about the significance of the question. "Um, well, it was this very morning. I'm afraid I don't remember the name of the beach – I'm not very good at remembering such things – but it was a sweet, deserted stretch, oh, I would say about three kilometers north of here. I wanted to find a spot away from everyone else – you know, somewhere to enjoy the quiet and really concentrate." Georg closed his mouth, and then said, "I'm blathering. Sorry." He began again. "Do you know it? This beach? The land dips in a bit – see there," he extended a brush toward the lower half of the painting, "that's where it forms a grotto. The water is brilliant there, like a deep aquamarine jewel. Have you been?"

Maxo's passion for walking had taken him over at least half of the island by foot. Much of the hilly terrain and cliff-edged shoreline had borne the sole of his boot. Everything had fallen under his scrutiny. The beach that Georg mentioned was an old friend, but one that required a stiff descent to reach its secrets. In fact, it was a marvel how the rocky bluffs unfolded into the smooth, wide plain of the crescent beach. Maxo, too, had stared into the depths of the aquamarine pool and been mesmerized by the sea stars, urchins and tiny fish that lived within. He, too, had admired the contrast between the bounding waves, the smooth swath of sand, and the whitish-gray rocks that rose like stone hatboxes stacked on top of one another.

On one of the few times he had visited the cove, the woman in the distance had appeared on the far end of the beach. In the mist from the waves, she had waited, watching, but never allowing him to walk any closer to her than twelve or fifteen meters.

Maxo stood upright and faced Georg, but suddenly found it difficult to put his question into words. Finally, he asked, "How came you to add this figure to your painting? The piece would have worked well enough on its own." Georg began to speak, but Maxo forestalled him. "That is to say, the figure actually complements the painting very well, but what inspired you to add it?"

By the time Maxo had finished speaking, Georg's sallow complexion had deepened to a dark red. "À la la, but there is the problem, Monsieur Vanka." One of Georg's teeth snagged his bottom lip before he could go on. "You see – I never painted her. I, I, I thought – though I did not truly believe you would do such a thing – I thought that for some reason you had painted her into the scene. Perhaps to give me a lesson? To demonstrate a better balance of the elements?" Georg cut himself off and drew a sleeve across his lips.

Maxo shook his head back and forth slowly. "Non, Georg, ça n'était pas moi." His eyes looked worried. "It was not me."

In the narrow bed, Maxo shook his head like he had so long ago. The mystery of the pretty woman in Georg's painting had never been resolved. Though he had taken all of his visiting students to task, no one could help explain her presence. Such an odd thing to happen, and now, here when he merely thought of the woman in the distance, disaster had played a heavy hand and ruined some of the good work already completed at the church.

Maxo's memory rehung Georg's painting before his eyes. The group had universally agreed that the budding artist should keep the figure in the picture. Others had liked it, too, and Georg had taken a small prize for the painting at a regional art show in Zagreb. Maxo's lips turned up in a smile. He cherished warm thoughts of his pupil and his success as an art student, but his heart still thumped when he recalled the figure that inhabited Georg's canvas. "Hardly surprising," Maxo huffed to himself, "considering she is the very portrait of the woman I saw distantly on many occasions, but never had the chance to meet."

The artist rolled over to face the wall. The lumps in the pillow nudged his head, and unconsciously, he sought a more comfortable resting spot. A ferocious yawn cracked his jaw, and Maxo pulled the scratchy, loden-green blanket over his shoulder. He began to doze, his lips moving in counterpoint. "Must tell." The words formed an urgent vow, as though sleep might erase them if they were not pronounced. "Must tell Father, as soon as the sun is up, my discoveries, and my suspicions."

The next morning, Maxo strode with determination into the kitchen. No one was there, and he observed that a lone place setting had been laid on the breakfast table. According to the cook, Father had hurried off to old Mrs. Laski's house. The ancient lady had fallen from her porch, and Mrs. Dobrovic had no idea when the priest would return.

"Lord be, Mr. Vanka," the cook said, stopping to peer into his face, "if you must speak to Father this very minute, why then, our Cara will run and fetch him."

Maxo grabbed her hands. Dishwater still dampened her fingers. "No, no, no. Please do not trouble the lovely Cara or yourself. It is nothing." His head nodded rapidly as if to convince himself that this was true. "Nothing that will not keep until later. I will catch up with him then."

Mrs. Dobrovic remained on the threshold of the kitchen door, her elbows cocked over her hips, and her lips pursed. She started to speak when Maxo said, "Come, will you not please pour me some of that fresh-squeezed orange juice you made this morning? I could smell its delicious blossom from my bedroom, and I have been longing all this while to sample it."

The cook flapped a hand before him as if to say "oh, you," and bustled to the counter where she fetched the juice. "Now, I've got a bit of eggs mixed with that ham from the other night, and how about some toast?" She plunked the juice glass before him and hurried away before he could respond, but he did call after her, "Is the tea kettle hot?"

CHAPTER SEVEN

THOUGHTS ROILED THROUGH MAXO'S MIND as he set up the scaffold to continue work on the second half of the *Battlefield* scene. The unspoken words that he had intended for Father's ears troubled him, but also, his morning plans called for the beginning of another disturbing painting. He climbed the scaffolding to the portion of the ceiling next to the seething Mother Mary. His subject on this side would match her in horror. In his sketch of it, soldiers slaughtered Christ on the cross, and then became terrified at the evil they had wrought. He considered details that he could add to the drama – perhaps a cross poking from one of the soldiers' pockets, and definitely, a crown of barbed wire for the Christ figure.

Maxo swallowed as he began to paint. All too readily, he sensed the barbed wire on his own head, piercing him with cruel reminders of his own terrible experiences during the Great War.

The road was no longer a road. Thousands of footfalls had obliterated its dimensions. Wagon wheels had scored its face with crisscrossed ruts that cut through each other in a patternless web of gravel and mud. Every fifty feet or so, Guil, the driver, swung wide to negotiate craters carved by the hundreds of shells that had exploded their wrath. The ground within the pits pulsed, an uneasy ooze amidst the constant repercussions.

The medics on the wagon hunched low in the drenching rain as even now, high explosives sang overhead.

"Allez!" the driver commanded the two horses. "Allez, allez! Move along now, my ladies. Go girls, go!" His tones bounced like anxious raindrops off their mud-streaked rumps as the steeds strained to pull the wagon. Behind blinders, their large equine eyes shone white as another shell whizzed by.

Guil managed to urge them past a deep groove in the mud, but the morass of a huge hole waited immediately ahead. The wagon slewed wildly and began to sink. Maxo grabbed the rail of the wooden seat atop the wagon where he sat with the driver. The cry of their single passenger followed by a dull thud reached their ears. Copper, the chestnut mare, whinnied as the slime climbed to her fetlocks. Both men jumped down to survey the situation. The orderly scrambled from the back of the transport rubbing his shoulder. A small lump shone shiny and purple above his left brow.

"Good God!" Guil flung his hands toward the mired wagon. "We'll never make St. Marin now!" Red blotches rose on his cheeks, and he rubbed the back of his neck.

Maxo clucked and patted his arm. "It will do no good, my friend, to work yourself up so. We must think of how to save the horses, and then, the wagon. It is of the first necessity to calm the poor beasts,"

"Though how that will be possible in this rain of fire," Guil gestured to the sky as more missiles zoomed by, " is anybody's guess."

The orderly, a young lad named Rune, cleared his throat. "Well, sir, you know, I am from the farms. I could unfasten those harnesses, but someone must hold the horses' heads to keep them quieted."

Maxo nodded and eased his way around the top of the crater. His eyes on the horses, his voice soft, he spoke. "Here, my pretties, here. Look this way. Tonton Maxo has something for you." In the same calm voice, he called back to Guil. "Look about and see what you can find in the way of boards, bricks, anything that can give the horses a place to stand."

Maxo saw two foot-sized stones by the side of the road. He plucked them up and plopped them in the mud before the horses. Now he had a solid foundation to reach the horses' noses. Crooning quietly, he let them snuffle him as he slid his hands tenderly down their necks. Soon, they nuzzled his shirt and allowed Maxo to comb his fingers through their forelocks. Bella, the big bay on the left, rested her chin lightly on his slight shoulder and sighed. Copper, in more peril, quaked a bit as Rune worked around her. As if by magic, Maxo produced an apple from his pocket. He bit off a piece and palmed it into Copper's mouth, and then another for Bella.

While Maxo walked toward the horses' heads, Rune had waded knee-deep into the sucking mud. Gently, he approached Copper, talking to her all the while. "There, girl, there." He stroked her side. "Let me just reach under here to grab the buckle." Rune bent in half below the horse's belly. Her skin quivered but she stood her ground. With his face inches from the unctuous muck, Rune unlatched the first of the fastenings, and then the second.

For a moment, Maxo lifted his face from the horses and looked around for Guil. He could not see the driver, but he could hear the squish of feet on soaking wet ground and the occasional epithet escaping Guil's mouth. He hoped the other man returned soon, before Copper could no longer be pulled to safety.

After finishing with Copper, Rune struggled to extract his legs from the sludge. He finally had to haul his torso up onto the wooden tongue of the harness to free himself. With chagrin, he stared at his bare left foot. "Oh, damn," he said with a low mutter, "where am I ever going to find another boot?" For more than a moment, he sat on the wood plank, unable to budge.

"Rune?" Maxo said. "Rune, we must hurry."

The young man clambered over the tongue and dropped down beside Bella. Here Rune crouched within easy grasp of the buckles. He unclasped the first, but as he reached for the second, his naked foot slipped. Maxo heard the succulent plop as Rune's buttocks connected with the muddy slop. Swearing in Flemish, the boy slipped and slid in his scurry to escape the hole. He turned on all fours to lift himself up and out as the weight of the muck pulled at his trousers. Suddenly he was screaming.

Both of the horses snapped their heads up as though they had been struck. They snorted, and their fright gave motion and strength to their legs as they struggled to escape the mire. Maxo clung between them, one arm hooked into the bridle of each. Bella broke free of the mud first, snapping the second harness buckle in two. Through sheer might, she pulled Maxo and Copper with her.

Panting, Guil appeared on a knoll beside the road, a bundle of sticks, boards, and guns in his arms. Rune had stopped screaming and lay shaking at the edge of the shell hole where he had skittered out of the mud. His breathing, jagged with panic, rasped in and out of his throat.

Fifty yards down the road, Maxo led the horses back toward them. Chomping a smatch of apple each, they walked calmly and readily down the ruined track.

From a different direction, Guil scuttled through debris until he stood within shouting distance. He began bellowing as he worked his way toward the orderly.

"Rune, boy, what is it? Whatever is it?"

The boy looked up for an instant and then leaned into his folded arms. Even from a distance, Maxo saw his shoulders heaving. He tugged the horses by their reins until he drew near enough to squat beside the thin form. He ran a hand over Rune's hair.

Rune tried to catch his breath, but the remainder of his sobs kept choking him. Finally, he drew a long, shaky sigh.

"Dear Rune," Maxo's voice soothed. "Do tell us. What happened just now?"

"I, I was just finishing the second buckle, you know, toward the rear of the horse, when, when …" he faltered.

"When?" Maxo coached.

"When I slipped and fell in the horrid mud. There was

nothing for it, but to get onto my hands and knees if I was ever going to stand up again, but as I was reaching out to get a hand-hold, I grabbed onto something soft and gooey, like a wetter kind of mud, only stickier, if that's possible."

Maxo swallowed as he pictured what the boy might say next.

"It, it was a man's face, only, only it was half rotted away, and what came up in my hands must have been, must have been his brains!" This last Rune blurted out loudly as though he could expel it from his memory if he spoke with enough force.

"Oh, my God!" Maxo and Guil exclaimed at the same time.

"But that, but that wasn't all. It, it was the smell. You think all this muck is bad, but that. Oh my God, I've smelled a rabbit before when it was dead in the field a week, but never, never, ever a stench like this, like all the rotten flesh in the world had gathered in one place. It was horrible. Horrible!"

The boy gagged and broke down again. Big Guil dragged him far from the hole and held him close while Maxo stared at the crater. He could see the yellowish scum of whatever bile Rune's stomach had ejected, but no sign of the monstrosity showed below the mud. His own throat constricted when he realized that they would have to return to the hole to rescue the stranded wagon.

Dusk fell before they could travel on their way again. In the end, strong Bella, with Guil's steady hand to guide her, dragged the ambulance from the rear to right it upon the road. Maxo helped Rune change into dryer pants, and Guil produced a pair of boots only one size too big that he had found in the nearby field.

They rode three abreast, crammed together along the driver's bench, but the arrangement afforded warmth and comfort. Maxo entertained them with a story or two from his student days and sang some Croatian folk tunes. Rune slumped on his shoulder as they bumped along, escaping to a deep sleep.

Maxo stopped his humming and looked at the boy. "Yes, sleep, young one, for now to escape the horrors of this day and this time. All too soon, we must wake to it again."

Guil studied the road ahead, but a hard glare shone in his eyes, and his jaw tensed as Maxo watched.

The artist wrapped his woolen cape as best he could about himself and the boy. Guil had waved away his share.

Thank heavens, it has stopped raining, Maxo thought and nestled further into the cloak. *It is actually possible to feel a little warm when we do not have to deal with the wet.*

As the horses clopped on, Maxo sank into their rhythm. The hoof beats and the rocking of the vehicle lulled him into a half-sleep where his thoughts took their own roads. Part of him contemplated how he would depict his wartime experiences once he resurfaced at the art academy. He had been studying in Belgium at the outbreak of the war, and like all the young men, had been conscripted to its service. Due to his beliefs, or so he thought, Maxo received an assignment to the ambulance corps. A modicum of medical training enabled him to apply first aid, and then safely transport battle victims to the nearest field hospital.

Because of their mission, Maxo's team never remained at the front for more than a few hours at a time, nor did they overnight in the trenches. Instead, they patrolled the deep ditches to retrieve injured soldiers from the staging areas, load them on the ambulance, deliver them to a field hospital, then return to the front for more of the wounded.

Maxo's mind retraced his steps on one visit through the maze of earthen corridors. A foot soldier with blood-soaked pant legs called to them for help in a quiet, controlled voice. As they lifted him onto a stretcher, he had shown Maxo a picture of his sweetheart. Backlit by the sun, her light curls formed an aureole around her face. "Why, she is an angel," Maxo had said and meant it. The man's face flushed with pleasure before he drifted into unconsciousness.

That took Maxo's thoughts to his last leave in Zagreb. His own angel lived there, and now his chest lifted in reminiscence.

The ebony hair tumbling down to her waist, the almost black eyes a deep pool for losing yourself, the moue of pink lips that blossomed into a huge smile when she was happy, the little chin sliding into a long white neck, the silken skin of her young breasts, small and standing at attention, the warmth of her belly, the curve of her thighs. His groin tightened, and he swallowed hard. *Dear God, only a memory now, but what a memory.*

The wagon jogged to a halt. As the remembrance whispered away, Maxo opened his eyes. A rudimentary field hospital located about a mile behind the front stood before them. Rune collected himself and released the horses so that they could be watered and fed. Guil and Maxo entered the big white tent to hear what lay in store for them the next day. A young soldier handed around crusts of bread, cups of wine, and a thin porridge for dinner. Then the men took what rest they could on the ambulance wagon's shelves. All too soon they would hold tomorrow's wounded as the medics headed to the front once again.

A thin drizzle greeted Maxo as he stepped from the ambulance van to relieve himself. He hustled into the hospital tent. Riding above the aroma of medicaments and antiseptics, he thought he could smell poached eggs. Surely, he still dreamed. But no, one of the aides told him that a grateful mother whose boy the head doctor had saved had brought two dozen eggs "pour le médicin." The juices raced around Maxo's stomach, and the roof of his mouth dripped with hope.

A nurse he had not met last night watched him, her cheeks rounded with amusement.

"Good morning, sir," she said in very correct French. "I am Sister Nora Whitson, and you, I believe, must be one of our good medics."

When he nodded, she said, "I'll be riding along to the front with you this morning. Unfortunately, we're expecting rather a lot of casualties."

"Ah, it grieves me to hear this," Maxo said, with a small bow to the sparkling eyes. "But it is no less than we can expect, I suppose, after what we heard last night." He studied the tilt of her nose.

Sister Nora blushed suddenly and said, "I suppose you'll be wanting some breakfast before we head out. Dr. Metvic has been blessed with more eggs than he can eat. Would you care for one?" She crooked a finger for him to follow.

Even in the midst of hell, heaven, Maxo thought as he wrapped his toast around the last morsel of egg. He glanced at Sister Whitson appreciatively. "I should no doubt say that I am sorry you have to accompany us to such a dangerous place, but in truth," he held up both hands, "I am not." They both laughed.

An hour and a quarter later, the laughter ceased as hard rain and zinging bullets filled the air. Instead, Maxo spat mud from his mouth before speaking from the bottom of a trench. "Pay attention, my friends, the footwork here, it is treacherous."

These trenches had nothing in common with the ones from Maxo's recollection. They had been hastily dug, and just as quickly, the rain had turned them into running sewers. A steady buildup of ooze underfoot caused them to flounder, and many of the trenches ran to dead ends clogged with the fallout from shells that had found their mark. Men worked feverishly to clear these passages, using only their hands for fear that human flesh lay trapped within.

Though shorter than the top of the trenches, Maxo still ducked as the giant shells sailed over. His hands pressed his ears hard against their thrumming whine. Wounded fighters littered the trenches, having slithered from the battleground and down the slippery trench walls. Some sat propped in place by their buddies, silent and sodden like wet sacks leaking blood, waiting for help.

Sister Nora hastened through the mud corridors with what speed she could muster, a large roll of white bandage under her left arm. She temporarily dressed wounds and gauged which men could make the trip on the ambulance. Maxo and Rune, Guil and whatever other recruit they enlisted manned the stretchers with their injured cargo, slipping and sliding their way back to the van at the open end of one trench.

When the eight racks groaned with prone men on either side of the ambulance, and a ninth man lay on the floor, Guil said, "That's it, lads, the horses won't take any more. Maxo! Rune! I'm afraid you'll have to follow beside the van. She's carrying too much weight as it is." Nora said she would walk as well, but Guil guided her up onto the driver's bench.

Maxo tied the flaps at the back of the vehicle for what little shelter they could afford the men, and then he and Rune brought up the rear as the horses pulled away.

"Bože moj!" Maxo exclaimed as shells blasted to either side of them. Again, he covered his ears, but nothing could shut out the thundering guns. He looked over at Rune. His face was pale beneath thick streaks of blood and mud, and his clothing was crusted with the muck from the trenches. Maxo began to laugh.

"What are you, crazy?" cried the boy.

"No, no, my dear fellow, it only struck me as funny. I was looking at you and feeling so sorry for the condition of your face and your hair and your clothing, and then," he chuckled, "I realized that I undoubtedly was looking at a mirror image of myself."

He walked closer to Rune and clapped him around the shoulders. "So, hey, we are all stuck in this together, are we not? And it is the height of the ridiculous, no?" But here his comments meant little to the boy who understood neither irony nor the politics of war. "Ah well, let us keep up with the wagon, yes?" and Maxo picked up his pace. Muffled cries issued from its depths every time the wagon wheels caught on a ridge of mud or bumped through a hole, and still it rained water and bullets.

As they reached the top of a slight rise, the sky lightened for a second. Maxo stood transfixed by the panorama before him. His heart quickened within his chest, and he found himself gulping for air. For as far as he could see, craters pocked the landscape in an unending pattern of rim-to-rim circles. Water filled some, and men, or what were once men, filled many more. Dead animals – hundreds of cavalry horses and messenger dogs, distended and horrible – littered the ground. The air choked with death and something else that tinged it with a dark edge. Maxo sniffed. Oh God, excrement – excrement mixed in with the mud and the blood. Jesus!

Then he noticed that through the masses, though death had come to call, a stirring of quick, tiny movements shivered the surface of the land. Abruptly, Maxo realized that rats – some as large as house cats – crawled among the carcasses and corpses, and they were feeding.

He jerked his eyes away and felt his gorge rise. By the roadside, Rune puked into the mud. Maxo spat to clear his throat and ran to help the boy. The skies re-opened at that moment and drew a gray curtain over the scene. Descending the next hill, it was as though they had never beheld it.

They marched past the next series of trenches, the first tranche after the front line. The shelling lessened here, though now and then something would whiz past to remind them that death lived only a breath away. From the front of the wagon, Guil's voice trailed back in gusts. "Come along, girls, whoop, whoop, get past … now. Come alo …, I know … can do it."

Maxo saw Sister Nora lean out and look back at them. She gave a little wave, and he saluted in return, tapping his combat helmet with two fingertips.

Inclined to restrict his eyes to the road in front of them, it did not take long before Maxo once more surveyed the landscape. He observed that, here, too, the enemy had blasted many of the trenches into oblivion, and that the forces had deserted the fortifications in large part.

As this thought occurred to him, the artist noticed an arm extending from beneath the debris of a nearby cave-in. "Poor soul," he muttered just before the fingers on the hand started waving. A faint moaning filtered from within the piled clods of earth.

"Good God, Rune, there's someone in there!" Maxo hurried toward the trench. "Someone alive, by Jove! We must rescue him."

He ran to the front of the ambulance. "Stop, Guil, stop!

There is someone buried, buried alive. We must help him to get out! Stop, I say!"

But Guil kept on driving. "Ne, ne. I cannot stop. Maxo, you know this. We are already over-filled with the sick and dying. There is no room for one more."

"Perhaps we could lie him here on the bench," Sister Nora suggested. "I can easily walk." Without a second thought, she leapt to the ground and followed Maxo back some twenty paces.

Guil continued for another hundred yards, and then he halted. "Mother of God, how can we help one more? These fellows will die if we don't get them back soon." He did not run back to help the other three, who now dug madly with their hands, but he did not carry on. Instead, he waited. *God, I want a cigarette,* he thought, *but lighting up was like sending an engraved invitation to the enemy. No, I do not want to get my face shot off today.* He peered around the side of the van.

Maxo spoke softly, putting encouragement in his voice. He tried English first, then German, but finally when he began in French, the buried man responded. "Au secours! S'il vous plaît. S'il vous plaît. Please, please help me. I want to live."

"Oui, mon ami, we could sense from your hand alone that this is true. We are carefully trying to dig so as not to hurt you. But can you tell me – are you badly wounded?"

Maxo maintained a steady stream of conversation, focusing on keeping the man alert while they worked to free him. They cleared from his arm up to his neck, and then like a beam of sunlight, his face shone through the mud. Sister Nora wiped the dirt from his eyes, nose and mouth with a white linen cloth, and he smiled up at her.

"Oh, merci beaucoup, Mademoiselle. You have saved my life. You have saved me." Tears glistened in his eyes though his lips smiled.

"But not at all, Monsieur." Nora replied in her schoolgirl French. "It was this gentleman here – Monsieur Maksimilijan Vanka – you have to thank. It was he who spotted your arm and heard your cries. It was he who insisted we stop and come back for you."

"But we could not evacuate you without everybody's help." Maxo nodded to his fellow diggers, graciously. "Quickly now, everyone, we must carry on to free our good friend here."

Maxo scooped rust-colored mud from around the man's leg. A vivid gash ran the length of his calf, and the cut dribbled fresh blood as Sister Nora daubed the wound. Maxo moved to the other side and in five minutes more, they had freed him entirely from the landslide.

They could tell from his uniform that he held a position of some standing. Though smeared with mud, gold braiding on his shoulders and a row of medals across his breast pocket indicated as much. He was either a French or Belgian officer.

Stretched out against the earthen mound in the open air, the man laid quietly, his breaths shallow as he fought to regain a sense of equilibrium. With a tender touch, Maxo extracted his own handkerchief and bathed the man's face with water from his canteen. As he did so, he noticed a dull twinkling of red, gold and green beneath the sludge that coated the officer's shirt and jacket. Curious, he slid his thumb across one of the colored bumps. A large ruby glinted back at him.

Maxo's eyes quickly returned to the face of the recovered man. His eyes were closed, and his teeth gripped his lips in a tight line, defying the pain of his wound and the position in which he found himself.

"Sir," for now Maxo could see that he addressed someone of importance, "Sir, we have to shift you soon. The Germans are attempting to move their lines forward and will be upon us if we do not depart."

"Of course, of course," the injured man breathed out.

"May we have your permission to escort you to our ambulance van?" Maxo said.

The man nodded and extended his arms as pain shot across his face.

"Many thanks, and please, sir," Maxo continued, "to whom do we have the privilege of speaking?"

With a tiny bow of his head and a frail smile, the man

responded, "I am the Duc de Sevigny of the Pierrefeu family. We have long inhabited and governed lands that border," he leaned his head in a northeasterly direction, "la Belgique and Bretagne."

"Ah, very good, your grace," Maxo bowed. "And now, if you will allow me. That's it, put your arms around my neck." With a small grunt, he hoisted the duke upright. Then, Sister Nora and Maxo each shouldered an arm and half-carried the man to the wagon. Guil helped lift him onto the driver's seat where eye-level to the task, Sister Nora bound the injured leg with gauze. With some flair, Maxo whirled the wool cape from his own shoulders and blanketed the duke as he hunched on the bench.

"Allons-y!" Guil called out, and they set forth once more.

Nora, Maxo, and Rune trailed behind the ambulance. After another mile, Maxo hoisted Rune to a sitting position on the rear-most board of the van's floor. He had noticed the boy limping more and more in the sloppy boots Guil had appropriated for him. Almost immediately, the youth leaned against the canvas flaps of the van and fell asleep.

Nora smiled at Maxo. "You are a man of conviction, Monsieur Vanka. And compassion."

"Please, Sister, please call me Maxo. This is no place for formality."

"But what about your behavior towards the duke?"

"Oh that. Well, it is what he has come to expect in his station, has he not? And I thought it would bring him some presence of mind – that he still held an identity despite all this filth."

"Ah, compassionate and sensitive - very honorable."

Maxo tilted his head and lightly shrugged his shoulders. "I merely try to do what feels normal for one in his position," he said.

With eyes only slightly hinting at mischief, she added, "And you must call me Nora if I am to call you Maxo, as I certainly have no interest in being your sister!"

Despite the rain and the barrage of artillery, their laughter rang out. They continued to chat long after the sun had set, and only the dim whiteness of the van lit their route. They easily remained apace of the ambulance as it negotiated the ruined road at a snail's speed. Guil cooed to the horses, "Go easy, my ladies, go easy," knowing that every bump, every lurch held pain for the injured soldiers aboard.

At two the next morning, he pulled the horses to a halt in front of the field hospital near St. Eloi. Maxo, Nora, and Rune hurried to unload the van of its weary and war-sick cargo. One man lay cold and close to death, so Nora suggested that they attend the others first. The duke kindly waited his turn, recognizing that his wounds required far less attention than the ones of the men in the back.

Eventually, Guil and Maxo helped him down from his perch, and the Duc de Sevigny leant against the wagon wheel, his weight propped on his remaining good leg. With some ceremony, he returned Maxo's cape and bowed as low as he could reasonably execute without toppling over. Maxo returned the courtesy, but as he stood again, the duke surprised him by extending his jewel-bedecked waistcoat.

"Pour vous, mon ami," the duke bowed again.

"Oh, merci, but non, non, non, non, non," Maxo said, "this is too great, too valuable a gift."

"What, my friend?" the duke asked. "Do you suppose a cloth of jewels can in any way equal the re-purchase of my life? For without you and your sharp ears and your sharp eyes, I would not have received this second chance at life." The duke was smiling but his face was firm. "I insist. It is little enough that I can do this, and when this blasted war is over, and we have won – and we will win, this I know – you must come and visit me at the Chateau Sevigny. Will you promise me this? Will you?"

Maxo grabbed the man's hand and arm. "It will be my greatest pleasure," the artist said. "And you so honor me, I am without words." Bending deeply from the waist, he accepted the vest of jewels.

The cloth weighed heavily in Maxo's hand. Over-sized

fleur-de-lis spelled out in rubies, diamonds, sapphires, and emeralds adorned its front surfaces. Golden threads united the designs. Nora could not peel her eyes away from the jewels, and unconsciously, she reached out a hand to finger a large, square-cut emerald. Maxo handed her the vest for closer examination.

"What a fabulous piece of clothing, Monsieur le Duc. How came you to be wearing this in battle?" she asked.

"Ah, yes, well, it was inherited from our grandfather by my brother who is the second son in our family and invalided at home. He insisted that I wear it for good luck," the duke said. "He said it had saved him, and that earlier it had preserved our grandfather during the Crimean War. Now it has completed its service to our family by saving me. Let us hope that it is the talisman that aids you in surviving this war unscathed, Monsieur Vanka."

The nurse handed the waistcoat back to Maxo and ushered the good duke into the field hospital. His wound had waited long enough. Time to rest his legs and begin the long journey back to health.

Around lunchtime, when the medical crew had done all that was possible for their travellers, they re-hitched the ambulance wagon to Bella and Copper. Rune joined Guil on the driver's bench while Nora and Maxo stretched out in the rear of the van for some needed repose. The wagon joggled as their return to the front for more wounded fighters commenced.

Though no one could overhear them, Maxo and Nora spoke in soft whispers. He asked her about her past life in England. Clearly, she adored her home on the southern coast, and she began to speak of its gentle climate and the abundance of roses and other flora that grew there owing to the mild, moist weather.

"Through the lych gate of the church, there is the most astounding row of hydrangea, perhaps twenty feet tall. The dense, lush growth is crowned with deep burgundy flowers like I have seen nowhere else." She sighed, and Maxo imagined the painting he could make with her leaning prettily to one side of the gate. Hers was a face of sweet angles and shadows, and the thought of capturing it on canvas stirred him deeply as he lay on the wooden pallet.

He entreated Nora to close her eyes and give him her hand. She giggled and asked why like an excited schoolgirl. But when she looked him in the face, Maxo's smile was soft and serious, and she calmed herself. Lying back, she closed her eyes and put out a hand, anticipating the kiss that would follow.

Instead, she felt two, three, four, no, five cold pebbles drop into her palm, and then felt the pressure as Maxo gently curled her fingers around them.

"May I open my eyes now?" she asked.

"Un moment." One moment more, then Maxo knelt at her side, kissing her forehead, her cheeks, her chin, and finally, deliciously, her mouth. For a fleeting second, heat washed over her, and the battlefield became as distant as the moon. At that moment, the van struck a tall ridge in the road and helplessly, Maxo fell across her, laughing at the absurdity of it all.

Her eyes never left his face, and he said, "Mademoiselle, you grant me much esteem, to look at me instead of what is in your palm."

"What?" she said. Then, she raised her hand toward her face and watched amazed as five precious gems tumbled from her open fingers onto the bib of her nursing apron. They flashed fire and ice and a shard of sea green. "What, what's this?"

Maxo held up a large round ruby. He kissed her. "Ruby – like your lips." Then, a sapphire. Kiss. "Blue fire for your compassion." Diamonds for her spirit, kiss, kiss; and lastly, the large square-cut emerald. Kiss. "Only rivaled by your eyes, the finest jewels of all."

Nora spluttered. "But the duke. I mean, these are yours. The duke - he gave the gems – he gave them to you."

"But they must be for all of us," he said. Earlier that afternoon, he had employed his penknife to carve away a handful of jewels for each of the ambulance workers.

Tenderly, he picked up Nora's other hand. "Did I not see the mud and blood caked under these nails as you clawed through the earth to save the Duc de Sevigny? Did not these hands bathe and bind his wounds? Was it not your sweet mouth and eyes and countenance that soothed him back to life? No mistake, my dear Nora. These gems are as much yours as anyone's."

And with that, he lay back down and cradled her in his arms while she clasped the jewels in her left hand. Her heartbeat fluttered in her chest like some small captive bird as she relaxed into his embrace.

Maxo drew in a deep breath, inhaling the musk of her hair and her skin. She closed her eyes as he twirled a tendril that had escaped her kerchief. Round and round and back again, his index finger spun the curl. His fingertip brushed her neck ever so lightly, and she could more sense than feel the delicate tension of his actions. Entranced, she thought it seemed completely natural when he began to hum. The old Croatian love song purred in her ear, and soon she slept.

"Da, da, dah, ta-dah, ti dum da dah da – garavuso kad bi moja bila, moja bi se zelja ispunila. Dark girl, if you would be mine, my wish would be fulfilled." Maxo still remembered the tune and a few of the words. He crooned them to the evening dusk as he lay prone on the high wooden scaffolding. *Is it the wooden planks at my back or all this painting of war-time scenes that has jarred loose the experiences – the terrifying experiences and the good ones – of my time at the front?* He thought that chapter of his life had long been closed, but now it revealed itself in the dark skies and frightened faces of this second half of the *Battlefield* mural.

Hardly surprising, given how much he hated the treatment the Germans once again exerted on his motherland. The stories that Louis – his good friend, Louis Adamic, the author – told stoked his mind with horror. The Germans continued to sweep through Slovenia and Croatia - entire villages wiped out, fathers and sons marched to the slaughter, their bodies dumped in massive unmarked graves, women and children routinely abused, sometimes tortured, sometimes killed without provocation of any kind, and houses and buildings leveled. Worst of all, the German propaganda had turned brother against brother, fomenting hatred between Serbs and Croats, urging the Serbs to commit the heinous Nazis' atrocities for them. *War now, war then. It was – it is,* Maxo corrected himself, *the epitome of mankind at his most despicable, his most detestable.*

With a start, Maxo realized that his right arm ached, and he gazed at the vivid slashes and streaks of thick black and gray painted across the sky. His brush splayed wide and be-straggled in his hand. He had nearly ruined it as he pushed his anger and disgust into the clouds of the mural.

Maxo tsked. It was small wonder if he harkened back to his own wartime experience. He had never felt any fear to match it since. Not even this ghost, this apparition of the church could approach the level of sheer terror that those ambulance-running days had inspired. Yet, he had developed a genuine fondness for the people he met, and in fact, had remained in contact with the duke for many years until his death two Octobers ago. Maxo had indeed visited his castle, and they had played baccarat and smoked cigars while discussing the issues of the day over excellent bottles of wine.

He bit his lip and wiped a smudge from under his eye. Sadly, he had lost track of the lovely Nora. Like so many wartime friendships, theirs ended when she was reassigned to another location. Miraculously, all of their small crew had made it through the war, though Rune suffered the loss of a few toes after the harsh 1918 winter.

Not for the first time that evening, Maxo shivered. A stirring, like a cold, flat plain of air, crossed through the room. He did not look down, but focused on mixing the somber shades on his palette. At the same time, as though with an independent will, his heart thumped high in his chest.

It seemed like the ghost knew when disturbing thoughts visited him. It drew on his anger and his fear and gained in power. Maxo licked his lips and swallowed. *Try to remember the good parts*, he counseled himself. And though his little Peggica skipped through his mind, and the bright colors of his Bucks County gardens paraded past his inner eye, he found it impossible to shove away the oppressive cold that had set in.

Once more, Maxo put his mind to figuring out the significance of this apparition. After all these years, the evidence indicated that the ghost appeared to him and only him. Maxo concluded that could mean only one thing. The spirit signified someone from his past. Someone who visited in order to what? Warn him? Deliver a message? Ward him away? What?

Before tonight, Maxo had not considered that the image might be somebody he had known during the war. The people he had become closest to – the duke and Guil the driver, and for a short time, Sister Nora – did not match up to his idea of a frightful ghost. Anyway, of those three, he felt sure that only the duke had died. But perhaps spirits are not required to issue only from dead people.

The artist thought of the many soldiers and the occasional civilian he had aided at the battle sites. A number of them had passed away, often before the medics could shuttle them to a remote field hospital, but the connection stopped there. How or why would they have wanted to remain in touch? They barely knew him.

He wondered how this spirit world worked exactly. Could it transcend the dual barriers of time and space all these many years later, over a vast ocean that probably few had sailed, into a land virtually unknown to them? Maxo thought it unlikely.

He slapped a thigh onto the scaffolding. Truly, all this speculation simply led to more questions. Time had trickled by faster and faster, and any answers at all about the apparition persisted in eluding him.

Impatiently, he sat up, his thin hair inches from the ceiling. His eyes bore into the darkness below, but if a darker figure reposed there, he could not see him. Maxo gave his head a little shake and reached for the chambray shirt that draped one pole of the scaffold. He put it on over his loose-flowing smock and instantly felt warmer. He took a breath. The air was lighter.

The dimness around him seemed to recede a fraction.

Maxo resumed his position to continue painting. The unfinished Croatian love song slipped back into his throat, and he gave it voice. He decided that the face of Nora, sweet Sister of the killing fields, would look well upon one of the angels he had still to paint on the eastern wall.

CHAPTER EIGHT

AS A MORNING STORM BREWED, the sun winked in sporadic spurts behind the massing gray clouds. Dabbing the last breakfast crumbs from his mustache, Maxo stood to watch the shadows chase across the kitchen linoleum. Shouting a hurried "Hvala" to the cook, he ran to his room and donned the stained peasant blouse that served as his painter's smock.

The darkening sky pressed him with a sense of its urgency. As he passed over the threshold and out into the yard, the breeze cuffed his ears. The wind streamed from the river straight up the steep incline of Maryland Avenue, and he sensed that severe weather threatened. Now the church moaned as the blustering airstream shuddered past its eaves.

High above the tallest peak of the church, Maxo spied a giant bird sailing the thermals. Its outline black against the thunderheads, the vulture soared in ever-widening sweeps across the hilltop. Two other vultures joined in, and they began an eerie, silent dance upon the wind. As they circled out over the industrial valley below, Maxo shook his head in wonder. *They must be at least a thousand feet in the air.*

Their presence did nothing to quell the growing tightness in his chest. Since childhood, he had always associated the vulture-like buzzards in Croatia with fear and dread. He could remember the heightened pitch of Mati Dora's voice, imploring them to seek shelter in the cottage whenever the dark birds appeared. Once they were gathered in, she would slam the door, make the sign of the cross, and then huddle with the children by the stove. Sometimes she told terrible stories of children losing eyes or fingers if they did not hide from the ugly scavengers.

"They are always hungry." Her waggling forefinger would chide the children. "And they never appear unless there is bad news. Why, only last week, old Moser fell dead in his field whilst the birds circled his corn."

Maxo knew now that the stories had been intended to ensure the children's obedience, but still, the sense of portent the vultures brought clung to his shoulders like an iron clamp. With certainty, he understood what their presence meant.

As he trotted toward the church, large, hesitant raindrops sprayed tiny fountains as they hit the hard pavement. A hot pink cord of lightning twisted through the sky, and the thunder boomed and boomed again as it echoed down the river valley. Maxo stepped inside the church door just as the rain sluiced in earnest from the sky.

Inside the church, the clouds painted an atmosphere of gloom that only the startling flashes of lightning relieved. The air closed around him, cool and choking. For a moment, Maxo stood to grow accustomed to the dimness. With a will of their own, his eyes scanned every wall, every pew, and every corner of the church. They searched as he did, positive that the specter hid in the shadows.

Maxo threw on the electric lights, but the murk seemed to absorb their incandescence. Still, the main chandelier lit his way across the nave and down the aisle toward the rear of the church. Maxo slipped a key into the door lock of a closet next to the church office. Father had insisted that he secure his painting materials and supplies here after the catastrophe involving the *Justice* painting.

So odd, Maxo thought, *that the only painting portraying true justice was the one so unjustifiably attacked.*

The left side of his mouth tightened as he reached into the

cupboard for his palette, a short stepladder, the work light, and his box of brushes, rags, and paint jars. He carried all of it to a nearby spot where he planned to return to work on the mural about greed. *A fitting job for today*, Maxo thought. The dark nature of the painting perfectly matched the outdoor turbulence and the indoor cheerlessness.

With some precision, Maxo arranged the spotlight to focus on the area where the man he thought of as "the capitalist" would be sitting. Next, he positioned the stepladder beneath the light beam as this part of the painting could be reached without scaffolding. With paints and paint cloth ranged on the ladder's platform and rungs, the work could begin.

As his foot reached for the first step of the ladder, Maxo caught his breath. Suddenly, he realized that as he worked, the entire church would be to his back, out of view. An unstoppable dread climbed his backbone. He spun on his heels, knowing he had to take one more look around. He could not imagine focusing on the painting when the creature might be staring at the nape of his neck, or worse, wafting its way towards him.

Walking slowly and softly, Maxo began tracing the indoor perimeter of the church. A small part of him half-hoped that the ominous pall of the day foretold a change in the spirit's behavior that might help unravel its mystery; another part doubted his readiness to confront the ghost. Feeling like the clamp from his shoulders had migrated to his temples, he paced past the painting of Mati Croatia in her corner spot and turned left to approach the chapel to the right of the altar. No sign of malice or mischief revealed itself. He crossed before the red-carpeted steps leading up to the altar and paused once again to take in the sight of the iconic Mother Mary floating high above. Her presence reassured him somewhat, and he smiled to himself. *Yes, I made a pretty good job of her – the peace and understanding in her eyes, the strength in her hands and arms – the way her face seems to bless you.*

His eyes searched the deep shadows behind the altar.

Quietly, he called. "Âllo, âllo. Monsieur le Fantôme? Êtes-vous là?" He had begun speaking in French, a language he always thought of as gentler than most, but perhaps the spirit would not understand. "Dobra dan," he sang in Croatian. "Yoo, hoo. Are you there, Mr. Spirit?"

The slight echo of his own voice bounced from the walls into the silence. Maxo cocked his head to one side, and then he shrugged. He continued his tour past the second small chapel where he lifted the velvet table drapes of its altar and probed the dark beneath. Nothing. He rubbed his forearms as though for warmth and proceeded to walk under the wall where *Justice* hung and a blank wall awaited his touch.

As he rounded the corner to head toward the rear of the church and today's work, cold wrapped his neck like a scarf, and a trace of wind lifted the hair at the back of his head. Maxo spun around, but saw only empty space. His shoulders shimmied to cast off the cold. Fear and anger gripped him at the same time, and he shouted into the soupy gloom.

"If you are not brave enough to show yourself to me, then, you will have to wait until another time. I have much, much work to do and cannot be bothered by you!"

He clapped his hands together three times fast, his final statement on the matter. Then, he turned to the back of the church where the painting of *Greed* awaited his touch. Above him, in the choir where he could not see, a tall, cloaked figure stood, still as death.

Within a matter of minutes, the artist became engrossed in the painting about greed. He wanted to achieve just the right balance between the poor supplicants of the mural – the servant and the mendicant black man – and the curmudgeonly rich man who dominated the scene. He should look wealthy, without a care, but perhaps not in the best of health. Now, ninety minutes later, Maxo buffed the wall around the capitalist's head with the side of his left hand. He wanted to endow the man's skin with a reflected duskiness that almost made his face appear white and skeletal.

"Is this man so mean, he can barely keep skin upon his

bones?" Father Žagar said, standing back from the mural.

Maxo clattered sideways off the ladder barely keeping his feet. "Za boga preplašio si me!" he swore. "Dear God, Father, you frightened me!"

"Dear fellow, dear fellow," Father Žagar patted the artist's back as he spasmed with cough. "I thought you must have heard me come in, that back door screeches so."

Maxo breathed one last cough. "It is nothing, my friend. It is, you know how involved I get in my work. I am in a different time and place when I paint. There is little that can disturb me at such times."

"Well said, and I understand that," Father said, "but clearly I did disturb you greatly." He stood facing the artist, their eyes level with each other. "Besides, Mrs. D tells me you were much concerned when you did not find me at the breakfast table yesterday morning. She felt you had something urgent to say."

Maxo's eyes studied a spider as it crawled along the church floor. A light sigh lifted his chest. "There is something," he said slowly, "but I would reserve it for a time when we both have more than a moment to discuss it."

"That sounds serious," the priest said. "I can make time for you right now if you need it."

"No, no, Father, no, no," Maxo held up his hands. "I know your days are no easier to set aside than mine. Let us talk when I have my bread and cheese tonight, when day is done."

"All right. It's your choice, but right now, it's not. Mrs. Dobrovic reminds me to tell you that lunch is being served, now!"

Maxo wiped his hands on a rag, and he loosely covered his palette with another piece of cloth before trailing the priest out of the church. Once more, his glance surveyed the gloom, and then, he closed the outer door behind him, careful to lock it shut. The artist did not often break for lunch, but the priest told him on the way to the rectory that the cook had prepared something special, something guaranteed to soothe his nerves.

Back in the church after the meal, Maxo smacked his lips as he savored the remaining flavors on his tongue from the chicken potpie and the cherry cobbler. Mrs. Dobrovic's formula had worked, and despite the thunder that continued to crash and roll through the valley, he could honestly say that his heart felt lighter.

He stepped down from the ladder to readjust the work light. In midafternoon, the gray atmosphere of the church had deepened to a slate fog. He pulled the lamp closer to the painting and redirected it at the dining table where the capitalist sat. There, a healthy repast spread before the man, though he was oblivious to everything as he studied the newspaper for stock reports that would augment his wealth.

Maxo could picture such a man. Darko's father had been one. On a visit to his well-to-do friend's home in his student days, he had swiftly gained an impression of Darko's father. The man had barely noticed the younger men as he sipped his morning tea and shielded himself behind the latest news edition. Any questions Darko put to him, the older man answered in grunts as his newspaper rattled with impatience. Later in the day, when a young servant dropped a teacup, Mr. Mislav demeaned the maid's abilities in chilling, hollow tones, and then dismissed her on the spot despite the protests of Darko's mother. Subsequently, he had stomped off to his library after delivering a sharp kick to the family dog whose only sin was being too old to move quickly enough from the autocrat's path.

Maxo's lips curled into a slight grimace. *Funny how people could be so different. My friend, Darko – such a loving, pleasant young man who liked nothing better than to socialize with his friends and to help out where needed. Perhaps he was the product of his mother's teaching. Certainly not his father's.*

Maxo stretched his face. In any case, the experience had helped shape what he now portrayed on these walls, though he felt certain Mr. Mislav would have disliked it intensely.

Maxo dipped a brush into his palette and worked on fine-tuning some of the details of the work. *It is essential to show the contrast between this rich industrialist and his poor counterparts*, the artist thought. He darkened the shadows in the room and brightened the tablecloth. *That would make an interesting reflection on the black man's face.*

His hand jerked as a clout of thunder seemed to clap him on the shoulder. An instant later, a fresh bolt of lightning seared down to the ground and flashed brilliance on the walls of the church. Maxo had no special fear of storms, but the closeness of this one tautened his chest. A thrill edged the nerves around his heart, and he discovered that he was panting.

A cascade of thunderbolts tumbled from the heavens, and the lightning dazzled his eyes. The smell of ozone reached his nostrils and the taste of wet stones coated his tongue. Maxo hurried down the ladder and thrust his palette and brush on a nearby table. He raced to close the office window he had opened earlier for some fresh air. He could see the big oak and the rectory in every detail as the lightning flared against them. Rain spat through the frame of the window and soaked Maxo's arm as he hastened to close the casement flung wide by the wind.

He shook his head free of raindrops, then looked around for something to dry his shirt sleeve. Father had left an old cardigan hung over the back of the desk chair, and one of its pockets contained a clean handkerchief. Maxo ran the cloth over his face, and then squeezed it around his sleeve to wick away the damp.

A loud clack sounded just outside the office door. Maxo's heart jolted sideways. Suddenly, his ears, his eyes, his hair, his every fiber tingled, alert and alarmed. He tried to tell himself that perhaps Father had returned to the church. He strained to hear anything else, but there was nothing else to hear.

Maxo's eyelids blinked in a slow rhythm. He leaned a hand against the wall beside the doorjamb. Two or three times, he inhaled, filling his lungs and fighting to regain a sense of balance and proportion. Well he knew that both dark and quiet could magnify sounds.

Maxo walked out of the office and into the back hall. He peered through the dark tunnel of the corridor to where it ended with a side entrance door, but saw nothing. He glanced at his work area. The spotlight continued to beam on the mural, the stepladder remained in place, and his brushes and rags perched where he had set them. His gaze swept the wide expanse of the nave where lightning still played between the windows. Nothing appeared different beyond the rows of wooden pews and the distant shine of the altar.

Maxo swallowed. His eyes blinked some more. There was no evidence of any wrongdoing or any wrongdoer, but he could not get away from the presentiment that had troubled him since morning. As he trod forward, something cracked beneath his left foot. Maxo knelt down. It was the brush he had been using right before the storm's force hit. Now the handle lay splintered from the weight of his footfall.

He fingered the damaged shaft of the brush as he continued to squat near the floor. His mind puzzled over how the brush had ended up there, or how it could have made such a loud crash, but somehow that did not seem to be the right question. The moment he thought that, a cold draft eked through the hallway. Maxo shivered as he stared, unseeing, into the dark.

Lightning danced through the window of the side door. Then, Maxo saw it. His palette, flipped facedown. Its pools of color glued the board to the floor. The cadmium red trickled from beneath – a line of blood creeping toward him.

Maxo staggered backwards until his shoulder collided with the office doorjamb. He looked at the table where he had placed the palette. *Could I have put it too close to the edge in my hurry?* He shook his head sharply to deny the idea. He spent far too much time mixing and deriving the subtle tints to allow for that kind of mistake.

A slow burn began to replace the ticklish nerves in Maxo's chest. He walked over to the stepladder to retrieve a palette knife. Back in the hall, he stooped to pick up the palette. He scooped the blobs of paint from the floor as well as he could with the straight-edged blade. With angry flicks, he shook each color back into its place on the palette. *This is really too much*, he thought. The onset of a headache bound his brow like a tight-fitting cap. *Two times now, my palette is destroyed.*

With a voice he did not know he possessed, Maxo bellowed, "Yi, yi! Enough, I tell you, enough!"

His next words froze in his throat as his work light dimmed to the power of one lone candle. Cold muffled his head and his neck and accented the ache above his ears. Maxo stood still as a statue straining to see whatever would come. He clutched the palette in grim protection, and the palette knife glistened in his right hand.

The thunder pealed, but more distantly now. Regardless, the lightning continued to dart in and out of the stained glass panes of the church windows. Sometimes, they disclosed very little; other times, it was as though a hundred spotlights shone in the sanctuary. The gilt haloes of the ceiling's angels flickered in the inconstant light. Down below, Maxo viewed only nave and aisle, apse and altar.

With the back of the hand that held the knife, Maxo rubbed his eyes. They had joined his headache, protesting from the strain of staring for too long.

It was there, waiting for him the second he stopped scrubbing his eyes. Maxo took a step back. His spine stiffened into a rod of steel. His eyes locked on the specter. Never before had the ghost met him on the same plane.

Curiosity and dread drove him to study the creature. It stood or floated – he could not tell which – about six feet tall at the head of the first pew, a place where Maxo had observed it before. Black cloth draped its figure from head to toe, and a deep cowl concealed its featureless face. If it had arms, no hands hung below the sleeves. A breeze rippled its cloak and skirts, but the apparition did not move otherwise.

Confounded, Maxo bit the inside of his lip. *Why appear if it intended to do nothing?* The tension and the cold built as the stand off dragged on. Maxo felt as though his head might split wide open. He wished this moment to be over.

"Phantom," he called. The word squeezed drily from his throat. He cleared it and began again. "Phantom, who are you? What is it you do here? Why do you come?" His voice gained pitch and volume as the questions flowed. "Why do you come to see me? Is there something I have done? Have I offended you in some way?"

Not even his draperies rustled as the ghost stood still and silent.

"Bože moj!" Maxo nearly shouted. "Answer me! What is it? What can I do to make you stop? What? What do you want?"

Like a wisp of smoke, the phantom slipped through the air as Father called through the vestry door, "Maxo? Maxo, are you all right? Did I hear you talking to someone?"

The lights rose in the church, and once more, the work light shone brightly against the mural. The air grew warmer. Maxo sneezed and shuddered. Carefully, he set the palette and the knife on the stepladder's shelf.

Father strode down the aisle toward him. "Maxo?"

"Ah, yes, Father, here I am."

"Good God, man, you look as though you've seen a ghost." As soon as the words escaped his mouth, Father Žagar gasped. "Oh my lord, you saw something, didn't you?" The priest eyed the artist, and then quickly swung his gaze around the nave. "Good lord, Maxo, I just stopped by to check on you. That storm that passed through, it was fierce, and well, I was worried about you. That the electricity might go out. That you might be plunged into darkness over here. But, but," his tongue searched for words, "I, I didn't expect. That is, I didn't realize, I didn't think I would find you in such a state."

Ticking his tongue, he placed a hand on Maxo's forehead. "My God, man, you're as cold as ice. And you look like you're about to pass out." Grabbing the artist by the left arm, the priest said, "That's it for today. Come along. We're putting you to bed with some hot broth."

With a weak voice, Maxo protested. "No, no. My palette. My brushes."

"Have no fear, my friend. As soon as we've gotten you into bed, I'll come back and clear things away. I think I know how to do it, having watched you so many times before."

He dragged on the artist's arm to overcome his leaden feet. When he offered to carry Maxo, the artist suddenly came alive. "No. No, thank you, that is, Father. I am quite able to walk."

"Good. Let's go," said the priest, looking around the church once more.

"Only, Father, please do come back right away for my palette."

"I will, Maxo. I promise. I will."

After seeing Maxo tucked into bed and stowing the artist's paints and tools at the church, Father finally returned to the work he had begun at his desk that afternoon. Not three seconds later, Mrs. Dobrovic tapped lightly on the open door.

"So sorry to disturb you, Father Žagar," she said, "but Sister Mary Martha would like a word."

"Oh?" Father looked vaguely toward the door as a brief flash of annoyance dashed across his face. "Mm, I'm rather busy." His hand finished the sentence by gesturing to the stacks of paper on his desktop.

"Well, it looks like a couple of the young lads may be in trouble," Mrs. Dobrovic said in response.

"Did she try Father Sebastian?"

"Remember, he's downtown at that civil society meeting you wanted him to attend." She wrapped one hand in the corner of her apron. "Shall I ask her to wait?"

"No, no, of course not," Father said. "It's not for you to worry about." He stood and came over to pat the cook's shoulder. "Ask her to come in."

"And the boys with her?"

"Oh, they're with her now? All right. Yes, certainly, they must come in, too." Father gave her a short, tight smile and turned back to his desk. He could hear some yelping from the kitchen as the nun escorted the boys down the hall to the study.

With purpose, Sister Mary Martha marched into the room flanked by two ten-year-old boys with reddened ears. She came to a stop at the exact center of the desk where she could face Father squarely.

With more decorum than he felt, Father set aside the paper he had been studying, laid down his pen, and rose from his chair. "Sister Mary Martha. Boys." He sat down again without offering them seats. "I hear you have something to tell me."

Sister Mary Martha's countenance had a way of looking offended, even at the best of times. Now a faint glow painted her cheeks as she began. Through grim lips, she said, "I'm sorry to report, Father Žagar, that I caught these two hoodlums up to no good, and of all places, in the church itself. I was able to grab them before they did any real harm, but I thought you should know about it as soon as school ended for the day. And," she added before the priest could interject, "I can't help but share that some people feel these paintings are having a bad influence on the young ones."

"Thank you, Sister, let's please stick to the matter at hand for the present," Father said, his eyebrows closing in on each other. "Leonard, isn't it? And Bobby? Suppose you tell me exactly what you thought you were doing in the church during the school day. Especially as I have forbidden anyone – particularly you schoolchildren – from interfering with the artist's work or going there without a teacher. I mean, you were actually in the church on your own, weren't you?"

Both boys stared at their toes and nodded. Bobby rubbed an ear. Without looking up, he said, "It was Louie's fault."

"Look at Father, boy," Sister said, "he can't hear your mumbling." She gave him a slight swat on the behind.

"Now what was that?" Father said.

Leonard took a deep breath and looked the priest in the eye. "He said it was Louie's fault, Father Žagar."

"Louie? Louie, the sixth grader?" Father's brows went up. "What, was he with you then?"

"No, it was just a dumb dare," Bobby said. Father waited. Bobby leaned from foot to foot. "You see, Louie told us there was a ghost in the church. We wanted to see it, but he said …"

"Who said?"

"Louie said we was too scared."

"Were too scared." Sister growled at him.

"Louie said we were too scared to go in there on our own, specially on such a stormy day. We said not, and so he double-dared us to sneak in at lunchtime."

"So that's why we went." Leonard tacked this thought on to reinforce Louie's role in the mischief.

"But I was in the chancel to fetch Mr. Vanka for lunch, and I didn't see you."

"If I may interrupt, sir," Sister said. "I believe the boys went in earlier and hid. As it was, I found them curled up below the first pew."

"So, were you locked in then after we came away for lunch?" Father asked the two boys.

"Yeah, and then we were scared," Bobby said. "Well, at least Leonard was."

Leonard, the smaller of the two boys, allowed two big tears to slip down his cheeks. "We're really sorry, Father," he said.

Father crossed his arms and stared at the two children. Finally, he said, "I hope you know that you will receive punishment for this transgression." Both boys hung their heads at the same time. "But tell me this first. Did you touch or handle any of Mr. Vanka's materials? His paints, his brushes, or God forbid, the paintings themselves?"

"Oh, no, Father," both boys said at once. Their voices tumbled over each other. "No, we wouldn't do that. We know not to do that. It really was just about seeing the ghost. That was all we wanted to do. And we were a little scared, but we still wanted to see it. Father, is there a ghost?"

"Enough, boys," Father said. "I've heard enough. And that question does not deserve an answer. I think you know the answer." He cleared his throat. "I need to get back to my work and you need to get home." He stood and walked around the desk with a ruler in hand. "So let's understand this. Hold out your hands."

He smacked the boys' palms sharply with the wooden slat. "One stroke for sneaking into the church against the rules." Another smarting slap. "Two strokes for not listening to me and disturbing Mr. Vanka's work." One sting more. "Three strokes for skipping out on school and trying to blame a classmate for something that was your own fault."

Through teary eyes, the boys listened to the remainder of their punishment. "Sister, please see that these boys remain after school for the next two weeks and help clean the rooms and chalkboards everyday. Give them whatever other chores you need done as well. And please be sure to inform their parents about this bad behavior."

"Of course, I'll take care of it," Sister Mary Martha responded. "Boys, you will wait for me by the kitchen door," and she gave them a shove toward the passageway. "Now, Father, about those paintings. Some parishioners feel strongly that they are blasphemous and that something must be …"

"Sister Mary Martha, that is all for today, thank you. As you can see, I am now well behind on my work."

With a stiff, straight back, the nun strode from the room without thanking the priest for his time.

CHAPTER NINE

THE CRASH AND FLASH of that afternoon's tumultuous sky had retreated. In its place, the clouds clustered like woolly lambs around the misty edges of the moon. Captivated, Maxo recalled seeing this moon another time. Lying in bed in Korcula, with one arm tucked beneath his right ear, he had stared at it through the bedroom window. The hour had been late. Even so, the moon shone high in the sky, a sliver away from being full.

What caught his attention, though, was the way its light diffused on the sea like a borderless blanket, silvery gray over the dark charcoal of the midnight waters. Only the gentle breakers evidenced the moon's true brightness as she picked out their curls in gleaming white trails that raced from the middle of each wave to either end.

Maxo sighed, quietly he hoped, not wishing to disturb his sleeping wife. She had reached out a hand anyway and felt for his shoulder.

"What is it?" The words caught sleepily in her throat.

"Ah, it is the moon," he replied. "Once again, she is playing her elusive tricks with me. I only wish I could capture the subtle depths of her reflections. To create the feeling I get whenever I see her like this."

Margaret propped herself on her right elbow so she could

see out the window over her husband's shoulder. The breeze blew soft on her face as she peered at the sea.

"Mmm," she said. "I see what you mean. Not the path of light the moon usually carves on the sea. More a hinting at the possibilities – a feeling that all is calm and good and beautiful – and yet, in its depths, a certain lurking of excitement or trepidation."

Maxo had rolled over and wrapped his arms tightly around Margaret. "Oh, my love, I am so happy that you can see it, too."

He kissed her lips – a deep, hungry kiss, but a moment later, he sprang from the bed. "Forgive me, my dearest, but you know, I must make some notes now if I am ever to generate – in some small way – what we see tonight." Without stopping for his dressing gown, he hurried from the room.

Glancing back, he saw Margaret licking her lips, still tasting the kiss. Then, she smiled at him and put her head on the pillow. Maxo knew she would go back to sleep. She knew better than to wait up for him.

He savored that image from long ago, his eyes filled with the light of tonight's moon. Margaret and her magic, the moon and her music. How he longed to have his wife here to help him sort out how to manage these strange occurrences. For though she embraced art and had a poet's appreciation for beauty, she was equally able to apply commonsense and rational thinking to most situations. He wondered what she would make of his mysterious visitor.

In the other rooms, Maxo could hear the clanking of pots and pans as Mrs. Dobrovic finished the dishwashing. The riffling of paper drifted to his ears as Father Žagar read or tidied up the church accounts. He angled the alarm clock to the light of the moon. Not quite nine o'clock. He rose with some decision and replaced the clock on the nightstand. Tiny tings vibrated from its brass bells.

Maxo switched on the lamp by his bedstead. He stooped before the small rectangle of mirror on the wall and smoothed back his hair with his fingers. His hands slid over his shirt to press out the bed wrinkles, and his feet donned the slippers that waited at the foot of the bed. His steps took him into the living room where, as he had surmised, Father Žagar hunched over some paperwork.

"Ah, there you are!" The priest raised a hand in greeting. "Feeling a bit better? Headache gone? Good. Let me see if Mrs. Dobrovic would be so kind as to make us a cup of tea before she leaves. Oh, Mrs. D!"

Maxo sank into the divan and propped a small pillow between his shoulder blades. "And what keeps you working so late tonight, my friend?" he said.

Father smiled. "Oh, you know, it's that time of the month again. Even a church has to pay its bills." He pointed toward a sheaf of papers. "And then there's the report to prepare for my council, of course."

Mrs. Dobrovic entered from the kitchen with a large tray. Steam wisped from the tip of the teapot, and beside it, she had ranged cups, saucers, and a plate full of fruits, nuts, and cheese.

"My word, you turned that out quickly," Father said, rubbing his hands together. "This looks wonderful."

The cook set the tray on the long table before the sofa. "Well, it's nothing," she said. "I've been keeping the kettle hot, thinking Mr. Vanka here might be waking up wanting something to warm his insides. And that plate of food there – well, I didn't expect you could make it through the whole night with only a cup of broth, did I?"

"As I always say, dear Mrs. D, you are an angel." Maxo kissed his hand and blew across it.

Mrs. Dobrovic's face dimpled as she waved a hand at the two of them. "Go on then. Enjoy. Time I'm getting home. Oh, and Father," she said, "don't forget, I'm taking a half day tomorrow morning. Cara's singing in the fall concert at school and has a solo. I don't want to miss that."

"Naturally. Please wish Cara good luck for us, and Mrs. Dobrovic," the priest said, "thank you so much for staying extra late tonight. Sure I can't walk you home?"

"No – no, no, Cara's meeting me at the corner. It's only

three blocks after all." She waved again. "Good night, you two."

"Good night!"

After the cook departed, Maxo reached at once for the teapot and poured brimming cups of tea for both of them. It was hot and black and with two lumps of sugar, perfect. Maxo drank thirstily, and then filled a small plate with apple slices, walnuts, and cheddar cheese.

Father sipped more slowly. He eased back in the armchair and watched the artist. There was no need to hurry into a conversation, but surely the time had come to discuss whatever it was Maxo needed to tell him.

The artist cleared his throat.

Ah, now. Here it comes. The priest leaned forward.

"Funny," Maxo said.

"Funny, what's funny?" asked Father.

"The young Cara."

"Cara?" One of the priest's eyebrows arched.

"Yes, so strange," Maxo said, "so strange to think of her as a soloist. Our quiet little chick in the corner of the kitchen, and yet, to hear Mrs. D tell it, one with the voice of a songbird."

The priest sank back into the wing-backed chair. "Indeed, it's true. Not a sweeter voice in the parish. With the timbre of a reedy flute." He sipped his tea. "I wish we could get her to sing here in the church, but her mother says she would never sing alone – without a chorus, that is."

The friends fell into a silence after this exchange. But unlike others they had shared, this one prickled with things unsaid.

Maxo sucked on the tip of an apple slice and studied the swirls in the carpet. He had stopped eating. Father noticed for the first time the fine lines around the artist's eyes and the deepening hollows of his cheeks. The priest folded his hands across his stomach and waited. *This would be like a game of chess,* Father thought, *if it weren't for the fact that I have no clue what the moves are.*

Father leaned forward once again. The movement caught

Maxo's eye, and he found himself face-to-face with the concern in the priest's eyes. He blinked and mashed his lips together. Then, he bowed his head.

"How long, Maxo?" the cleric said. "How long has this been going on?"

Maxo's long fingers steepled across his nose, and his index fingers pressed in on his sinuses.

"My friend, please tell me." A pause. "I feel certain this is why you were looking for me this morning, wasn't it?"

The bent head nodded faintly. Slowly, Maxo raised his head. The steeple slid down to his mouth, where his fingers tapped his lips as he considered the two questions. His eyes clouded.

"Father, I hope you know that I would never wish to add to your daily concerns, nor would I ever wish to be the source of worry or disturbance."

The priest shook his head quickly. "Of course not."

"But, the other week, the first time my palette was destroyed, and, and - " here Maxo searched for words, "and you chose to question the parish people about it, well, I felt badly about that. Because – because I knew it was nobody's fault."

Father Žagar waited. Leaning on his left knee, he listened to every word.

"As I believe you guessed in the church this evening, the ghost has returned." Maxo breathed out a long whoosh of air as though he had opened a relief valve on his secret. The priest closed his eyes for a minute, and his chest moved up and down as he drew breath. He rolled a hand over in the air indicating that Maxo should continue.

"It is the same apparition. Tall, silent, clothed in black, no face to be seen. You came within inches of seeing him today, but when he heard you enter the church, he vanished, like so much smoke in the air." Maxo pursed his lips and blew toward the ceiling, as though exhaling cigarette smoke. "But that was what was so unusual. The specter has never put in a daytime appearance before."

The painter ran a hand across his head. "Always, always before, he shows up in the dead of the night, when no one else is about, many times when I have fallen asleep, always when I am most alone."

"Tell me," said Father Žagar, "how do you know when he is there?"

"Well, it is much like what I originally described to you in 1937, you know, when I asked you to talk with the spirit and ask him to leave?"

"Yes?"

"So it is that the very first thing I notice is a feeling of unbearable cold – either someone breathing across my neck or my face, or feeling chilled to the bone. Then, my trusty work light sometimes flickers, but mostly, it simply fades to a dull glow. If any lights are on in the church, they dim as well." Maxo licked his lips and reached for his cup of tea. He drained the cup and clacked it onto the saucer.

"Then, my eyes uncontrollably search and search the dark to find the specter. Sometimes they are successful, and other times - " The artist held up his palms and shrugged.

"Do you believe that the ghost is looking for you?" Father asked.

"That is the puzzling thing. A few times, I can see nothing in the darkness. Many times, when I do see the apparition, he is seated in the first pew or his back is to me." The artist swallowed. "What is more frightening though, are those times when it appears to be watching me; and once or twice, it has drifted toward me before evaporating into the shadows." A tremor shimmied down Maxo's torso. "Unh! It is terrible to think about."

"I agree, it sounds awful. But, Maxo, I have to say that today is the most frightened I've ever seen you. What exactly happened? I take it that something different was afoot."

The muralist related that late afternoon's misadventure – struggling with the open casement window, mopping up the damp, hearing the loud clack, and running out into the hallway to find his brush and palette slammed to the floor. "This, this was no small thing on its own, Father, and I have to tell you I was two parts angry and only one part afraid as I scraped paint from the floor, and then stood to face the demon."

Maxo coughed. "But, that was when I truly became unnerved. It was the very first time I had seen the ghost in daylight – such daylight as there was between strokes of lightning – and on the same footing with me. Every other time, I had been lucky to be above it, somewhere on the scaffolding. But now it rose, dark and silent and menacing, a foot taller than me, staring me down, floating toward me. My blood froze then. I remember shouting all the same, but it would not answer me. It never does."

Maxo wiped his mouth with his handkerchief. "Thank the great heavens, Father, that you walked in the door when you did. I tremble to think what might have happened."

Father Žagar reached over and patted Maxo's knee. "Dear fellow, you have been through an almighty trial today and these past few weeks. I do wish I could have learned of these events earlier, but no matter. Here we are now, and we must sort them out, even though it doesn't seem a case where logic can apply."

Father rose from his chair and walked over to his desk in the next room. He pulled a tablet from the center drawer and found his fountain pen under the scattered papers on the desk's surface. He returned to sit beside Maxo on the sofa.

"Now, a few more questions, and then we figure out a plan."

By the time they were done, they had consumed another pot of tea, and Maxo had finished the fruit. Father urged Maxo to tell him every detail of every visit that the specter had made to him that year. He also inquired about what Maxo was doing to solve the mystery. Maxo shared an abbreviated litany of the memories he had been combing through for answers.

"An excellent approach, my friend," the priest said, "especially when you consider the sensitivity of your nature, which I gather has been yours from birth. It seems likely that you can attract spirits as well as birds and children!"

They both smiled a little at that. Father encouraged Maxo to continue his pursuit of remembrances with a caveat. "Start to write down anyone who might fit as an obvious suspect."

Father summed up what they had established about the apparition. "With the exception of today, your specter only materializes in the deep midnight hours, and his malice never seems to extend beyond creating an icebox atmosphere and high-level eyestrain when it lowers the lights, is that right?"

Maxo tipped his head in agreement.

"So there is, in fact, no proof that the spirit may have meddled with your paintings or your palette?" the priest said, his mind leaping back to his earlier interview with Sister Mary Martha and the two wayward boys.

"Well, my friend," Maxo said, "if my own observations are what comprise the facts of the case related to this creature, then no, I have never actually seen him near either the murals or my paints and painting equipment."

"That doesn't rule it out, of course," said Father, "but for me, it does open up some fields of speculation."

"Such as?"

"Well, such as the possibility that some person, much as I suspected before," Father said, "is responsible for these damaging acts."

"That would be unnerving to dwell on for me," Maxo said with tight lips.

"Right, but do think about it for a minute," Father continued. "You've just said that the specter only appears at night, and that it doesn't seem to possess any corporeal characteristics. That would make it hard to wreak any physical havoc, wouldn't it?"

Maxo opened his mouth, but Father went on. "Now, we also have no evidence that the damage was committed at night-time. This afternoon, for instance – it was what, no later than five o'clock when your palette and brush fell to the floor?"

"Something like that." Maxo fumbled with the handkerchief in his lap.

"And the destruction of the face of *Justice*, which worries me far more, happened at a time when no one was watching the place. That could've been a daytime event, too."

Maxo's head jerked to attention, and he interrupted the cleric. "But this one, I feel there is something else that concerns you about it. What is it?"

The priest's lips pulled into a line and twitched as though they did not wish to free the words. "Well, the other option we have to ponder is, in your rush to close the office window, you just may have slung your palette too close to the edge of the table. After all, you told me you were in a gosh-awful hurry. That's a pretty narrow table, and the stacks of paper on it could have caused the palette to slide."

"But -" Maxo began.

"Maxo, we have to consider that the palette and brush could have fallen on their own." The priest over-rode his protest. "But we can hardly say the same for the *Justice* painting. She did not destroy her own face, obviously. No, my friend, I believe our culprit is a man." Father stopped and shook his head sadly. "And most likely, one of our own."

CHAPTER TEN

A RECTANGLE OF SUNLIGHT painted the blanket on Maxo's bed. He yawned and glanced through the bedroom window. The sky harbored not a single cloud, and its blue rivaled the cerulean on his palette. A sigh of relief climbed his chest. Today's weather would be the polar opposite of yesterday.

He hummed a Croatian folk tune as he gave his body a good scrub in the bath. After dressing, he donned a jaunty neckerchief that set off his fresh chambray shirt. The smell of rashers greeted him as he walked into the kitchen, a clean painter's smock draping his left arm.

Father flipped the bacon strips in a frying pan on the stove and looked up as Maxo came in. "Greetings, my friend, and good day to you. I'm afraid you'll have to settle for me as cook this fine morning. How do you want your eggs?"

"Ah-h, that smells heavenly. Eggs?" Maxo said. "On such a day as this, I have to say – what is your expression? Sunny-side up!" He laughed and slapped Father Žagar on the back. "Only I insist, if you are on cooking duty, then I am the clean up committee."

"Fair enough," said the priest, and he slid two eggs onto a plate along with three pieces of bacon. "The toast will be along in two shakes."

In short order, the priest joined Maxo at the table, bearing his own breakfast and four slices of toasted rye bread. For a while, they chewed in agreeable silence, but the priest stole glances at the painter once in awhile. He took a sip of coffee.

"Mmm, mmm, that was a good breakfast, if I have to say so myself!" Father said. "Made even better by seeing you so hale and fit this morning. Does this mean all the demons are back in their place?"

"It is more simple than that, Father," Maxo said. "I am merely in tune with the day – a brilliant, clear morning, a sun that burns bright – and so do I." He laughed again, easily.

"And if our sorting out last night helped foster that, then I am glad," said Father. "More coffee?"

Though it was a cheerless picture, Maxo bent his mind to finishing the *Greed* mural once and for all. Somehow, working on it today seemed easier. The sun suffused the nave in golden light that reflected into the back hall. *Quite a remarkable change*, Maxo thought, *after the drear of yesterday*.

He viewed the mural in the bright light and saw which areas of the wall still needed attention. *Well, at least I can paint most of this on foot*, Maxo thought as he carried an old straight-backed chair from the church office to hold his painting supplies.

As he worked, his mind clicked back over Father's points from last night. In the light of this clear, new morning, they made sense. They comforted him even though he knew that one possibility implied that some mischief-maker was actually creeping into the church behind his back. The specter mystery remained a question mark, but he had promised Father to continue to give it some serious thought. *As if I could do otherwise*, Maxo grunted to himself.

Once again, the painting on the wall drew him in. He brought all of his powers of concentration to bear in recreating the mendicant's face. He wanted to make sure that people could feel the man's hurt, and his fear and wanting. Ah, dear Babić, if only he were here to advise him. Whenever Maxo thought of him, he remembered his friend's consummate skill at portraiture. To gaze upon one of his portraits was like holding a conversation with the inhabitant of the frame – inviting, delightful, deep.

The glasses clinked as the butler set the tray on the side cart in the drawing room. Babić rubbed his hands together. "Ah, here are the drinks now, my friends. What will you have, Miše, Becić? And you, Vanka, what about you?"

"Živio, bless you, I am thirsty," Maxo said, "but in such an elegant room as this" – he revolved, his arms outstretched to take in the Rococo furnishings and the paintings that adorned every wall surface – "I think that it must be champagne. We should toast our good fortune to be in such a beautiful place with such a wonderful host."

Ljubo Babić smiled. Coming from anyone else, he would have considered this remark over the top, but coming from Maxo, he took it at face value. "As always, my dear Maxo, you are too gracious with your words and your compliments. Champagne it is then! Bertrand! Champagne, molim. Hvala!"

There were no objections from Miše or Becić, and the four friends gathered in a small circle between the sofas. Vladimir Becić raised his glass. "To the future of art!" he boomed. "To the future of art," the other three chorused, and then they all laughed.

"Please, please be seated," Ljubo invited, "and do feel free to smoke," he added as Vladimir was busy placing a long brown cheroot in his cigarette holder.

Maxo shook his head at his bearded friend. "I have never understood how smoking can improve the taste of champagne," he teased.

"That's because you have never understood me." Vlad pretended to pout, then leaned his head back and roared lustily.

"You are a man of many tastes, to be sure," offered Miše, quietly stroking the gilt arm of his chair. "I am thinking of the lovely Lucinda, ey?" He stretched his lips into a smile.

Becić smacked his tongue against his lips. "Oh, her, yes. Beautiful and tasty!"

Babić feigned to cover his ears. "Please, spare us. No more tales of your bordello visits. Really Becić. When we have so many more important things to discuss. Like the weather!"

Everyone laughed and clinked their glasses together again.

A half hour later, they were embroiled in a debate that mixed politics and art in an eternal argument. Shirt collars loosened and faces lit with champagne and heat, each sat leaning forward vying for a chance to voice his opinion.

Babić was talking. "Listen, is art about beauty, or is it about making statements? I, for one, have moved beyond thinking that art must have a photographic quality. It is much more important, nay, an obligation on the part of the artist to portray what he truly sees when he paints a person or a plant or a view of the land."

Becić scoffed. "Well, isn't that what the Impressionists have been doing all along? I say it is time for us to go beyond such representation. Art needs to be – cries out to be - something more!"

"What then?" Maxo cut in. "Are you beginning to follow Diego Rivera, and what he has been doing in Paris and now in Mexico? I, for one, think that his work is brilliant, and that he has brought a whole new meaning to what art can be."

"Certainly, certainly," Becić said. "Rivera is a prime example of the power of large scale work and how it can affect us."

Here, Miše interjected in calm but certain tones. "Art, whether about beauty or politics, should be executed so that the viewer feels something. So that she or he is moved, emotionally as well as intellectually."

"Oh, I absolutely agree," Babić jumped in. "I merely posed the question because I believe that some people try to take a straight line on these things, and I am not at all sure that is possible."

"But I think I understand what is pulling at you," Maxo said. "Because it pulls at me, too. I see a look in someone's eye, I hear a laugh like tinkling bells, I taste a pastry whose butter runs over my tongue, I watch the joy of a child skipping rope, and I ask myself, can I translate this to canvas? Is it possible to capture such rapture, such depth? This, this, is it not, purely about beauty, about art? At the same time, if I am successful, will it not move the person viewing my painting? Will they not feel something? Do we really have to choose between beauty and message, in other words?"

"Thank you, Maxo, that is very clearly put – for me," Babić said. "I find that I rarely begin a painting – a portrait, especially – with the idea of communicating anything other than the impressions I see there."

"That may have something to do with who is paying you," Vladimir joked.

"Yes, well, obviously that is a factor if the sitter, the model, wants to recognize himself after the painting is completed," Babić smiled back. "But as someone who always wanted to paint, who has always been driven to paint, I don't want to have to make excuses for what my painting is or is not."

Maxo considered Babić to be the best artist of their Group of Four as they had dubbed themselves. "Never, never should you worry about such things, Ljubo. It is you I look to for how to improve what I wish to communicate with my canvases. That is, like you, I do not always set out to send a message through them, but in your case, your skill is so consummate, that every time I see them, I can hear your paintings talking to me."

"Ah, hearing things now, ey?"

"Do you speak back to them? That's the real danger!"

"Can I talk to them, too?"

As he brushed paint onto the mural, Maxo laughed as he remembered the good-natured chaff of his fellows. He also recollected how Becić had turned the conversation to a more serious note afterwards.

"I am glad that you mentioned Diego Rivera awhile ago, Maxo, for two reasons," Becić said. "One has to do with the sheer nature of art itself, but the other reason is a more practical consideration." He paused to light another of his tiny cigars.

"On the one hand, I think we all saw the exhibit that showed off Rivera's charms, now that he has returned to a more humanistic or natural style. He is equally capable of portraying the beauty of a woman, the fragrance of a flower, or the delight of a small child, much as any traditional artist. But he seems to be ahead of us all when it comes to demonstrating his beliefs as well as his observations in his work." Vlad puffed between sentences.

"Here it comes again," Miše spoke up. "Yes, we know all about his feelings, and your feelings on the role of art and how it can serve the cause of the revolution – that great time when we will all be equal." He mimicked Maxo's earlier gesture, waving his arm and drink around the luxurious room. "Really, ever since you spent time at Montparnasse, you seem to think of nothing else."

"You may make fun," Maxo interrupted, "but I think that Rivera is on the right track in at least this one way, if not many more. I like his notion that art belongs on public walls. That it is not some privilege for the upper classes to keep locked away in their private galleries. Art is bigger than that, better than that. It should belong to the people. Whether it can spawn or should spawn revolution is another matter entirely."

He sipped thirstily from his glass as Becić broke in. "But, he has been successful. Look, they've started a mural movement in Mexico. People are seeing the work. They're beginning to realize that they deserve more. Why, I credit him with the rise of the working class in Mexico."

"Gentlemen, gentlemen," Babić pushed into the conversation. "This is all well and good, but you mentioned practical before. Who is going to pay for all of this, er, public edification?"

At the same time, Miše said under his breath, "Sounds like you've been reading too many of Rivera's autobiographical – or should I say apocryphal – stories!"

Becić heard the remark and flushed. "Okay, forget what I said, and let's just go back to our original discussion. It was about art as beauty and message. Has not Rivera proven both can unite? And has he not made a good living doing so? Obviously, someone with deep pockets believes he is onto something."

"And as for the practical side of things, I was headed in a different direction altogether in my thinking." Vladimir stabbed the stub of his cigar into a nearby ashtray. "Actually, it had much more to do with us."

A tinge of surprise traveled across the other three artists' faces as they looked toward Becić.

"We're all ears," Babić said.

"It's just this," Becić said. " Croatian artists should be receiving the same due as Rivera and the French artists." He pounded his fist on a nearby table. "Have not all of us studied in Paris and the great European art capitals at some point? Should we perhaps consider how to achieve fame and deliver a message through a public mural project in Zagreb? Who can help us? Perhaps Bela Čikoš-Sesija, our old teacher, indeed he will have ideas." He paused for breath. "Babić, surely you can work some of the same magic that you have used to organize other exhibitions of our oeuvre!"

Becić's enthusiasm was catching, and the conversation drifted far into the night, through a hastily assembled supper that Ljubo had been obliged to order, as more ideas shot around the table.

Maxo set his brush upon his palette and put a hand to his cheek. He cast an objective eye at the mural, but at the same time he thought, *lord, how I miss those gatherings. I miss that gang.* While he and Margaret had settled in a community that supported the arts, he had never again identified peers or colleagues that could measure up to the Group of Four. That kind of kinship was rare.

Once again, he wished for Babić's presence. His colleague always had provided concrete but kind criticism of his painting, and Maxo felt he could use his advice on the mural. He was not entirely satisfied with how it was unfolding, but it seemed to have taken on a life of its own – somewhere beyond his control.

He shook his shoulders. It was almost as though here was another place where the specter was intervening. *That's another instance where Babić's good head would be useful*, Maxo nodded to himself. He had always relied on his friend for a certain level-headedness whenever problems arose. *I wonder how he would advise me about this ghost.*

It occurred to Maxo that he had not considered any of the Group of Four as factors in the specter's appearance, unlike the host of other memories he had raked through over the weeks. Perhaps there was some merit in thinking about them, but he could little imagine any of them as a malevolent presence. Besides, as far as he knew, every one of the group was still alive.

It was funny that he had recalled that particular scene at Ljubo's palača, considering the very issue he was up against with the *Greed* mural seemed to be much more at odds with beauty, and much more in agreement with message. Now in his own mind, he revised his notions of beauty. *It does not mean that the thing is and of itself beautiful, but that it may be a beautiful representation of a concept.* Picasso's *Guernica* came to mind. The giant mural's somber tones portrayed the horrors and grief of war and the utter confusion and desolation resulting from battle. *The physical battlefield as well as what rages within our own heads.*

The artist raised his chin to study his latest mural with that thought in mind. He pondered what Babić might say to him about it. *Maxo, clearly this is the very representation of ideas that we have been discussing. Tell me, do you feel the parts of the painting work together to convey your intent?* Maxo slapped his thigh. Suddenly, he felt it would work. The rich man centered in the picture controlled the action. The chalky pallor of his head rising above his black garments while his eyes carefully focused on no one gave Maxo a hollow feeling. *An entirely appropriate reaction*, he thought. Genuine suffering emanated from the other figures in the painting, and the hand floating above the wealthy man added the precise intonation of evil required.

Maxo's hands rasped as he slid one over the other as

though bathing them without the advantage of water. He waggled his head, concurring with his own thoughts. The mural was complete, and as the central figure generated the emotions of the scene, he would rename the painting *The Capitalist*. Surely, Father would agree with that.

Maxo tidied away his paints and his rags and his brushes and the chair. Evening light still slanted through the westerly windows, so he took up a position in one of the pews toward the back of the church with pad and pencil. He faced the wall where *Justice* and a remaining blank panel flanked the long panes of stained glass. Until now, he had not had the heart to return to the *Justice* painting, but fortified from the successful completion of *The Capitalist*, he felt it was only fair to restore *Justice* to her former glory.

He leaned his back against the wing of the pew and crossed his legs so that his sketchpad could rest on his lap at an incline. Before beginning, Maxo's eyes roved over the mural of *Justice*. Her gentle pose persisted, undisturbed. The white robes furled in soft folds that dropped from her waist, and in her hands, the scales of justice remained balanced. Perhaps no one had actually dared to disturb the depiction of the Lord's love and fairness.

But her poor face, ah, that was a different matter. Maxo's neck contracted as he willed his eyes to look above the neck of *Justice* and gaze upon the damage. In truth, there was nothing much to see. As far as he could tell, no fresh paint had been applied the night the destruction took place. Somebody or something had simply utilized the damp tempera he had applied that day to ruin his work. *What fury had possessed someone*, Maxo wondered, *to go to the trouble of erecting the tall ladder and climbing the scaffold in order to reach, and then smear the face into oblivion?* The medium had been driven back and forth, up and down, and round and round in sharp thrusts that blended Maxo's carefully chosen colors into muddy puce. *They must have used a rag,* Maxo noted, *as though to expunge every detail. They were strong, whoever they were.* Any brushstrokes had been flattened except where the tempera had been pushed into a sort of piping that lined the slashes of paint.

Maxo shifted his glance to the sunset-heated reds and golds of the windows. His right hand stroked his throat, and his lips pulled into a tight line below his moustache. He cleared his throat and sat a little straighter. As he began to draw, the paper in his lap crinkled when his sleeve caught the corner of the page. In his mind, the artist made a promise to the painting. *I will put this right. I will make you more beautiful than you were, though you shall have a new face. And I will find out who did this to you.*

A half hour later, Maxo held the tablet in front of him. It was a good sketch and tomorrow, he would put it into action. In the gathering dusk, a fleeting smile crossed his face, and he rose to exit the church and lock the vestry door behind him. It pleased him to think that he would have a few precious hours away from the murals that evening. Even so, when he reached the door, he rubbed the back of his neck and spun toward the nave. A wild sensation that a pair of eyes had followed his retreating form possessed him, but he could see nothing.

The evening was unseasonably cool, and after they finished dinner, Father lit the small gas heater that sat within the hearth of the chimney. The two armchairs with graying upholstery sagged like old men on either side of the fireplace. Maxo took up a position in one, and Father joined him in the other wingback after asking Mrs. Dobrovic to bring their coffee into the living room. Both relaxed into the evening. The warmth of the heater and the lingering aroma of that night's beef stew and potato bread hung around them, adding to their comfort. At about the same time, both men stretched their legs toward the hearth.

Father chuckled as he extended his arms and then crossed them behind his head. He sank into the familiar cushions with a satisfied groan. He watched the reflection of the tiny flames as they feathered shadow and light on his friend's face.

"Ah, thank you, Mrs. D," Father said as she placed a steaming cup of coffee and a plate of Apple Betty at his elbow. "That was an exceptionally delicious dinner tonight, just exceptional," he said, patting his stomach. Her face twisted into that peculiar look of pleasure and embarrassment that she sometimes wore. She handed the artist his coffee and quickly exited the room.

"Hvala!" Maxo called after her.

"So, a successful day, then," Father said, his mouth full of the crumbly dessert. "Yet another mural completed and a title for it, to boot."

"Yes, yes," Maxo replied, "you must come and see it in the morning light and adjudge whether you feel it is truly finished."

"Oh, well, that's all right. I mean," the priest licked a drop of apple filling from his finger, "I'm happy to see it once again – I look forward to it – but I think it's rather up to you to decide when these paintings are completed."

"Yes, and no, Father," Maxo said. "Regardless, I would value your opinion."

They agreed that they would visit the church and *The Capitalist* mural tomorrow after morning song. When that was settled, Father picked up the newspaper, and Maxo reclaimed his sketchpad and began once more to draw.

For a while, only the click of the heater's hot metal and the sibilant slide of pencil against paper could be heard. Occasionally, the newspaper interrupted the silence as the priest rattled to a different section. Maxo's slurps of coffee seemed more pronounced in the still. The china clinked as he replaced his cup in the saucer. All quiet again.

From his chair, where he had curled his legs like an Indian fakir, Maxo chortled. Father raised his head as the breathy snort came again.

"What? What is it?" Father became infected with the laughter. "Are you going to let me in on it?"

Maxo rose from his side of the fire and placed his sketchbook in front of Father's newspaper.

"Ha, ha, ha. You've caught the scene very well, my friend," the priest laughed out loud this time. "That spindly, wavy ladder captures exactly how I felt the one time I ventured up it to rescue you." Good-natured sarcasm tinted these last words.

Looking at the cartoon drawing – a depiction of Maxo climbing down from the high scaffolding in the church via a very wobbly ladder – the artist said, "I suddenly realized that I have been slightly out of touch with my family. Too absorbed with things here. Allowing things to trouble me too much, when there are many things I would share with them." He rubbed an itch beneath his nose. "I have drawn this for Peggica to give her an idea of what her old papa is up to."

"Well, as far as it goes, it's quite realistic," Father said. "I like how you've depicted the church with its murals, and it's quite fun the way you appear to be juggling your balance and your materials on the ladder like some kind of circus clown."

Maxo grinned. "Yes, I look clever, but silly, too." He was clearly pleased that his caricature of himself and his surroundings had gone over so well with the priest. He made his way back across the room. "Now I must get busy on a letter to accompany my chef-d'oeuvre!" He climbed back into his chair, and propping the sketchpad on the protrusion of his knees, he jotted his note on the next sheet of drawing paper.

Father returned to his news, Maxo scribbled, and the mantel clock ticked by the minutes, and then the half hour. A soft purring began to emanate from behind the newsprint. The space heater clicked.

A bang outside the front window caused Father to bolt upright. Before he could say, "What was that?" a tinkling, like the sky raining glass, followed the crash. Priest and artist flew from their seats and dashed out the door toward the church. Father snagged the umbrella from the hook on their way, thinking some sort of weapon might be worth carrying.

"I think it came from the church," Maxo shouted, as the one who had actually been awake to hear the loud noise. The men raced to the church door nearest the rectory, but it was locked tight. Neither had remembered to grab a key.

"Let us circle around," Maxo suggested, "I do not think the sound came from here exactly." He motioned for Father to go one direction while he headed clockwise toward the parking space behind the church.

Suddenly, the flap, flap, flap of leather soles against pavement could be heard. They were in a hurry. Maxo sped around the corner from darkness into moonlight and nearly ran into the priest.

"He's gone down the hill," Father panted.

They both strained to catch a glimpse of the intruder, but it was impossible to say whether they saw him or only the trees waving their shadows beneath the moon's shine.

Father placed a hand on his chest to catch his breath and slow his heart. With the other hand, he reached over to Maxo's shoulder. "Come, my friend, it's not for us to give chase. We need to make a telephone call."

In no less than fifteen minutes, a policeman was walking the perimeter of the church with Father Žagar and Maxo Vanka. Something crunched underfoot as they rounded the rear of the church. The officer shone his flashlight on the ground. Shards of glass sparkled back at them, a localized storm of miniature icicles. He swept the light around the parking space and the berm that bordered the church. A chunk of brick in the grass arrested the flashlight's ray. He stooped to examine the brick more closely, but wasn't sure if its surface glittered from glass or the materials from which it was made.

"Hadn't we better look at the church itself?" Father urged.

The officer's light crept slowly up the brick wall of the church. A jagged twinkle greeted the beam where the office window should have been.

"What part of the church is this?" the policeman asked.

"It's the church office," Father responded. He was scratching the bald spot above his forehead. "Why the devil would somebody bother with a window fifteen feet off the ground?"

"A good question," said Officer Dimwiddie. "What do you have in there?"

"Well, nothing I would've thought worth stealing," Father said. "I keep the church records in there. You know, the registry of births and deaths and banns and marriages, and so on."

"Is there a safe?"

"Do you mean, do we keep money there?"

The policeman nodded.

"No, any collections or school tuitions or donations come with me to the rectory." The officer looked slightly alarmed, so Father added, "Don't worry. There's no risk, believe me. One of our members who's a banker donated an old vault-type safe for our use. It resides in the basement, and only I and one other council member know its combination. Oh, and it's much too large and heavy to be carted away."

"So, no money then. Any other valuables?"

While Father explained what might be of value in the church to Officer Dimwiddie, Maxo continued to patrol the churchyard near the incident. He had nothing specific in mind about what to look for. He merely listened to that inner voice that had been his companion over the years. Now it told him there was something else to find.

He walked over to where the drive of the church entered Maryland Avenue, the road that curved steeply down the hill. A slice of lawn lay in a triangle between it and the avenue. Maxo closed his eyes. The scent of moist earth filled his nostrils along with the green of summer grass, still young from the late spring. He opened his eyes and looked down. The night was so bright, he could almost detect colors, though the translucent blue of the moon's borrowed light coated everything. In the middle of the green swath, he could clearly see disturbed earth and a dark depression no bigger than the size of a man's foot. *No specter this time then!*

"Father!" Maxo called. "Father, come here!"

After securing the spot with a large galvanized tub that the priest retrieved from the rectory cellar, the police officer took the brick chunk as evidence and made his departure. He promised to return in the morning light. Maxo and Father entered the church, and heedless of the cost, threw the switch on every sconce and chandelier. They worked together to nail a board across the broken office casement, though it was hard to imagine how anyone could squeeze between its leaded panes, much less reach the high window. Then, they swept away the fragments of glass that had blown inward from the impact.

"Hmpf! The brick must have ricocheted when it encountered these lead surrounds." Maxo traced the dark gray metal that held only glass teeth where panes had been.

"Well, I hope it fell back and hit him," Father said, "but at least, the leads protected the church from any damage the brick might have done if it had come through." Air rushed out his nose as he bent and picked up the last dustpan-full of glass splinters.

For safety's sake, Father decided to gather all of the registries and take them back to the rectory. Between them, they toted the bulky books through the kitchen door and down the cellar steps to the security of the vault.

The mantel clock chimed 11:30 as they climbed the stairs to the kitchen. Father closed and locked the cellar door, and eying the clock, said, "I think that a sip of sherry might be in order, and there's just time before the day runs out."

They regrouped before the living room hearth, and Father turned the heating device one notch higher to chase the chill that was tickling his spine. Both men's faces appeared long and drawn though the living room lamps continued to exude their cheery glow.

"Well," said Maxo, but he did not seem to know how to continue.

"Well," the priest responded as if to one of his own litanies. "There is a bright side to this, you know, Maxo. Sort of, that is." He sipped the wine and waited as the liquid warmed its way to his stomach. "Now we know for certain that an actual person is responsible for the damage to the church. Your specter notwithstanding, someone – and God, I hope it's no one from this parish – someone is intent on ruining your work and hurting the church." Neither man took much comfort in these words as they bid each other good night.

CHAPTER ELEVEN

LATE THE NEXT NIGHT, Cara tiptoed into the living room. Her mother had retreated from the kitchen and gone home with a sick headache. Cara had promised to make sure the evening coffee and food tray would be delivered when Mr. Vanka finished work for the day.

As she entered the room, the lights were low and the air was still. Cara started when she caught sight of the two men, their heads bowed in prayer. Embarrassment flushed up her cheeks at having intruded, so she quickly placed the tray on the table between their chairs and soundlessly slipped from the room.

A moment later, Maxo straightened his neck and breathed in the roasted bouquet of the hot coffee. "Pour you a cup?" he asked Father, but the priest shook his head.

"Tempting, but as a new day is so close to beginning, I will drink my water, thanks!"

In fact, neither man had been praying. Cara had simply caught an odd moment when they both had bent their heads in deep thought. It had been a long day.

Maxo had spent the whole of it, with minor interruptions, constructing his platform, and then reworking the damaged painting from the scaffolding. The figure of *Justice* stretched far higher than he could reach with a stepladder, and he was determined to restore her face today. He had been touching up her eyes when Father called from below to say that the policeman had returned and could Maxo help them for a moment?

"Of course, though I am not sure that I have much more to add than what we discussed last night." When he had tucked his palette into a safe corner and wiped his hands, he clambered down the scaffold. As he joined Father Žagar on the ground, he whispered, "Not the best timing. As you can imagine, I am reluctant to leave her," he leaned toward the painting, "even for a moment."

"I tell you what," Father said, "we'll hold the conversation right outside the church door so that you can glance in now and then."

With this, Maxo had to be satisfied, and the policeman was agreeable.

"I've already surveyed the area again by light of day," said Officer Dimwiddie, "and there's precious little else to find. You'll be happy to know though, that we can identify the make and size of the shoe that made that mark over there." He directed this remark to Father, who said, "Really?" with as much appreciation as he could muster.

"Yep, men's lace-up oxfords, size 10 ½ , slightly pointy toe, maker – Jarman."

A beet red climbed from Father's collar and suffused his neck and cheeks. He choked slightly. "How can you be so sure?"

Maxo patted the priest on the back. "Father, are you all right?"

The policeman carried on. "Well, you see, Jarmans have a very distinctive stitching on the bottom of the shoe, plus they stamp a tiny J right where the sole meets the heel. It was a good footprint. We could see the little J very clearly."

"But, but," Father sputtered. "Every other man on the street wears oxfords, and, and," he pulled up the hem of his pants, "what you've just described could be me." Below his pant leg, a scuffed black oxford stared up at them.

Disregarding the priest's upset, the policeman let out a hearty guffaw. "Oh, Father!" He slapped a knee. "That's a good one, but I reckon we won't find any mud trapped in the seams of your shoes, will we?"

Immediately, Father bent double as he reached with both hands to examine his footwear. He hopped a little to regain his balance as he stood on one leg to examine the bottom of his right shoe. The faint outline of a scripted J was all that the sole revealed.

"There, there," Dimwiddie said. "We'll catch him, don't you worry. I've taken a sample of the earth beside the road, and we'll be interviewing the neighbors to learn if anybody saw anyone. Plus the print tells us that this is not a tall man – probably someone of average height, but maybe with a little weight on him, given the depth of the mark."

He explained to them that no trace of the perpetrator had been left on the brick Dimwiddie had carried away the night before, and that he'd like to examine the office and parts of the church for fingerprints. What he really wanted to know from the two of them was whether any other incidents had taken place in the past six months or so.

The priest and the artist exchanged looks, which were not lost on the law officer.

"Mr. Vanka, now, I understand you spend a good part of every day and every evening painting inside the church." Officer Dimwiddie did not phrase this as a question. "Certainly you would've noticed if something was amiss, wouldn't you?" The policeman waited while he flipped to a new page of his notepad. "Ever hear anything?"

Maxo's face sagged. He slid his gaze across the ground and up to Father's face. The priest shrugged ever so slightly.

"Officer, yes, you have heard correctly. I am alone most days in the church," Maxo said. "Often I begin at nine in the morning and do not stop until midnight or later."

"Phew, that's a long day!" the officer said. "Ever get lonely or drowsy or both? I could imagine some strange things myself, I think, if I were shut up with these characters staring at me every day."

"No, no, never lonely. You see, Officer Dimwiddie, I become immersed in the work, and before I know it, the hours have flown by." Maxo took a breath. "But yes, on occasion, I have dozed, and at other times, I have heard things." A hint of reluctance crept into his voice at this last point. "But more to what you are asking, there have been," Maxo hesitated for the fraction of an instant, " incidents."

"Incidents? What sort of incidents?" Dimwiddie asked.

"Two times my palette has been disturbed," Maxo said. "You need not look at me like that. It is the most important thing to an artist, particularly if he is midstream in a painting and has mixed unique colors expressly for that painting."

"Point taken," the officer mumbled and glared at his pad.

"And worst of all, somebody defaced one of the murals right after it had been painted. In fact, if you care to step this way, I can show you the restoration I am performing right now."

Dimwiddie's face showed that he had been suitably impressed after viewing the *Justice* mural. He said as much, and then added, "Someone went to a lot of trouble to mess up that painting. Not an easy climb." He expressed his doubts about discovering any fingerprints in the area of *Justice*, but noted other locations in the church might reveal a clue. "We have a fingerprint specialist on the force. I'll send him by a little later."

Maxo excused himself while the policeman mapped out a plan with Father Žagar. He did not want to miss out on the afternoon sun. It was some of the best light that had shone over the past several days, and he intended to take full advantage of it. With practiced ease, he swung himself onto the ladder and ascended to the scaffold.

He returned to painting the eyes. With a dark mixture, Maxo drew charcoal strokes around their rims, making them appear large and serious, and possibly, a trifle worried, as if she knew how difficult it would be to balance the scales of justice in a world gone crazy with warmongers and despots.

Maxo outstayed the sun in his post, reframing the angel of justice's face with soft curls and mounting a white flame upon her forehead for purity and cleansing. Only two more interruptions disconnected him from his work. Once, he had to go fetch his work lamp as the natural light waned. Another time, the police asked him to descend and show them exactly where the ruin of the second palette had taken place.

Long after dark, the artist descended for one more look at the refurbished mural. It was the nature of the beast. He must climb up and down, up and down as he worked on the large murals in order to gain perspective. Performing the close work necessitated only being able to see a small portion of the painting at a time.

Maxo closed his eyes and squeezed his shoulder blades together. He cocked his head from side to side and wondered if anyone else could have heard the pops and creaks as the kinks eased out of his neck and spine. Then, with deliberate slowness, he opened his eyes to regard the *Justice* mural afresh. His cheeks relaxed, and a shine ventured into his eyes. Though he would not be willing to repaint every mural in the church, he had to admit that the new face graced the *Justice* figure far better than the original one ever had. He felt he had captured just the right elements of compassion, trustworthiness, and caution.

When he finally arrived in the rectory living room that night after putting away his materials, Father already occupied the old chair to the left of the fireplace where he appeared to be in deep deliberation. Maxo slid into the chair to the right and joined him in contemplation. That is, until the food tray arrived, and suddenly, he realized what an appetite the completion of a painting could create.

In addition to the coffee, the artist reached for some bread and cheese and a golden apple with just a hint of blush on its cheeks.

Father could tell from the look on his face that Maxo had been successful in restoring the *Justice* mural. "So, it's good then?" he asked.

With a wad of bread in his cheek, Maxo nodded. He chewed, swallowed, and smiled. "Yes, yes, I think that it is. I hope you will agree, and I look forward to hearing what you feel about it." Juice spurted from the apple as he took a large bite. "Sorry." He wiped his mouth and the flecks on the table with his napkin. Swallowing again, he asked, "But my good friend, what finds you so plunged into thought this evening?"

"You can no doubt guess," said the priest. "It's this confounded not knowing. Not knowing who in the Lord's name is making such a nuisance. No! More than that. Not knowing who is posing such a threat to the community of our church." He drank a sip of water. "And the police, while well-intentioned, haven't been exactly helpful. They haven't learned more than you or I knew already or could discover."

"In truth, I have to admit that I became too absorbed in my work today to give any of it much thought," Maxo said, crunching on another bite of apple. "In fact, I was rather put out that the Officer Dimwiddie believed he needed to interrupt me twice, especially when I had so little to tell."

"Well, I know you weren't all that keen to reveal what you've heard and seen in the church," Father said, "but that is quite a separate matter, of course, from the damage to the painting and palettes."

Maxo drew a circle around his empty plate twice. "It is not the sort of thing I want to share with anybody, really, except for you. Not to mention, I am doubtful about whether he and others would truly believe me. After all, I am somewhat foreign, an exotic element to most people here. I know they wonder about my paintings, and it is as likely that they would be dubious about my mental state if I started talking about ghostly phenomena."

For a few moments, both men gazed into the cold grate of the fireplace. Then, Maxo added, "Truthfully, for me, though, it goes beyond worrying what anyone thinks of my actions or my behavior."

"Yes," Father said, nodding, "that's never really bothered you before."

"It is this sense – this intuition, if you will – that in appearing to me and only me, this specter is both a personal and a private matter. Do you see what I mean?"

"I can entirely understand your feelings." Father Žagar looked Maxo in the face. "I know you to be a good man, a kind man, and it would be completely out of character for you to conjure up something like this if it were not real. And since I have faith in you, then I must believe it is real, and that it has something to do with your past or your present." As an afterthought, he added, "Though I am inclined still to think it is something from your earlier years. That puts it squarely in your hands – a personal matter, as you say."

Again, they lapsed into silence. Only the ticking minutes on the clock dropped into the quiet, like tiny pebbles tinkling the surface of a pond.

A small laugh spluttered from Father's mouth. "And anyway, if this story were to get out, everyone would think we were both crazy, and that would be no help at all."

Maxo chuckled along with him, and the room became brighter.

"Father, did not we begin by talking about what deep thoughts possessed you earlier?"

"Yes, yes, indeed we did." Father laughed anew and wiped the corner of his eye with his sleeve. Maxo waited.

Father took a deep breath and said, "I was actually running a list through my head of all the possibilities. I was particularly looking at all of the men – for it seems now that if the footprint tells us nothing else, it tells us that the perpetrator is a man – here, or in this very church, who for some reason, might bear some rancor toward you or me or the church."

The priest chewed on his bottom lip. "But all that I find I am really doing is running my mind around in circles. I'm usually more logical than this, but I fear this thing has thrown me for a loop. Nothing like this has ever happened here before. At least not in my time."

Maxo sighed. "Dear Father, I do hope I have done nothing to bring this on, but in my turn, I fear that I have. But perhaps I can be helpful. May I borrow your tablet?"

Father Žagar handed the writing pad to Maxo, and the artist turned to a blank sheet. He picked up the pen that lay on Father's side of the table.

"Now, this will be our own query sheet," Maxo began. "Let us start with what we know about this man from what we have witnessed so far."

"But what do we know? That's just it." The priest spouted the words hotly, but Maxo raised his hand in a stopping motion.

"We know quite a bit. One moment, please." Maxo drew some columns on the sheet. "This first column shall list what we know. You see, once we can identify some characteristics, then you will have a much better chance to narrow the field of, of – "

"Suspects." Father clamped down on the word as though it were something bitter that he had to eat. He downed a long draught from his glass.

Under "Characteristics," Maxo started writing words while he said them out loud. "Average height, somewhat heavy set, size 10 ½ shoe, some physical ability (can climb high ladders and scaffold) …"

Father interrupted. "Can we infer from those facts that he is middle-aged or younger?"

"I will put middle-aged, question mark," said Maxo. "It could possibly be true, though in the old country, I knew many who were old and yet active. Now, what else do we know?"

Father sought answers in the fireplace. Without looking at Maxo, he said, "Angry, someone who is angry – at us, at you, at the church, or all of the above – angry to the point of violence. Willing to be destructive, as in *Justice's* face, the palettes, the office window."

The pen scribbled down the page. "This is good, Father, this is really good," said Maxo. "I would add, someone who is secretive, perhaps clever."

"Oh, my gosh," Father slapped his forehead. "It has to be someone who knows his way in and out and around the church." He whistled – a long, low note. "Boy, that narrows the field some."

"Perhaps we can get more specific yet," Maxo said and wrote down, "Known to have hard feelings toward (1) the church, (2) the priest, (3) the paintings, or (4) the artist. Did not you tell me you have heard some complaints now and then?"

"Well, yes, yes I have," admitted Father, "but I never took them seriously."

Maxo looked up from his writing. "Hmm. After last night, I think you must."

The discussion reminded Father that he had yet to share the story about the two miscreant boys. He recounted the story to Maxo and also added that he had later called Sister Mary Martha back in for a word.

"I wondered if she had seen anything amiss when she went into the church to apprehend the boys," Father said, "but as she only traversed the nave as far as the first pew, she said she hadn't noticed anything."

"Ah, that is too bad," Maxo said. "She might have acted as a key witness if only she had walked to the back hall."

"Well, I think her chief concern, and rightly so," and here Father stifled a yawn, "was to take the boys in hand. Though she did take the opportunity when I talked to her to remind me again that she has received several complaints from people about your paintings. It seems they feel the artwork may not be an entirely good influence." Father sighed and stroked the worn brocade of the chair arm. "I tried to explain to her that she must educate these plaintiffs about the real meaning of the work, but whether she will or not is anyone's guess."

The artist sighed. "Always it is impossible to please everyone." A powerful yawn slid from his mouth, and he stretched. "Oh my goodness, time for bed. I am afraid the next column on this sheet – Potential Suspects – people who match these characteristics – will be up to you, Father, as I simply do not know that many people here."

Father shook his head in agreement and took the tablet

from Maxo's hands. "Yes, but this list will help immensely. Come, time for us to sleep on it." He clicked off the lamp next to his chair and turned toward the hallway to his bedroom. "Good night, my friend."

"Good night, good dreams."

"Papa, Papa, come play with me!" Peggica dragged on his arm, tugging him away from – what was he painting? Some sort of beast, a large dark figure peering from behind a tree with slanted yellow eyes that sliced through the night like two beams.

"Papa."

"Yes, my love, I am coming."

She led him to a bench near the big oak that shaded his studio. Along the rim of the seat, she had lined up the little animals he had shaped for her from caramels. He clapped his hands. "Hura! Have you taken me to the circus?"

Little Peggy giggled as they knelt together beside the bench. She stopped abruptly as her father's face darkened. "No, no, this does not belong here. It is dangerous," he said, and immediately popped the figure of a dire wolf into his mouth and chewed it into oblivion.

Peggica began screaming as though he had bitten her instead.

Her screams woke him. Maxo jerked from sleep. *What on earth,* he thought. *Why would I dream such a thing?*

Maxo passed a palm from his forehead across the top of his head. The sweated twisting and tossing of the dream had knotted his hair into thick mats. "Za boga miloga!" he whispered to the room. "Dear God!"

He rose then and went to the bathroom where he could splash cool water on his face. For added measure, he ran a damp cloth over the back of his neck. He cupped his hand below the faucet to sip the water as it grew cold. All the moisture seemed to have left his mouth for his scalp.

"Oh, that is better," he exhaled. He returned to his bedroom and switched on the bedside lamp. He sat in the ladderback chair where he usually hung his smock, placed a hand on each knee, and focused on nothing. He blinked his eyes and swallowed some spit that had formed on his tongue, trying to quench the confusion that clouded his thoughts.

The dream might have been the result of last night's late night discussion with Father Žagar, but Maxo rather thought not. It was much more likely that the unfinished business with the specter still hid in the corners of his mind. While he had experienced no more physical encounters with the ghost over the past week, he did not for one moment believe that the creature was gone.

This guided his thoughts to another possibility. Of late, Maxo felt that he had brought a stronger degree of confidence to his own presence in the church. He had painted with more vigor and conviction over the past few days, perhaps as a reaction to the unexplained incidents regarding his paintings and his paints. A sea change had blown through his mind, and Maxo understood now that he had come to a decision. He was not willing to tolerate any further interference with his work, from vaporous apparitions or from malefactors of more material form. He realized he was prepared to fight for his right to be in the church, should it come to it.

Maxo sat a little straighter in his chair as this thought came to him. He looked across the room at the crucifix that glowed at him in the soft light of the lamp. Surprise curved his brows into arches, and a sniff issued from his nose. *Funny, everyone at university, and school, for that matter, had always seen me as the peacemaker – the one they could count on to remain unflustered when chaos was all around. The least combative person anybody knew.*

But these circumstances were so different. Maxo did not think that his art, his métier, his vocation had ever been challenged like it was now. He had a specter to deal with as well as a real-live person who clearly intended to do him or his work harm.

Maxo sighed. *So I must turn into a fighting person.* He shook his head. It would not be his choice, but he knew he would stand tall in the face of future challenges of this kind. He wondered vaguely if this was how wars began and became the more sorrowful that circumstances now pushed him into this corner. How contrary that after painting anti-war messages on the church's walls, forces continued to press him into battle mode to complete the work.

Maxo grabbed his head as though to squeeze out this painful thought. "No," he vowed, "I will never aggress against anybody anywhere, but if forced, I will defend my stance." With that, he had to feel content that a true difference lay between the two positions.

Still the mystery of the specter lingered without resolution. Maxo promised himself to re-focus his efforts in that direction in the morning. With that, he slipped into bed and a more soothing sort of sleep.

The gift of another sunny day encouraged Maxo to begin a fresh mural. Time began to weigh on him as he realized only a few weeks remained before the festival and the end of his contract. Three murals awaited completion. The golden flare pouring through the large eastern panels boosted his belief that he would be able to accomplish the work in good time and in good style.

Today's subject contrasted sharply with the bright atmosphere in the church. It did not dampen Maxo's mood, however, as he hummed about making his preparations. Like the mural of *Justice*, this painting would be rendered entirely from the scaffolding, but with his own two feet planted firmly on the boards. His heart gladdened at this small favor even though his back would be turned to the wide expanse of the nave.

While the light was good, Maxo climbed the scaffolding he had erected in the early hours and began to sketch in the painting that would oppose *Justice* on the wall he called the New Testament. He already had titled the mural *Injustice.*

Stroking with a dry brush, Maxo outlined the figure. A head, shrouded and sinister, a gas mask strapped where a face should be. Hands raised like *Justice's*, but holding a bloody sword and scales far out of balance as gold outweighed bread. Dark garments clinging to legs so thin they appeared skeletal.

He flanked the disturbing figure with floating sets of hands that supplicated, that begged, that pleaded for help.

Such was his concentration, that Maxo never noticed the passage of the sun over the roofline of the church. He did not see it merge into a mass of clouds that had formed to the west. The lunch hour had long since passed, but he climbed down to drink from his jar of water and noticed that Mrs. D had left a plate of ham and cheese rolls with pickles on the pew nearest his workspace.

Munching on a sandwich, he stood back to gauge the effect of his sketch. In form and stature, it complemented the *Justice* figure well and provided the distinction he was hoping for between the two figures. Maxo's lips twisted as he chomped off a piece of pickle. It was sour and delicious –garlic dill, his favorite. He finished the meal with a great gulp of water, and then buzzed about, getting ready to paint.

First, he lugged the work lamp up to the highest level of the scaffold. Next, he connected several lengths of extension cord to reach the electrical outlet at the back of the church. Finally, he devoted some time to creating a new palette. The colors *Injustice* required must contrast sharply with the dulcet tones of *Justice*.

The clock tower struck half past the hour of five as Maxo completed his first pass at *Injustice's* head. He shuddered as he assessed the result. The eyes staring through the gas mask goggles chilled him with their cold watchfulness. He could feel his nerve ends tingling just beneath his arm hair, and as the former brightness of the church descended into an even dusk, it magnified the darker aspects of the painting.

As if anticipating trouble, Maxo's head performed a slow surveillance of the apse, the altar, the nave, and the back hall. Further than this, he could not see. A deep quiet had moved into the building, but nothing seemed out of place – an ordinary summer's eve.

Maxo breathed out and extended his arms far above his shoulders. Returning to his paints, he continued to detail the head and neck of the figure. Anxiousness propelled his brush to finish this section and move onto the hands, which he imagined would add a significant punch to the drama of the mural's message.

Time ticked on by, and Maxo did not even hear the chimes at seven o'clock or nine. The portrayal of the hands proved delicate even for the experienced artist, and his focus locked him in deep communion with the details.

Far below him, a light breeze scattered papers in the hall. They feathered toward the floor, whispering like leaves from an autumn tree. The wind fanned up to the church ceiling and tickled the paint rags on the scaffold. When it rippled across Maxo's sleeves, he noticed. He paused, his ears straining. His gaze whipped around the church. Nothing. No sound, no chill, no specter.

Cobwebs in the corner of the nearest window danced as the breeze came again. Maxo grunted and stamped his foot, impatient with himself. He had forgotten to close the vestry door nearest the rectory when day turned to night, and now this pleasant little breeze had come along to remind him.

"Ah well, time for a break anyway," he told the mural. Weaving his fingers together with palms outward, he extended them away from his chest. Then he shook his hands and arms, limbering up for the climb down.

His feet had just touched the floor when what sounded like a drawer sliding shut reached his ears. His body reacted and slipped below the scaffolding, standing as still as a shadow. Now light footsteps pattered from the rear of the church, moving up the aisle behind the light of a lantern. Maxo discovered he was holding his breath.

As the figure passed him, he could see past the light. An "Oh!" escaped his mouth before he could restrain it.

The figure spun around and held the lantern higher. "Who's there?" a female voice inquired. It did not quaver over the syllables. Maxo relaxed then and stepped out from under the boards of the scaffold.

"It is Maxo Vanka, the artist," he said. "And you are Sister, Sister Mary Martha, are you not?"

"Well remembered, Mr. Vanka," the head nun replied. "I did not wish to disturb you, but as I saw the lights and the open vestry door, I came in to make sure everything was all right. Also, I wished to retrieve a book I had left in the office." She raised her hand. Her fingers clasped a small book with a red cover. Maxo nodded. "Frankly, I'm surprised you would leave the door open, even on so fine a night, given the disturbances we've had lately."

Maxo opened his hands to her – an apology perhaps, or an admission of guilt. "Funny you should mention that," he said. "I had this moment realized this oversight myself and came down from my painting to close and lock the door." He shuffled a few steps closer and looked into her face. "I have to say you rather surprised me. I am not accustomed to late night visitors. If you would be so kind," he said as he ushered her to the door, "should you need to enter again some evening, please greet me. I would be most happy to know you are here."

Sister Mary Martha dipped her head briefly in what could have been a nod and exited into the fresh night air. Maxo leaned against the doorjamb watching until she had entered the door of the convent opposite the church.

CHAPTER TWELVE

MAXO AND FATHER ŽAGAR did not have time to compare notes until late the next night. *Injustice* had so enthralled the artist the evening before that he did not return to the rectory until the early morning hours. By that time, only the dim lamp in the hall greeted his arrival. And though Maxo rose early, the priest woke before him and rushed to administer the last rites to one of the elders of the parish.

Another sun-fired day blessed Maxo's work, and he could vouchsafe that the *Injustice* mural was already halfway to completion. Father Žagar, though saddened by his early morning duties, reported that activities had crammed his day, too, including, "what I'd call some very good detective work." He smiled over his steaming cup of cocoa at Maxo's face, which stretched in appreciation.

"I am impressed, Father, do tell me, what has happened?" Maxo sliced into the fresh loaf. He put the bread and a healthy slab of Braunschweiger on his plate.

"Well, it's not so much what has happened as what I've been able to find out," Father said. Since midnight had not yet struck on the clock, he allowed himself a tiny taste of the liver pâté and some of the olives Mrs. Dobrovic had provided.

"Go on," Maxo said.

"That list we made the other night?" Father began. "It

really helped straighten out my thinking; though as you already know, it forced me to look at the problem from an uncomfortable angle." He scraped the last of the liver from his plate with the heel from the bread. "I suddenly realized that the one doing all of this – the perpetrator, as the police call him – had to be one of our own. Someone who had access to the church. Someone who knew the church inside and out. That is, they could find their way around. They could figure out which windows were which, even from the outside. Worst of all," Father wiped his mouth with the linen napkin from the tray. "Worst of all, it has to be someone who acts as a trustee of the church. Somebody who would have a key."

"Ah," said the artist. "So, along with all the other attributes we listed the other night, this is a person who holds a position of trust. Someone who presumably cares for the church, and who has been cared for by others." Maxo scratched an eyebrow. "It all feels more confusing to me, somehow, when we know this."

"Oh, you mean because the suspect who loves the church is at the same time trying to destroy parts of it?"

"Yes, it does not add up for me." Maxo set his coffee cup in its saucer. With his left hand, he stroked his cheeks above his beard line, as though he could shove the problem out of his head via his mouth.

The priest shrugged. "Actually, that doesn't trouble me so much. I can reconcile the two within my own mind. See here. Say a person feels he's given his lifeblood to the church for the past two decades – raising money, serving as a council member, assisting with projects – you know, pretty much anything the church needs doing. Then along comes this youngish upstart priest," he bowed from his chair with a little salute of his hand, "who decides that the walls of the church are too plain. That they need to sing in praise of the Lord and on behalf of his teachings. The man may not agree."

Maxo started a sentence, but Father carried on. "I don't know if I ever mentioned it before – it didn't seem worth mentioning actually – but there was never a unanimous vote in favor of installing the murals. One, or no, two people held out during the secret balloting of the council as to whether or not to move forward with the initiative. It didn't matter as the other thirteen voted a resounding yes, and off we went to hire you and begin the process."

Father poured another half cup of cocoa for himself and blew across the top of his cup. For a few moments, all was silent save the sipping of the chocolaty brew.

Maxo looked at the priest, and when he caught his eye, he said, "That is helpful to know in understanding these events. Part of me rather wishes I would have known sooner, but rational thought tells me that there would have been little I could have done to prevent the – the transgressions. Especially," he added, "if we are dealing with somebody who is not particularly rational."

The priest's head jiggled slightly, a quick nod to this possibility. "So, in considering all of that, I spent a good hour or so yesterday making a list of probable suspects and then narrowing it down." He sifted through the papers on the table next to him and pulled out a sheet. "As near as I can tell, there are three potential perpetrators. Lord, I do not care for that word," he said in an aside. "It makes it all sound so terribly worse."

"Worse than what, Father?" Maxo's eyebrows shot up. "If we have someone who is intent on inflicting grievous harm, then it is our responsibility to take this search for them very seriously. After all, an innocent person may well have been hurt if that brick had sailed through the office window and hit somebody."

Father Žagar rested a hand on Maxo's arm. "There, my friend, I'm sure you're quite right. But here," he handed him the paper, "have a look at this and tell me what you think. Oh, and by the way, all three men wear oxfords though it remains to see if any of them are size 10 ½."

On a fresh sheet of notepaper, Father had drawn three columns, one devoted to each of the individuals he had identified. Their names ranged along the top line. Below them, in his neat block print, he had written characteristics from the list he and Maxo had generated the night before last.

Maxo perused the list. Three names – Lou Tumach, Stephan Graški, and Johnny Petak – headed the page. Only Johnny's name sparked an association for Maxo.

"Did not Johnny help build the first set of scaffolds in 1937 – the big ones we used at the front of the church?" he asked Father.

"Yes, that's right. What a memory you have, Maxo!"

Maxo continued reading. His lips twisted as he neared the bottom of the page. "Father, did you not find this exercise interesting? It seems for the most part, that these three men could be like identical twins. Only there are three of them," he laughed.

"Yes, I was struck with the same thought. Like heights, all a bit podgy from their wives' cooking, all middle-aged and reasonably strong, all in similar clothes. And every one of them served as altar boy here when they were growing up, so their relationship with St. Nicholas stretches back much further than mine. Frankly, I couldn't draw any real distinctions until I reached the bottom of the page and got into what you could call the fine detail."

Maxo looked down at the sheet again. "Yes, I see that Johnny is your sexton, and as such, has keys to the church. Lou and Stephan have both served on council and acted as officers of the church. Hmmm, Stephan is your current treasurer, and both he and Lou have fulfilled duties as lector when needed. That appears to entitle Stephan to keys, as well. But can Lou get into the church?"

"Truthfully?" Father said. "There are probably more keys out there than I care to admit, but during my tenure, these are the people that officially have keys, although only Johnny has a full set. Stephan merely uses the back door to get to the office, so he has one key for that. And I think Lou, as past Chair of the Council and head lector may have keys to both the back door and the vestry."

"I like what you have labeled 'attitudes'," said Maxo,

pointing to a spot on the notes. "This gives me a much better sense of the men and of what they may be capable."

Father Žagar's lips pulled into a straight line that was not quite a smile. "Yes, I think this is where we really begin to separate the men one from the other. Johnny I have always known as fervently devout. He attends daily services, and then carefully straightens any little disorder in the pews left behind by others before he leaves. He reads the Lord's word in the Bible and in his missal every day. I know because he frequently asks questions that come from his readings."

"Yes, he has even asked me to explain some of the murals," Maxo said. "I mean, not this time, but in 1937, I remember we had quite a good chat one day about the mothers in the companion mourning pieces. He seems thirsty for understanding."

"True. Johnny is not an educated man, but he works hard to improve himself. He's asked me questions about the murals, too, but I don't recall that there was ever any malice behind them. I mean, I think he felt the paintings were a bit dark, and that they might scare the little ones, but other than that," the priest shrugged. "He's a hard worker. He has his own garage down in Millvale, and when he's finished a whole day of repairing automobiles, then he'll come here to look at the boiler or fix the gutters. You know, whatever needs attention."

"So, he would have plenty of opportunities to enter the church on his own," Maxo said, propping his chin on his hand, "but seemingly without any motivation to do any damage, especially if he is the one that repairs everything around here."

"That's right," Father said. "In fact, he's coming up this evening to mend the office window. If we have to look at all sides of things, though, I suppose he could've broken the window as a ruse to throw us off."

"But Father, from what you have just said, would he be sophisticated enough to think of such a plan?"

"I doubt it." Father shook his head.

"Just so. Onto the others, who look rather more promising." Maxo checked the columns again. "You note that

Lou has the longest affiliation with the church and may have feelings of ownership because of it. You also mention that even though he is no longer chair of your church council, he still acts like he is and tries to control the decision-making. He also believes his opinion is of the highest value and can be derogatory when others express theirs." Maxo paraphrased what Father now pronounced.

"I believe the words I used were curmudgeon and narrow-minded." They both laughed. "I could certainly see Lou becoming upset if he was one of the two people that had been outvoted about the mural project."

"Do you really think, though," Maxo asked, "that he could stand at the lectern and read spiritual passages in good conscience, if he were guilty of these deeds?"

The priest spoke to his chest as he dusted a few crumbs from his shirtfront. "My dear Maxo, I am sorry to say that I have seen much worse than that as a practicing priest. People who are intractable - " The artist gave him a questioning glance. "People who are extreme in their views and unwilling to change can engage in actions that fall well outside their religious beliefs, though they may rationalize them through the church's teachings. We could go into a deep discussion here about the misuse of Christian beliefs throughout history – the Inquisition, Bloody Mary's reign in England, Joan of Arc's sacrifice, the Salem witch trials – but that is rather far off course for tonight's conversation. Let me just say that, yes, it is possible. But the truth of the matter is that we don't know how Lou voted."

Each man digested these ideas for a while. Finally, Maxo spoke up.

"All right, then. What about this Stephan Graški? He is your treasurer. Surely he is trustworthy."

The priest wiped a sleeve across his brow as though to rub away thoughts he would rather not have. "Ah, this is a tough one for me. I've always considered Stephan to be one of my better friends here in the parish. He's kind, enjoys a good laugh, and has helped me numerous times with tasks no one else wanted to take on."

"But?" Maxo said, "I can hear a 'but' coming."

"But," the priest said, "he is what I would call a strict Catholic, and he has been very open with me about his dislike of the murals, particularly this new set. It's a stretch for him to see an anti-war painting as the word of God. He would have our walls covered with angels singing the Lord's praises. Stephan has gone so far as to tell me he believes some of the murals are idolatrous."

Maxo set his plate quietly on the side table. "Oh dear."

Abruptly, Father stood and paced in front of the hearth. "So here we have an excellent man, one I know to be the author of many good deeds, and without whom I would be lost when it comes to the church's finances. But he harbors hostile feelings about the murals and is unapologetic in his criticism of them." His voice dropped. "I don't know if I could actually say he hates them, but he's made so many negative comments over the years, he makes me think so." He paused, running his fingers over the edge of the mantel. "So, you see, I have no choice but to include him on the list."

Maxo sprang to his side. "My friend, I am so sorry. I do not like to see you hurt in this way. Shall we call it quits for tonight?"

Father smiled. Maxo's occasional use of American colloquialisms always tickled him. "No, because I think you have something to tell me, don't you? But, I do need to take a quick break." He moved toward the hall that led to the bathroom.

While he waited, Maxo piled the soiled crockery onto the tray and carried it to the kitchen. He had this odd sensation that somehow the commonplace had evolved into something strange and uncomfortable this evening. *Such are the ways of men*, he thought. *Completely ordinary people can be capable of perfectly extraordinary evil.* He sighed and turned on the tap for the dishwater.

The mantel clock struck midnight before the two friends sank back in their chairs before the cold fireplace.

"Father, are you sure you would not prefer to discuss this tomorrow?" Maxo asked. "Your face tells me you are weary."

Father Žagar folded his hands across his stomach and extended his legs onto the short footstool in front of his chair. "Weary or not, Maxo, I have to admit that I don't think I'll get a proper rest anyway until we can figure out who's behind these disturbances."

Maxo nodded and resting his elbows on the arms of his chair, he canted forward to impart his discovery from the night before.

"As I think I mentioned earlier, Father," he said, "I seem to be blessed with new energy to complete the murals. It is as though the specter senses it and has kept his distance. Or absence, I should say." Maxo stroked the end of his moustache. "In any event, that energy is channeling into remarkable progress on the murals – a happy instance for you and for me."

"All of yesterday and last night, the mural of *Injustice* engrossed me. You know how I can become. I was deaf, blind, and senseless except for the painting before me. I forgot to eat or drink, I did not take a break, and I neglected to close the vestry door after dark. I had left it open all day to enjoy the sunny breeze that blew through the church."

Father cleared his throat when Maxo mentioned the open door. "I'm not sure I want to hear what happened next."

"Yes, yes, well, I do apologize. It was foolish, and I promise it will not happen again. But under the circumstances, it may have yielded a valuable clue for us, or at least more evidence to consider about these infractions against the church and my art."

"Really?" Father Žagar sat upright in his chair.

"Yes. It was when I had finally realized that the wind still chased through the church. It had actually picked up and gusted to the ceiling, rustling my rags and my sleeves. I climbed down the four levels of scaffolding and within seconds of reaching the ground, I became intensely aware of other sounds beside the wind." The artist's eyes widened. Father licked his lips and blinked.

"I braced for the inevitable chill of the phantom, but it did not come. Only the warm air of the balmy night blew past my ears. Still, I remained on the alert – a little mouse in a big, dark church ready to run."

"And then?" the priest asked, urging Maxo on.

"And then I heard the very definite sound of a drawer sliding shut in the office."

Father's brows shifted up in surprise. "The office? Again? A drawer?"

Maxo nodded briskly. "Yes, my thoughts, too. So I hid beneath the scaffold and stood as quiet as that little mouse, waiting, waiting. Very soon, footsteps could be heard marching through the hall and up the center aisle. I could just make out a dark figure behind the beam of a lantern, and then, all of a sudden, there was her face."

"Her face?" The priest's own face became a question mark.

The words spilled rapidly from Maxo then. "Yes, it was Sister Mary Martha carrying a red book. In the shadowy light, I have to admit she looked tall, dark and menacing, but such is my imagination when I am half frightened. I revealed myself right away, of course, and received a dressing down for it, as though I were the night-time intruder."

"Did she say anything else?" Father said.

"Yes, she talked about coming to fetch the book from the office, but I felt as though that was an after-thought, because she also mentioned that she had come to check on things once she had noticed the open vestry door."

"Well, that seems in good order as far as it goes," Father said.

"But Father, why come and check at all when she knows I often work late at night?" the artist cried. "And why not notify me once she was in the church and could see that I was on the scaffold? And what was she looking for in the church office? Surely a book would have been located on the nearest shelf. And last, but not least as far as I am concerned, were you aware that she shoes her large feet in black oxfords that very closely resemble the style of the men?"

This last revelation stunned Father into silence for a moment. Then, under his breath, he uttered, "Sister Mary Martha? Sister Mary Martha?" shaking his head all the while. He slumped into his hands and rubbed his face up and down as though he were giving it a good scrub. Between his fingers, the priest asked, "Are you sure, Maxo? Are you quite sure it was her?"

"Now, Father, you know you do not need to ask me this." The priest's head twitched in agreement. "I know who she is, but even so, I said her name out loud, and she concurred that it was she. Of course, she had no idea I was observing every detail about her – an artist's boring habit, I am afraid – and you are aware that I can sense things about others. In her, I sensed that the level of her admonishment of me was pitched to draw attention away from something else."

Red blotches coated Father's cheeks as he raised his head to study Maxo. "And did you later explore what that might have been?"

"You will understand that I was a bit unsettled after the encounter with the Sister," Maxo said. "After I watched her walk home, I closed and bolted the vestry door. Turning around to the dimness of the church, my energy deserted me, and I have to confess, I lost my motivation for investigating or painting that night. With aching limbs, I climbed the scaffold once more to fetch my palette and brushes. I switched off the lamp, but left it in place, and then, once more, I descended to the floor."

"As I had to lock my things in the closet near the office anyway, I thought that I would have a quick look around. First I gathered some papers that lay in the hall before the door. They must have blown down when the wind was brisk. I flicked the switch to the office, and the overhead light blazed into being. The desktop appeared in no greater disarray than usual, and the window had been repaired so that it still opens even though the new glass is not yet installed."

"I stepped around like a cat that does not wish to get his paws wet. The bookshelves revealed nothing except a slot in the row of missals where one was missing. All but one of the file drawers on the desk could be opened, but for the life of me, I found nothing that seemed in the least suspicious."

Father's eyes narrowed as though he were resisting a bad pain. This was not news he wanted to hear. Something of a more concrete nature would have been helpful at this point.

"As I was shoving the last drawer shut, my skin prickled with cold," Maxo continued his tale. "I thought, 'this is all I need on such a night,' and before anything could materialize, I turned off the lights, scampered down the aisle, and escaped through the vestry door."

"And of course, you ensured that it was locked behind you," Father said.

"Of course," Maxo responded with a tilt of his head toward the priest.

Silence oozed between them – an oily, gelatinous sludge that seemed to push their chairs apart. The discomfort Maxo had detected earlier had come to perch between them.

Except for the cook pattering around the kitchen the next morning, once more Maxo ate breakfast alone. The milk coiled in a sour ellipse on top of his tea, and he coughed more than once on the dry toast.

"Looks like we're in for a spot of rain today, Mr. Maxo," Mrs. Dobrovic said as she scrubbed the pots in the sink. She cleared the plates from the table. Maxo noticed the moustache of beaded sweat that clung above her mouth. "Lord knows, it's humid enough."

Maxo viewed the clouds through the kitchen window. Slabs of gray slate piled one on the other, stretching across the entire sky. "It does not bode well for good light," he said. "I had best get moving to take advantage of what I can before the storm darkens the church further."

"Wait, Mr. Maxo!" she shouted after him, "I've got two jars of water for you this morning. You'll need them."

He retraced his steps quickly, gave Mrs. D a peck on the

cheek, shouted "Hvala!" and rushed to the church.

Ten minutes later, Maxo stood on the high platform putting the finishing touches to *Injustice's* head. With any luck, he could complete it within the next two hours, and then move to the third level of the scaffold. *Thank heavens!* The heat might abate a few degrees if he could get away from the church's ceiling.

Maxo slipped the bandanna from around his neck and wiped his forehead. He bent to sip from the first water jar and to pour some more black onto his palette. As he mixed some colors for the shroud, a fleeting movement from below caught his eye. It was the priest.

"Father! Felicitations! I am glad to see you!" he shouted.

"And I, you, my friend," the priest said. "I don't wish to interrupt your work, but I wondered if we could have a small discussion, say in about an hour's time. What do you think?"

"Make it an hour and a half, and I will be more than happy for a little rest," Maxo said.

"Done!" said Father. "See you in my study at ten o'clock."

At the quarter chime, Maxo once more descended from his lofty perch. He would regard his work from the bottom when he returned and determine whether or not the topmost piece was finished. He made a beeline for the rectory bathroom where he splashed cool water on his face after scrubbing the paint from his fingers with the bar of Lava soap reserved for him. It felt so good, he splashed some more cool water over his head and the back of his neck and toweled off. Then, he combed his hair neatly into place.

At ten sharp, he relaxed into one of the chairs in front of Father's desk. Father took the other one so they were facing each other without the slab of the oaken desk in between.

The priest hemmed in his throat. "Maxo, I feel that I owe you an apology for last night." When the artist began to protest, he raised a hand. "No, no, I do. It's just that I think I experienced something like shock or maybe a whack over the head with a board." He smiled. "There was never any real reason to rule out that the culprit could be a woman, and at that, a woman who is close to the church, but suddenly, it all came crashing in on me. The disturbances, the suspicion of some of the best people in the parish, too many unknowns. I shut down."

"And understandably so," Maxo said. "Father, please. We are friends. Perhaps I could have been a bit more, umm, tactful in how I presented my story."

"No. It is best to have these things straight out. That is a gift I value in you, Maxo," the priest said. "You are always forthright with me, and too few people are. Anyway, you may be happy to hear that I have taken action on account of it."

"Oh?" Maxo said.

"Yes." Father thumped his right hand on the arm of the chair. "I immediately set forth this morning to hold a long interview with Sister Mary Martha."

Maxo bit his bottom lip. "Oh, tell me it is not her, nor that you have accused her of anything."

Father laughed. "Well, despite what I just said about being straightforward, you can rest assured that I was appropriately circumspect with the good sister. I'm not sure you know that she is the head of our teachers here, which means that she is also in charge of all of the nuns. While ours is a small community, she takes her responsibilities very seriously. For this reason, since the disturbances began, she has conducted a personal surveillance of the church on random evenings, especially when she noticed things that seemed out of line. She may have heard complaints about them, or may not agree with or even like all of your paintings herself, but she has great respect for the parish council, and as such, feels she has a duty to uphold its decisions. This certainly includes protecting the church and its artifacts." He paused for half a second. "Or so she vows, and I have no reason to disbelieve her."

"A relief for me, and for you, Father," Maxo said. "I was concerned lest I unfairly exposed her in some fashion."

"Not at all, Maxo," Father Žagar said. "It is as well that you told me about her late night perambulation. In truth, she should have informed me that she had undertaken such a task, but now we have been able to clear the air as to that point, at least."

"What do you mean, at least?" Maxo asked.

"Well, we had a good conversation, Sister and I," the priest's eyes became distant for a second as though he were trying to recall the words, "but I couldn't help feeling that while all of her actions were well intended, she seemed to be holding back a piece of the story. I wasn't clever enough to probe further about it without sounding accusatory at the time, so I suppose a second conversation will be in order."

Maxo rolled his head around on his shoulders. "Did you ask her if she had any ideas on who might be causing the damage?"

"Not in so many words, I'm afraid." Father shook his head in admission. "She spoke more generally about her suspicions, much as we have done over the past weeks until we had something more definite to go on. And before you ask, I did not share any of our discoveries with her. Which leads me to the other reason I wanted to speak with you this morning."

"Oh, yes?"

"Maxo, we created a fairly good list of suspects last night, but we didn't get so far as to make a plan of approach. I have to say, I am feeling out of my depth here, particularly when it involves trustees and valued members of the church. What do you think we should do?" The priest drummed his fingers on the desktop as Maxo thought this question over.

"We are two lambs lost in the wood on this one, Father." Maxo gave the priest a small smile. "I'm thinking, thinking, but nothing is coming just at the moment. Will it make much of a difference, do you think, if we postpone this discussion to later this evening?"

Father responded right away. "Actually, I was really hoping to get started on something today. I have some time, and the sooner we can get on top of this, the better, in my book."

"Ah, I see, and I understand," Maxo said. "Let me bargain with you then, to re-meet at lunchtime, say, one o'clock? I do some of my best thinking while painting, and I promise to have some suggestions when I return."

The priest shook his head in agreement. "I suppose I am asking the impossible, to hope for some instant, miraculous response from you, but," and he laughed a little at himself, "that doesn't keep me from hoping."

Maxo trotted back into the church before the first lashings of the threatened storm could begin. The rain pelted the stone sidewalk and splashed in at the door, forcing Maxo to shut it tight. With no open windows or doors, the atmosphere in the church closed in on him, humid and gloomy.

Maxo stepped to the light switches and brought the main chandeliers into play. That was better. From the ground, he studied the figure of *Injustice* for a few moments, then eagerly, scaled the scaffolding and positioned the work lamp so that it illumined the head of the figure. *Surely, another hour will finish the job*, he thought. With his fine sable brush, Maxo painted deft, quick strokes, filling in the final details of the gas mask and the shrouded eyes.

The gas mask he could complete from memory, having seen so many of them during the war. But his aim was not only for it to look realistic, but to frighten the viewer when he considered how damaging the powers of *Injustice* could be. Once more, Maxo's thoughts swam into the painting, and minutes passed like fleeting seconds.

When it came this time, it shocked him as though a bolt of electricity had passed through the back of his neck. The chill omen of the specter's presence clashed with his sweat-soaked neck to send a shivering current down his spine. He came close to dropping his palette. Slowly he turned as the lights dimmed throughout the church. Automatically, his eyes searched the first pew, and they were rewarded: the unmistakable black cloak and cowl, the invisible face staring above the altar, staring at nothing.

Maxo breathed out through his nose, a heavy breath as though he were pumping out all the air in his lungs. His lids dropped over his eyes for the space of a few seconds. When his body waved out toward the abyss of the nave, and his head spun with sensation, Maxo forced his eyes open and stepped back to press his shoulders hard against the New Testament wall. *It must be the heat to give me this reaction,* he thought.

He looked to the pew. The phantom had not budged. *I had a feeling about this day,* he said to himself, *as soon as I saw those clouds through the kitchen window. Perhaps M. Fantôme has heard me talking too large with Father Žagar, and comes back to teach me a lesson.*

The question became, what could he do about it now? Maxo rubbed his arms to bring some warmth into them and his hands. If he attempted to climb down, he would have to be able to feel his hands on the bars. *Should I make a sound? That sometimes worked. Oh where, oh where is that confidence that I have been feeling all week?*

It came to Maxo as he quivered in the heat that he had never really spent any serious time during a normal hour to consider actions he could take when the specter appeared. Now, he cursed himself for this thoughtless oversight.

Maxo slid his back down the wall until he could sit. Keeping in mind that the appearances never lasted that long, he decided to wait out the specter.

The cloth rubbing against the wall as he sat aroused the ghost's curiosity. It turned to face the New Testament wall, but did not appear to look in Maxo's direction. Never the less, Maxo tucked himself into a small ball outside of the faded circle of light thrown from the work lamp. *Would this never end?* Maxo thought – hoped – that Father would come to his rescue once again when he realized that he was late for the promised luncheon discussion. In dismay, he silently pounded a fist against his forehead. He had completely forgotten to develop some ideas for that discussion!

In his distraction, Maxo did not observe the phantom as it exited the pew and floated down the aisle to disappear beneath the choir.

CHAPTER THIRTEEN

WITH HIS FACE BURIED IN HIS HANDS, Maxo berated his own absorption in the painting of *Injustice.* Not only was he stuck on this high shelf with that thing down below, but he had failed to make good on his promise to the priest. His toes curled inside his boots, and his fingers dug into the sinuses above his eyes. Now did not seem a propitious time for developing some sensible suggestions on how they should proceed with their investigation. *Oh, Maxo!* This time, he felt as though the specter's appearance was entirely his own fault.

It did not keep him from wondering how long he would have to attend the phantom's whim. No sooner did he think this than he realized that the air around him had grown warm again. The next thing the artist knew, the church brightened as the electric lamps flared anew. Shooting his eyes to the front of the church, Maxo blew a heavy sigh. Ignoring the cries of his cramped joints, he scrambled down the boards and ladders and charged out of the church.

"Whoa!" Father Žagar shouted, and then, "Ouch!" as he cracked heads with Maxo when the two men collided. Father collected himself, and rubbing his forehead, asked, "And to what do I owe this lump on my noggin?"

"Oh, oh, Father, oprostite! Oprostite!" cried Maxo, pressing the heel of his hand against the red mark at his hairline. "A thousand, thousand pardons!" He grabbed the priest by the shoulder. "Are you all right, Father Žagar? Bože moj, I am so very sorry."

In return, Father laid a hand over Maxo's. Its reassuring warmth passed up his arm. A sigh stuttered from his lips. "Oh, I am so glad."

"It's nothing at all, my friend, not to worry," said Father. "It's not like it's the first time I've butted heads with somebody." He chuckled at the mild joke. "And I confess, it's partly my fault. When the mantel clock chimed the half hour, I suddenly suspected that something was wrong over here at the church, so like you, I was speeding on my way when you burst through the door."

He put an arm around Maxo's shoulders and guided him back toward the rectory. "Come now. I can see that something has happened, and I'm thinking a cup of coffee with a soupçon of whiskey in it might not go amiss."

Maxo allowed himself to be led into the kitchen, and then on to the living room where between them, Father and Mrs. Dobrovic removed his smock and propped him in the corner of the couch with a couple of pillows.

"Dear Mrs. D, strong, black coffee and some of those delightful apple turnovers you made this morning might be perfect about now," the priest said turning to the cook.

Mrs. Dobrovic darted a concerned look toward Maxo, pinching her lips between her teeth. Then, with a quick tip of her head, she hurried back to the kitchen where already the kettle whistled for her presence. Father moved to the cupboard behind his desk and pulled out a bottle of Seagram's.

By the time he reached the table between the sofa and chairs, Mrs. Dobrovic was entering the room with a clinking tray. She placed it squarely between them. "Now, them peaches are fresh from my garden, Mr. Maxo. I don't think anything will fix you up better than those." She smoothed her hands down her apron and stood there until Maxo reached for the coffee pot. "Here, let me get the sugar for you. Three teaspoons today, and drink it as hot as you can. That'll put the energy back in your blood." She spooned a generous amount of the white crystals into his cup as he poured.

Maxo gave her a weak smile. "As always, my dear guardian angel. Hvala, my dear. Hvala a million times."

As if his thanks were what she had awaited, Mrs. Dobrovic returned the smile and exited the room. The boards creaked a farewell as her solid figure passed over them.

Along with the sugar, Father splashed a dram of whiskey into the cup. "With all of this, you'll soon be doing cartwheels about the room," he said.

Maxo pulled a long draught of the hot liquid into his throat. "Hoo! What do you call it? A good jolt?" He took another sip and sat up straighter. "I think I am all better now," he said, and both men laughed.

"But," he added, "I fear I have let you down, Father. Once again, I have allowed my mind to become entirely immersed in the painting. I am afraid I completely forgot my assignment – my promise to you." He opened his palms toward Father Žagar. "And so I come empty-handed to this meeting. Or empty-minded, as the case may be."

"Again, Maxo," Father said, "I don't want you to worry. It is enough for me if you can spare this small spot of time to bounce some ideas back and forth. I think I've come up with an approach, but I'm anxious to have your opinion."

"Ah, well, you know, I am always ready to give an opinion." And for the first time since entering the rectory, Maxo's smile was big and bright.

"I knew I could count on you." Father smiled back at him. "But before we begin, do you want to tell me about it? Do you want to tell me what happened in the church just now?"

"It is not necessary to get it 'out of my system', as you might suspect," Maxo said, "but I can tell you in brief that the ghost has paid another daytime visit to me." He coughed into his hand. "For some reason that I cannot derive, the daylight visits are equally, if not more frightening than the ones at night, perhaps because I know for a certainty that my eyes are not deceiving me. I can see him much more clearly, there was even a hint of a face this afternoon, and maybe because the day is hotter, the chill he brings seems that much colder. I thought I would freeze to death just now. And then…" Maxo stopped and rubbed the back of his neck.

"Yes?" Father asked. "And then?"

"And then, I became angry with myself – something I do not often do."

"Angry?" Father's voice posed the question in tones that sought understanding.

"And annoyed, very annoyed with myself," Maxo said. "You see, not only did I let you down by not giving two thoughts to your concerns from this morning; but it came to me that I had made no preparations about what I would do if the spirit reappeared. Much as you wish to make plans to solve our earthly mystery with direct action, so I think I need an outline of what I will do to confront our spiritual one." He sniffed. "It struck me as so, so foolish to have not made such a plan by now."

The artist's ears wiggled as he gulped his regret. Father watched the line of his jaw grow straight and taut. "Another drop?" He moved the whiskey bottle within reach, hoping it could erase that line.

"No, no," Maxo replied, shaking his head rapidly like a dog freeing water from his fur. "That is, not if you expect me to do any more painting today. The brushes, and for that matter, the ladders, will not cooperate if I take any more." With his eyelids half shut, he glanced sideways at the priest. "Perhaps later though!"

"Good enough," said Father. "Then, let's get down to business."

"Yes, let us do so!" Relief crossed Maxo's face to be able to square off with a problem so different from his own.

"Where we left it this morning," Father said, "was that at least three men of trusted position have keys to the church and can pretty much enter any time they want. What I was hoping for were some ideas about how to approach them reasonably – to find out what we need to know without arousing their defenses. That's about where my mind goes blank."

"Not surprising, Father. You simply are not one to mislead others," Maxo said. He passed an index finger across one brow and then the other. "It is not a question of lying, however, or being evasive. Not really. Hmm. Let me see your tablet again."

Propping it on his knee, Maxo turned to a fresh lined page. "Maybe it will help if we can jot down the questions we need answered. Then, perhaps, they will suggest a pathway to finding the answers."

"Well, one is, we need to know the size and type of their shoes," Father said.

"Right." Maxo made an entry at the top of the page. "We also want to know where they were at the time of the palette and painting destruction and the night that the office window was broken." Beside this question, he wrote down the respective dates of the incidents.

"Is it helpful to probe their feelings about the art in the church?" Father asked, chin in hand.

"My first impression? I think such questions might seem too obvious. They might suspect where you are going with such a line of inquiry. And they might not like it."

"Okay, right. Um, what else? It seems like there should be at least a third question, but I'm blessed if I can think of it," said Father.

"It may be that if you begin with these questions, others will naturally arise. It will be up to you, Father, to make sure that you ask them objectively."

"Lord, I hope I can do that."

"I feel positive that you can, my friend." Maxo leaned over to grip Father's wrist. He took the pad up again as he said, "So, as we have been talking, a small idea has been forming in my head. Would you like to hear it?"

"Yes," Father replied. "I'm still confounded if I can think of an approach."

"Well, there are two things that suggest themselves to me,"

Maxo said. "Regarding the shoe size, a tiny taradiddle may be in order. Could you not say that you are trying to clothe a family that needs help, and that in particular, you are seeking men's old oxford shoes, size 10 ½? I mean, it is not so far from the truth as it seems to me that you indeed often collect clothing for those in need."

Father Žagar slapped his knee. "Ha! By George, Maxo, you've hit the nail on the head. I won't even have to make it up. We've just learned of a family in Millvale whose house burned down last night. It would be easy enough for me to include the shoe request in among the other things they need. And by way of not singling anyone out, I could put out the request to several of the parishioners that I think might help. I could talk to some of them personally, including our three – "

"Yes, those three men," Maxo filled in. "Exactly. And who knows? It may eliminate one of them or perhaps, all of them." For a moment, the artist made some notes on the sheet.

"Now, regarding the dates, times and places question, that is a bit more challenging. But, what do you think of this?" Maxo looked into the eyes of the priest. "What if we recruit these three, or however many are left after the shoe question is answered, to help you investigate? Get them to inventory the other men as to their whereabouts on the dates in question."

"And naturally, they'd have to include themselves in the inventory," Father chimed in. "Or I could say that I'd need to interview them, since they'd be interviewing everyone else."

"That is brilliant, Father, just brilliant!"

"Better yet, they could help me design the questions and how we verify the answers we're given. Like – like everyone would have to provide a witness, or, or something that shows where they were." Father scratched his head. "Hmm. This isn't quite as easy as it first sounded."

"No," Maxo said, "but I do think it can work, and it is something you can organize quickly, expressing to the men that there is some urgency to resolve the issue."

"All right!" Father smacked his hands together and rubbed them back and forth. "I'll begin this minute."

"Just a moment, my friend, there is one other thing." The artist held up one finger. "Things should be done in a certain order. First, the clothing and shoe request." Father nodded. "Then, the inventory of where people were on the nights we are thinking about."

With profuse but hurried thanks, Father grabbed the notepad from Maxo's hands and scurried to his desk. He flipped to another blank page and began a letter of request for the family who had lost everything.

Maxo slipped one of the apple turnovers into the pocket of his smock, grabbed a peach, and made his way back to the church. It was midafternoon, and at last, the sun had managed to carve its way through the cloud cover. Strips of sunlight streaked from the gray cumulus and lit Maxo's heart.

This must be what old Mati Dora called bone weary, Maxo thought as he ended the long work day by hanging his smock on the hooks in the cellar stair. He turned the blouse in on itself, taking care that none of the paint splatters touched the wall.

His feet dragged along the carpet runner as he walked toward the bathroom where he would wash and hopefully feel half human again. He was not entirely surprised, however, when Father Žagar accosted him before he could get to the sink.

"Maxo, greetings!" It felt like the priest was shouting in his face. "I am glad to see you. What a day this has been."

"Father," Maxo said, "if you have not noticed, we have already moved into the next day. You are up very late." Then, he relented. "But I can see you have much to tell. Give me five minutes, and I will join you."

"Of course, of course," Father moved aside so Maxo could step into the bathroom. "And in the meantime, I'll make sure the kettle's hot."

Face and hands scrubbed, Maxo slumped into the chair on the right hand side of the fire. A small tray perched on the table between the two chairs, offering the promised tea plus a banana, an early apple, and a wedge of Schweitzer cheese.

Father had already arrived and turned his chair so that he could better face Maxo. "May I slice you some cheese?" he asked.

"In a moment, Father. At this minute, nothing seems better than to lay back in this chair and stretch my legs." He pushed his toes further toward the unlit hearth. "But as it is so very late for you, please tell me all that has happened. And no matter if my eyes are closed, my ears are not."

"So, I take it you have made good progress today," the priest said.

"Yes, remarkably, my luck seems to have turned this afternoon," Maxo said in a soft voice. "No more disturbances, no more distractions, and a plenitude of late afternoon light. The *Injustice* mural is all but finished. It somehow demanded my full and concentrated attention." The artist stifled a yawn with his left hand. "Tomorrow, I will give it a critical eye and fine-tune some details, but then, then he will be done."

"Congratulations, Maxo! I think that's the fastest you've ever completed a mural here. Well done! Sounds like we will be in very good shape for the festival." He smiled at the artist. "I'm happy for you, especially if you get to go home a little earlier than you thought."

"We shall see," Maxo murmured. "But, please, what is your news? Quick, before you burst."

"First of all, my friend," the priest said, "I have to tell you that I could not have done this without you. I know I can always rely on your creative thought to help me work my way through a problem. And your suggestions today couldn't have been better."

Father stopped to pour the tea, which he judged had steeped enough by then. He handed a cup to Maxo.

"So, as you saw, I wrote out a request to several of the parishioners that I expect do have a little extra in the way of clothing and household items, asking for their help with the Bock family. Oh, the Bocks are the people whose house caught fire. As it happened, I did have a list of some of the family's dress and pants sizes, so it did not seem unusual to include shoe sizes as well."

He brought a glass of water to his lips, but before he drank, Father said, "I went to families in Millvale and Lawrenceville, the two closest to the fire incident, but also the two places where our three men live." He took a long sip and wiped his mouth on his hanky.

"We were extraordinarily successful in raising goods as well as money."

Maxo smiled. He had often heard from the parishioners he knew that it was almost impossible to say no to Father Žagar, no matter what the request. *A fund-raiser and social activist extraordinaire*, Maxo thought. "That's excellent, Father," he said through the steam from his teacup.

"I'm saving the best for last, though." Father beamed.

"Oh, yes?"

"Yes! Because it turns out that our Johnny – Johnny Petak – was most apologetic that he could not donate shoes. It seems that he has inherited his papa's size 11 ½ despite his short stature!"

"Oh, Father, that's great news!" Maxo clapped his hands. "I know that brings you tremendous relief. I have to say that in my own head, I was finding it hard to believe that Johnny could ever be culpable of such deeds. I am so glad to hear this."

"Yes, I'm breathing a little easier tonight, my friend," the priest admitted. "I even think that we might recruit him to help us, if it comes down to that." He tapped his thumbs together in his lap. "There is more. A sort of post script that doesn't make me especially happy, but it does help me to think that we are making some progress."

"What is that, Father?"

"It appears that both Stephan and Lou wear size 10 ½ oxfords made by Jarman, no less."

"Ah, I see." Maxo twiddled his moustache for a moment. "Well, Father, it would seem that you have two investigative partners."

"Amen," the priest replied. "I've already spoken with

them, and we start the inventory tomorrow."

Cued by an enormous yawn the artist could not hide, Father Žagar said, "I did have one other thing I wanted to discuss, but my dear fellow, it looks like your bed is calling you. Shall we plan to chat again at breakfast?"

Pushing both arms of the chair, Maxo heaved his body onto his feet and nodded.

"No later than seven, okay?" Father said. "I want to be ready early when Lou and Stephan come by."

"For certain, Father," Maxo yawned as he shuffled off to his room. Mustered by courtesy, a breathy good night sighed from his lips.

The next morning, Maxo mumbled through a mouthful of toast. ""Well, what about the nuns, then? Have you found nothing out?"

"It was you who first said I should wait to question them further," Father said. "Honestly, Maxo, you can't have it both ways." He tapped his knife on the edge of his plate attempting to dislodge some excess butter from its blade. "You seemed so worried when I had been too quick to speak with Sister Mary Martha, and now you're acting as though I've been slow on the draw." The butter flicked backward onto his rabat.

"Oh, Lord!" The priest daubed at the spot on his chest, and then scrubbed as the grease spot doubled in size. He threw down his napkin. "Bother!"

"So sorry, I fear I have poked into a spot that is sore," Maxo said. "I did not mean to sound expectant. Or, or impatient. I was just wondering." He dunked his napkin into the glass of cold water at his place and proffered it to the priest. In a soft voice, he said, "Father, listen to me. All will go well today. You will surely have some answers by day's end." He leaned back in his chair and watched his friend.

Having repaired his shirtfront, the priest returned Maxo's napkin to the side of his teacup. With his lips stretched into a taut line, he took a deep breath through his nose. Finally, he released it, and his shoulders dropped. "I am certain you are right, Maxo, but somehow, with the hour upon me, it feels like something may go wrong. And I *am* worried about how to address the situation with Sister and her charges." As an afterthought he added, "If indeed there is one. I can just hear Sister Mary Martha asking me, 'What situation, Father?' Mmph!" This time the air gushed out of his nose. "That was the other thing I wanted to talk with you about last night."

"Father," Maxo said, "Whether we call it a situation or something else, we both have sensed that Sister Mary Martha does not tell us all. There is a piece of story missing that may be important for us to know. Tell me, do you ever hold staff meetings with the good sisters?"

"Yes, as a matter of fact, I do." Father cast his eyes up to the left. "I believe our next meeting is a week Thursday."

"Oo, could you not make an exception for an urgent matter and hold the meeting earlier?" Maxo asked. "I do not think waiting will forward our cause, so to speak."

"Of course, I can do that, but what do you have in mind?"

"I am thinking you begin such a meeting with the usual business matters of the school and the church," Maxo said, "but then, I think you solicit their help – like you have with the men – in thinking through the raft of incidents that have occurred. After all, more than anyone, they are in and about the church, preparing for services, tidying, rehearsing the choir, and so on."

"But like we did with our two male suspects," Father asked, "should we list what we hope to discover? I mean, the obvious first thing is that one of them knows something – something more than she's telling."

"Yes, I agree, that is of the first importance," Maxo drained his teacup, "getting her or them to tell us. Then, I also think it is all right to reveal that Sister Mary Martha has been patrolling the church at night and find out if anyone else has been similarly engaged."

Father watched his fingertips slide back and forth over the glossy oilskin of the kitchen tablecloth. They skimmed over bright red cherries, emerald green leaves, and the white space in between. "Maxo," he drew out the "o" in the artist's name,

"I wonder – what do you think of coming to the staff meeting with me? I think the sisters would be sympathetic to your troubles and might speak more openly than they would just to me. It would also give me the benefit of your extraordinary sensory gifts."

The artist inclined his head and looked up at Father Žagar from below his brows. "If you believe it would truly help, and that I would not prove to be a hindrance, I would be most happy to attend." He gave a little bob of his head, bowing to this idea.

"Then, it's settled." Father clapped a hand on the table. The silverware jangled in chorus. "Could you spare some time tomorrow morning?"

"My word, Father, but never do you waste any time." Maxo's lips curved in a gentle smile. "Yes, of course I can come then – the earlier the better, I say!"

At quarter to eight the following morning, Maxo sat alone in the living room of the rectory in preparation for the meeting with the sisters. Father and he had carried a few extra chairs in from the dining room and formed a circular seating arrangement between the upholstered chairs and sofa. The artist sat in one of the straight-backed chairs with his back to the side window of the room. He had selected it for its vantage point and the light. He should be able to see every face and any hint of - w*ell*, he thought, *any hint of whatever was to be seen.*

At the moment, he curved his back into the chair in a relaxed pose and hummed to himself. Yesterday had proven deeply satisfactory, and aside from wanting to help his priest friend, Maxo felt entirely justified in taking a few hours away from his painting. The day before had gleamed pure sunshine, and before dusk, he had been successful in completing the painting of *Injustice.* The atmosphere in the church had been comfortable, quiet, and embracing. No visitors in earthly or spiritual form had come to disturb his peace. Well-being had been his partner all day and night, and it continued to collaborate with him now as he turned his mind toward the meeting to come.

Soon, he heard the rustle of skirt and habit as the eight nuns and Sister Mary Martha entered the rectory at the kitchen door. Through the archway of the living room, he heard Father Žagar.

"Good morning, Sisters, good morning! Please go through to the living room. Mrs. Dobrovic and Cara will follow with refreshments in a few minutes."

Father led the way, but at the sight of Maxo, the head nun paused for half a second, causing the rest to stack up one against the other like bottles blocked on an assembly line.

"Come now, Sisters," Father invited. "You all have met our good friend, the artist Maxo Vanka. I've asked him along to share in our conversation today. Please, sit wherever you like." He gestured toward the circle of furniture. Father purposely sat two chairs away from Maxo, and the nuns filed in, filling the seats furthest from the artist and the priest first.

Quick on their heels came the cook and her daughter with two enormous trays: one held teapots, cups, plates, sugar, milk and spoons; the other groaned with pastries, including thick slices of Mrs. Dobrovic's specialty – kolache – fresh baked that morning. The air rolled with aroma – nuts and honey, apricots and poppy seed, warm sweetbread.

"Let us pray," Father said, and everyone, except Maxo, crossed themselves and bowed their heads as he thanked the Lord for His generosity and for the Dobrovics whose skill and labor had set forth such a magnificent breakfast.

There followed five busy minutes of clanking china, burbling liquid, and smacking lips as the tea was poured and the confections were chosen and sampled. Once everyone had settled back in their places, Father quickly dispensed with some minor scheduling issues. He then took a long sip of tea as the nuns' curiosity and trepidation descended on the room like a lowering fog.

Father sat a little straighter in his chair. Maxo unobtrusively stretched his spine and sharpened his focus.

The priest began. "First of all, many thanks to Sister Mary Martha and to all of you for assembling this morning on such short notice. Once more, I truly appreciate your willingness to serve. In fact, I thank the Lord every day for the gifts that each of you brings to our small parish."

"So, today I call on you to bring those talents to bear. As you know, our dear St. Nicholas church has been the recent victim of a number of what I will call attacks. For this reason," and the priest gestured toward Maxo, "I have asked Mr. Vanka here to explain to you the nature of some of these incidents as he has personally endured hardship on their account. Maxo?"

Maxo edged to the front of his seat and sat very tall. "Thank you, Father Žagar. Sisters, please let me first add my grateful thanks for any help you can give us on these matters," and he went on to retail the events and their dates of occurrence: the destruction of the first palette and the ruin of *Justice's* face, the damage to the second palette and his brushes, and the breaking of the church's office window. He related his story with a simple passion, but one that reached out to the sisters' feelings.

"I know that not all of you understand or maybe even like my paintings, but equally I understand that you can empathize with how very personal these attacks feel to me, especially as at some point they may interfere with your own ability to serve the church." Licking his lips, he continued, looking at each nun in turn. "Having my paintings or my palettes destroyed was like depriving me of my beliefs – what I believe I am called to do by a higher power. Do you know that I think of these murals as my gift to America? That is how very, very momentous this job, this mission is to me." Quietly, he added, "I – I do not know what would be similar for you. Perhaps you have been given a sacred family crucifix or a set of rosary beads that is sentimental. One day you find that this precious item has been crushed to powder under foot by some unknown attacker."

Several of the sisters gasped, and at least four clutched the rosaries that dangled from their hands – an action observed by both Father and Maxo.

"Worse yet, you have no understanding of why the assailant would target you or your precious artifacts – the 'tools of your trade,' if you understand my meaning."

A nervous thrum ran around the circle as though the nuns' blood threshed through their systems at a greater pace. Only Sister Mary Martha sat silent with her fingers woven across the protrusion of her old woman's belly.

"Hush!" she said to the sisters in tones of admonishment. "No more drama, please. Listen, and let us hear what Mr. Vanka thinks all of this has to do with us."

Maxo flushed red at the veiled accusation, but before he could respond, Father Žagar took the floor.

"Sister Mary Martha, all of you, please, I know that what you have heard is unsettling. Believe me, it has kept me up most nights now for weeks and weeks. What we – me and Mr. Vanka, and many others, frankly – are seeking is some assistance from you. Can you believe your priest if I tell you that we truthfully have no idea about who is committing these crimes? And that we truly, truly need your help?" Father stared into Sister Mary Martha's face before gathering in the entire circle with his glance.

A number of the sisters nodded to him, communicating their belief in silent accord. Several hands played with the tassels of their woven belts. Many eyes beneath lowered lids surreptitiously sought Sister Mary Martha's reaction.

The old nun did not look away from the priest's gaze. Nor did he melt under the steely glare of eyeglass and unflinching brown orb. "Sister, if you have something to say, now would be the time," the priest said. "And," he hesitated for the breadth of a heartbeat, "perhaps you would like to share with your good sisters how you have already been helping the church through this difficult period."

Another riffle of sound rippled around the group. Sister Mary Martha shifted her sight out the window past Maxo's shoulder. The artist thought he could hear gears churning inside the tall wimple on the iron-grey head.

The starch stiffness of her cornette snapped as she abruptly turned back to the group. "I have not had the opportunity to say as much to all of you, but Father knows that

I have been embarking on late night strolls in and about the church, hoping to identify or perhaps surprise whoever is responsible for these dark deeds. St. Nicholas has been my home for far longer than any of you," and she included the priest in this remark, "and I believe it is my obligation to see that the church is protected at all costs. With no commentary intended on your work, Mr. Vanka, it would seem that these incidents only occurred after your arrival. I have to feel that in some part this working at all hours of the day and night, and leaving the doors and windows of the church open when they had ought not to be has contributed to reaping these misfortunes."

Maxo stirred in his chair, but again, Father leapt in before he could comment. "Thank you, Sister, your point is quite clear, and I am happy that you have shared your practice and beliefs with the group. It certainly seems the perfect opportunity to open the floor for discussion for any of you that may have seen or heard anything that has seemed, well, unusual or out of place." He went on, " And one small clarification. Mr. Vanka has only once allowed the door of the church to remain unlocked at night while he worked, and he came to tell me right away of his error. I can assure you that it has not happened before or since that time.

"Now, for purposes of complete disclosure, I want to share that the police found only one small piece of evidence the night of the office window breakage." The circle grew smaller as the sisters leaned in to listen. "Some unknown person ran away from the scene that night, but we know that he – or she – wore a size 10 ½ oxford shoe." Like someone had hit a switch, feet scurried beneath habit skirts – rabbits hiding in the tall grass.

Father cleared his throat and clapped his hands. In unison, the group jumped in their seats. "So, my friends and colleagues – now you know everything that we know. Please think. Is there anything you can share that might shed light on these problems?"

The priest studied the faces before him and waited. Sister

Margaret Claude meditated upon her toe tips. Sister Alfreda Magdalene pulled in her lips, a frightened gleam in her eye. A younger nun, Sister Mary Helen, looked eagerly into his face, but a movement to her right let her know that Sister Mary Martha was watching. She dropped her eyes.

After two full minutes of silence had passed, he said, "Very well. I understand that it is hard to recall things upon demand. But now that you know the tough position we are in, I hope that you will feel free to come to me if you have some news or any thoughts. No matter how inconsequential you think they may be, they just might help." He stood up to dismiss them. "We had best get on with our days, everyone. The school children are arriving." He did not add his thanks.

Chairs scraped the floorboards and long black skirts exited the room whishing softly against each other. A curious silence fell behind them. Maxo was about to clear away the chairs when he noticed that Father had resumed his seat. His hands had assumed a prayerful attitude and pressed flat against each other before his mouth and nose. Irritation sketched the priest's forehead, and his eyes pursued far away thoughts. Maxo went to his chair and waited.

In a few moments, Father's attention returned to the living room. "Oh, excuse me, Maxo, no need to detain you from your work." When the artist's face questioned him, he said, "Just trying to think of what my next steps should be." He wiped his brow. "Whew! That was a stinker of a meeting!"

"Stinker?" Maxo asked. He pronounced it "stink-air."

A short laugh barked from the priest's throat. "Yeah, something that smells really bad, like rotten fish." No mirth from his eyes joined the laugh.

"Ah yes, it smelled of many things," the artist agreed. "Fear, suspicion, secrets, perhaps even lies. The Sister Mary Martha –"

"Yes, we should've strategized more about how to handle her," the priest said, running his handkerchief across the back of his neck. "She holds much stronger sway over the sisters than I would've thought. It's almost like she said something to them first, before they ever came into the room."

The priest squared his shoulders. "But you represented the situation quite well, thank you, Maxo, and now I must be off. Old Joe Blake is in the hospital again, and not doing so well this time, I hear." He began shifting the chairs back in place. "Maxo, let's keep thinking of these things during the day and meet up later. Will that suit you?"

Maxo held a dining room chair in his arms. "Yes, of course, Father, whatever works for you." He set the chair down and clasped his hands in a gesture of solidarity. "It appears the art of detection is not for the faint at heart, eh?" Then, he turned his back, picked up the chair, and left the room.

CHAPTER FOURTEEN

LIKE THE THIN STRAINS of a reedy flute, her voice came down the wire. "Papa, hello, hello! Papa?" In his delight to hear little Peggica's voice, Maxo's own voice caught in his throat, choked between laughter and tears. "Papa?"

Finally, he spoke. "My dearest darling, is it really you? I thought perhaps a tiny bird was calling me on the telephone."

"Oh, Papa, of course it's me," Peggy said. "Mama said I could call today. You know why, don't you?"

"Because the sky has turned green? No? Or perhaps the kittens have learned to bark?"

"No, ne, ne, Papa," Peggy giggled.

"Wait! Allow me one more guess, please," Maxo said. "Let's see. Is it because you have grown too tall to fit in the school house?"

"Oh, Papa, you're full of beans!" Peggy hooted.

"Full of beans? Full of beans? Who says this?" Maxo faked an angry voice.

Peggica laughed even harder, and then she said, "Grandpapa, that's who!"

They chuckled with each other over the long distance call.

"Oops, Mama says I need to hurry now, but Papa," Peggy said, "all of your guesses were wrong. I'm calling to wish you a happy birthday! Happy birthday, Papa!"

"What? It surely cannot be my birthday yet!"

"Well, it is. You've been there painting so long, you probably painted right through your birthday," Peggy explained. "Anyway, I wanted to let you know that I'm sending you something in the mail. Mama says I have to go now. Bye-bye, my Papa."

"Au revoir, my little sparrow. Keep well, and thank you, my darling, thank you for calling."

"Love you, Papa. Bye!"

The line clicked as Maxo whispered, "I love you, too" into the mouthpiece.

He set the phone back in its place on Father Žagar's desk and walked through into the kitchen. Stringing green beans at the kitchen table, Mrs. Dobrovic raised her head. "Everything all right at home?" she inquired.

"Indeed, yes, hvala," Maxo said. "Thank you so much for fetching me from the church for the call. It was my dear little daughter, Peggy, or Peggica as I call her."

"Peggica. That's cute," Mrs. Dobrovic said.

"She is mignonne, very cute," Maxo told her. He picked up one of the green beans and crunched it between his teeth. "It appears that I have missed my own birthday. Peggica called to give me her warm wishes."

"Oh, Mr. Maxo," the cook slapped her cheek. "There now, I wished I would've known. I would have whipped together a birthday surprise for you." She looked around the kitchen as if hoping one might appear.

"Good Mrs. D, there is hardly any need for that, as well as you feed me every night and morning." Maxo's face reflected reassurance. "In truth, while I am glad I was born, as the years go by, the day does not hold as much meaning unless I have my Peggica to celebrate with me."

"Very likely, I'm sure," Mrs. D's loose bun bucked at the nape of her neck as she nodded in vigorous agreement. "Will you be back off to the church, then?"

"Indeed, yes," said Maxo. "I have begun work on the last great piece, and as I must range across the entire ceiling of the apse, there is not an hour or a minute I can sacrifice at this stage. A bientôt, Mrs. D, see you later!"

The sunset shot fiery peach shards through the silhouetted branches of the trees as Maxo crossed from the rectory to the church. September and early October had brought a blazingly hot Indian summer to the Pittsburgh region, but now as the sun sank, the feel of autumn hinted cool and restless around the edges of the heat.

No chance I will leave the church doors open tonight, Maxo thought. *I will want to preserve any warmth that I can.* And thinking this, he pulled the vestry door to and latched it behind him.

He flipped on the light switches, and the tall skeleton of an enormous scaffold appeared in the center of the church. It balanced carefully in the central aisle, its opposing struts taking up the better part of the pews to either side of the upright. From where he stood near the door, Maxo leaned back to take in the view. The intent of the ceiling mural would be to depict the transcendence of Christ, but he also hoped that it would encompass and draw together all of his works to date to show that even the worst that life had to offer could be surmounted through conviction and faith.

It was by far the largest mural that Maxo had undertaken at St. Nicholas, though perhaps not the most powerful. None-the-less, he believed it was the critical piece needed to finish his work in the church.

Looking up, he surveyed the two long ceiling ribs that bisected each other as they sprang from their supporting columns. The architectural structure created the space for four scenes of equal dimension. Between the beams, a night sky glimmered down on him. Thousands of stars peppered the spaces, and Maxo could see that the effect worked well.

He had already laid out the places for dozens of angel faces along the ribs, but tonight's work would involve completing at least one of the four sketches that would fit within them. He would begin in the quadrant furthest from the altar. It made sense to him that this area would depict Christ's descent into Hell. Its corresponding panel, closest to the altar, would epitomize Christ's victory over death, and His final ascension into Heaven.

The work only required a simple palette since Maxo painted the faint outlines in blacks and greys. Regardless, soon the drawing occupied him completely. The apse hummed with his voice as Maxo trolled out the lines of a Croatian folk tune, then some ditties he had learned during the war, and finally some of the jazzy ragtime revivals his friend, Louis, had exposed him to in the clubs of New York. As he guided the brush in broad strokes, his shoulders moved fluidly, as though they danced to his music making.

However, when it came to adding the fine detail, Maxo's voice dropped to a low hum and sometimes stopped altogether while he concentrated on achieving just the right touch. He settled into a comfortable pattern. Broad strokes. Song. Detail. Hum. Climb down, check progress. Assess effect. Climb up, make changes. Broad strokes. Song. Detail. Hum.

So the evening drifted by, and into this pattern dripped thoughts from earlier that day. *Father certainly has his work cut out for him. No answers on anything yet, except Johnny, bless him. The men are still conducting their interviews of the male parishioners. And Sister Mary Martha.* He shook his head. *Something more complex there than either Father or I could have imagined.*

He outlined the flames of Hell and at the same time, reflected on the faces that had sat around that morning circle. *Not that I associate them with Hell,* he chortled to himself. But his decision to place his back to the living room window had worked out well. Every face had been defined by the early sunlight, and he had seen perhaps more than the nuns intended to reveal.

The gleam of suspicion in Sister Mary Martha's eye had not escaped his notice, and he considered her pose an act of defense. She had consciously chosen to fold her hands on top of her large belly, the picture of complete relaxation. *Too bad her spine gave her away,* Maxo thought. *A ramrod shoved through it could not have been stiffer. Yes, her posture was defensive. Prepared to repudiate the unknown: where the conversation might lead and what it might force her to divulge.* "Had not she said as much when she challenged me?" The artist threw out the question to the ceiling.

Maxo's memory moved on to the other nuns' faces. Many had stared into their laps, but even these faces could be read. They looked smooth but drawn. Lips clasped shut for fear words would escape. Tiny lines of tension creased foreheads, tugged eyes, and pulled mouths down in unintentional frowns.

Maxo stopped in mid-song as he recalled Sister Alfreda and Sister Claudetta. Alfreda's gaze had bounced all over the room like a rubber ball searching for a place to land. Claudetta's eyes floated from place to place, seemingly of their own will. Neither nun ever sought the face of another person in the room. Without meaning to, the two sisters had stirred something unwanted within the artist – a sort of apprehension that things were off kilter, out of balance. In any case, the roiling in his stomach did not prevent him from taking their measure.

Sister Alfreda's eyes appeared rheumy and reflected the light in a way that made him think she might burst into tears. *She is afraid of something, the good sister Alfreda,* Maxo thought, *but what? Sister Mary Martha? Or something more frightening? The knowledge of wrongdoing? Surely not the specter! Her tortured expression might well represent that kind of fear.*

Sister Claudetta's face held his interest longer. He estimated her age to be in the early fifties, and though somewhat heavy-set, he would not say she was overweight. Her face was broad. In fact, her cheeks appeared somewhat squeezed by the wimple, and more than once, he had caught her lips in motion, like they were giving her advice. Her eyes struck him the most. They reminded Maxo of the eyes of warhorses – wide, dread-filled, unblinking and unfocused. *That one, I believe she is in her own world most of the time,* Maxo said to himself. He wondered what, if any danger that could portend.

Two young nuns had sat together directly across from Father Žagar. Sister Mary Helen and Sister Catherine wore the simple head drapes that made him think they might be novices. They possessed the smooth skin, bright eyes, and pink lips of youth. Despite the head coverings, Maxo could see that both young women were quite beautiful. He could have kissed the high Slavic cheekbones and large almond eyes that made him think of his sisters in Croatia. The young women had been attentive, even eager, to learn what Father and Maxo had to say. *They certainly seemed to want to contribute to the dialogue,* Maxo thought.

He paused in his reflections to squirt more black onto the palette, and with a long, dry brush, he continued to complete the scene before him. As he thought back on the morning gathering, he shook his head. *Perhaps a group meeting had not been* the *best way to go. For sure, if they had been on their own, the two novices, or at least Sister Mary Helen, would have spoken. Come forward with her ideas.* Maxo frowned. He hoped they had not ruined the opportunity to learn something more from the nuns by acting too hastily.

Then he smiled a bit as he sketched the feet of Jesus. They had learned something, in any event. All of the nuns, whether young or old, wore black oxford shoes, and some of them possessed feet as large as any man's. He looked forward to sharing these thoughts with Father later that night.

Well past midnight, Maxo finally recognized the ache that wrapped his spine like a snarled vine. The pain, though not debilitating, reminded him that once more he had pushed his body to the limit. Time to bid the church good night. He closeted his things, extinguished the chandeliers, and trundled toward the exit at the front of the church. Just as he opened the door, a loud scrape sounded from the back of the church. A start of surprise rushed up his back. His thoughts had already flown to the rectory, the warmth of the living room, and the enjoyment of a light snack before bed, so the disturbance caught him off guard.

Now the moment seized him, arresting his back muscles and his steps. He stood silent and motionless, straining to listen for what would come next. He could hear his heart banging against his ribs, but could anyone or anything else hear it, too? A deep breath slid into his lungs, attempting to slow his heartbeats. In the next moment, they raced to a higher pitch yet.

A low moan issued from the back hall. It lasted for the length of a day. The muscles on the back of Maxo's head gripped so tightly, he thought his scalp might tear apart. With infinite care, he reached for the nearest switch.

Light restored silence. Maxo craned his head around, but seeing nothing, he looked back through the open door to the garden and rectory beyond. A sigh stretched through his rib cage, and he turned to drag his feet toward the rear of the church. In the back hall, he flipped on another light, and then another. They illuminated the quiet, empty corridors and nothing more.

Maxo knew he would have to enter the office. The scraping had sounded very like a piece of heavy furniture being forced across the floor. Perhaps the desk or a bookcase had been shoved out of place. He reached around the doorjamb to throw the light switch before he crossed into the room. The broad back of the old oaken desk presented itself and appeared untouched. However, when he circled around the desk, a flurry of folders and papers skittered under his feet. Then he saw the file drawer. It had been removed and shoved – no – jammed underneath the desk till it had wedged hard below the shelf that usually held it.

Maxo ran an open hand over his moustache, mouth and beard. It caught under his chin as he studied the disarray. He crouched to get a closer look. They appeared to be ordinary files. Some detailed the church's expenditures, others stored past sermons, and still others listed the church personnel.

He was predisposed to tidy the mess before Father arrived the next day, but a stronger instinct told him to hold off. The scattered files meant nothing to him, but perhaps Father would be able to interpret them.

Maxo had just arrived at this decision when a swish and a slam jerked him back to the present. This time, he did not hesitate. He ran from the office, down the side aisle, and up to the front of the church. The vestry door had clapped shut, but he did not believe for one second that the wind had propelled it.

This time, the artist was quick to turn off the lights and firmly close and lock the vestry door. He jiggled the handle for good measure, and finding all in order, quickly traversed the sidewalk leading to the rectory's kitchen door, anxious that no second be wasted. This time there was a good chance of catching someone.

Maxo flounced through the kitchen, shedding his smock like an old cape and tossing his hat on the back of a chair. He rushed into the living room, where a silence as deep as the church's greeted him. A tray of fruit and cheese awaited him, along with a teapot huddled under its cozy. Next to this, he spied the note.

10:45 PM. Dear Maxo, it began. *It seems whenever we find ourselves on the brink of discovery, I am called away to somebody's bedside. Home as soon as I can. F.Z.*

Maxo re-read the note, and then sank into the right hand chair of the twin wingbacks flanking the fireplace. He half lay on his back, shading his brow with his right hand and running a forefinger over the worn brocade pattern on the chair's arm with his left. He shook his head. That sort of note usually meant he would not be seeing Father until breakfast, if then.

Was there someone else he could enlist? Maxo sensed the minutes speeding by along with the probability of capturing anybody. He poked around the fruit and cheese tray, consumed a small lump of cheddar, and drank only a half-cup of the lukewarm tea. Fatigue fell over him like a drop cloth. Disappointment rimmed his eyes.

"Ah well, there is nothing for it but to talk with the good Father in the morning," Maxo confided to the room. He raised himself from the chair and shambled off to bed.

A chill drizzle greeted Maxo when he crossed from the rectory to the church the next morning. He was glad for the companionship of his felt fedora, but his turned up shirt collar had done little to protect him as he stepped beneath the dripping roofline of the vestry door. As he had predicted,

Father Žagar had not yet returned.

He examined the lock on the latch. No sign of tampering. He had been concerned that the intruder may have decided to return last night. He was pretty sure he had interrupted him. *Or her*, he reminded himself.

Once inside, the assortment of odors found in old buildings when rain and must collude assaulted his nose. The light from the chandeliers did little to dispel the dinginess of the interior. The clouds outside mounded at the windows as though trying to muscle their way in.

Maxo looked up at the rickety pile of scaffolding with considerably less enthusiasm than he usually felt. "Most would say, a good day for staying in bed," Maxo said to the empty space.

"But that's not your style, is it?" Father said from the entryway. He paused for a second to shake the water from his umbrella, and then thrust it into a nearby stand.

"Father!" Maxo said. "At last, you return. I was very sorry to have missed you last night."

Seeing that Maxo was bursting with something to say, Father sat on the nearest pew and gestured for Maxo to do the same. The story of last night's intrusion came pouring out of the artist's lips.

"Imagine my surprise, Father," he said, "after such a peaceful evening of work. To be shaken by the noise, the mess made by the papers, the proof that there is indeed a perpetrator of flesh and blood, that is d-d-doing all this." He waved his arms indiscriminately around the church.

Father leaned over and placed a hand on Maxo's shoulder. "Once again, I'm so sorry that these things always happen to you." Then he adopted a more practical tone. "But, perhaps we should have a look at the church office and see what's what."

Together, they bent over the papers on the office floor. Father's voice sounded cramped as he stooped to pick up some files. "In any event, if we needed more evidence of a living, breathing culprit, you've found it."

"But, Father," Maxo said. "Should we not leave these

things *in situ* for the police?"

"Truthfully, I think that they'd tell the officers very little," Father replied. "For one thing, there would be many sets of fingerprints on the files; and for another, as you told me earlier, there doesn't seem to be any mystery or reason behind which files were tossed." He studied the floor. "In fact, this looks like a pretty random act of nonsense. All it really does is give me another tedious couple of hours of work straightening files. Come, help me stack them on the desk at least, and save my poor back from grief."

In short order, they organized the files by category on the oak desk's surface.

"Great, thank you!" Father clapped his hands. "This will give me a good head start this afternoon. I'll come over and work alongside you on this dismal day. As you observed, a good day for being tucked inside."

The two friends walked toward the front of the church. "Oh, Maxo, I nearly forgot what I came in to tell you."

"Oh, yes?"

"I've had a note from Sister Mary Helen. She's requested a meeting right after school tomorrow."

"Really?" The artist could not keep the surprise out of his voice.

"Well, it appears," the priest said, "that Sister Mary Martha will be spending tomorrow afternoon downtown and won't be back till late."

Maxo could not help feeling excited at this news. "Excellent! Any chance I may listen in?"

"Of course. We'll plan it for tea time, if you feel you can pull yourself away for a break then." Father also assured him that he would be up and about until late that evening, if they wanted to have a talk over Maxo's midnight snack.

When Maxo had retrieved his palette and climbed the scaffolding, he noticed that the atmosphere in the church had lightened. The clouds, though still present, had released their clutch on the church by several degrees. He began sketching in earnest then, vowing to complete the drawing of the descent into Hell by the end of the day.

It felt even better when, true to his word, Father returned after lunch to see to the files in the office. Maxo wiped his forehead and basked in a renewed sense of well-being. Though as an artist he conducted most of his work alone, in this particular case, he now realized how much more comforting it was to have someone in the church with him. There would be no random appearances of ghost or transgressor while they were both there.

Up on the top level of the boards, Maxo put the finishing touches on the first sketch. He stretched and cracked his knuckles. Down below, he could hear the quiet shuffling of paper and the off-key whistle of the priest as he worked. For one who could sing the mass so perfectly, Maxo wondered where his whistle had gone wrong. Never the less, the small sounds soothed him, and he felt more peaceful than he had in a long while.

Maxo checked his palette and then walked to the opposite side of the scaffold. He had elected to sketch Christ's ascendance into heaven next before painting either scene. He wanted to be able to verify that each appeared in proportion to the other when viewed from the church floor. From his arsenal of brushes, he plucked one with a three-foot handle. It provided his only means for reaching the higher parts of the ceiling.

The afternoon wore on, and Maxo's sketch descended from the heights to a point where he could sit cross-legged on the wooden boards to continue to paint. He could hear Father chatting on the telephone. At least, he assumed he was not talking to himself. *Not like me*, Maxo laughed.

An old Croatian lullaby that Mati Dora used to sing crooned in his head. Soon he was humming it out loud and reminiscing about his early days in the Croatian countryside. As a young artist, he had toured along the Kupa River gaining sights and sounds and smells that he would later weave into his work, but those youthful days in the Zagorje Hills, though tough, had left their imprint on his mind. Views of steep hills rolling away one behind the other to the distant blue mountains hovered before his eyes. Closer to home in the Jugova garden, he could see green grass, baby birds, and tiny forget-me-nots. Though small, the garden had yielded a rich feast for the eyes, especially in the spring. Once more, he was Mikula, dressed in his finest shirt, hanging over the front gate, waiting, watching for the woman in the distance. She arose in his mind's eye, beautiful, young, a picture of high fashion and allure.

A sudden gust rattled the church windows and sent a draft caroming around the rafters. It drove him back to the present, sharply aware that he may have triggered a change of some kind. Maxo looked below and around the chancel and choir. Seeing nothing, he refocused on the work before him. He heard Father tinkering with something in the back hall.

As swiftly as the wind had come, so a thought flew into Maxo's mind. *I can tinker, too.* It dawned on him that no major plan to confront the specter of the church need be drawn. He would simply summon the ghost and contest his presence there. *Instead of him coming to haunt me at a time of his own choosing,* Maxo thought, *I will decide the time and circumstances of our next meeting.*

Maxo grabbed the top of his head with both hands as his brush dribbled paint on his trousers. All at once, he had figured it out. *This is what happens when you only think of something indirectly*, he told himself silently. *Understanding comes on its own terms.* Now, he realized that the spirit generally put in an appearance whenever his thoughts drifted to the woman in the distance. For reasons he could not explain, thinking of her attracted the ghost's attention.

He vowed to exercise his plan the very next evening, when he would be alone and locked in the church by himself. He would see to that. No point in having his plan confounded by friend or intruder. Only Father Žagar would know what he was trying to prove.

The simplicity of the plan astounded Maxo. How had he not thought of it before? Satisfaction filled his chest. At once, the challenge of the ceiling mural became easier, and Maxo's spirits soared to the boss that secured the highest point of the ceiling. He knew now that he could finish the painting with time to spare.

Father Žagar did not harbor the habit of pouring cold water on someone else's ideas, but he did not want Maxo to overlook an important point. That night as they stretched their feet toward the fire in the hearth, Maxo had shared his idea for calling up the ghost.

"My friend," the priest said. "I can't tell you how glad I am that you've finally hit on a plan for dealing with the apparition. I know how much it has plagued you these past weeks."

Maxo could sense another one of Father's famous "but's" about to surface.

"But," he smiled, "what is your plan once the spirit has actually materialized?"

"You know, Father," Maxo replied, "I have been giving that much thought." He scraped the last bit of cheese onto his bread. "One of the things that I have learned from previous encounters is that the ghost does not respond at all to shouting or sharp questions."

"Right, so you've said," Father agreed. "Nor, according to you, does it put in an appearance on the days when you are feeling particularly confident."

"That is the head of the nail, Father. You have hit it," Maxo said in a loud mumble as he chewed. He swallowed. "I believe that I must conjure him by thinking thoughts of the woman in the distance, and then when he comes, I must treat the spirit with respect and – and a certain degree of humility."

"I think that would strike just the right note," Father said.

"Then I will try my hardest to do as my Mati Dora's grandmother – her baka and mine – used to do. Speak gently – gently, but firmly. Try to understand why he is here. Help *him* to understand that it is all right for him to rest." Maxo dusted the crumbs from his hands onto his plate.

"So, basically, you'll try to get in tune with the spirit, and then offer your help," Father summarized. "I think that's quite admirable, Maxo, really, considering the amount of grief he has caused you."

"Truthfully, Father?" Maxo looked into the priest's eyes. "I am not sure that I did not inflict much of that fright and worry on myself. But in any event, it is of less consequence now. This plan is simply a matter of what makes the most sense, I think," Maxo said. "If one can make sense of these situations. Clearly he seeks something. Somehow it has something to do with this woman in my past. Perhaps he was a man from my past, but now, it feels futile to me to go on trying to figure that out. I am not even sure it is really that important."

Father nodded.

"What is most important is that he go to his rest," Maxo said. "Just as my baka helped spirits to lie down, so will I assist this specter to find his resting place." He folded his napkin and placed it on the tray.

Father got the signal. "Well, then," he said, rubbing his hands together, "how would you like to hear what I've discovered today?"

Maxo's eyes sparkled. "Ah, so there are new developments? I would love it if you would tell me." He poured some more tea into his cup and settled into his chair.

"Good," Father said. "First of all, we are meeting with Sister Mary Helen and possibly Sister Catherine tomorrow at 3:00 p.m. Second – and I've known this for about a day now, but we haven't had a chance to talk – my investigative team has finished their survey."

"Oh?"

"And without exception, without exception, I tell you, Maxo," Father slapped a knee, "not one of the men could have been involved in the incidents at the church. Lou and Stephan have assured me that in every case they were able to verify the men's locations on the dates in question. So, unless one of their spouses or friends is covering for them –"

"Covering?"

"Shielding them from discovery," Father said, "they're all in the clear. Innocent, that is. Innocent, by God, and thank

Heaven."

"Are you including Lou and Stephan in this innocent category, too?" Maxo asked.

"Yes, that's the best story of all." Relief spilled from the priest's eyes. "Lou and Stephan were together. On the night that poor *Justice* had her face ruined, they were together celebrating."

"A mid-week celebration?" Maxo's eyebrows arched in doubt.

"Yes," Father said. "It seems that their blessed children decided that it was a propitious time to announce to their respective parents that they are engaged to be married. When she heard, Tilda – that's Stephan's wife – pulled together a special dinner to which the happy couple, their siblings, and all of the parents were invited. It's not the sort of occasion any of them would miss."

"And are they happy? The young couple? And the parents with this news?" Maxo said. "I know that I am not very strict about these things usually, but when it comes to my darling daughter, I expect Peggica's love to ask my permission for her hand."

"Not to worry, Maxo," Father laughed. "Old Lou would scarcely part with his daughter if he didn't think the young man was suitable, and I expect Stephan Junior understood that. He did the thing properly, and yes, I believe everyone is quite happy about the prospect. Young Stephan is already an associate accountant at the company that hired him, so Lou can look forward to his lovely Maria being well looked after."

"A toast, then, to the happy couple!" Maxo clinked his cup against Father's water glass, and they sipped their drinks.

"To the happy couple," Father said.

For several minutes, they both sat back in their chairs and stared into the fire. Finally, Maxo opened the discussion. "It seems much has happened since yesterday morning."

"Indeed," Father said.

"Why, we have not even had the chance to talk about the meeting with the sisters, and now it very much looks like …"

Maxo's voice trailed away.

"Yes," Father said. "Yes, it does."

The flames whispered in the hearth as the conversation lagged. Then, their voices clashed as they both spoke at once.

"Did you notice their shoes?" Father asked at the same time Maxo said, "What is it that is so strange about Sister Claudetta?"

"Oh, oprostite, Father," Maxo said. "Molim, please, you first."

"Well, I was simply making a point about their shoes. When I talked about finding the shoeprint, did you notice how every one of them tucked their feet up under their habits?"

"For certain, I noticed," Maxo said. "It was rather like the day when you felt that perhaps you would like to hide your own shoes from the police officer. Like you, they all wear black oxfords. And at a guess, I should think that at least two or three sisters have feet that are size ten if not bigger."

"Yes, it was a funny reaction, because it's not as though we don't see their shoes every day. Although," Father scratched his head, "they had not become objects of interest before this, it's true."

"But in measuring their feet from memory," Father cast his eyes to the left, "I can think of three sisters for sure whose shoe size I'd like to know."

"Yes, me as well," Maxo said.

"Sister Mary Martha, Sister Claudetta, and Sister Alfreda."

Maxo nodded his agreement. "Exactly whom I would have picked. But to the right of Sister Catherine, who was that? She, too, has sizable feet."

Maxo watched Father's eyes search around the circle as though the nuns still sat before them. "Oh. That was, um, Sister Frances Geraldine. I don't think you've met her. She's the Latin teacher." He pursed his lips. "I suppose we will have to add her to the list, to be fair."

"Yes," said Maxo, "though it is far easier to attribute negative actions to the other three, if one were to be perfectly honest. Sister Mary Martha is defensive and somewhat aggressive. Who does she protect or what does she hide? We have asked this before."

"Right," Father said. "And Sister Alfreda. She's so nervous she makes me nervous. What's that about, do you think?"

"Perhaps she knows something as well and is truly frightened about knowing it," Maxo said. He sucked his moustache over his top lip. "Maybe she has been threatened, though I really do not think so."

He pressed a crumb on his plate with the tip of his finger. "Then, there is Sister Claudetta. That one, she does not make me nervous, but she disquiets me all the same. She is not quite right, is she?"

Father said, "If I remember correctly, there is some history with her – some nervous condition. Its name escapes me. For the most part, she behaves normally, but I think when she feels pressure, then these odd behaviors come out, like the unfocused eye or the way she flutters her hands. And those muttering lips. Br-r-r. She can give you a funny feeling, that's for sure."

Father readjusted his posture in the chair. His thumbs tapped together in a point above his lap.

"So, what about this Sister Frances?" Maxo asked. "Aside from rather big feet, I only noticed that she stared into her lap for the space of the meeting, though she did help herself to a rather large plateful of pastries and fruit at the beginning."

"How do you ever remember such details?" Father laughed. "I have to confess that I didn't really start my observations until after the breakfast was consumed."

"It is my habit, as you know." Maxo leaned his head to one side and looked at Father. "But in and of itself, there is nothing very culpable about eating a substantial breakfast, is there?"

They both chuckled at the thought. "No, if that's the worst she can do, I think we can safely eliminate her."

"Excepting that she has nothing to tell us about someone else, that is," Maxo added.

Their eyes drifted back to the firelight. Father blinked at

the onset of fatigue.

Maxo leaned over. "Father, is it about bedtime?"

Father licked his lips, then yawned. "Mm, it is, but I have one more thing I'd like to tell you."

"Yes, I am happy to stay and listen if you feel you can remain awake for five more minutes." Maxo regarded the priest kindly.

Father Žagar raised his head. "Of course. Of course, I can. But first, what's this I hear about your receiving a phone call yesterday morning."

"Ah," Maxo laughed. "I had a cheerful, pleasant work day," he said, "made even better by a phone call from my dear little daughter. You see, it appears that it was my birthday."

"Oh, Maxo," the priest said, "I'm so sorry that I missed it. We'll make it up to you on the weekend, I promise."

"No, no. No need, really, just telling you as part of why my day was so agreeable," Maxo said. "All day I worked, and the sketching came along well. In fact, I painted deep into the evening, even though I was only making the outlines. Eventually, a petite ache in my back reminded me that it was time to stop."

"Mm," Father said. "And that's when all this noise and bother began, right?"

"Yes," Maxo said. "I was just longing for my talk with you, and then my bed, when it all happened."

"Well, the other thing I wanted to tell you about is related to that disturbance," the priest said.

"Interesting," the artist replied. "And you know, the more I think about it, the more I believe that whoever was here last night – in the church, I mean – wore a long skirt. It could be that it was a nun's habit, but of course, it could also be a chasuble."

The priest's mouth curled into what could have been a wry grin or a frown. "In any event, it turns out that the files did tell me something after all. I pretty much had to take them all apart to set things right, but it helped to have them sorted into general categories."

He lifted his water glass to his lips. "I was thankful to see that none of the financial reports were missing. While the church has no secrets, I don't think my council would like it if their business papers ended up in the public domain. Nor would I."

"Yes, this is the business only of the church members," Maxo said.

"On a bright note, I was able to organize my past sermons probably better than ever before," Father said. "Usually I'm in such a hurry following Sunday mass, that they just get tossed into a file folder which I always think I'll get to later and seldom do."

Father Žagar's face clouded over. "But of deepest concern to me were the personnel files. They contain details about every employee associated with the church or the school, and seem to be the ones that were the most scattered." He gulped some water. "So much so, that I began to form a theory. I believe the other files were mixed in to hide the fact that it was the personnel files the culprit most wanted to destroy."

Maxo waited. He could sense that a revelation was coming.

"You see," said Father, "once I had put all of the staff files back together, I found that two were missing. That's why I was at the church for so long today. I double- and triple-checked through all of the personnel files in case I was mistaken. But every other folder was in order. I couldn't find any misplaced items that might really belong in the missing files." He threw up his hands.

Maxo's ears prickled.

"Those files belong to Sister Claudetta and Sister Mary Martha." Father punctuated the sentence with a thump on his chair arm. "They detailed their background and their experiences at St. Nicholas. Sister Mary Martha's file was probably our oldest and most valuable, given her tenure here. That's not to say I don't value every file, and naturally, they should all be kept very, very private." The cloud on Father's face turned thunderous. "Maxo, someone has really crossed the line this time."

"But, Father, that is bizarre. For what reason would they be taken? Were there incriminations in these folders?"

"I don't think so, Maxo," the priest sighed. He threw his head against the chair cushion. "I just don't know." After a little while, he added, "For tonight, though, I have to admit that my mind is too tired to think of these things more. I'm really not coming up with any answers. Let's rest on it, and see what reveals itself in our dreams."

"Yes," Maxo agreed, "and remember, we still need to hear what Sister Mary Helen has to say tomorrow. I have the feeling it will be something important."

CHAPTER FIFTEEN

IT REQUIRED A STRONG ACT of determination to concentrate on his painting the next day. All of the discussions Maxo had held with Father Žagar over the past several weeks took turns prancing through his mind as he willed himself to focus on the ceiling. He had much yet to sketch and paint. He had so many questions still to be answered.

Observing Father Žagar at breakfast, Maxo thought that he appeared to be in worse shape than himself. Over the morning toast, the priest shared with Maxo that his dreams had rankled his nerves. One dream in particular reappeared again and again. In it, he was chasing someone. Every time he came within inches of catching him, the figure always disappeared over the next hill. He could never quite see who he was.

"That's why I'm so tired this morning," Father said. "I actually feel like I did all that running."

"In a way, you did, my friend," Maxo said. "It sounds like perhaps the dream was a necessary prelude to coming events." He had patted the priest's shoulder. "Do not be over anxious for today's meeting. Surely, it will take us one step closer to the truth."

He wished he could have been as sure himself. Maxo had to admit that his anticipation about the talk with Sister Mary

Helen had grown well out of proportion. He knew he was pinning far higher hopes on her information than it probably warranted. In addition, he had not forgotten the promise he had made to himself. Tonight would be the night. Tonight, he would confront his own demon.

At the thought, Maxo's stomach flopped around like a fish on land. The brush fell from his hand and clattered down the three stories of scaffolding. "Dovraga!" he muttered under his breath. He passed a hand across his forehead as though to rub out any more bad thoughts. Maxo never wished any day away, but he realized that he could not wait until this one was over.

In a stronger effort to pull his thoughts far from the impending encounters, he began to rework the ascension of Christ with a fresh brush. *This must be a painting of sparkling wonder. One that will spur hope and fill the viewer with a sense of light and peace*, he told himself. The trick worked. As he opened the door to more positive thinking, Maxo glided into a state of engagement with the ceiling sketch that remained undisturbed until Cara came from the rectory to fetch him.

"Mr. Vanka," she called softly, her face aimed at the distant ceiling. "Mr. Vanka?" she said again, her voice raising a note higher in question.

Maxo's face slid into view, floating above the boards of the scaffold. "What is it, anđeo?"

She blushed even though she had heard the artist call all of the children angels. "Father says to remind you that it is fifteen minutes before your afternoon meeting. He thought you would like to know."

"Ah, yes, already?" Maxo said. "Thank you, dear Cara, tell him I will come momentarily." He smiled, and then spun around to gather his brushes and palette. Quickly climbing down, Maxo retrieved the fallen brush, stowed his materials in the locking closet, and ran out the door. He arrived in plenty of time to wash his face and hands and don a new shirt before the young sisters knocked at the door.

Father hurried to greet them and ushered both Sister Mary Helen and Sister Catherine into the living room. A steaming pot of tea and a dish of cookies stood waiting for them on the table before the divan.

"Please, please, come in," Father said. "May I pour you some tea? And you must try some of these oatmeal cookies." He bit into one and caught a crumb from the corner of his mouth. "You really must. They're loaded with nuts and raisins. Mm, delicious!"

The two young women looked at each other, then at Maxo, and then back at each other. "Forgive me," Father said. "Let me formally introduce you to Maxo Vanka. I do not believe he's had the pleasure of your acquaintance before. Mr. Vanka, this is Sister Mary Helen." Maxo bowed over her hand. "And Mr. Vanka, Sister Catherine." Again the brief, polite bow.

"Please, please, let's all be seated," the priest said. "I've asked Mr. Vanka here again as a measure of propriety and because, as you heard the other day, he has been intimately involved in the occurrences at the church."

The nuns sank as one onto the sofa and accepted the teacups Father held out to them. Maxo and the priest sat opposite in two upholstered chairs.

"Now," the priest began, "if there is nothing else needed to make you comfortable, let's get on with our discussion. And Sister Mary Helen, please let me say how very grateful I am that you have stepped forward to speak with us. Of course, anything that either of you say will stay within the confines of this room. You have my promise, and," Father looked in Maxo's direction, "Mr. Vanka's pledge that we will not speak of these things to anyone except ourselves."

"We understand, Father," Sister Mary Helen said. She was a year or two older than Catherine, and took the lead in the conversation. "It's just that, well, with Sister Mary Martha, there wasn't a chance to say these things before."

"Did she forbid you to talk to me or to us?" Father gestured toward Maxo.

Sister Mary Helen nibbled at the edge of a cookie. "Well, not in so many words. But we got her meaning all the same, didn't we, Sister Catherine?"

Pale and blonde, Sister Catherine nodded and then dropped her eyes to her lap.

Father smiled, though to Maxo's mind, the tight line of his lips looked rather stern. "Look, I don't want you to worry about Sister Mary Martha right now. I know she's your superior, but I am hers. That gives me the right to speak to anyone on staff that I wish. Do you understand that?"

Both women nodded.

"All right," Father folded his hands and leaned back slightly. "What is it you wish to share, Sister Mary Helen?"

Sister Mary Helen licked her lips and explained. "There's a reason I brought Sister Catherine with me today. I mean, I can tell you what happened, but I thought it would be best if you heard it from her, since she's the person who actually saw it."

"That sounds reasonable," Father said. "Please, continue."

The young nun ran a finger down her cheek. "If I remember right, it was the night that Mr. Vanka's painting got ruined. I don't know if you know it or not," this remark she addressed to Maxo, "but the younger nuns do some housekeeping for the older nuns. I'm assigned to Sister Alfreda and Sister Mary Martha, and Catherine does Sister Frances' and Sister Claudetta's rooms."

"Anyway, that night Catherine found Sister Claudetta's room in more of a mess than usual." She glanced at Father. He waved her on. "Sorry, I feel a little like a traitor saying all this. Anyway, Sister Claudetta's not the most organized person, and so it involved picking up her things, folding clothes, putting them away – that sort of thing." She glanced at Catherine. "Maybe you should tell the rest."

When Sister Catherine hesitated, Father said quietly, "So, you found something."

Sister Catherine fingered her rosary beads, and then regarded the priest's face. Her bottom lip caught between her teeth for a second before she said, "I was straightening her habit when I noticed something sticky on my left hand."

"Wait," Maxo asked. "Where was Sister Claudetta at the

time?"

"She was in the washroom," Sister Mary Helen answered for Sister Catherine. "That's usually when we get into their rooms – when they're out of them – so we don't disturb their prayers or their sleep. That's the idea, anyway."

"Yes, that's right," Sister Catherine dipped her head toward Sister Mary Helen. "I was cleaning while Sister Claudetta used the washroom."

"So, what was this sticky substance on your hand?" Father asked.

"Well, as you know, the lights aren't very bright in the nuns' cells, so at first I couldn't tell," Sister Catherine said. "But when I brought my hand right under the light, it was streaked with red." Her eyes shone with horror at the recollection. "At first, I thought it was blood, so I felt a little faint. I've never been much good around blood. That's why I decided to teach instead of nursing at some hospital."

Father waited, though Maxo had uttered a low "oh" at the mention of the color.

Mary Helen, impatient, jumped in. "But, when Catherine turned her hand over, she realized that there were also smears of blue and brown and black on her hand."

Sister Catherine resumed her own story. "So, I knew then that it had to be paint, and that it must have come from Sister's habit. I pulled the material off the hanger and went over it inch by inch under the light." She paused to sip her tea thirstily.

"And?" Father's folded hands tightened their grip on each other.

"At first I couldn't find anything." Breath hissed from both men. *Was there no real answer forthcoming?* Maxo thought.

"Then, I suddenly remembered that I had to turn the sleeves of Sister Claudetta's habit right side out to get it on the hanger. They'd been rolled up, and they were all wrinkled." She paused again, and Maxo thought perhaps she did it for effect.

"Then?" Father's tone was tinged with impatience.

"I turned them inside out again, and sure enough, the left sleeve seemed to have all the colors of the rainbow smeared inside of it. I touched it carefully, and the paint felt quite damp."

Maxo jolted back in his chair but did not interrupt Sister Catherine's story.

"Then, all of a sudden," and here Sister Catherine swallowed so hard they could see the muscles bulge in her throat, "I realized that footsteps were coming down the hall. And voices. Not just Sister Claudetta's –" Again, she looked to Father.

"Yes, we know that Sister sometimes holds discussions with herself."

"Yes, so," Sister Catherine continued, "there were two voices this time – Sister Claudetta's and Sister Mary Martha's. I was scared then and didn't know what to do. I should've been done with the room by that hour, and I didn't want to get caught, especially with paint on my hands. But, but there was nowhere to hide, as you know."

"What did you do?" Maxo said gently.

"In the end, I decided I'd conceal my hand as well as I could and just apologize for being so late with my work, *and* take the punishment Sister Mary Martha would be sure to give me. I was rehanging the habit, with its sleeves right side out again, when both Sister Claudetta and Sister Mary Martha came in."

Sister Catherine stopped then and licked her lips. She looked down into her teacup. Her mouth twitched, first at one corner and then the next.

Father leaned forward. "Sister Catherine, is there anything else you wish to tell us?"

The bottom lip returned to its place between her teeth, and Sister Catherine, without raising her head, shook it.

Sister Mary Helen rubbed a circle around the younger novice's back. "It's all right, Catherine, I can tell the rest. You've done well."

She looked into Father Žagar's eyes. "There was one other thing – it could be a small thing or not." She reached for Sister Catherine's hand.

"Sister Catherine told me," said Sister Mary Helen, "that when the two older nuns came into the room – well, Sister Claudetta was her usual, kind self. She said, 'hello, dear,' or something like that to Sister Catherine and floated over to her bedside. Sister Mary Martha couldn't have acted more differently, however. She didn't exactly fly into a rage, but in a voice as cold as steel, she said to Catherine, 'What are you still doing here? I'll see you in my office at eight a.m. sharp. And give me that!' She snatched Sister Claudetta's habit right out of Catherine's hands and jammed it into a ball under her left arm."

Sister Catherine began to weep. The tears slid down her cheeks without a sound. Maxo whipped a fresh handkerchief from his pocket and handed it to her across the table. "There, there," he said. "There, there."

Father Žagar sat straight and cleared his throat. "Thank you. Thank you both," he said. "You have told your story quite clearly, and there is no reason to be afraid any more." He replaced his teacup on the tray. "Sister Catherine, I am so sorry for the anguish and suffering you may have endured because of this situation. I ask you only to find it in your heart to forgive, if you can. Please be assured, your secrets are safe with me. It is only fair to tell you, however, that I will take action because of what I have learned here this afternoon. I hope you can find some peace in knowing that you did the right thing. God bless you both, and thank you for asking to see me."

He stood to walk them to the threshold of the kitchen and was glad to note that despite their distress, both young women stopped to thank Mrs. Dobrovic for the afternoon tea. The cook uttered some pleasantry in return as she closed the door behind them. The mantel clock struck four.

Father rubbed his hands together as he returned to the living room. "I'm sorry to ask for so much of your time, Maxo, but if you would be so kind, let's take a minute to sort through what we just heard. I can see that you have something to tell me."

"With pleasure, Father," Maxo said. "It has been such a

strange day already, I am not sure I can redirect my thoughts to the mural at this moment. So, my time is your time, as it always is." He gave a smile and another little bow and followed Father as they moved into the wingback chairs opposite the fireplace.

"How about that?" Father's voice chimed out. "We progress, my friend, we progress!"

"Yes," said Maxo, "a most remarkable story."

"What? Don't you believe them?"

"Two innocents such as these? Yes, of course, I believe them." Maxo rocked his chest and shoulders in agreement. "I cannot think that there is any guile within either of them. It is simply that –" He hesitated.

"Simply what?" Father crossed his arms.

"That, now that we have heard it, the story sounds so obvious when we put it together with all the other factors." He held up a hand, its fingers wide. "One," he pointed to his baby finger, "we know that Sister Claudetta is capable of strange behaviors from time to time. Two," his ring finger, "she is a woman of some size and strength. Three," middle finger, "we have believed that Sister Mary Martha has been screening or as you say, 'covering up' for somebody. Four," his index finger, "Sister Mary Martha has been found in the church at unseemly times; five," his thumb came into play, "someone has taken pains to make specific personnel files vanish, and six," he slapped his palm. "Suddenly, in one big swoop, we have our two antagonists appearing in the same scene together." He massaged the end of his nose. "It simply strikes me as too flawless." As Father began to retort, Maxo said, "No, no. No, no. I do not mean that it is a story that will not hold the water, but I feel – it is a feeling only – I feel that there is something deeper within it that I do not yet see."

"But, Maxo, since we have already eliminated the men, we both agreed that the perpetrator is most likely one of the nuns that resides here." Father did not like the bloom being knocked off of his conclusions. "At the very least, Sister Claudetta has had opportunity, and what about that weird hooting you heard the other night in the church? Who would be most likely to make such a noise?"

Father shook his head in a wide arc. "No, I am afraid that Sister Claudetta's ailment has resurfaced in a most unsavory and perhaps dangerous way. I only regret that I've been rather out of touch with the sisters. You know, I let Father Sebastian do most of the school-related work, and I feel confident he would have told me if he'd noticed anything peculiar among them. They have been very, very careful to shield this from anyone's view."

Maxo's eyelids closed halfway, and he stretched his neck this way and that on his shoulders.

"I can see that you are not entirely satisfied, Maxo," Father said, "but I feel that I must take steps soon. And it is looking like we may need to find some good care for Sister Claudetta."

"I appreciate your sense of urgency, Father. The situation is not at all pleasant, and as we have found, quite frightening for someone to be causing such havoc in the church. But –"

"Before you go on – well, maybe this is part of what you were going to say next – but Maxo, what caused you to bolt upright when Sister Catherine was talking?" the priest said.

"Yes, that is an important thing, and it is part of why I suspect something more complicated is going on." Maxo's eyes roved the distance, regarding something beyond the rectory walls. "You see, I have always thought that the damage to *Justice's* face was caused by somebody that was left-handed."

"What? Why didn't you ever mention this beforehand?" Father sputtered. "We could have easily narrowed our field of suspects had I known. Honestly, Maxo!"

Maxo raised a hand to stop the torrent of words. "Father, I would never mention such a trait and perhaps falsely identify someone unless I felt very sure about it. How does one tell if something is caused or created or destroyed by a left-handed person? In the case of the *Justice* mural, I noticed that most of the marks started on the left side and shot up and to the right. In places where the smears circled around, they always went in a clockwise direction. Both cases made me think, hmm, this could be the work of someone left-handed. And I did not even think it was somebody trying to purposely mislead us by using his left hand instead of his right, because the strokes were too strong and too bold."

"That's a grand piece of observation, Maxo," Father said, "but is it of any use now that you've repaired the painting? It's not as though we have a photograph of the damage." He held his hands before him as though he were snapping a picture. "But, say it is true. Why bring it up now?"

"Because of Sister Catherine's story," the artist said. "If she was not mistaken in her description, paint residue coated the inside of the habit's left sleeve. She did not report any on the right sleeve. I have to believe that Sister Catherine knows the difference between the front and the back of a habit."

"I'm sure you're right about that," Father agreed. "But, Maxo, Sister Claudetta isn't left-handed. She's right-handed, for sure. Only the other day, I came upon her grading papers, making her thick, red marks with the pencil held in her right hand."

"That is as may be. But I noticed one thing else about left-handedness as Sister Catherine's and Sister Mary Helen's story unfolded."

Father turned his head over his left shoulder as though looking back on the two young nuns. Then, he smacked his forehead. "Maxo, do you mean the part when Sister Mary Martha balled the robe and stuck it under her left arm?"

"Yes," said Maxo. "Yes. That is exactly what I mean."

Father's shoulders drooped, and he sank lower into the old chair beside the fireplace. A silence dropped into the room, and only the mantel clock appeared undisturbed as its rhythmic tick-tock clacked out the minutes. Maxo fiddled with a loose button on his shirt and wished to silence the timepiece. Ripples across his jawline exposed the clenching and unclenching of his teeth.

His eyes shifted to the priest's face. His jaw pulsed again as he took in the mass of furrows on Father's brow and the hurt bewilderment that nestled deep within his eyes. In a voice one shade above a whisper, Maxo said, "I'm so sorry, Father."

That tripped some flashpoint in Father Žagar's mind. "Well, don't be!" He blustered the words in a loud voice. "Don't be, because I'm not buying it."

He straightened in his chair and looked at the artist. Remorse bit him as soon as he took in the sorrowful look on Maxo's face. Red-cheeked, he instantly returned to his normal speaking tones. "Maxo, look, it's just that Sister Mary Martha has been with the church and the school for a very long time. I have known her as St. Nicholas' most stalwart defender, in good times and bad. I also know that below that tough surface, she really does care for her charges, be they nuns with problems or schoolchildren. What you're suggesting is tantamount to some kind of sabotage."

Maxo hung his head. "An ugly word, that."

"Yes, yes, it is." Father nodded rapidly in concurrence. "That's why I'm having a very hard time even thinking of it as a possibility."

He took a quick sip of water. "I'll admit there are signs that point to someone using his or her left hand for some of these deeds, but I'm not quite ready to say that it's definitely someone who's left-handed, although your point about the swirls on Justice's face is a good one. As I sat here, I was thinking about how I use my right hand. If I'm wiping the kitchen counter or erasing a blackboard, I recall that I use a circular motion, but it is counter-clockwise – very normal for a right-handed person, I assume."

"Yes, I believe so," the artist said.

"So, to think about a left-handed person making clockwise circles seems plausible. But as to your other thought about Sister Mary Martha tucking the soiled habit under her left arm, I can't really agree with it."

Maxo's eyebrows arched. "Oh?"

"You see," the priest continued, "I thought of the countless times I've come over to unlock the church with an armful of books or bulletins or files, and had to shift them to one arm to use the other for the unlocking. Always, I put whatever I'm carrying in my weaker arm – my left – so that my dominant arm – my right – can do the job." Here the priest chuckled. "To tell the truth, I'm not even sure I can unlock a door with my left hand, it feels so uncoordinated most of the time!"

Maxo smiled, too. "Yes, I have heard that it is a funny, rather helpless feeling. I do not suffer from it so much myself as I often have to switch the brush from hand to hand in order to reach certain spots on a wall. But yes, I am in accord that the bundling of the habit under Sister's left arm is no solid proof, but what I would offer as a mere suggestion."

The priest scratched his neck. With a look, he appreciated the artist's willingness to step back from his earlier conclusions.

Maxo spoke again. "But, Father, while you were thinking about all of this, it seemed to me as though you looked very troubled. What is it that we should also be considering?"

"Ah, my friend, there is little I can hide from you," the cleric said. "At the same time I was thinking this through, I also felt a deepening concern for Sister Claudetta. She is a very sweet person, and in the past, has made significant contributions to educating our young people, but the fact is, her – well, I'll call them fantasy spells – her spells seem to be growing more frequent." He shook his head. "Also, there was something that I didn't tell you about as I placed no importance on it until this story came out today from Sister Catherine."

Maxo leaned in, giving Father his full attention

"After the breakfast meeting with the nuns, I was working in my office when a gentle knock came on the door. To my surprise, Sister Claudetta came in and asked for a word. She looked incredibly sad, and I tried to put her at her ease, but the whole time she sat before me, she fidgeted with her rosary beads and stared past my head for so long, I turned around to see if someone else was there, listening. In the end, I really couldn't get much sense out of her, except that she kept saying how very, very sorry she was about the incidents in the church, and how dreadful and frightening it must be for you and me, and for everyone, really. It was a bit pathetic but frustrating, too, because I couldn't get her to tell me if she'd actually seen anything."

Father rubbed the back of his head. "In the end, I concluded that her regret was due to her long-time feeling of responsibility for the church, and not necessarily because she'd had anything to do with these nasty occurrences, but it struck me as odd just the same. And I couldn't help myself, as she left the room, I looked at her feet, and if her shoes are not the same size as mine – 10 ½'s – then I'm a monkey's uncle."

"What?" Maxo said and barked a short laugh.

"Just an expression, Maxo. I mean, more fool I if her shoes are not the exact same size as mine," the priest said. "It gave me a little turn, actually. Mostly what it left me with, however, was a worry that Sister Claudetta's spells are getting worse. And now, of course, after today's revelations, I don't feel I can rule her out as a suspect."

"But, Father, do you truly feel Sister Claudetta would have the sophistication to plot out some of what has happened?"

"Well, the problem with some of these disturbed people is that they are very cunning. I would never have said that she was the type, but her mental state alters what I might think I know about her."

Both men ruminated on this for a short while. Then, Father added, "And since Sister Mary Martha fits the bill for having been in or near the church for some of these occasions, one very likely conclusion for me is that she is taking care to cover Sister Claudetta's tracks. And we both know that I would be the last person she would tell if she suspected one of her nuns, one of her charges, as the person behind all these grievous acts."

Once more, the room wrapped them in an ominous hush, and strangely enough, the clock was silent, too.

CHAPTER SIXTEEN

HIS BODY BOGGED HIM DOWN as Maxo heaved himself onto the scaffolding in the late afternoon. Clouds congested the sky once again, and their accompanying dreariness descended on the nave and Maxo's spirit. He never rejoiced at wrongdoing, and the fact that he knew these people – *ay!* Regret rained down that was far heavier than the gloom. While Maxo recognized that they were nearing a solution to the church's mystery, it did not eliminate the guilt he felt.

He slid his palms down either side of his trousers, and then selected a brush. Time to carry on with the sketching. He had yet to depict the angels that would flank the two Christ panels on the ceiling. Steadily, he outlined their fantastic wings. Feathery and full of light, and more than twice the body length of the figures, they signified the jubilation of the angelic company at Christ's resurrection.

Contrary to his usual sessions with the church walls, Maxo painted mechanically. For once, his absorption ranged away from the mural before him and back into the series of events that had brought him to this point. *To the place where it may be my finger that has done the pointing,* Maxo sighed to himself.

The destruction of *Justice*'s face rose first before him. *And to think*, he shook his head, *I nearly convinced myself that it was the specter's doing. I would sooner it was him than to cause Father all of this grief.* He jabbed dark spots between the fronds of the feathers. *It cannot be at all pleasant for Father to have to confront one of his own.* Jab, jab. *Far better if it had been a stranger.*

It struck Maxo as odd now that he could have believed it was the ghost's fault, but he understood why, in retrospect. Had he not generated one of his worst encounters with the spirit when he had painted that face? *The face of my – of the woman in the distance,* Maxo recalled. *Without fail, the specter appears whenever I think of her, and that time was no exception. In fact, actually having painted her face so beautifully, so exactly, I thought it had led the apparition to his first physical act of hatred towards me.* Maxo rested his brush on the palette and swept his sight back and forth across the ceiling. His eyes confirmed that the new figures matched the earlier ones in proportion. *Small wonder if I became more frightened each time he visited after that.*

In rapid succession, the other scenes flowed back through his mind. There had been the second incident of his palette and brushes falling victim once again. Then, the rock had been thrown at the office window, and they had made the discovery of the shoe print. What followed was learning that Sister Mary Martha had been lurking about the church at random hours, and that someone had left behind a mess of papers and documents in the office. Always sprinkled in and around these events were the ghost's appearances – his dreaded cold, the dimming lights, his growing boldness as he appeared to Maxo in the daytime and began to approach him. *Hardly amazing that I confused what the causes of these happenings might be,* Maxo thought. *Or at worst, some very clever planning on the part of Sister Mary Martha or yes, Sister Claudetta, to play upon my fears and confound the situation.*

For the space of a moment, Maxo hoped that somebody would get what she deserved, and if he were truthful, he hoped it would be Sister Mary Martha. On second thought, he began to regard whoever it was as an object of pity. *What rational person would behave in such a way?* He was sure that the good Father would try to find the right sort of help for her derangement.

He thought of poor, old Sister Claudetta. While her

behavior did appear to be offbeat at the best of times, from what Father had said, it sounded as though never a bad intention had found its way into her heart. *If it has, then she is a much darker horse than we believed. Of course, perhaps she carried out, what would one call it, her obsession – yes, an obsession – as a messenger from God. Yes, that would explain rather a lot.*

Somehow this last thought settled Maxo's mood. He retrieved his long brush and moved across the scaffold to work on the opposite panel. Here, too, angels would parade and celebrate the victory of life over death. His shoulders relaxed as his painting gained momentum and drew him into the work. He did not notice that the sun had set, and he was only slightly distracted by the movements below as Father and the nuns came in for evening prayer.

The service had ended, and silence refilled the nave. Maxo clicked the cramps out of his neck, and extending his arms behind his back, pulled his shoulders into a satisfying stretch. As he bent over to pick up his palette, he saw Father re-enter the church. He waved.

"Good evening, Father! And how are you?"

The priest smiled, but no teeth appeared in his usual broad grin. He shrugged his shoulders. "I'm doing as well as I can under the circumstances. Mrs. D cooked me a good supper, and I feel braced for the evening ahead. It looks as though it will storm later."

"Oh?" Maxo crouched to blend some more gray. "In my usual way, I am afraid I have not noticed the weather, except that I called to one of the altar boys to switch on the big lamps slightly before you came in for evening prayers."

"Maxo." The priest's voice held a question.

"Yes, Father?" Maxo said.

"My dear man," Father said, "I feel like I have placed so many demands on you recently that have nothing to do with why you came here, but –"

"My friend," Maxo said. "Never should you worry about this. How can I help?"

It was Father's turn to crack his neck before averting his

face to the ceiling. "It's just this. I've scheduled a meeting with Sister Mary Martha this evening, and since it is never appropriate for me to meet alone with a nun – that is, actually, Maxo, I would really value having you at my side when I talk with her."

He passed a hand over the back of his neck. "I know it won't be easy," he said, as though Maxo had objected, "but your being there will give me strength. You don't need to say anything. Just being there will be enough."

"All right. Rest easy, Father," Maxo called from the ceiling. "I will be happy to be there if it will be of any help to you. What time shall we say?"

Maxo watched Father depart. He had shot a silent wave to the artist and walked toward the side door with the steps of an aging man. "Poor Father," Maxo murmured to the angels. "Such is the life of a priest, eh?" He set aside his own disappointment that he would have to wait another night to engage the specter. After all, how could he compare that with the raw need that his friend now demonstrated?

Maxo arrived in the priest's office early per Father's instructions. Father had arranged three chairs in a crude circle, but he did not sit down. Instead, he paced back and forth in front of his desk.

"You know what bugs me the most?" It was a rhetorical question to the room rather than one directed at Maxo. The artist waited. "It wasn't just the destruction of property. And it wasn't that Sister Mary Martha lied to me – to both of us – on more than one occasion, and did a great job pretending to cover up for someone else." He pounded one fist upon the other. "It was how hard she tried to pin the blame on Sister Claudetta." His eyes smoked with anger as he connected with Maxo's face. "Now that's iniquity."

"Whoa, whoa, Father, hold the horses," Maxo said. "This is a change of heart from our last discussion, is it not? I left you pondering how you intended to help Sister Claudetta recover her balance. Now, in a seeming instant, it appears you have pinpointed Sister Mary Martha. Is this true? What made you change your mind?"

"I found evidence."

"Evidence?" The artist looked puzzled.

"I remembered that Sister Mary Helen said that Sister Mary Martha would be gone all afternoon," Father explained. "I made a flash decision to do something I never would've dreamed of. I resolved to search Sister Mary Martha's room. I had to find that habit, I just had to. I had a feeling about it."

Maxo sank back slightly in his chair and tucked in his chin. He cringed in fear of what he would hear next – what he already suspected.

"First of all, I made sure that no one saw me going into the convent," Father said. "I'm not interested in someone being able to give Sister Mary Martha any kind of warning about tonight."

"Anyway, I found her room spotlessly tidy. Not surprising for someone whose penchant for order borders on the compulsive," Father said in a factual tone. "As you've already heard the young Sisters say, there's really nowhere to hide anything in the nuns' cells. However, Sister Mary Martha, being head of the school, possesses a room that is marginally larger than the others. It affords her the space for a small desk, a chair, and a tall dresser and bookshelf combination."

Father licked his lips. "Initially, I didn't see anything that appeared disturbed. Clothing was neatly folded in the drawers, the books were lined up alphabetically, and the made up bed would've passed muster with the military." Father sat down next to Maxo. "I was about to give up, I'll tell you, thinking she might have already disposed of the habit, but I decided to have one more search around the room. Something had caught my eye the first go-round, but I couldn't seem to grasp what it was."

His eyes flicked to the top of the bookshelf in his study. He stood and pointed up to the highest shelf. "Suddenly, I had it. On the topmost shelf of her dresser, one book, a big book, stood slightly out of line with the others. I pulled her desk chair over and stood on it to reach it – a volume of prayers, as it turned out. More importantly, the space that was left revealed a bundle of black cloth stuffed behind the row of books. I grabbed it, and I've got it in the closet," Father gestured toward the study door, "right now."

"Does it still carry the paint from the palette?" Maxo asked.

"Well, that will be for you to determine from the colors," Father said, "but it certainly has crusted, dry paint in a variety of hues plastered onto the lower half of the inner left sleeve of the habit."

"Mon Dieu," Maxo said placing his fingers in front of his mouth. "But how - ?"

"How do I know it's hers?"

Maxo nodded.

"From the laundry tag," Father said. "You see, having no large washing facility here, we send the habits out once a week to the laundry. Since they all look alike, each sister sews her initials on a tab at the back neckline of the habit so that the right robes can be distributed to the right nuns. The label on the habit I found read M M. No one else in the convent has the initials 'M M' except Mary Martha."

A knock at the back door stemmed any other conversation, except a quick whisper from Father. "We have only to verify these actions with Sister Mary Martha, and then I will know what to do."

Maxo breathed out. *Would that it could be as easy as that*, he thought.

Mrs. Dobrovic showed Sister Mary Martha into the room, and then returned with a tray of tea things.

Sister Mary Martha dusted away Father's offer of refreshment with her hands. She pushed her chair back from the two men and sat straight and tall. She laced her fingers below the girth of her belly.

"Father," she said, cutting in before the priest had time to begin, "I really hope this won't take too long. It's a school day tomorrow, I've had a long and tiring trip to Pittsburgh, and I still have some papers to grade before the morning."

"Be that as it may, Sister Mary Martha," Father Žagar said, "what we have to discuss here tonight is of over-riding importance. Otherwise, I never would have intruded on your schedule." He stopped to pour tea for Maxo and himself. Sister held her pose so quietly that her chest barely moved up and down. She stared at Father in flinty silence.

"Sister, we are an open community here, and I am very disappointed that you did not feel you could bring your grievances to me, no matter what they involved."

"I'm sorry, Father," Sister Mary Martha said without a drop of sorrow in her voice, "I don't know what you're talking about. What grievances?"

So this is how it is going to play, Maxo thought. Father must have thought it as well. His next words were designed to shock.

"Your hatred of Mr. Vanka's art work. Your disrespect for our church. Your victimization of a helpless person."

Sister Mary Martha had maintained her stone face until this last comment. Anger burnt out of her eyes and a foreign smell tinged the air, not entirely pleasing.

"How dare you?" She stood.

"Please, sit down at once, Sister Mary Martha," the priest said, directing a finger at her chair.

Quivering, she retook her seat. She sniffed deeply. "I haven't the faintest idea what you're talking about. And as for Mr. Vanka's paintings," she spat the words, "if he cares to leave the doors and windows open, why, anyone could come in and damage the work. How dare you shove the blame that is his onto me?" Above her crossed arms, her face had turned an ugly, mottled purple.

"I dare, as you call it," said Father in a quiet, but firm voice, "because I have evidence."

"Let me guess." Sister Mary Martha tapped her elbows with her fingertips. "Sister Mary Helen and Sister Catherine, out of the goodness of their hearts, and knowing that I would be absent this afternoon, trumped up some story to tell you. And because they are young and beautiful, and I am but an old

– older than you – nun whose loyalty to St. Nicholas has never been questioned, you choose to believe them."

Father Žagar leapt to his feet. "That is quite enough, Sister Mary Martha." He flew to the closet and returned with the soiled habit. He exposed the paint-streaked sleeve to her view. "No more of your prevarication. How do you explain this?"

The purple slid from Sister Mary Martha's face and was replaced with dull alabaster. Her eyes continued to blaze beneath her brows. "Sister Claudetta," she said. "No doubt the young people have told you about finding it in her room. I only meant to protect her by taking it away."

"And by hiding it, I suppose," Father snapped. "You never thought to come to me with this – that there might be a seriously disturbed member of our community. It was your judgment that I should not be told, and you threatened the others if they spoke of this." He coughed with disbelief. " I can't think of any explanation you could offer that would excuse that. Truly, I cannot."

Maxo whispered in his ear as Sister Mary Martha composed a retort.

"Never mind that," Father stopped her in mid-breath. "Please come over to the desk and write your name for me on this piece of paper."

The nun did not leave her chair. "And if I refuse? I mean, it looks as though you have already tried and convicted me without bothering to hear my side of the story."

"I'll listen to your story," Father said, assuring her, "but if you have nothing to hide, why not write your name for us?"

Sister paused for a moment, dabbing a handkerchief to her eye. "Only an eyelash," she said and standing, walked over to the desk, took the pen in her right hand, and scrawled her name. It was barely legible.

"All right, thank you," Father said. "Now, write it again please with your left hand."

She scribbled her name once again. It was loopy and irregular on the page. Father labeled the signatures as right and left, and dated the paper.

"Again, thank you," Father repeated. "Please have a seat and tell us what you should have mentioned many months ago."

With no apology, the sister told a tale that was crisp and clear in detail. No date, time, place, or incident was omitted. Her story was remarkable for its chronological accuracy, and it occurred to both men that she must have been constructing it for some time in the event that she would have to meet with them.

The gist of her representation was that Sister Mary Martha, in shielding Sister Claudetta, had inadvertently implicated herself. It was Sister Claudetta who climbed the scaffold after purloining Sister Mary Martha's habit, who ruined Maxo's work and his palettes, who broke the office window and scattered papers, who stole the files that were missing. Sister Mary Martha only wanted to maintain peace at the church and prevent Sister Claudetta from being tossed out on the street with no one to care for her.

"That is all very well, Sister," Father said when she had finally concluded, "but you should have brought these facts to my attention many weeks ago. It's clear to me that help is needed." He stopped to choose his next words. "It makes me sad, Sister Mary Martha, that you could imagine I would throw Sister Claudetta to the wolves. I've never given you any reason to believe that."

Before she could retort, Father stood up. "I think that will be all for tonight, Sister. Thank you for coming, and thank you for sharing this information. I will give all of this further thought and speak with you again." He showed her out of the room, but not before she glanced one more time at the signature page on the desk.

"Where's Mr. Vanka?" Father Žagar asked Mrs. Dobrovic as he settled into his chair at the breakfast table the next morning.

"Oh, lord, he was in and out of here like a flash." She skipped one hand off the other to show how fast the artist had passed through. "He snagged one of them muffins there and a jar of water and said he had to make tracks." Mrs. Dobrovic smoothed the tablecloth in front of Father Žagar and set a large bowl of Cream of Wheat before him. "There, something to warm you up. It's turned downright chilly outside. Probably have a frost before too long." She huffed as she fetched a spoon that had fallen down the side of the stove.

As if Father had responded, she added, "Well, he didn't exactly say 'make tracks,' but you know what I mean. He was in a big hurry to get painting. Said he had in mind to get at least one full ceiling panel painted today."

Cautiously, Father sampled the hot cereal, and then blew on his first spoonful. "Very well," Father said between puffs. "I'll go and see him later."

"Oh, will you?" the cook said. "Because if you wouldn't mind taking it when you go, I promised him a thermos of coffee. I wouldn't ask, but it's cleaning day here, and then I said I'd help with the clothing drive this afternoon."

Father had picked up the morning paper. From behind it, he said, "Of course, just leave it in plain sight so I don't forget it when I go over."

Inside the church, Maxo had been busy on the scaffolds since the early hours. He had painted through mass unbeknown to Father, and the chanting of the age-old ritual had appeased him. He had woken feeling raw from a night that had been tempestuous, tossed with tense dreams and fitful half-waking. He had been more than glad when daylight came, and he could depart his bed.

Maxo could not say that his disturbed night surprised him. He went to bed brimful of trepidation and emotional strain. His mind cast back on the lengthy discussion that had followed Sister Mary Martha's departure from the rectory last evening.

After she left, Father had suggested a room change. "I'm going to turn on the gas hearth and pour us a warming drink which we'll enjoy by the fireside in more comfortable surroundings than this." His arm waved in a circle about the room to dispel the negative atmosphere the senior nun had left behind.

"If by a warming drink you mean something more powerful than hot tea," Maxo said, "I am all for it! Brrr!" his lips trilled.

Father smiled, appreciating the injection of a little humor, and led the way.

With Maxo to his right, they extended their legs from the wingbacks toward the fire. Each cradled a snifter of brandy in his right hand. Maxo held his glass aloft. "To discovery, and creative thought."

"Here, here," said Father, and he downed his first nip of the caramel liquor. "Ah, that's the ticket," he said, licking his top lip. The fire crackled in response as the artificial logs grew hot. "Well, we've gone and done it now, Maxo," he said, "but I give Sister Mary Martha full marks for persisting with her campaign of innocence." He took another sip. "I have to admit, her act was good enough to throw some doubt into my own heart from time to time during the interview. You?"

Maxo dampened his forefinger with the brandy and watched as it skated around the rim of his glass. "I think I had some reservations going into the conversation. For instance, I did not have the time to tell you my further thoughts about Sister Claudetta."

"Oh, what were those?" Father studied his snifter and the way the brandy coated the glass.

Maxo looked into the fire. "I was having difficulty picturing Sister Claudetta as an evil-doer when the only possible explanation struck me. If, in fact, it is true that she has some sort of mental disturbance, could she not think of herself as the right-hand of God or something, and carry out dark deeds in His name? I believe that sort of religious mania is not unheard of."

Father rubbed his chin where a new day's whiskers were beginning to sprout. "That is a thought, Maxo, to be sure, and one that I had not considered. It could clear up a number of points. Still."

"Still," Maxo joined his thought, "there is much now that presses in, after tonight's conversation, that sways me away from Sister Claudetta, disturbed though she may be." He sniffed his brandy and took another sip. "Back to Sister Mary Martha, I think for certain that we must never underestimate the high intelligence that resides beneath that wimple. I daresay she may be planning her next move as we speak."

"Much good it will do her," Father shook his head. "Unfortunately for Sister, she's left a rather wide trail of breadcrumbs for us to follow."

Maxo scratched his head for a moment. "Oh, breadcrumbs. You mean like the tale of Hansel and Gretel. But in this case, let us hope there is no flock of forest birds to eat the evidence."

"I don't think we'll have any worries there," Father said. "After all, I have the tunic of her habit, paint-spattered sleeves and all. In fact," he pulled himself out of his chair, "I'll go get it so you can judge for yourself."

Maxo could hear Father rummaging through the hall closet and swearing softly under his breath. "Damn it. Confound it, where did I put that thing?" Maxo swirled his brandy, while a weight of stone grew in his stomach. *Was nothing straightforward any more? Could Sister Mary Martha have somehow re-appropriated the garment?*

He could hear Father storming into the kitchen. "Mrs. Dobrovic!" he called. By now, Maxo was out of his seat and hurrying down the hall.

"Father, Father, she said she was going home as soon as she had cleared the tea from the nine o'clock meeting."

"Oh, Hades, so she did." Father's face looked stricken. "Maxo, the habit is not in the closet." He paced the kitchen. "I must telephone Mrs. Dobrovic no matter how late it is."

"One minute, Father," Maxo took him by the shoulders. "Think, where did you last see it?" The men searched each other's faces for an answer. "The study!" they both cried and flew down the hall. However, a quick search of the small room revealed no black vestment of any kind, either carelessly flung across a chair or thrown upon the floor.

Father slapped the surface of the desk hard. The signature

page flew to one side from the force. The priest captured it in one swift movement. "At least, we've not lost this." He moved to the telephone and lifting the earpiece, spun out the numbers on the dial as quickly as it would turn.

Maxo slumped into a chair feeling slightly ill. Father held his hand to his chest willing his heart to stop pounding so hard. On the other end, the phone rang five times, six times, seven. "I'll let it ring ten times," Father said.

On the ninth ring, Mrs. Dobrovic answered the phone. Father could hear her panting. "He – he – hello?" She gulped for air.

"Mrs. Dobrovic, it's Father Žagar. My apologies for bothering you so late, but I need your help." The words spilled out of his mouth.

Maxo could hear the cook's loud voice echoing tinnily from the phone. "Good gracious, Father, are you all right? You don't sound yourself." Her quick breaths clipped the words. "Excuse me." It sounded as though she were taking a sip of water. "I was just down in the cellar and only heard the phone this minute."

"I'm fine, I'm fine," he said. "Actually, I'm not fine at all, Mrs. D, I seem to have lost something here at home, something valuable."

"Lost something? Something dear? Oh, Father, I'm so sorry to hear that. How can I help?"

"This evening when we were talking to Sister Mary Martha, I had carried the tunic to a habit into the study," he said. "I thought I'd left it draped over a chair, but when I checked just now, it was gone."

"Oh, sure, I remember that," Mrs. Dobrovic bawled down the phone line. Relief rang in her words. "Here I thought you said it was something valuable you were missing. But I did see it, and I thought, what's that grubby thing doing here, cluttering up Father's study? 'Course, I looked for the initials right away, and seeing it was Sister Mary Martha's, I chased after her with it."

"Oh, my God," Father moaned.

"What, what is it?" Maxo said, unable to hear all of the conversation.

In a side whisper, Father said, "She found the habit and gave it back to Sister Mary Martha."

To the phone, he said, "What? What was that you just said, Mrs. D? Could you slow down and tell me again what happened? You said you chased after Sister Mary Martha. Did she take the habit from you?"

"Goodness gracious, Father, I hope you know me better than that," Mrs. Dobrovic's voice adopted a note of pride. "I wouldn't give the head sister a wrinkled-y, spotty habit like that. She said she'd take care of it, but I said, 'No, no you won't. You have far more important duties. I'll clean it up for you and deliver it proper. I just wanted to let you know it was over in the rectory, and that it was safe. That we had it.'"

"Wait a minute," Father said, "you mean, she didn't take it from you? You still have it?"

"Lord, no, Father." Father's face fell. "I don't have it. Not here at home. I stuffed it in the laundry bag I keep in the cellar way there at the rectory. I'll do it with the rest of the rectory clothes tomorrow."

"Hold on one second, Mrs. D," Father said. "Maxo, go check the laundry bag hanging in the cellar steps."

In thirty seconds, Maxo returned with the soiled garment. Father Žagar returned to the phone. "Mrs. Dobrovic, we've found it. Thank you very, very much. And I know you won't understand this, but I do not want you to wash the habit by any means, nor return it to Sister Mary Martha. I'll explain everything to you in a few days."

Maxo could hear some muffled protests squawking from the phone.

"Yes, yes, I understand. No, it has nothing to do with your housekeeping or cooking which is always wonderful. Please don't worry. I'm very thankful that you found the habit and put it in a safe place." He paused. "No, no bother. Right. Oh, and Mrs. D, I'd appreciate it if we kept this to ourselves, okay?" Maxo could hear some mumbling through the phone.

"All right, thanks again. We'll see you tomorrow. Have a good night's rest, and God bless you."

Father hung up the phone. His eyes looked like they might pop out of his head. He glanced at the clock. "I don't know about you, Maxo, but I have time for another drink before midnight, and I think I can truthfully say this draught will be medicinal."

Maxo looked at Father's flushed face and agreed. Together, they retreated to the living room, carrying the habit and the signature page with them.

"I swear, I'm going to sleep with these two things tonight," Father said once they were settled back in their chairs. "That's definitely more excitement than I was looking for at the tail end of the day."

"I do not know about sleeping with them," Maxo said, "but I would certainly consider placing them in your locking trunk and putting the key under your pillow."

Father clinked his glass against Maxo's. "I'll drink to that."

Once more, they sat staring as little blue and orange flames leapt in the hearth. "I was hoping," Father said, "that we would have some time this evening to analyze our visit from Sister Mary Martha. Are you game for staying awake for another half hour?"

"Absolutely," Maxo said. "I doubt that I should sleep if we do not. I believe we were talking about breadcrumbs." He smiled and tipped a dram more brandy into his snifter.

CHAPTER SEVENTEEN

WHAT A NIGHT, Maxo thought now as he blended the colors that would define the *Descent into Hell* mural. The two friends had discussed Sister Mary Martha well past the half hour mark. With mixed feelings and despite the evidence that might be ascribed to Sister Claudetta, in the end, they could deduce no other explanation. Sister Mary Martha appeared to be the culpable party as far as the vandalism to the church and paintings was concerned. Their justifications always seemed to return to the same points.

There was the habit itself. Maxo read the sleeve like a long lost palette. To Father Žagar, he pointed out the different paint tones that he had used to create the first face of *Justice*. "See here, this is where I mixed cadmium red and China white with some sienna to create her flesh tones. And this grey-green was what I used to outline her beautiful eyes." Despite the fact that the paint had dried into angry-edged chips, the hues remained easily identifiable.

Maxo stroked the colors of flame onto the ceiling of the church. Of course, they had already realized that Sister Mary Martha wore black oxford shoes. A quick measurement of the footprint before her chair in the study had been taken. When compared with the sole of Father's shoes, it told them that those oxfords were the same size as a man's 10 ½ shoe. She was, after all, a big woman.

A yawn seized Maxo's throat, and he had to pause his painting for a moment to let it pass. His night had been too short, but for good reason. It had been essential to examine the facts related to Sister Mary Martha's behavior closely and to arrive at the correct conclusion.

He had argued passionately to Father Žagar about two items that seemed to indict Sister Mary Martha irreversibly.

Maxo remembered saying to the priest, "After all, if I am to be very truthful, someone else could have donned Sister Mary Martha's habit to destroy the painting in the church, someone else could be left-handed, someone else could wear size 10 ½ size shoes. But no one, no one at all except you and I know about the missing files, Father. We took a care not to tell anyone else of that particular misadventure. So how was it that in delivering her litany of accusations against Sister Claudetta, Sister Mary Martha knew that the files were missing?"

That had made Father sit up straight.

"And then there was the matter of her handwriting. She did not fool me or you when she at first hesitated to write her signature."

"Yes," Father said, "I got the impression she was calculating whether she could pull off writing her name with her right hand."

"Right, thus, the eyelash in the eye, to 'buy time' as you put it."

It had been all for nothing in the end. Sister Mary Martha had not factored in the artist's powers of observation. The writer's bump on the middle finger of her left hand was evidence that the nun had overlooked, but that Maxo had not. *She could not make that vanish in an instant, could she? And if she was not the culprit, why seek to disguise her own handwriting?*

As a final note, Father and he had agreed that it had been the Sister's own intelligence that had given her away. While the infractions were not complicated in nature, it would take someone with ample wit and bravado to determine the when and the wherefore of each offense. Plainly, Sister Claudetta possessed neither. *Hers is a simple soul*, Maxo thought, *untroubled by guile or malice; her intellect unlikely to plan and execute anything more complex than a lesson plan.*

Sister Mary Martha's actions in this regard troubled Father more than anything else. "I thought I knew her, Maxo," Father had said. "I never would've guessed she would sacrifice an innocent colleague for the sake of her own wicked ends."

Maxo flexed his shoulders and grunted as the stiffness cracked out of them. Holding the paintbrush above his head for so many hours sometimes played havoc with his neck and shoulder muscles, and it looked like this was going to be one of those days. Never the less, he thought that the job of painting overhead, no matter how long a task, would be far easier than dealing with Sister Mary Martha.

He did not envy Father Žagar the steps he must take next. All of his skill as a church leader and as a counselor would be required. He had to balance finding good care for Sister Mary Martha while firmly separating her from her duties at the school and the church. He told Maxo he would pray for grace and guidance to handle the situation so that no repercussions came back on the church community.

Maxo shook his head. *A daunting assignment*, he thought as he raised his brush to fill in the detail on the loincloth with which he had garbed the Christ figure. But he also believed in the power and goodness of his friend. *If anyone can manage it, Father Žagar will.*

Like the little sparrow that often snuggled in his shirt pocket when he took a break in the garden, the thought warmed Maxo's heart, and he held it close. It allowed him to turn the full force of his attention to the completion of the first panel.

Though Maxo showed him descending into Hell, the Christ figure's face glowed in beatific splendor. Unclothed and vulnerable, He appeared to know that He must travel through this trial by fire before ascending to the glories of Heaven, and He rejoiced in that knowledge.

How strange and how wonderful that it occurred to me to paint this panel at this time, Maxo thought, *when I am only a few hours away from descending into my own sort of Hell.* He was certain that part of last night's restlessness linked directly to his anxiety over meeting the specter, especially since his plans had been postponed another full day. Now the hour approached when he must put some action behind his intent, and it left his mouth as dry as sunbaked sand.

Maxo stared into Jesus' eyes as he detailed the angel that supported Him in His descent. He plumbed the dark orbs for courage and calm. "I must," Maxo said to himself, "I must – I have to believe that facing my tormentor from these past weeks, and yes, four years ago – I must believe that it will lead to something better." He wiped a sleeve across his nose, lighting its tip with white as he sniffed to himself. "Perhaps I think this because things cannot surely get any worse."

The thought gave but cold comfort, and Maxo vowed to tuck back into his work before the afternoon light evaporated. He had come to the realization that he would need to conceal the starry sky in this quadrant of the ceiling. If the painting truly depicted a trip to the netherworld, there would be no stars there. Instead, he mixed his most somber colors – black, gray, brown, blue – and with a broader brush, spread clouds in a wide V below Christ's feet. They reached from edge to edge of the panel. The fantastic, burgeoning billows climbed on each other's shoulders with the menace of a great storm about to crack the heavens.

The viewer will be left to determine whether the clouds represent the smoke of hellfire or an impending storm of say, Biblical proportions? Maxo smiled to himself. He enjoyed creating the mood – the uncertainty that these clouds introduced. His brush flashed across the sky, working at a furious pace. The energy seemed to fly down his arm and out the brush. At times like this, Maxo believed himself to be the servant of the brush. *I am a means of reaching the ceiling or a wall or whatever surface requires its touch.*

A flush rose upon the artist's face, and his feet danced across the scaffold as he rushed to and fro to convey the message of the clouds. Maxo darted down the framework to resupply his palette, and just as quickly, climbed again to continue the work. The clots of cloud mesmerized him as they pulsed and spread beneath his brush. Certitude expanded his chest, and it was not until Father Žagar had thrown the switch on the chandelier for evening prayer that Maxo realized the sun had set some time ago.

"That's impressive," Father called up to him. "And a bit frightening. You've had a busy day, my friend."

"Yes," said Maxo. "In a few strokes more, I will finish this panel, so if you do not mind, Father," he bowed from on high, "I will remain during your service, but quietly as a mouse, I promise."

"Of course, Maxo, please." The priest waved a palm upwards to bless the continuation of the work, and then turned to walk toward the vestry and his preparations for prayer.

Much later that evening, Maxo revived himself at the lavatory sink. His face emerged from the hand towel, pink and fresh and smudge-free. His nails had been scrubbed till the whites shown, and only the cuticles betrayed dim traces of paint. Back in his room, he donned a clean shirt, a dark blue tunic in the peasant style he favored. Its neck and placket glimmered with the rich embroidery of Croatian handiwork. Maxo stooped before the mirror and tied a soft, silk scarf around his neck.

He peered around the corner of the study before setting off for the church. Father studied the artist for a moment and nodded. "Looks like you're ready," he said, and raising his right hand, crossed the air before Maxo. "Blessed be your journey, my friend. Fear not, and find what understanding you can." As Maxo turned away, the priest added, "I plan to work late."

Maxo bobbed his head. "Thank you, Father. Thank you. For everything."

Then, he was away. Swiftly, he crossed the rectory yard. Reaching the vestry door, he opened and shut it again behind him, his movements quick and quiet.

Inside, the hush of the darkened church wrapped itself

around him – a stole of smoldering fate waiting to embrace him. He breathed in the cool air. Its musky breath met his own. He took his time. This was a night to handle everything with deliberation.

With the doorway as his mantle, Maxo allowed his eyes to adjust to the dark. Once more he thought how unfamiliar the familiar became in the absence of light. For all the hours and weeks he had spent in the church, for every inch of wall and ceiling he had faithfully covered with paint, the shapes and forms he had come to know now disguised themselves in shadow, receding into strangeness, disappearing in the murky atmosphere.

He squeezed his eyes shut and opened them again. The atmosphere lightened ever so slightly. Maxo had learned that trick in the war when the night was at its darkest, and it had been so important to see before being seen. Objects began to emerge through the dusk. Below the Pieta, several votive candles flickered red within their glass holders. They flamed on after their parishioners' prayers had been uttered, long after the memories they evoked had surrendered to the night. They gave him comfort. The warmth of human touch still hovered in the cool vastness of the nave.

Padding across the stone tiles, Maxo faced the center aisle between the two rows of pews. He stroked the wooden rail before the left-hand bench and sat. From this vantage point, the lit votives before the Crucifixion mural caught his eye as well as two large candles that blazed within glass hurricane lamps on either side of the altar.

"Bless you, Father!" Maxo whispered.

The lamps threw enough light for him to view the first few rows of seats and the skeletal scaffold that stretched to the ceiling. However, only one pew mattered to Maxo – the first one right of center where the specter most often sat.

Maxo wiped a hand down his mouth and beard and cleared his throat. He shifted his buttocks to tuck against the back of the pew, making him sit straighter and taller. *It is time*, he thought.

Taking a deep breath and shifting his legs to the right, Maxo focused his gaze on the middle distance – that place between earthbound reality and conscious thought. He allowed his mind to empty save for one thought.

She took all of him now. The pouf of her dawn gray dress rested against the edges of his mind. The slim lines of her bodice rose from the soft folds to the slender neck, the shining dark coil of hair at her nape, and the perfect profile. Her head turned and two beautiful dark eyes poured into his, taking him in, trying to see all of him, to understand who he was and what he had become.

Maxo uttered a low moan and swayed in his seat. Never had she come to him like this – the woman in the distance. She had never dared come so close. As her outline blurred, he nearly cried out. He struggled to stay with the vision. He struggled to keep her there.

A plink like someone dropping a pebble on the floor called him back. Immediately, his eyes focused on the front pew. No one was there. His glance darted back and forth across the apse, up to the ceiling, and past the altar. He turned and probed the back reaches of the church, raising his eyes to the choir, peering into the back corridor, studying the black corners at the rear of the church. Nothing revealed itself.

As though someone had flicked lemon juice into it, his left eye twitched, and the sting of salt tears trembled at its corner. "Oh," he breathed out. Disappointment and dejection swelled the syllable to bursting point. Maxo slumped in the pew and tapped the crown of his head against the wooden backrest. *I was so sure, so very certain that if I could find a time like this when quiet and dark reigned throughout the church – I was so sure that if I thought of her, if I thought of the beautiful woman in the distance, he would come.*

Maxo pressed the tears from his eyes and with lowered lids, studied his outstretched legs. After a bit, he licked his lips and sat a little straighter. He thought, *I am good at waiting. I can wait. I will wait tonight and tomorrow night. And the next night, and the next night, if that is what it takes.* He shook a fist at the ceiling, and aloud he shouted, "Do you hear me, ghost? I can wait! I will wait!"

The notes of his voice rumbled around the room and returned some courage to his breast. After all, it was not yet late tonight. He could afford to stay a while longer. *Did not the specter often appear around midnight or later?* He could do this.

Immediately, his thoughts reverted to the vision of the woman in the distance. *By God, she was so real*, he thought. *I felt as though I could trace her cheekbone or caress the silk of her dress.* He closed his eyes, remembering. *I will hold this image close, for its own sake and also, because it may help me in the future.*

The faintest whiffle of air breathed past his face. Maxo opened his eyes. He could not see anyone or anything, but the candle flames on the altar trembled. Something had disturbed their steady burn. He knew he had not invented the breeze.

He ran his hands through the hair on either side of his head and readjusted his position. The bench seemed to be growing harder. At first, he tried thinking of the woman in the distance some more, but this time she remained a faraway speck at the crest of a hill or a tiny figure on the curve of a beach. Again, no specter appeared.

After a bit, Maxo sighed and gave it up. For a short time, his thoughts turned to the mundane, and he planned his painting schedule for the next few days.

The church tower chimed the half hour. Eleven-thirty and still nothing. *I will keep vigil for another hour, maybe a little more,* Maxo reckoned, unsure that he could remain awake for longer without some sort of activity to keep him going.

To his own surprise, a small blip of laughter escaped his lips. He wondered if some day, people would say he was crazy for doing this. That the phantom was a figment of his over-ripe imagination fueled by wine or fatigue or both. Chuckles burbled out of his lips though they did not smile.

"It would be so easy to discourage myself if I believed such things," Maxo told the church, yet at the same time, a tiny thought niggled at the rim of his consciousness. Could he have conjured the specter from severe over-work or for some other reason? What answers did he seek in the wee hours that might have put significant pressure on his late-night nerves? When he was all alone and sometimes quite helpless, did something from his past push his imagination over the brink?

In the next moment, Maxo shimmied his shoulders to chase such doubts away. "No one would say such things if they had endured what I have here. The drafts, the intense cold, the dimming of the lights, the deep feelings of dread and yes, fear. Ha!" Again, the artist spoke out loud to the eyes and ears of the church. "I wonder if many others could have sustained the work as I have done if they had witnessed such terror. Few would have the stomach for it, I daresay."

He folded his arms across his chest and contemplated the Mother Mary hovering over the altarpiece. As ever, her gaze assuaged and comforted him. Maxo's thoughts drifted to his dear great-grandmother in the Zagorje. "Baka always told me that spirits only appear to those that are open to them. I remember her saying how chill and drear her meetings with the ghosts were, and that we should never be afraid of this. It seems they take a great deal of energy to show themselves to us. That is where the light and heat go whenever they appear."

Said aloud, the words rang with sense, even logic. Maxo nodded to himself. *What reason would the old woman have had to deceive me? Both she and Mati Dora told me I had a special gift for attracting spirits, whether they lived in little birds or in thin air.*

Maxo considered the number of birds and animals that he had befriended over the course of his lifetime. Even now, a sparrow – the miniscule Prepelica – graced him with his friendship here at the rectory; and at home, at White Bridge Farm, wrens, sparrows, and finches numbered among his friends.

And had not he seen the woman in the distance many times since her passing? And what about the man in the woods behind Mati Dora's house? These things had never been explained.

"And so," Maxo told the Mother Mary, "it is not impossible to think that if a ghost lives here, I am able to see it."

Midnight. Maxo and his thoughts trailed away across the years. He recognized that he had never really identified a likely candidate for the ghost of the church though he had raked through so many memories.

The faces rolled through his mind like a cinema film being cranked by hand. Mati Dora, the only mother he had ever known, loved and beloved. Parted from the tenderness of her arms all too soon. His two sisters, Doritska and Maritska, whose current fate eluded him. How he hoped they had escaped the Nazi scourge. The vicious Baldo and his sidekick son, Juro. *May they both rot in Hell. How Mati Dora ever loved Baldo is beyond dreaming.*

His face switched from frown to smile as Maxo remembered the delightful Colonel Salvić who had transported him to his new life and the beginnings of his passion for art. Boyhood friends, school friends, and university friends marched before his eyes. *It was completely unlikely that any of them would haunt me now – to what possible end?* he asked himself.

Far more likely, some villain from the war, he thought. But overall, Maxo had to admit that the fellows he had encountered during the great conflict – the badly wounded and the half-starved – were good men trying to hang on until the day they could go home, until the time when they could begin to live again. *Maybe it is the Duc de Sévigny or the good nurse Nora who comes to warn me of something*, he postulated. He regarded both of their kind faces with a sad smile – happy to have known them, and sad that they were lost to him.

Actually, he thought, *it is much more likely that someone from the Group of Four would have the chutzpah and force of nature, and perhaps the sense of humor, too, to send his spirit forth to pester me.* That theory evaporated as soon as it came to his mind, however, as Maxo remembered that all of those colleagues were still alive, or so he believed.

He had a tendency to think that the specter represented someone from the Croatian community that had helped build this church, excepting that, *excepting that the spirit often appeared when I thought of the woman in the distance*, Maxo told himself. *Not always, but often enough that I must conclude that there is a connection.*

Another half hour chimed. Maxo barely noticed as he undertook a dispassionate examination of the woman in the distance. When he thought about it, her beauty and grace were just as remote as the day he had first glimpsed her from the Jugova garden gate. Perhaps his mind had played tricks on him over the years, embellishing the impressions of a young boy. The dark chestnut locks, the creamy white face with the merest hint of rose clinging to each cheekbone, the fine patrician nose, straight from a Grecian vase, the stylish frocks of rich and pale colors, all bustles and ruffles, the frilly parasol to match. It would be what a boy might wish his mother to look like in a fairy story.

For without being told, Maxo knew that the woman in the distance was his birth mother. He had sensed it from the beginning. The cues were evident now that he thought about it – Mati Dora so anxious he should appear clean and well, the tense hug she would give him before pushing him out the front door, the fact that she never accompanied him to the gate, the invisible string that seemed to extend between the boy and the woman.

Mati Dora had never spoken of his relationship with the well-to-do woman in so many words, but Maxo knew that the Jugovas were not his true family. He knew, thanks to Baldo Jugova's crude remarks and ill treatment, that he had been adopted. The young Mikula never pressed Mati about this, but as he grew older and more independent, he vowed to learn the truth of the matter.

For the woman in the distance had still visited to observe him from time to time at his boarding school, and once at university. In point of fact, he felt certain that one time he had been introduced to her at an exhibition of his own works. But having never seen her close to, they both behaved at the time like the amicable strangers that they were – ones with a mutual appreciation of art.

Maxo stood and stretched, and exiting the pew, he walked in circles in the space before the steps to the altar. He did not track the time as he continued to contemplate the question of the woman in the distance. Years after his formal training, when he had begun to make a name for himself in the European art world, he had been able to verify that his birth mother had been of Austro-Hungarian descent and a noblewoman, no less. Try as he might, however, Maxo never managed to meet her formally nor understand why she had surrendered him to a peasant family, except for the obvious reasons.

Now he wondered if by the time he was instructing his students at the art institute, she had passed away. It would explain why he had seen her occasionally strolling the secluded Korculan beach where he liked to walk and sketch. The fact that Georg had seen her there, too, lent credence to the idea.

Surprising him again, Maxo's eyes began to smart, and his chest heaved with unreleased sobs. However, his tears fell for Mati Dora and not the attractive woman who would forever be a stranger to him. Truly, if he thought about it, only Mati Dora deserved his consideration. He knew with certainty that she never would have parted with him if she had had a choice, but finally, the pressure of a wealthy relation and the assurance that the petite Mikula would have a better life than she could ever give him had loosed Mati's hold on the young Maxo.

The woman in the distance, however - she had chosen. Chosen a rich, respectable life unfettered by a tiny fachook, an unexpected baby, a child with no father. The spit collected on Maxo's tongue, but he swallowed the bile and his resentment as he turned his thoughts once more to Mati Dora.

"Mati Dora," he voiced, lifting his eyes to the celestial ceiling. "Mati Dora, I swear to you upon all of these works that surround me and to which I have given my heart and soul. I swear that you are the only mother I have ever had. If you can hear me, know that you are my most beloved Mati and will be forevermore." His eyes shone wet and silvery as he gazed at the painted stars. "I love you," he whispered and dropped his head.

Silence slid into the place where his voice had been. The

utter quiet folded its arms around him, and peace nestled within his chest. Only his heartbeat thumped in his ears. Softly it came but rapid like the pulsing he felt when first he had cupped a tiny bird in his hands.

In a twinkling, it dawned on Maxo that the atmosphere in the church had lightened and warmed. The dusky shadows had lost their intensity. His breath came more easily. Raising his head, he turned to face the altar.

There it stood. In front of the altar rail, upon the lowest stair, the specter towered. Still and silent, draped in its black robes and hood, it appeared to contemplate the air above Maxo's brow.

Of its own volition, Maxo's head jerked back, but the artist did not step away or say anything. He forced his hands to hang at his sides though their palms sprouted moisture and begged to be dried on his pants. Never once did he move or remove his eyes from the black hole where the ghost's face should be.

For what seemed the space of several days, they confronted each other, the ghost and the man. A waft of air brushed the skirts of the specter's black robe and cooled the air between them. Though Maxo awaited the freezing dread that usually accompanied the breeze, none came, and his heart beat warmly, steadily, unfettered by any feelings of terror.

Maxo hungered for answers or some kind of sign, but he compelled himself to remain still and more importantly, quiet. He recalled how often he had chased the spirit away with his voice. *This is not about words*, he counseled himself.

Finally, he opened his hands to the specter in a gesture that contained both invitation and question. At the same time, he dipped his head gently toward the spirit. He held his hands open for about fifteen seconds, and then rested them at his side.

Another draft passed between them, riffling the sleeves of the specter's cloak. But no, the phantom had moved. He had glided a step closer to Maxo and brought both of his arms together in a gesture of prayer. Like a maharishi returning a blessing, Maxo reflected the gesture.

The creature's movements completely mesmerized Maxo. He breathed in shallow, noiseless mouthfuls, his eyes pinned to the ghost's hood. Within, he thought he could discern the minutest gleam staring back at him.

The spirit was once more in motion. It raised its sleeves to the walls and the ceiling, taking in every painting, every face, every angel, every message. It folded its would-be hands in prayer again. Maxo repeated his salute.

Then, the spirit astonished Maxo by sailing right through him. A cry escaped the artist's lips as his mind strained to send forth his thoughts. *Please come back. Do not go. Not yet. I do not know what you want, or what you need.*

With little hope, he spun around to trace the phantom's trail. The ghost had stopped immediately behind him, facing the rear of the church, its spindly arms upstretched once again. They pointed to either side of the choir loft where the empty, cream-colored plaster faintly reflected the candlelight. For a long while, the artist contemplated the blank walls and the spirit's reach toward them. Then, Maxo closed his eyes and nodded. He understood now. He knew what was wanted.

When he opened his eyes again, the spirit was no longer before him. Maxo peered into the darkness, craning his neck and willing his eyes to see, though there was nothing there. There was nothing to be seen.

He turned back to the light of the altar. The specter had repositioned itself on the first step. As Maxo watched, the candles burned low and blue, and a deep cold permeated the nave. White mist formed before his lips as he exhaled and then pulled in another icy breath. At the same time, the ghost's figure darkened to a deeper black than the artist had ever mixed, and it lengthened, growing tall and nearly blotting out the illumination of the altar. Awestruck, Maxo stood as still as one of the church's pillars.

The phantom hovered so for only a second more. Then, bowing forward with one arm outstretched, its image began to fade. The disappearance astounded Maxo as much as anything he had yet seen. As though the very air absorbed its molecules, soon the spirit became transparent, a wan shade of its former self.

It was then that Maxo realized he had been holding his breath. Now he breathed it all out in a deep sigh. As if that were the wind for which the spirit waited, it vanished before him – a wisp of smoke that slipped toward the starry ceiling, through the apse above the altar, and into the arms of the Mother Mary.

CHAPTER EIGHTEEN

MY DEAR MAXO,

Greetings, my good friend, and Merry Christmas to you and all of your family, or Happy Hanukkah. Whatever it is you celebrate there, I hope the occasion was joyous, and that you were blessed with many happy times together after so many months spent apart this past year.

I am pleased to share that we are all well here, and that your magnificent murals shining down upon us enlivened our own Christmas celebrations. Maxo, there are not enough words in my vocabulary to thank you for creating this living, breathing masterpiece in our church. Its images and messages will live on far beyond our own short lives. I feel blessed every day as I work among the murals and the stories they tell.

The only down side to our holiday had to do with – you can guess – Sister Mary Martha. While I made arrangements for her care some weeks earlier, still, thoughts of her troubled mind tinged my personal Christmas joy with a bit of sadness. Do you know, she was adamant till nearly the end about her innocence and would have left me in doubt, except that we found further evidence of her disturbed thinking in her convent cell. After her removal to the Beneficent Sisters, a good order that helps incapacitated nuns, Fr. Sebastian and I made a thorough search of her room. In it, she had hidden a missal whose under-linings and marginal notes quite vindicated what we had suspected – a sort of mania for anything she considered ungodly and how it should be treated. Some ugly language, really. I'm glad you didn't get to read it, but I'm afraid that it included most of your paintings, Maxo.

Ah well, she was a mysterious case indeed, and I am saddened when I think of all the good works she fulfilled for the church, and yet how she may have influenced so many tender minds over the years. Let us hope there is no malingering damage for her protégés and that someday, Sister Mary Martha can enjoy good mental health again, as it is certain she will never hold a position of trust in the future.

One last note on this subject, I have to say that the remaining nuns have really risen to the occasion. Sister Frances was a wonder in leading the school term to its close with barely a ripple, and she will be helping me to find someone else to fill in at the school. I'm hoping to convince her to take on the leadership role.

Father paused in his writing to take a sip of coffee. He broke off a piece of pizzelle inside the Christmas cookie tin Mrs. Dobrovic had left on his desk. Flipping the sheet, he continued to write.

Oh, but I haven't mentioned what is probably most important to you. My apologies – it has taken me entirely too long to do so. How do the weeks fly by so fast? I was truly sorry that you could not make it here for the fete of St. Nikolaj Tavelić. Of course, you remember we'd planned all along to unveil your paintings in their full glory in honor of our patron saint.

The weekend was a tremendous success. How I wish you could have been here. Each day, we had huge crowds, and the acclaim for the murals was, to say the least, enormously gratifying. Naturally, there were those who missed the symbolism, but overall, it seemed to me that everyone appreciated your works. You should have felt your ears burning, you were talked about so much. Many accolades belonged to you those days, I can tell you. Not only did we have the full Croatian community in attendance, but also several professors of art and art history came from the universities. We were delighted to welcome them all, and Mrs. Dobrovic led a triumphant team of volunteers to create one of the best feasts this parish has ever seen.

By the way, I'm enclosing some newspaper clippings that were written here in our local paper and in the Pittsburgh Press. You've achieved quite a bit of fame, Mr. Vanka, and we are all proud to have known you.

Now the church seems an extra special place for festivities because of you. We've had four baptisms and three weddings since you completed your work. But I have to confess that some of my fondest moments are when I am in the church alone, and I can spend time with the murals without interruption. They speak to me then, and every time I study them, I see more.

Closest to my heart are the two figures you painted in the choir as your last hurrah.

Father crossed out the last phrase and replaced it with *as your final gift.*

The priest stopped for a minute and chewed the top of his pen. He thought about the astonishing story that Maxo had told him the day after his nocturnal adventure in the church. He had filled him in at the breakfast table, since the exploit had taken him far past Father's bedtime the night before. He remembered how the artist's eyes had shone as though lit from within, and the way a renewed confidence seemed to radiate from his pores. Eagerly, he had spouted, "I know now, Father! I know now what I must do."

And he must have. On his last day in the parish, Maxo had been treated to a farewell dinner that Mrs. Dobrovic had put together. Father Žagar smacked his lips as memory tasted the roast lamb and rosemary potatoes, all smothered under a hefty dollop of gravy. His contribution had been a bottle of French wine – a good, stout burgundy. Cara and Mrs. D had joined them, but as they were clearing away the dishes, Maxo leaned over and said, "I have been meaning to tell you, Father – she is gone."

"What?" Father had asked. "She? Who?"

"The apparition," Maxo said. "That night – the night she decided to show herself to me, the night I understood and vowed to fulfill that understanding – the specter vanished. Poof! Gone, like a wisp of smoke. Gone to her rest hopefully."

The news flummoxed Father for a moment. He had never

seen the ghost for himself, and he had to admit, he had not given it any more thought in the days following that incredible night Maxo had shared. "Really? Wh – well, that's excellent news, Maxo. It must have made these last few weeks a good deal more tolerable." Internally, a spurt of relief traveled along his windpipe, and Father had cleared his throat. "That's it then. The last of our mysteries cleared away." He had clinked his glass against Maxo's and swallowed the remainder of his wine.

Father shook his head and re-read his last line, then began again.

Closest to my heart are the two figures you painted in the choir as your final gift. St. Francis of Assisi has always been my favorite saint, and now, because he reminds me of you – of your ways with animals and children, and grownups, too – he is even more endeared to me. And St. Clare, that tender caretaker of St. Francis who personified his philosophy and pledged her life to propounding his teachings – your portrayal of her speaks everything of hope and beauty, goodness and light. It is the pinnacle of your work here at St. Nicholas, and I marvel every time I think of what you told me – that you created her in the image of your own dear Mati Dora. I love the sublime connection between her as the earth mother facing the mother of Heaven, our Mother Mary of the altar – two powerful and constant sources of love and protection over Heaven and Earth. Together, they are the crown jewel of your work here. Bless you, bless you for making it so.

He paused for an instant and rubbed his eyes. Strange, but wonderful how the two murals moved him every time he thought of them. *Lord, I miss him,* Father thought.

Before you think I go on too long, I will draw to a close – soon, I promise. But dear Maxo, I have to tell you that I miss our late evening chats, and the chance to wrangle with ideas that range beyond the daily cares of church and home. I miss your smiling face, your quiet jokes, your point of view (some would call arguing), and your counsel. These past months with you, and the weeks in 1937, have marked an extraordinary time for me. I only hope that we may enjoy your company now and then as you find yourself in Pittsburgh. You will always be welcome here at St. Nicholas.

Mrs. D says to tell you she misses you, too, and that she cooked shrimps for her visiting family last week. They all loved them.

Dear Maxo, please do let us hear from you from time to time, as the "spirit" moves you.

God Bless You and Keep You, My Friend,

Yours ever,

Albert Žagar

ABOUT THE AUTHOR

THE MURALIST'S GHOST is Karen Mocker Dabson's debut novel. Some of her short stories and poems have appeared in the anthologies of the Columbia Chapter of the Missouri Writers Guild and the *Story Circle Journal*, and she has received writing awards from both organizations. Originally from Pittsburgh, Pennsylvania, she resides in Columbia, Missouri with her husband, Brian, and Jack the Dog.